PHOENIX

PIPER STONE

TERMS USED

Burnout—Fires set to burn areas between control lines and the main fire

Crown Fire—A fire burning hot enough to continuously spread through the tops of trees

Firebrands—Large embers or chunks of burning, airborne material

Fire Devil—Whirlwind of fire

Firestorm—A mass conflagration of fire, a blowup

Fusee—Railroad flare use to light burnouts and backfires

Helitorch—A firing device on a helicopter that is capable of starting a fire

Jump Ship—Smokejumper aircraft

Mud—Aerial fire retardant dropped by aircraft

Zullies—Missoula smokejumpers

PROLOGUE

*B*rothers in arms.

Bad boys, cowboys, soldiers, sailors, airmen, and Marines.

We'd been labeled delinquents, incapable of redemption.

And we'd gone our separate ways.

Heroes. Monsters. Sinners and saints.

Above all we were men honoring our country even while a terrible secret loomed just below the surface.

There were those who would never forget, praying we'd never return.

Others would stop at nothing to prevent us from doing so.

We were intent on finding salvation by protecting those we loved.

But demons from a single act would never allow us to forget.

Six men determined to right the wrongs from our past.

Six men prepared to do what it took.

No matter the cost.

Together in life.

Together in death.

CHAPTER 1

 hoenix

"What the fuck is wrong with you?" Maverick's voice was muffled, the sound lost completely as an explosion of fire erupted in the forest.

"We're surrounded on all sides!" Gage yelled from behind.

Fuck my life.

I stood staring at the fire as wind carried embers high over the thick canopy of trees. I'd always been mesmerized by fire, the beautiful blue hue mesmerizing. Even now, the heat oppressive, I couldn't break away from the intensity of sensations rocketing through me.

"Riggs. We have to get the hell out of here." Houston snapped as he flanked my side, holding his arm over his face as the thick, acrid smoke rolled in billowing clouds. When I said nothing, he grabbed my arm, trying to lure me away.

"No fucking way." I jerked from his hold, anger burrowing deep inside. "No one will be left on this mountain. Do you fucking hear me?" I lunged forward through the wall of flames, a furnace blast of heat stealing my breath. After jumping over several fallen limbs, I glanced up at the canopy of trees as the fire exploded all around us. How the fuck had this happened? There was no sense calling out, the bellow of my voice unable to filter through the raging fire.

Already disoriented, I turned in a full circle, struggling to concentrate. Where the hell did you go? Why? Why had this happened?

I heard another sound behind me and ducked seconds before another limb fell from thirty feet above. I jerked to the right, but it wasn't fast enough, the limb crashing down on me. Fuck. Fuck. Fuck. Scrambling, I crawled away, slapping my smoldering jeans. When I noticed a figure just ahead, I bolted forward, tackling Colt to the ground.

"Jesus. We're can't get through this," he yelled, panting as I rolled him over, dousing the flames as he kicked out, almost frantic.

"Stop. Breathe. I got you," I told him, pitching him over one last time.

"This is crazy. We can't do this," Colt moaned.

"Yeah, we can." I was no longer so certain.

Ricardo appeared from the shadows, struggling to move forward. Wheezing, he dropped to his knees. "I can't... I tried... No. Use."

I was frozen for a few seconds, agony tearing through me. "We have to. I can't. I won't."

"Fuck, no. Get out of here. I'm not coming back until Belle is found. Do you fucking hear me?" Before I had a chance to head deeper into the forest, Maverick tackled me from behind.

"No! We're not losing you too. We're getting the fuck out of here."

"No. No..."

Gasping, a crackling sound dragged my attention. I blinked furiously, shoving the horrible memory aside. I couldn't do this. Not now. Not here. Fuck. Fuck...

Get your head out of your ass, Riggs Wentworth. That's what my father would say. Shaking, I allowed anger to sweep through me as wild as the fire raging in the distance. Fuck the images.

Fuck the past.

Fuck everything.

The anger burned deep inside, my muscles aching from tension and self-hatred.

I hoisted the ax, slamming it against the fallen limbs. Then again.

And again.

I moved from one broken limb to another, the remnants tumbling in the wide ditch we'd created.

Still, there was no relief from the pain, an anguish that had haunted me for years. Being a helicopter pilot, chasing down insurgents hadn't dulled the heartache. Being shot down then tortured for four full months, every inch of my body electrocuted, beaten, or whipped hadn't eased the guilt. Facing infernos had done nothing but feed the beast.

So I swung the ax several more times, one brutal swing coming after the other.

"Jesus, Phoenix. I think that's enough."

I took a deep breath, turning my head in the hotshot's direction. They called him the Firecracker because of his explosive nature. I called him asshole. When he started to laugh, my grip on the ax tightened, daring the son of a bitch to take a single step closer.

A sharp crack drew my attention, dozens of massive limbs falling off several of the trees, spearing the ground as if digging their way to the center of the earth. Another vision flashed in front of my mind and every sight and sound was dragged from me, sucked into a dark abyss.

"The entire top of the mountain is on fire, Riggs. Listen to me. We did everything we could do," Ricardo implored, the wild look in his eyes exactly the way I felt.

I turned and stared as the fire consumed everything in its path, flames licking up to the heavens. As I lifted my fist toward the sky, the others did the same. Together in life. Together in death.

Forever.

. . .

I took a deep breath, drifting back from the fog.

The crown fire had burned hotter than any of us had expected, and I had no doubt the damn fire had been purposely set, an accelerant used. The stench was godawful and nothing created by nature.

"Time for a burnout. Let's get this fucking fire under control," Captain Zephyr called from behind the line of jumpers.

After wiping soot from my face, I turned in a full circle. We'd done a damn good job of steering the raging inferno from the campsite, but if the winds continued to change, we'd lose control again.

"Wentworth. I need you," the captain called. At this point, I was considered the explosions expert, something I'd learned during my time in the Marines. However, I was on loan, my expertise meant for a seminar, not facing the beast hundreds of miles away from my team.

I lumbered forward, this acrid smoke getting thicker. As soon as I approached, there was something about the position of the trees that sparked another memory. For a few seconds, I shut down, trying to control my breathing.

"Help me. Help..."

Fuck. I closed my eyes briefly, only able to hear the rapid beating of my heart.

"You okay, buddy?" Zephyr called.

His loud voice cut through the fog, and I shook my head. "Just dandy, Captain. Let's get this shit controlled." I barreled forward, grabbing the bag of explosives and several fusees, handing the rest to two other jumpers. Hopefully, the railroad flares would be enough.

As I barreled into the woods, I could hear the captain screaming that I was supposed to wait for backup. That wasn't my style. I was a loner, damn good at what I did, and no one was going to tell me what to do at this point in my career.

I turned in a full circle, determining the direction of the wind then shifted to the right. As I jumped over a fallen long, I tripped on debris on the other side. After tumbling forward, the fusee popped free of my hand and I immediately scrambled to grab it. As I jerked to my feet and turned around, all the breath was sucked out of me.

Two men lay face down on the ground. As I walked closer, the stench of blood and brain matter mixed with the smoke, bile immediately forming in my throat.

The two victims had been bludgeoned to death but only after they'd been shot several times.

* * *

"Ask any woman in an arranged marriage. Love is the least stressful way out."

—Fay Weldon

Wren

"You have a date for the wedding. Mother won't take no for an answer."

That was the way my sister started our conversation. A date? Over my dead body.

"Then I'm not coming," I told my baby sister, even if that wasn't an option. I would never disappoint her. She'd been through far too much in her life and deserved all the happiness karma could provide.

"You're my maid of honor."

"You can find another." I knew this was going to happen. Goddamn it, I hated my parents. They'd been trying to rule both our lives since birth. And they'd been far too effective.

It was Cammie's wedding, but I was the one being fixed up, likely with the intention of pushing me into marrying the selected choice. I had no doubt the candidate of choice was a man of wealth, capable of providing me with a huge house and all the amenities while I provided a passel of kids.

I wasn't mother material. I wasn't interested in marriage either. To hell with my parents.

Marriage.

How could anyone stand to get hitched? Being stuck to one person the rest of my life wasn't on my bucket list. Now, if the union was more like a lease on a car, allowing someone the capability of getting out in seven years, then maybe. However, my little sister was a romantic. She'd been the little girl to believe in fairytales, her pink room and pretty little white canopy bed suiting her personality. Meanwhile, I was the girl who shoved her long hair under a ball cap, insisting on playing outside with the boys. My skills playing baseball along with being a late bloomer had allowed me to fit right in.

Much to the chagrin of my parents.

Then I'd developed curves and suddenly, not one of the boys wanted to play those kinds of games.

"Very funny, big sis. You can handle it," Cammie told me. "You're superwoman."

Uh-huh. I'd lived on my own since college, but my parents still treated me as if I was their possession. My sister had called a superhero for as long as I could remember. I hated it because most of the time I felt as if I was a complete failure. Even though I'd found the courage to move away from my home to another state, I'd still followed the Tillman family rules as if they were gospel.

Sighing, I stared out the windshield into the darkness as the snow began to pick up in intensity. Then I quickly glanced at the GPS on my phone, cursing the fact I'd taken advice from someone I didn't know who'd ensured me that this road was a shortcut. It seemed I was driving into the middle of nowhere. And where had the storm come from?

"Are you still there?" Cammie asked. Even the lilt of her voice screamed she was in love. Wait until after the honeymoon when all the romance was tossed out the window and reality set in.

"I'm here. Just watching the snow coming down."

"That's why you should have flown."

"I wanted to see the countryside."

"That's a lie. You just don't want to spend any extra time with Marcus and me," Cammie retorted.

No, I didn't. To see them fawning over each other, making out at the table when I'd been stupid enough to come back for their huge engagement soiree had been enough to turn my stomach. "I had some time that I needed to take off and thought, why not. It's been a wonderful few days."

Like hell it had been. I'd driven through thunderstorms, hail, now ice and snow.

"What are you driving?"

"My car," I snapped, instantly hating my terse tone.

"You mean the sports car that shouldn't be on snowy mountain roads?"

"I like my Trans Am."

She snorted. "You could buy anything in the world, yet you drive an old Trans Am. Why?"

Because I adored muscle cars and always had, even tinkering under their hoods from time to time. "Relax, Cammie. I'll be there before you know it. Is everything ready to go?"

"You know how Mother is, always making a change here and there."

Our mother had a penchant for detail, especially when she threw one of her lavish parties, which had been far too often considering our father required maintaining a certain image. He was a United States Congressman, after all. How many times had he reminded us of that fact?

"It'll be over soon. Where's the honeymoon?" While I realized that avoiding the subject couldn't last for long, my mind was already conjuring up how I could avoid being forced to endure the unwanted attention. As I gritted my teeth, I turned up the defroster. The scenic route had taken me through Billings, Montana, which had seemed like a good idea at the time.

"Italy. A whole month. Can you believe it?" she squealed.

I knew my father had checked out her fiancé top to bottom, likely hiring a private investigator to ensure he was the right man for his precious daughter. Marcus Owens was from a very wealthy, powerful family out of Texas. Since I worked in Dallas, I knew just how influential they were. The coupling would allow both families to become even more powerful, owning dozens of corporations in the west. Their meeting had been arranged, Cammie encouraged to accept his marriage proposal, even if she didn't want to admit to it. "Good for you."

"He's not bad."

"Who?"

"The guy Daddy set you up with."

She was baiting me, which Cammie was good at doing. "Who is he?"

"Lincoln Daniels."

"Lincoln Daniels? Are you freaking kidding me? He's fifty years old." Dear God, my father had dropped to the bottom of the barrel. Lincoln had also made one too many passes at me, acting as if I'd be lucky to get him. The thought of spending a single minute of time with him made my stomach turn.

"But he's rich."

"I don't care about money." Even as I said the words, I knew they sounded ridiculous. I had a trust fund worth millions of dollars that I could access either when I married or the day I turned twenty-eight. That was over three years away and good ole Mom and Dad were insistent I find a husband before then. Perfect.

"Well, I don't think you can avoid it unless…" She laughed, the tone changing into her conniving tone. We'd both learned to be little deviants when necessary.

"What are you thinking?"

"Bring a date. Maybe he could be your fiancé. Fake dating is all the rage. Find a hunk with huge muscles and absolute sex appeal. He doesn't have to talk, just…"

"Camille!"

She laughed hysterically.

Oh. My. God. I'd been reduced down to finding a fake date? My life was obviously in shambles.

Huffing, I almost retched just thinking about her idea. "What am I supposed to do, call one eight hundred rent a date?"

"I'm certain there are male escort services. At least it would get Daddy off your back for a little while."

As much as I hated the idea, she had a point. Seeing my father twisting in his greed and pompousness would make me as happy as a little bird. It could work. Maybe I could find a glorious movie star or a famous racecar driver. No, what if I found a regular guy who was down on his luck? Wouldn't that turn my father's stomach? Ugh. I had two days to come up with somebody. The problem was that he'd need to be a stranger since Mother and Father knew every family in town. "I'll think about it."

"I just thought I'd warn you." Her voice now sounded like a soft drink commercial.

When she sighed, I knew she was about to drop another bomb and it always involved our parents and a new rule that had to be followed.

"Incidentally, you've been asked to stay at the house over the weekend."

"I rented a cabin not too far away."

"That's not good enough. It's not a request," she continued.

"It's a requirement for the good of the family," we both repeated in unison. I groaned and felt the tires losing traction. The conditions were getting worse. "I'll deal with it." I'd rented the cabin specifically to allow myself some peace and quiet, taking a full three weeks of vacation to relax, maybe start writing the book I'd always talked about doing. The truth was I hated my career, the pressure starting to get to me. Being a financial advisor meant I worked long, arduous hours and my client list included members of the Fortune 100 club.

Translation. They were arrogant as hell, demanding I take their calls at all hours of the day and night, always a pain in my ass.

Shuddering, I turned up the heat and continued on, praying I wouldn't get stuck. Mile after mile I'd seen nothing but trees and hillsides, the road so narrow I was terrified I'd careen off a cliff. That's what they had in Montana, right? I tried to keep myself awake, but the exhaustion was starting to get to me. I wouldn't be doing a cross-country trip by myself again.

"I'll see what I can do, but don't you mention a word to either one of them," I told her.

"Who, me?" Cammie giggled. "I can't wait to see the hunk you find. That will take the pressure off of me."

"Uh-huh. You just go back to your little snookums or whatever you're calling him now."

"Honey drop."

Oh, dear God. I was going to be sick. "I'll call you when I get into town."

"Be careful. The roads up here are getting slick."

While I didn't want to stop for the night, I might have no other choice. "Stop worrying."

"You're my sister. I'll always worry about you."

I tossed the phone on the seat, my entire body tense from anticipation. The last phone conversation I'd had with Mother should have been a red flag warning.

"You aren't getting any younger, Wren. You need to settle down." I was twenty-four, for God's sake. I wouldn't call that being a spinster in any language.

I chuckled and turned the wipers onto high. Now the snow was really coming down. Shit. I had several hours to go. I had to face the fact that if I came to a small town, finding a hotel for the night was the best choice.

Maybe my only choice.

My mind started to wander, creating the perfect hunky date in my mind. He had to be tall, buff, and rugged. I didn't care if he could barely put a coherent sentence together. As long as he looked good in a suit, I could go with that.

Stop thinking about it.

How could I? Maybe there was a service I could use. I certainly had the money to pay for an escort. Ugh. What would he want in return? Hell, no. There wouldn't be any touching, no kissing. Well, maybe a peck or two to convince my parents, and they'd be watching closely.

I rounded another corner, a shadow crossing in front of me, which forced me to put on my brakes. Shit. As the car started to swerve back and forth, I almost panicked.

Hold it together. Foot off the brake.

Even though I followed the little voice, the tires couldn't maintain traction, ice pellets hitting the windshield a good indication of why.

Breathe. You'll be fine.

This was supposed to be a celebration and all I could think about was finding a good-looking man who could walk and talk just like my father. Did that man even exist?

There wasn't a perfect man in the universe. None.

Forced to pull the car to the right, the windshield starting to fog, I realized I was losing control. As the car spun around in a full circle, I kept both hands crushed around the steering wheel. At the least the car was slowing but...

Oh. No. No!

CHAPTER 2

"In order to rise from its own ashes, a phoenix first must burn."

—Octavia E. Butler

Phoenix

"Fuck!" I slammed my hand on the steering wheel, cursing Mother Nature. "What are the road conditions in Missoula?" I should never have agreed to the bullshit assignment in the first place.

Gage Beckham laughed. He'd been known as the Iceman while serving in the military, but for some reason he'd refrained from using it since his return. Somehow, I couldn't stand the thought of using my real name any longer. "Borderline dangerous."

"Great." Just fucking great. I was in no mood to screw with a snowstorm. I had shit to get done back home.

Yeah, like what?

By his tone alone, I knew I was in for a shitstorm if I attempted to make it all the way home. "Hunker down, bud. The storm came in early. From what I can tell on the radar, it'll be out of range in six hours, but it's gonna pack a wallop. The roads are already getting icy. Even that big four-wheel drive you have won't get you here."

I was afraid that would be his answer. My buddy should know given he was the sheriff of Missoula. "Fine. I'll get a motel for the night." Yeah, in bumfuck Montana, which was where I was headed. 'I know a shortcut,' one of the smoke-jumpers from Billings had told me. I'd bought it, exhausted from the unexpected firestorm I'd been forced to help fight. If I had to guess, I'd say the son of a bitch had purposely led me on a wild goose chase.

"I heard about the fire," Gage added.

"Purposely set. Burned almost four hundred acres before we were able to contain it." I couldn't get the images of the two unknown men out of my mind. After dragging them away from the burnout zone, the captain had made a calculated call to go ahead with the controlled fire, which meant destroying any evidence. There'd been no other choice or the fire would have consumed the campsite on its way toward the city limits. To think I'd been a guest speaker for a workshop hosted by Billings' elite smokejumping team, who the Zullies considered their rivals. Then all hell had broken loose.

19

"We've had too many of those lately," Gage said with a grumpy sigh. He'd been called out on several of them over the last few months.

"Yeah, I know. At least the blaze didn't torch any buildings, but two lives were lost."

"Shit."

There was a quiet tension between us, the reason personal. However, we both knew better than to drag up the past, a conversation that had been forbidden to surface ever again.

"I don't know how you do it," he commented.

"Cause it's my damn job."

He snickered. We'd been friends for years, my return to the area as if I hadn't bailed from Missoula for years in search of something I'd never be able to find.

Salvation.

He'd stayed, fighting the good fight against criminal activity. "You're a damn good Zullie. No wonder they call you Phoenix."

Exhaling, I turned the wipers on high. I loved being a smokejumper, but the long days had started to take a toll. "Not according to my captain." Stoker Hansen was a tough son of a bitch, one of the best smokejumpers in the business, but the man had it in for me. I was too old, according to some of the guys, but I'd tested out just fine, top of the list. That had pissed a lot of other jumpers off. Fuck them. Staring into the eye of the beast as it threatened to consume everything around it was all I was meant to do. The rest had been nothing but a placeholder until I'd gotten my shit together.

"You do love to break all the rules. Look, the roads will be clear late tomorrow. Consider it a vacation," Gage said then laughed.

Some freaking vacation. I hadn't gone on one in more years than I could count. In my mind, I didn't deserve days off. That didn't mean I wasn't feeling the effects of exhaustion. While I loved my job, the rugged danger I faced almost every day, I hated the politics I'd been required to play. At least volunteering to be a mentor would get me off the shit list.

Or so I'd been told.

"Yeah. Yeah. I hear you. Keep warm by a fire while I suffer in a bedbug motel," I told him.

"Jesus. All doom and gloom as usual. Find a woman. That will improve your mood at least, you insufferable bastard," he chortled.

"Women are the bane of my existence." I had reason to think that way. I'd sworn off women. Forever.

"I'm not talking about a relationship, dude. Just find one you can fuck."

"There are always strings attached."

"After one night?"

"Especially after one night."

"Fine. Go sulk in your whiskey." His laugh was a reminder of all the things I was missing, but women weren't on my radar.

He ended the call, and I immediately dialed another number. The smart thing to do was to hunker down for the night.

At least there was some small town I'd already forgotten the name of only ten miles away. After turning up the heat in my truck, I slowly made it around a curve. The Ram could usually get through anything, but the icy mixture made for treacherous driving for anyone. At least she answered on the first ring. "Betty. Unfortunately, I don't think I'm going to get back tonight."

I could tell she was irritated, but she knew the time spent for my job wasn't controllable.

"The roads are getting slick. Don't worry. Everything is fine here."

Sighing, I had a sense of relief. "How did tonight go?"

"As well as can be expected. Stop worrying. I'll be right here until you get back," Betty said, obviously trying to convince me.

"You're an amazing woman."

"I know," she said, half laughing just before ending the call. At least one thing was under control.

With the snow falling rapidly, it was tough to see outside the windshield. God help anyone in a small car. Huffing, I was determined to make the best of it. Maybe I could finally get a good night's sleep. I rounded another bend on the hilly road, the headlights illuminating a car up ahead. I slowed to a crawl as I neared, craning my neck to determine the problem. What in the hell was some idiot doing out in an old Trans Am in this kind of weather? They were either a danger junkie with a death wish, or a damn tourist who'd underestimated the ever-changing weather conditions.

I rolled down my window as I slowed to a stop. There was no one nearby. Maybe they'd realized the error of their ways. Snickering, I continued on, traveling about a mile and a half when I noticed a blip in the distance. "You have to be kidding me?" As I looked closer, I realized I was witnessing a train wreck, the idiot from the muscle car making an insane attempt to seek help.

Oh, fuck me. The driver was obviously trying to make it to a house or a commercial business to get help. The guy would need to walk another eight miles to find a single soul. While the last thing I wanted to do was have this kind of interruption on top of dealing with the icy conditions, I couldn't allow the poor soul to continue walking.

Whoever was walking noticed my headlights and turned around. Just as I caught a single glimpse of the guy's face, he collapsed onto the pavement. "Shit." I glanced into the rearview mirror, passing the poor guy then pulling to a stop just a few feet away. I was no damn hero, but I couldn't in good conscience let a man die on the side of the road.

As I climbed out, grabbing my flashlight from my gear bag, ice pellets hitting me in the face, I cursed Mother Nature for a second time. Damn, I didn't like the cold. I yanked the hood of my jacket over my head then trudged through the snow, the crunching sound another reminder the late winter blast was perilous.

As I approached, shining the light just off to the side, I realized there was no movement, not a single sound or flinch. Jesus. If the guy had died on me, it was really going to fuck up things. I crouched down, slowly rolling him over and shining the low beam over his face.

Only the person with a death wish wasn't a man.

The lone figure who'd fallen into unconsciousness was a woman, her face reminding me of an angel. I was momentarily mesmerized until I realized her lips were already turning blue. What the hell? She was dressed in jeans, a light parka with a thin hood, certainly not attire meant for this kind of weather. She wore no gloves and instead of boots she wore shoes without socks. What in God's name had this girl been thinking? I pressed my fingers against her pulse. It was thready. I had to get her warmed up or she'd go into hypothermia. She was already unconscious.

What in the hell was she doing all the way out here? The road wasn't a thoroughfare for a single major tourist destination, and it was clear she wasn't a local.

There was no way I could leave her here to die in the wilderness. Grumbling, I scooped her up into my arms, holding her tightly against me. She seemed so frail, as if the life was draining from her small body. When she moaned, her eyes opening briefly, I cursed the day I'd returned to Montana. I preferred sun and surf, not mountains and snowstorms. At least that's what I'd kept telling myself. As I eased her into the passenger seat, I shook my head. This was going to turn out to be a very interesting night.

When she moaned again, her fingers falling across my hand, a rocket fire of electricity shot through me. I shifted my gaze, once against captured by her eyes. While the light on the cab was dingy as hell, there was no doubt she was staring back at me with stunning lavender eyes. My cock twitched, a stark ache appearing out of nowhere. I could easily fuck her.

What the hell are you thinking?

"You're going to be just fine," I told her, driving my raging libido back into the darkness, as I grabbed the fire blanket from my bag. Maybe it would help keep her warm until I found a place to land. I shoved it around her shivering body, taking a few seconds to brush wet hair from her face. When my cock hardened even more, I chastised my body's reaction. So she was beautiful. So the hell what? I had no room for romance, especially from a wayward stray on the side of the road.

As I eased onto the driver's seat, I took a deep breath, shooting her one last look before pulling onto the road. She had no idea how lucky she was I'd found her.

She remained still, her breathing ragged as I continued on the road, the conditions becoming more treacherous with every mile. When I finally saw lights up ahead, all I could do was hope there was some sign of life, a single motel in the small town. After driving another mile, I noticed a half-lit neon sign just up ahead. The marquis reminded me of the old ones that I used to see when my parents had driven through whatever secluded location they had to get through in order to fulfill their need for adventure.

As I pulled in, I debated getting two rooms. Nah. I'd need to watch over her for a few hours to make certain her condition didn't worsen. There was something ominous about the crackling sound the sign made as my boots hit the snow-laden pavement.

Half laughing, as I walked directly under it, I half expected the damn piece of glass tubing, metal, and plastic to come crashing down, shattering all around my feet. When I reached the door of the small office, I threw another look toward the truck, shaking my head.

The dude behind the counter was obviously surprised to see anyone in this weather. I'd been forced to rouse him from snoozing in front of whatever game show he was watching on Nickelodeon.

Then I had no choice but to carry her plus my gear bag up two flights, struggling to slide the old-fashioned key into the lock given her dead weight pushed against my chest. Before I walked inside, I gathered another whiff of her perfume, which turned my balls hard as rocks. It had been a long time since I'd held a woman in my arms. I kicked in the door, struggling to turn on a light.

The room was nothing special, but it appeared clean, and the heat was working. That's all I gave a damn about. After yanking down the sheet and tattered comforter, I put her down. She was still trembling, the wet clothes part of the problem. Christ. The last thing I wanted to do was invade her privacy, but I had to get the wet clothes off her body, or she'd never start to warm up.

There were about a dozen reasons I hesitated, including the fact I wasn't used to undressing helpless women for any reason. I couldn't seem to take my eyes off her face, furious with myself for finding her attractive while she could be close to death. I yanked off my coat and gloves, tossing them aside and raking my hands through my hair. Right now, there couldn't be a worse scenario.

"Get a grip," I hissed then turned away abruptly, yanking my gear bag onto the dresser, riffling through it until I found what I was looking for. As I held the bottle of bourbon in the dingy light, I shook my head. I could make all the excuses in the book for needing a hit of liquor, but the truth was I was terrified of having her die right in front of me. The ugly, helpless feeling was overpowering, more so than a single moment since arriving in Montana. I'd returned home to start afresh, refusing to fall into the demons that had kept me in a stranglehold.

I took a huge swig as I listened to the sound of the howling wind. I'd left my job as a damn EMT because it hadn't soothed the beast crawling inside. I preferred the danger and rugged terrain where I usually didn't need to deal with people other than my smokejumping team.

Much to the chagrin of my father, who was waiting with bated breath for me to accept the vice president position that had been on the table since I'd been ten years old. I hated the corporate world, but Pops had been pushing hard for years. With him being in bad health, my mother was now calling me once a week.

He had no understanding of why I needed to do this and there was no way of explaining it to him even after all these years.

When the mystery girl's body started to shiver uncontrollably, I was forced back into reality. The girl needed my help. I took another mouthful, slamming the open bottle onto the scarred surface before moving toward her. As soon as I touched her, a moan slipped past her lips, her eyelids fluttering open again.

"Don't fight me, sweetheart. I need to do this." I wasn't known as a gentle man, but I did what I could to be one as I peeled her jacket from around her, carefully pulling her arms from the sleeves then tugging it from under her. After easing off her shoes, I still couldn't believe she wasn't at least wearing any socks.

The fact she remained unresponsive troubled the hell out of me. It was time to stop acting like some teenager and get the rest of her wet things off. I held her head in my palm as I pulled the sweater over her stomach, stopping just before lifting the material over her breasts. This was getting ridiculous. I'd seen dozens of people in the worst possible light, sometimes forced to remove their clothing in order to provide medical assistance. Why was this any different?

Because you're a hungry, lonely asshole.

That might be the truth, but for all I knew she was married with six kids. I tried to remind myself what I was doing then pulled the sweater over her head. When my eyes drifted to her red lace bra, I almost lost it. Every muscle inside my body was tense, blood coursing through my veins like wildfire.

I sat down on the bed, rubbing my sweaty palms on my jeans before unfastening the top button on hers. Because they were wet, I had to struggle to get them past her hips, concerned when she didn't moan or cry out from my rough actions. When I finally wrangled them away, tossing them onto the floor, I immediately yanked the covers over her, avoiding gazing at her long legs or matching crimson panties.

You're a very bad man, Phoenix. You're never going to rise from the ashes.

That was certainly my reputation. I'd been called everything under the sun over the years.

Including a killer.

I searched the small closet, finding another blanket. The damn ratty pieces were far too thin to matter. Given her condition, she might need more help than I was capable of providing, but God only knew if there was a hospital or urgent care within fifty miles. If only I'd brought my emergency kit I kept at the house. After she was tucked in, I stood staring at her for a full minute before returning to the bottle of booze. At this point, I needed something to calm my nerves.

I hadn't been this anxious in as long as I could remember. The slight burn from the cheap liquor as it slid down my throat was justified, punishment for my waves of desire. I had no idea how long I stood staring at her but when her breathing became less fitful, I finally took a deep breath. Still, she wasn't out of the woods yet.

After a few seconds, I checked the pockets on her jacket finding nothing. There'd been no bag or purse I'd seen. Not only had she driven into the middle of a snowstorm, but she'd also walked into what would soon become whiteout conditions without any identification or money. What had she been thinking? She'd been better off staying in her car.

Yeah, but for how long?

I rubbed my eyes, finally noticing I stunk to high heaven. I hadn't bothered showering at the fire depot, preferring to jump into my truck heading back home. I certainly hadn't planned on seeing anybody in the dead of night. I took another belt of bourbon, realizing she would be out for several hours. At least I could take the time to grab a hot shower.

Another moan slipped past her lips, and I walked closer, unable to stop myself from brushing hair from her face, rolling the tip of my finger down her cheek. She was still so cold, but her temperature had improved slightly. That meant she'd made damn good time walking through the four inches of snow to where I'd found her. That could mean the difference in the poor girl getting frostbite.

I took a few minutes to rub each of her hands, checking on her feet before backing away. She'd had a guardian angel looking after her.

And that certainly wasn't the wretched bastard who'd carried her from the snow. No, that man could only be considered a devil.

As I headed toward the bathroom, I released a long, exaggerated breath. Maybe fate had finally decided to come back and bite my ass.

* * *

Wren

Warmth and softness.

Shifting, I slipped my arm to the side, trying to make sense of what I was feeling beneath my fingers. I tried to open my eyes, but they were heavy, as if I'd had too much to drink, only I knew that wasn't the case. But what... Mmm... I rolled on my other side, inhaling slowly, uncertain what scent was filtering into my nostrils. Then I realized what it was, the stench of smoke. Moaning, I tried to sit up, willing my eyes to open. A rush of images slammed into my mind.

Snow and ice pelting against the windshield.

Darkness so dense and ominous the headlights did nothing to mark the road.

Trees so thick I couldn't make out anything else.

Oh, God. Where was I?

I blinked several times, trying to focus, swimming up from the pit of blackness that had held me down. As my eyes slowly began to focus, I finally managed to ease to a sitting position, every muscle aching. *Where the hell am I?* I scanned the location, finally realizing I was in a hotel room. Wait a minute. Hold on. How had I gotten here?

And why was I under the covers?

When my eyes fell onto a pile of clothes on the floor, I jerked the covers against my chest as if that was going to do me any good. I was almost completely naked. Oh, God. What had I done? As I took shallow breaths, I realized my pulse was racing. Why had my clothes been removed? Fear slipped into my system, and it almost became crippling. There was nothing worse in my mind than waking up in a hotel room and having no idea how I'd gotten here.

I closed my eyes, trying to bring back the last memory. The storm had come in so fast. One minute it had been dry, some sun in the sky. Then the clouds had rolled over, suffocating the light. Within minutes, it had started snowing. That's right. I... my car. Oh, no. The car had skidded on the ice and I'd driven into a ditch.

Then I'd started walking.

Then headlights and... nothing.

But as the scent of smoke filtered into my system once again, my skin began to tingle. I freed my arms from the covers, staring down at the goosebumps covering both as I remembered something else.

A man's strong arms holding me against his chest.

A husky voice telling me it was going to be okay.

And imploring eyes the color of the Aegean Sea.

When I heard a noise, I turned my head. That's when I knew I was in deep trouble.

A pile of clothes was on the floor near the bathroom. Men's clothes. Oh. My. God. Please don't tell me I'd fallen into the hands of a twisted man who'd taken advantage of me when I'd been unconscious.

Don't panic. There must be an explanation.

This couldn't be happening to me. I was a good girl, well, at least for the most part. I obeyed all the rules, tried to be kind to strangers, and gave to charities. Why this?

Stop thinking so irrationally.

How could I?

Maybe I had been a silly girl to drive my sports car. Montana weather was unpredictable in March. I knew better. Even though I'd tried to erase most memories from living in Missoula, I wasn't stupid. Or maybe I had been. Wrecking the car served me right. Panic reared its ugly head, enough so I couldn't breathe for a few seconds.

I threw back the covers and an instant bite of cold rushed into my arms and legs. Shuddering, I peered down in a strange combination of horror and relief. At least I was still wearing my underwear. A benefit. And I didn't smell like sex. A definite benefit. Whoever the son of a bitch was, he hadn't fucked me like some wild animal.

Oh, I was definitely lost in the fog from before. There was no other explanation for my crazy thoughts. One thing was certain. I had to get out of this room before *he* came out of the bathroom. I immediately reached for my clothes, so lightheaded I almost tumbled to the floor. Whew. It took me three tries to grab my jeans. They were soaking wet.

Okay, maybe that was why mystery man had removed them. I tried to remember even a glimpse of his face. Unable to do so, I envisioned him as a monstrous man with wild hair and an unruly beard, capable of ripping a man apart with his bare hands. And to think the gruff bastard had brought me to a cheap motel like this one? I certainly deserved a lot better than to be treated like a whore.

When I took a single step, it was too quickly and I felt back on the bed, gasping for air. How far had I managed to walk? I could barely remember anything but the bitter cold, winds whipping through my jacket. I'd been so stupid to try to make it the rest of the way. It wasn't like I'd been dying to return.

When my heart stopped thudding against my ribcage, I carefully rose to my feet, still wobbly but stronger than before. While I could tell the heat from the unit under the window was on full blast, a burst of cold skittered into me, icy tentacles sliding through every muscle. My underwear was damp, so cold against my skin that I couldn't breathe. I had to find something to wear.

A bag. I noticed whoever the predator was had brought in a bag. I carefully made my way toward it, determined to snatch a shirt. *Are you crazy? You're going to put on something that belongs to a crazed killer?* My inner voice wasn't helping in the least. I certainly wasn't going to stand in a flaming red thong and lace bra while Mr. Serial Arsonist cleaned soot and grime from his body after burning down some-one's house.

Yes, you are.

No, I wasn't.

There's no other way to try to get out of his clutches.

There were times my inner voice did make some sense. Tonight was one of those nights. I was a strong woman. I'd left my comfy home for Texas all by myself. I could certainly wear clothes I had no business wearing.

My rational brain had yet to be thawed.

As I started riffling through his bag, I could swear I heard the shower being cut off. Shit. I didn't have much time. I tossed various items onto the floor. Rope. A flashlight. Protective eye goggles. No clothes yet. A small ax. A mallet. A…

A moan escaped my lips, and I immediately slapped my hand over it as I tumbled backwards. This was a gear bag of a mass murderer. Get a grip. *You can do this. Do it!* I walked closer, staring down at the sharp blade, horrible thoughts and disgusting visions filling what was left of my mind. I was shocked it wasn't covered in blood.

I just knew I was going to die.

Sucking in my breath, I threw a look toward the bathroom, fear now turning to terror. I had to find the courage to get the hell out of the room.

I reached in again, finding something soft. When I managed to pull out a huge tee shirt, I almost cried with relief. Wet underwear or not, I didn't have time to lose. He'd be coming out the door any minute. I threw on the shirt, spinning in a full circle, noticing a thick, fur-lined parka. Oh, thank God. I grabbed it, noticing Killer Boy had worn boots. I jammed my feet inside, not bothering to tie them, then stumbled toward the door.

Why weren't my legs working right?

No, hold on. The ax would come in handy.

I flipped around, losing my balance and crashing into the dresser. Pain tore through my hip, my mind almost returning to the wretched fog from before. Oh, no. I wasn't going to lose it. Not now. I could do this. Panting, I fought my way back to the duffle bag, grabbing the handle of the ax.

All I had to do was get to one of the hotel staff and they'd call the police. When I tried to unlock the door, I realized I couldn't feel my fingers. Door. Did I just hear the creaking sound of hinges from the monster opening the bathroom door? Maybe he'd taken another weapon inside with him. Now he was going to carve me up for dessert.

I hadn't realized I'd been holding my breath until I finally managed to throw open the door.

Then I heard his voice, the deep husky tone shattering the last of the polished steel armor.

"You're not going anywhere, sweetheart."

CHAPTER 3

 *hoenix*

She smelled like trouble, my traitorous body responding immediately.

Even the glint in her eyes screamed of trouble, the worst kind.

I wanted to fuck her.

At least a few times.

But that would get me into all kinds of trouble I didn't need.

As she stared at me with those same damn gorgeous eyes of hers, my mind went to every filthy place it shouldn't have gone. At minimum, I wanted her voluptuous lips wrapped around my cock as she looked up at me.

The mysterious guest remained frozen, the same mouth I wanted to deep throat finally pursing into a perfectly rounded O. Her eyes were as wide as saucers, staring at me through the dim light as if I was an alien being. When she slowly started to lower her gaze, her breathing more ragged than it had been when she was unconscious, I allowed myself to ponder the situation.

For a woman who I'd feared was on her deathbed, she'd managed to toss my things on the floor before deciding to steal some of my clothes. And she stood in my boots and coat with my ax in her hand. What the hell was she thinking?

When she shifted from one foot to the other, placing her other hand on the ax handle and lifting it into the air in front of her, I tried not to laugh. Even though the wind howled, blowing snow into the room, the blast of cold air didn't seem to bother her in the least.

"Come back inside and close the door," I told her, trying to keep some sense of levity in my voice even though I was exhausted.

"Na uh," she said, already shaking almost as much as she'd done before.

Na uh? Really? It was easy to see I'd been right in my assumptions. "Give me the ax." I threw out my hand and walked closer. The woman growled, an actual animalistic sound. What did she think was going to happen by a man standing in nothing more than a towel?

"Nope. If you come any closer, I'll… I'll cut your balls off."

I wasn't certain whether to be shocked or amused. If I weren't so bloody tired, I'd likely be furious, but given the circumstances, I tried to remind myself to give the girl some slack. "Give me the ax and come here. You're going to freeze to death."

"That's better than being cut into pieces, charbroiled for dinner."

Fuck. She'd misunderstood what my bag was for. Now I was definitely amused and would have teased her relentlessly under other circumstances. "Look. I'll ask nicely since I'm about to freeze to death myself. Come inside. *Now.*" When venom flared in her eyes, my cock twitched. She was a feisty one.

Her mouth twisted as she glared at me, her grip tightening on the handle of the ax. I had the distinct feeling she'd make good on her threat. I took another step closer, and she lifted it by a few inches, growling like some damn she-wolf.

"My patience is wearing thin, little girl."

"Look, grumpy bastard. I don't know who you are. And I'm not a little girl."

"The man who likely saved your life. How's that?" I retorted. Grumpy bastard? Yeah, maybe I was.

She finally seemed to sense a storm was raging outside, taking a jerky step further into the room and quickly glancing over her shoulder. I noticed she was shaking even more. At this point, she was going to fall to the floor and God knew what would happen if she still had the sharp ax in her hand. I'd purposely sharpened it while waiting for the hotshot's captain to sign me out. Somehow, I doubted she was the kind of woman who knew how to wield the powerful tool.

No, she was far too soft and feminine with a luscious hour-glass figure and perfect skin. Ah, shit. Here I went again thinking like a bastard.

When she finally closed the door, I cocked my head. Then I beckoned her with a single finger. "Come here, sweetheart. I'm not going to hurt you." What I wanted to do was turn her over my knee, teaching her some manners. "You're better off with me."

"Na uh."

Who the hell said na uh? Sighing, I could feel the frustration building to the point I was about to say something totally out of line. Then again, I'd never been known as the kind of guy to watch my mouth or curb my anger. "Sweetheart, if you don't come here and hand me that ax, I'm going to need to punish you, even if you almost fell into hypothermia. I don't like your attitude."

Her eyes remained open wide. Then she narrowed them sharply, her mouth twisting. "And I don't like yours. I don't know who you think you are, but if you dare try and lay a hand on me, I'll cut it off after I've handled your testicles."

Jesus Christ. The woman was serious. This was getting us nowhere fast. "I'm going to come closer so you and I can have a discussion. Why don't you place the weapon on the dresser. I won't touch it if you agree you won't touch it. Fair enough?"

"Who are you? Where's my beautiful car? Why did you remove my clothes? What did you do to me when I was out of it? And what is that horrible stench?"

She was starting to sway. This was getting out of hand. I took a step closer and she almost panicked. I could see it in her eyes.

"My name is Riggs, but you can call me Phoenix. Your *beautiful* car, which was a stupid choice to bring to Montana this time of year, is stuck in the snow. The reason you're standing in my tee shirt is because you were soaking wet. What I did to you was remove your wet clothes so I could bring your body temperature up. And the stink is from remnants of smoke from a huge fire I was battling along with some other smokejumpers. Now, are you satisfied enough I'm not an ax murderer, so you can put that down before you really do get hurt?"

"What kind of name is Phoenix?"

"One I got in the Marines." I could tell she didn't believe me. "See the tattoo?" I stuck out my arm, flexing my muscle.

While she lowered her gaze, the smirk remained. "For all I know you could have carved that yourself."

"First of all, it's not carved, it's ink. Second, my knife skills don't include dancing along skin for fun." Great. Now I was fulfilling her ax murderer fantasies.

She hesitated, but slowly eased the handle onto the edge of the dresser. "What's your last name?"

"Social security number too?"

"I'm cautious."

"Uh-huh. Now that we're playing twenty questions, you're going to answer mine. What's your name? Why in God's name were you out in the middle of a snowstorm in a car with zero capability of making it through ice in barely any clothes? And where in the hell were you headed on a dark, lonely road leading to nowhere?"

She glared at me with defiance in her insanely gorgeous lavender eyes, but in those few seconds, a jolt of electricity shot into both of us at the same time, the crackling energy unlike anything I'd ever felt before. She certainly seemed to experience the same thing, her gaze shifting into a foggy lust. When she started to speak, she dragged her tongue across her lips and God help me, I wanted to crush my mouth over hers, pulling her tightly against me.

There was no chance the thin towel managed to hide what I was thinking, the ache in my balls severe.

"I'm... I'm..." she stuttered, her eyes falling to my groin. She swallowed hard and pushed her hand through her strings of hair, struggling to return her gaze to my eyes. "My name is Wren Tillman. My beautiful Trans Am was a gift to myself for all the shit I've been through recently, so I certainly wasn't going to leave it behind in Texas. I listened to the weather forecast this morning and there was no mention of a storm rolling in." She stopped briefly, her chest rising and falling. "And where I'm headed is no business of yours, except I'll tell you the destination is because of a ridiculous family event that I can't miss for anything. Does that satisfy you?"

I thought about what she'd said and sighed. "Texas, huh? Well, this isn't the best way to get to Missoula."

"I'm from Missoula, so I obviously know what I'm doing and where I'm going." Goddamn, her attitude was rough around the edges, which made me want to show her who was really in charge. "And why are you staring at me like that? You're not a very nice man."

"Nope. You're right about that." I lifted my eyebrows, wanting nothing more than to keep fucking with her since driving my cock deep inside wasn't an option. I was one bad man.

Her face turned beet red. "Okay, maybe I've never been on the road before but I trusted my GPS."

I decided to take another two steps closer, and a slight hint of fear returned on her face. "Well, it was wrong."

"Fine. Do you want to tell me all the things I've done wrong?"

"Like you shouldn't have been walking in the snow? Maybe if you were a smart little girl, you would have stopped for the night? Would you like me to continue?"

She bristled, her entire face depicting vile and ugly thoughts while all I could think about was wondering how tight her little asshole was. She purposely closed the distance, glaring at me with so much venom it was all I could do not to burst out laughing. "Fine, Mr. Smokejumper, if that's what you really are, then you're right. I'm a long way from home and I just..." When she faltered, I cupped her jaw, digging my fingers into her skin. I didn't blame her for not trusting a

43

man standing in a towel, but I needed a drink and good night's sleep, not a ferocious tiger standing over me in the middle of the night.

What I wasn't expecting was her quick actions as she cracked her hand across my face. From there, everything happened in a split second as I snapped my fingers around her wrist, the hand the one that had been holding my towel in place. Then I shoved her against the wall, pressing my naked body against her half naked one. My reflexes were what I normally did when anyone dared to attack me.

I came out fighting.

"That wasn't nice of you, little girl."

"Yeah? Well, I never said I was a nice girl, especially around an ax murderer." Wren wiggled, managing to slam her foot against the back of my knee. Then she pummeled her small fists against my chest, her lips full and pouting.

"So you like it rough, do you?"

Her eyes lit up with a fire I hadn't seen in a long time. "If you think you have what it takes."

She had no idea what she'd just done by opening Pandora's Box.

"Be careful what you ask for, little girl."

I pressed the full weight of my body against hers, pushing my fully erect cock into her stomach. And in those next few seconds, I knew I had a choice to make.

One. I could be a decent man and pull away, getting dressed and encouraging her to lie down and get some sleep.

Or two. I could do all the filthy things to her that were rolling around in my mind like wildfire.

Since I wasn't a decent guy by anyone's standards, I make the only choice a bad man like me could make given the circumstances.

I captured her mouth.

* * *

Wren

Holy smokes.

I was being kissed by the most gorgeous man on the face of the earth. No, he wasn't just good looking. He was a model-on-the-cover-of-a-men's-high-fashion-magazine   only wearing a leather jacket kind of sinfully good looking. Even the ink covering a portion of his body was attractive. It also managed to hide several scars.

Phoenix.

The name rolled off my tongue. A Marine. Did that mean he was trustworthy?

I was flabbergasted and that wasn't like me in the least. Granted, I shouldn't have slapped the man who'd probably saved my life, but his brazen attitude and threat to punish me had gotten under my skin.

He wasn't just a grumpy asshole either. He was an arrogant son of a bitch, just wrapped in the most incredible muscular layering. While he was older, likely in his late thirties, the age had turned him into a masterpiece.

I'd teased him, which wasn't like me, but it had felt so damn good, as if I'd opened the floodgates of passion. He was rough and tumble, and I had a feeling he wasn't going to let me go unscathed.

As he crushed his body against mine, there was no doubt what he had planned. Maybe he'd concocted the scheme when he was in the shower, or when he had picked me up in the snow. Whatever the case, I had to get away from him.

Only my body didn't want to in the least. Now he smelled of soap and testosterone, the scent rushing straight to my pulsing core, the needy bitch already driving me crazy. When he'd grabbed my chin, pussy juice had trickled into my panties. Now I was breathless, my vision blurred from a crazy moment of desire and need furrowing inside of me. I'd never been so overwhelmed by the presence of a man, my sense rattled to the point I was more lightheaded than before.

I couldn't control my reflexes or my inner bad girl and I wrapped one arm around his neck, tangling my fingers in his thick, dark curls, arching my back as he explored every centimeter inside my mouth. No man should taste this delicious, a hint of bourbon mixing with a tiny smidgen of peppermint.

My God, he was hard as a rock, his shaft throbbing, which matched the way my pussy was quivering, the scent of my desire wafting between us. This was crazy, ridiculous on so many levels. I didn't know him. He could be married or have just escaped from a prison. He could have made up the story about being a smokejumper for all I knew. Then why save me? Because I was the first woman he'd come in contact with?

You're thinking crazy thoughts. Stop it.

I couldn't breathe as the moment of passion kicked up in intensity. He was so powerful and strong, visions of him carrying me to his vehicle popping into my mind. As a roar of electricity shot through me like a thunderbolt, I knew I could get lost in this moment. I moaned into the kiss as he dominated my tongue, his masculine scent filling me completely.

When he lifted me off my feet, I involuntarily wrapped one leg around his, enjoying every second of the way I felt in his arms. How long had it been since I'd been with a man? Oh, yeah, a lifetime ago and the few times I'd been with the jerk had almost turned me off of men completely.

But the desire had just come roaring back.

I was hungry for attention, more so than I'd ever been in my life, all sense of rationality swept away. My heart was beating so fast I was certain I would have a heart attack and when he broke the kiss, I gasped for air, blinking several times in order to try to focus.

What the hell was I doing? Acting like some crazed school-girl enamored with a boy. I couldn't do this. I had better sense. But as he lowered his gaze, his green eyes penetrating mine, I also lost myself once again. No. Hell, no. I couldn't do this.

Phoenix made the mistake of backing away a few inches. That was all the space I needed. I gave him a hard shove then cracked my hand across his face once again, managing to swerve under his arm toward the bed.

"Not so fast, sweetheart." He wrapped his fingers around my hair, swinging me around to face him once again, throwing his arm around my waist. The look in his eyes was primal, as if he was going to eat me alive.

Dear God, a part of me wanted him to.

"You need to let me go."

"That's not going to happen. We're stuck together all. Night. Long."

Shit. Shit. I hadn't thought about that. "No way."

He smirked and lowered his head. "Oh, yeah."

I wiggled until I was able to jerk out of his hold, struggling with the girl inside who wanted to be set free, if only for a single night. I backed away and when he took a step closer, I slipped my leg in such a position that the second he took another stride, he toppled over.

His growl was a clear indication I'd crossed a line. Maybe I was being foolish or maybe this had become a predatory game. I wasn't certain. But when I jumped over him, he grabbed my arm, tossing me onto the bed, once again crushing his body against mine.

He rose onto his elbow, shaking his head. "Tsk. Tsk. Now I'm going to need to punish you."

"For what?"

48

"For being a bad girl."

"You're crazy." I glared at him in shock.

"You got that right." When he swept his gaze down the length of me, I hissed.

"And you're a pig."

His laugh was deep and so husky that it sent vibrations dancing through me. A part of me wanted to take a swing at him and the other to seduce him.

"I've been called so many things in my life I've lost count." His tone was far too sultry, reeking of danger.

He didn't give me time to object, rolling over and sitting up on the edge, jerking me over his lap in a split second. I was so shocked I didn't react at first, gasping when he brought his palm down on my mostly naked bottom.

Why, oh, why had I worn a thong that morning? Maybe because I had no clean clothes left, preferring to wait until I got to my destination to do so.

When he smacked me four times in rapid succession, the heavy fog started to lift and I pushed up from the bed, using what little strength I had left to almost pitch myself off it.

Phoenix seemed surprised, muttering under his breath before throwing his leg over mine. "That's going to cost you." He ripped down my panties with enough force I heard a ripping sound.

"No! Don't you dare tear them."

"You should have thought about that when you fought me."

He managed to drag the lacy material down to my knees then resumed the spanking. I was mortified, heat building in my cheeks as fast as the skin on both sides of my bottom. Nothing could have ever prepared me for the incredible burst of pain tearing through me. I panted like some dog, clawing the ugly bedding in a vain attempt at getting away from him. He was far too big and too strong, his muscles sculpted as if from the hardest stone.

The moment the tiny towel had slipped from his waist, floating to the floor, my mind had gone into a state of permanent desire. His cock was long, thick, and gorgeous. I even envisioned taking the tip into my mouth, sucking until he filled my throat with his cream.

What was I thinking? That was crazy. Maybe I had a head injury from the hard jolt when the car was tossed into the ditch. Yes, that had to be why my mind had been taken prisoner by lust.

He peppered my butt with hard cracks of his hand, the sound exacerbated to the point my ears were ringing. Or maybe that was from the constant crackling of electricity shooting through me like a live wire. Either way, it didn't matter. I couldn't want this. Not ever. Harsh discipline had never been a part of my life. I abhorred the thought.

And I hated him.

Then why was I so turned on, my nipples aching to the point of pain as they brushed against the lace material roughly? I had no answers. I keep going back to the possibility I wasn't in a right state of mind.

"Let me give you a hint, sweetheart. When a man saves your life, it's best not to make him angry."

"I'm not your sweetheart!" God, the man was infuriating.

"You're going to be exactly what I tell you to be right now."

Holy shit. That man thought he could be in charge of me? Not a chance. "Never."

"Then you'll learn the hard way."

He brought his hand down at least six more times, developing a rhythm. I tried to kick my legs but couldn't budge even a little bit. I closed my eyes, doing what I could to control my breathing and my nerves. Another vision of his naked body swept into my mind and my pussy clenched and released so many times I was certain I'd have a climax.

Oh, God. Wouldn't that be embarrassing?

"I'll give you a hint," I said breathlessly. "Don't have an ax when you take a stranger inside a hotel room."

"Duly noted."

I heard the amusement in his voice and squirmed again, gasping several times when I realized how wet I was. Jesus. Was I dripping juice on his legs? I cinched my eyes shut, trying to block out the moment.

Then my pussy muscles betrayed me more than my body had. Clench. Release. Clench. Release.

No. No. No!

As an orgasm suddenly rolled through me, I lifted my head, doing everything in my power to keep from allowing him to know. When a series of moans rushed up from my throat, he stopped spanking me. Suddenly, he was caressing my heated skin, rolling the rough pads of his fingers in circles from one side to the other.

He eased his leg from mine, adjusting my knees so they were spaced further apart. Then I heard his heavy breathing.

"Are you wet for me, Wren?"

When he said my name, the strangest sensations of swooning swept through me, his tone entirely different than before. He was as aroused as before, maybe more. I was so turned on by the sound of his voice I couldn't answer him.

But thoughts jetted into my mind that were wild and crazy, exciting and terrifying.

He was going to touch me.

Lick me.

Fuck me.

Oh, sweet Jesus, I couldn't believe this was happening.

Bad girl. Bad girl. Bad girl.

No, I was worse than that. I was a terrible woman for allowing a stranger to touch me in an inappropriate manner. I was about to share that with him when he slid his hand between my legs, rolling his thumb around my clit.

I dragged my tongue across my lips, my heart racing as he slipped his other fingers past my swollen folds. Then I pushed up from the bed, tossing back my head. There were so many things I should say, but in that moment, there was nothing more I wanted than to feel alive again, to experience the kind of passion that had eluded me for years.

No, for my entire life.

I didn't need to know anything about him, and he couldn't care less to learn about me.

I wouldn't see him again, the state was too big, and that would be just fine.

But on this night, maybe, just maybe I could allow myself to live.

Hold on. Maybe he could be my date.

What are you thinking? He's rough around the edges. Hmmm… Maybe that would be perfect. But I certainly couldn't ask him at this moment. He'd laugh at me.

When he rolled me over onto the bed, he planted his hands on either side of me, peering down. His eyes were glassy, but the color was like looking into shimmering pools, a deep lagoon that I could fall into and feel safe.

That's what he made me feel, as if nothing and no one could ever hurt me.

He lowered his head until our lips were mere centimeters apart, his eyes darting back and forth across mine. Then he said the words that both titillated and terrified me at the same time.

"This isn't a good idea, but I don't give a shit about rules. I *am* going to fuck you. Not just once but the entire night. And you're going to scream out my name every time."

I pressed my hand against his chest, digging my fingernails into his skin as I took a deep breath. We both knew exactly what this was, two people needing to find solace in the middle of the night, satisfying a hunger that knew no bounds. And in that moment as I nodded once, I could sense nothing else mattered but the taste of him, the feel of his muscles against my skin.

He pushed me into the center of the bed, crawling over me, his chest heaving as he narrowed his eyes. Then he ripped at my bra, jerking down the straps, reaching under me and deftly unfastening the hook. As he tossed it aside, I rolled my fingers down his chest, marveling in his tight abs and perfectly sculpted body. He was rock hard everywhere, his days spent fighting fires honing his body. I no longer wanted to think about anything else. Just the moment.

Just him.

Just our needs.

As he cupped my breast, I arched my back, flashes of light skipping past my field of vision. This was wild and wonderful, something I would never forget. Then again, the experience would be something I wouldn't want to remember. I wasn't this girl.

Tonight, I shoved aside the anguish and anger, exchanging it for sin and filth.

And it felt good.

His growl was that of a predator and as he slowly lowered his head, his eyes seemed to change colors, his irises shimmering in gold. The second he darted his tongue around my already taut nipple, there was no way of keeping a moan from escaping. He was nothing more than a beast, but his roughness ignited every ember. When he pulled my hardened bud into his mouth, I grasped his shoulders, digging my fingers in as juice trickled down the inside of both thighs.

I could tell by the carnal expression on his face that he knew exactly what he was doing to me.

"Oh... Yes." I tossed my head back and forth, unprepared when he bit down on my tender bud. The slice of pain awakened the last of my senses and I was the one who'd become a ravenous beast. I brushed my fingers down his chest, reaching for his engorged cock, but he was having none of it. He yanked one arm over my head then the other, shifting onto his knees as he grasped both wrists in one massive hand.

I was his prisoner, a possession he could do with what he wanted. Panting, I watched as he rolled his lips to my other nipple, taking the time to lick and suck before pulling the tender tissue between his teeth. Every part of me ached, my muscles incapable of reacting. I had no strength left, no sense of wanting to get away, but I could tell the man was dangerous just by the look in his eyes.

As if he had secrets to hide, dark deeds that had stripped him of a portion of his humanity. That made what he was doing that much more exciting. When he was finished teasing my nipples, he dragged his rough tongue all the way down my stomach, using his knee to push my legs open wide. Then he flicked a single finger back and forth across my clit until it was so sensitive that I cried out several times.

"Yes. Oh, God. I…"

"Soon, you'll be shouting my name, sweetheart." His growl was so deep, the intense baritone skipping through me, that I lost all ability to breathe. He had a way of making me feel as if we'd done this before, our needs escalating every time.

Phoenix switched his finger to his thumb, rolling it around my clit as he toyed with my pussy, darting his fingers inside. And the look on his face couldn't be described. I wiggled in his hold, trying to free my arms, but it was no use, his hold that tight. As he pumped his fingers inside, keeping them flexed open, I knew it wouldn't be long before I had an explosive orgasm.

"Mmm… Oh…" Every strangled sound skipping past my lips seemed to turn him on even more. As least I was able to bask in the beauty of his cock, my mouth watering to suck him dry. I'd never want to take a man into my mouth and throat so much. It was another crazy moment in my mind, but I couldn't rid myself of the dirty images.

"You're so wet for me. Am I the only man who can make you this hot?" he asked, the wry smile on his face one of dark mischief.

"Yes. Oh, yes."

As he laughed, he thrust his fingers in hard and fast, driving me to the point of madness within seconds. Nothing had ever felt so scintillating, my breath captured in a vacuum that I never wanted to leave.

I couldn't hold back any longer, the orgasm unlike any I'd ever felt before.

"Yes. Yes. Yes!" My scream was high pitched, and I couldn't seem to stop the sound from echoing in the room. I could only imagine what other guests were thinking. Or maybe they were hungrier than they'd been before. One climax drifted into a wave, and I lolled my head to the side, no longer able to think clearly.

"That's a good girl," he muttered, and I could barely understand what he was saying. When he released his hold, I couldn't move, not wanting to lose the fabulous moment.

But he had other things in mind, yanking me off the bed and into his arms. He shoved me against the wall with so much force the lamp on the nightstand rattled, jarring my senses. I clawed his back, trying to hold on, wrapping my legs around him. He kept the same smile, so dark and dangerous that I was almost concerned about what he was doing.

Then he wasted no time driving the entire length of his cock deep inside. My muscles stretched, my mind blown as my pussy clamped and released, struggling to accept his huge girth.

"Yes. Yes!" Another scream popped from my mouth and this time he stopped it, capturing my mouth as he rolled onto the balls of his feet.

He began fucking me like a wild animal, driving deep and hard, slamming me into the wall as he dominated my tongue. I continued raking my nails up and down his back, the sensations overwhelming, the moment savage.

There was an almost desperate need inside of him, the longing as great as my own. He continued pistoning inside of me, sliding me up and down the hard surface. The scent of him became intoxicating and I knew my skin would be tainted with his aroma. As he sucked on my tongue, I closed my eyes, shifting into a moment of raw bliss. He continued for what seemed like twenty minutes, his stamina unlike anything I'd ever experienced. How could he keep going this way?

Phoenix abruptly ended the kiss, gasping for air before nipping my lower lip then dragging his tongue from one side of my jaw to the other.

"Are you still cold, sweetheart?"

I barely heard him, only able to nod. The chill had driven into my bones, but the surface was hot as a wildfire.

"Hmmm… then I guess we need to do something about that." He pulled me away from the wall, taking long strides toward the bathroom.

"What are you doing?"

"What I need to get you nice and hot all over." He ripped back the shower curtain, stepping inside and turning on the water.

"You just had a shower."

"Yeah, but we're going to get so damn dirty I'll need another because after I'm finished fucking that sweet pussy of yours, I'm going to take you in your tight little ass."

The instant blast of cold water didn't lessen the heat we'd already generated. There was something so dirty about being in an ugly motel room decorated in shades of tan and orange to make the experience seem even filthier. He pushed us both under the stream, his breath labored as he ran his fingers down my side, allowing his gaze to fall at the same time.

"You are one beautiful woman."

"You're not so bad yourself, for a rough and aggressive man."

"Baby, you ain't seen nothing yet." He lifted and pushed one leg against the shower wall, tickling my clit before wrapping his hand around his shaft. As he pressed the tip past my swollen folds, I took a deep breath and held it. This time, he eased inside slowly, allowing my muscles time to expand. That didn't make it any less intense, my mind blown by the way my body reacted, electrified sensations coursing through every muscle and tendon.

The fire building between us would not be denied. When he was fully seated inside, he threw his head back with a deep roar. When he finally dropped his gaze, locking onto my eyes, I was mesmerized even more than before. He allowed me to stroke his chest, running my fingers up and down aimlessly for a few seconds. The moment was pure joy, the exploration one I could do for hours.

"Grasp the showerhead and do not let go or I'll be forced to punish you again."

His commanding words would have put me off only hours before. I'd always hated men who thought they could lord their power and strength over a woman, but with him, nothing was the same, everything new and fresh.

And I wanted to obey him.

Maybe later I'd try to determine why, but right now that was the furthest thing from my mind.

I did as he demanded, wrapping my fingers around the cold metal, holding on for dear life as he pressed his hand against my thigh, holding me in place and fucking me more brutally than before.

The heat continued to build, steam rising in the small space, beads of perspiration almost immediately forming over the top of my lip. I was no longer cold, the fire burning between us threatening to get out of control.

He pulled all the way out, thrusting into me then repeated the move, all the while watching my reactions. My eyelids were half closed, the pleasure spilling through me inde-scribable. The man was so powerful and masculine, his purpose only to provide the ultimate roar of ecstasy.

I was shocked with an orgasm flashed through me without notice, exploding into every synapse, the ache building to a bolt of ecstasy.

"Oh. Oh. Oh. Oh. Oh."

"Do you want more?" he asked, his voice barely audible.

"Yes. God, yes."

"Then tell me, sweet Wren. Tell me what you want."

"Fuck me. Just fuck me."

"Soft?"

I opened my lazy eyes as wide as they could go, shaking my head.

He tweaked my nipple, pinching and twisting until I cried out in pain. "Not good enough. Tell. Me. Now."

"Fuck me hard. Drive your big cock deep inside."

His nostrils flared, his growls more animalistic and he did as I asked, driving his cock so deep inside that I thought I'd lose my mind. My body was shattering from his touch, every molecule broken down to its base, and he was slowly rebuilding it again piece by piece. How could sex be so life changing, reducing me to my most primal self? I writhed in his hold, trying desperately to follow his command, but my fingers were slipping.

Slipping.

Falling.

When I grabbed his shoulders, he took a deep breath, narrowing his eyes. "You disobeyed me."

"Yes." And I'd do it again. And again. My fingers were on fire, seared from brushing against his skin.

"Then I have no choice." He pulled all the way out, pinching first one nipple then the other, his breathing ragged as he watched me.

I was shaking from head to toe, no longer in control of anything. My body. My mind. My soul. The mystery savior had yanked them from me, claiming them as his own. When he pressed my legs as wide open as possible, I bit my lower lip, blinking several times.

He ran a single finger between my breasts, taking a few seconds to roll the tip around my belly button. Then without hesitation, he smacked my pussy lips over and over again.

An instant rush of agony poured into every cell. "Oh. That is… it hurts."

"That's what bad girls get." He repeated his actions several times until my mind was blown from the way the pain shifted into pure nirvana. How could experiencing this kind of agony feel so damn good?

"I'll be good." The words blurted from my mouth before I could stop them.

"I don't believe you." He slapped his fingers against my pussy lips six more times then dropped to his knees.

As the water splashed down over us, he engulfed my pussy lips with his hot mouth. There were no words, no sound coming from my pursed lips, the pleasure that intense. As he licked and sucked, I pressed the back of my head against the shower, water trickling into my mouth. My legs were trembling so much I would have fallen had his strong hands not been holding them in place.

Gasping, I couldn't seem to get enough air in my lungs as he drove his tongue inside, lapping my cream. He was savage with his actions at first, then shifted to sweet tenderness, pulling me so close to another mind-blowing orgasm that I wasn't certain I could stand the pleasure. He feasted as if he were a famished man, issuing husky growls the entire time. I laughed and moaned, no longer able to focus, the heat in my system becoming explosive.

"Come for me. I need to taste all of you."

There was something about his command that couldn't be denied. Almost instantly I complied, obeying him like a good little girl. The moment I was swept away by the most powerful orgasm, I thought the man was going to eat me alive. He licked furiously for a full minute, maybe more. I could no longer think clearly and didn't bother trying. I was completely lost in ecstasy.

I was vaguely aware he'd risen to his feet, stroking the side of my face. When he turned me around to face the shower wall, I didn't try to shift to another position.

"Open your mouth," he whispered in my ear before nipping my lobe.

I did so instantly and when he drove his fingers inside, I sucked without being told.

"Do you see how sweet you are?"

"Mmm…"

"Make them nice and wet for me."

I sucked and licked as he pumped them in and out, still tingling all over. When he pulled his hand away, I rested my face against the cool surface, panting so hard my heart was thudding against my chest.

"Now, open those sweet ass cheeks of yours," he growled.

Everything about the command was maddening, but I arched my back as I eased my arms around my hips, splitting open my ass cheeks.

"Yes. Perfect. You're such a filthy little girl. Aren't you? You need a man to fuck your asshole every day." He rolled a finger down the crack of my ass then rimmed my dark hole, the action forcing me to pant. I'd never been taken in the ass. Not once. It had felt dirty and horrible. When he breached my hole, gently sliding a single finger inside, I licked my lips in anticipation. I wanted to be a filthy little girl. I craved being taken like an animal.

He pushed his finger even deeper, driving past the tight ring of muscle. As he started pumping, a wash of pain flashed through me as I gasped. When he added a second finger, I tensed but within seconds the discomfort shifted into a carnal need. I arched my back even more, bucking against his fingers.

Chuckling, he added a third finger, thrusting harder. And harder.

"Now, I fuck you." He replaced his fingers with his cock, pushing the bulbous head just inside. Then he planted his hands on either side of me, pressing his chest against my back. "Do you like it dirty?"

"Yes."

"Good." He slipped another inch inside, then another.

I gasped, shivering against him as the vibrations became even more electrified. When he thrust the last few inches in, every muscle tensed, and I gave him exactly what he'd wanted.

I screamed out his name.

"Phoenix! Yes. Yes."

He pressed the full weight of his body against me, holding his cock in place for a few seconds. Then he started pumping in earnest in a nice, steady rhythm, allowing my muscles to get used to the thick invasion. But within seconds, he couldn't hold back any longer, pulling out until only the tip was inside then driving deep inside.

"Yes. Oh…" I could no longer put a coherent sentence together, my mind blown from the intensity of his actions.

But it felt so damn good that I never wanted it to end.

He placed his hands on mine, entangling our fingers as he continued the lewd act, shifting his hips and thrusting brutally. Our ragged breathing was the same, our bodies molding together as one. Harder. Faster. I wanted more. More.

And he gave it to me, fucking me until the water finally started to turn cold. Only then did I sense he was close to coming.

I closed my eyes, still panting, my mind on cloud nine. Then I squeezed my muscles. There was nothing more enticing than hearing his deep roar as he filled me with his seed.

 *ren*

I'd learned two valuable aspects about myself in the last three years since graduating college a year early. One: I hated a typical corporate structure. Two: Sexy, rugged men were tempting but usually came with baggage. The second had proven true on the few dates I'd gone on. Every man had some complex they kept hidden until the third or fourth date. Either they were a control freak, had to prove themselves to their buddies, or acted as if women were objects.

That made the decision to try to hire Phoenix easier than I'd expected. Okay, so we'd had sex, seriously incredible, mind-erasing sex. In fact, my body still ached from his roughness, his needs insatiable. He'd taken me two additional times, waking me from deep slumbers. Not that I was complaining. I'd never had so many orgasms in my life. However, it could never happen again. Once I made up my mind about something, I never altered my decision.

Ever.

"I'll take you to your car. I should be able to dig it out," Phoenix said almost in passing. He grabbed his bag, his gruff demeanor returning as soon as the sun had risen.

Suddenly, a woman who'd never had trouble finding her voice couldn't form words in a coherent fashion. I stood where I was, staring at him. Granted, he was lovely to gaze upon under any circumstances, but I felt like a failure all of a sudden, needing to pay a man to date me for a couple of days.

Even if the circumstances required me to jump out of my comfort zone.

When he finally turned to face me, he narrowed his eyes. They were so deep green that I was lost in them for a few seconds. "What's wrong, sweetheart? Cat got your tongue?"

"Um…" As he started to walk closer, the same heat swept through every muscle in my body like a wildfire.

"Do I make you nervous, little bird?"

As he crowded my space, I tried to keep a rational mind, finally sidestepping him.

"I have a proposition for you." I couldn't look him in the eyes. I'd never felt so humiliated in my life, but my sister's idea made sense. No strings.

"Hmm… When a beautiful woman says she has a proposition for me, my mind goes to some very dark, kinky places." His laugh sent a shiver down my spine.

"So look. I'm just going to say this." Before I lost my nerve. "I'm returning to Missoula for my sister's wedding and I'm the maid of honor. Now, you don't know my parents, but they're the oppressive type who want me to follow this path they laid out for me in grade school. You know the one I mean. Get straight A's. Be the most popular kid in school. Work for the family company then allow them to hunt down the perfect man to spend the rest of my life with, popping out at least three kids while living in suburbia with a white picket fence and a damn dog in every holiday photograph." I finally took a deep breath, realizing it was ragged.

Meanwhile, he remained quiet as a church mouse.

I still couldn't look him in the eyes. *Get to the proposition.*

My inner voice wasn't helping.

"I'm not the marrying type. Hell, I don't even like men. I mean I like them. Big and rugged, with sex oozing from every pore, but that's not my life." I wasn't making any sense, the fact my cheeks were so hot I could barely breathe affirmation. "So, what I'm saying. No, what I'm asking is that since my parents have a date ready for me in the hopes another engagement announcement can be made at the reception, would you be my date?"

There was total silence in the room.

I wanted to crawl under the bed and die.

68

"Um. I'll pay you. Now, you'd have to endure a couple days around my family, and that's no easy task, but I think you can handle it. All I need is to pretend we're close. Really close. I'm not suggesting you buy me a ring or anything, of course not. But my mother can pick out a lie from a thousand yards away. I figured since we had sex, we might be able to pull it off. That is if you can still stand me this morning." Now I was almost out of breath. And I still couldn't look him in the eyes. What was wrong with me?

"Who's the date?" he growled possessively.

"So, this guy my parents have known for years. He's older. Not like you where you're a lot older than me but not too old. He's really old, like fifty. I don't want to marry a fifty-year-old man. Okay? I'm young. Carefree. I have my whole life ahead of me and he'll want kids right away. I can't do kids. Nope. Not me. There is no clock ticking."

Shut up. Just shut up.

Oh, God. I felt his presence. He was standing right behind me. I knew he was. A lump formed in my throat, which was so unlike me. This was much more difficult than I'd imagined.

"I know it's a lot to ask but I'll pay you a thousand dollars. We can negotiate if you need to. I'm pretty flexible in all areas so—"

Phoenix whipped me around to face him, cupping both sides of my face. Then he captured my mouth, the move so unexpected I was frozen in place. His fingers dug into my skin as if he was determined to take what he wanted. The taste of mint toothpaste sizzled my senses almost as much as the massive hunk who held me in his arms. I pressed my hands against his chest, curling my fingers around his shirt. He had a crazy effect on me, which was disconcerting as hell. Somehow, I knew this was his way of refusing.

When he finally broke the kiss, a sly smile crossed his face. "Did anyone ever tell you that you talk too much, sunshine?"

"Sometimes. Okay, often."

He backed away, turning toward the door.

Shit. He was going to blow me off.

"Um… was that a yes or one of those 'nice try' moments?" I asked, biting my tongue after doing so. Great. I looked desperate. Now I wanted to crawl in a huge hole in the earth.

"Thousand bucks, huh?" he asked.

"Yes."

"What's the catch?"

Shit. I hadn't wanted to tell him the rest just yet. I thought I could hook him then grovel when he found out he'd need to stay at my parents' house. "Um. I hope you own a suit? I mean, a rugged man like yourself probably doesn't need a suit very often, but it's a formal affair. You'll understand when you meet my mom and dad. Everything has to be just so, especially since it's my baby sister's wedding." When he cocked his head, glancing over his shoulder, the darkness in his eyes created another sense of arousal. I needed to shut that off right now.

"Stop talking. I have a suit. What else?"

I remained quiet, dragging my tongue across my lips. "Oh, you want me to answer. Well, you need to stay with me at my parents' house for the weekend. That's a rule."

The smug look on his face returned. "Fine."

"And one more thing." I stood taller, refusing to back down on this. I couldn't allow the night I'd spent with him to cloud my judgment or interfere with my future plans. "And we can't do this again."

"This," he repeated.

"You know. Sex. We can kiss, a chaste kiss or two. That's fine. But definitely no sex."

He lifted a single eyebrow before allowing his gaze to fall all the way down to my useless shoes. "You have yourself a deal, little bird. But I have one condition myself."

Oh, God. I could only imagine what he was about to say. "Okay."

"You will do as I say."

"Meaning what?"

"Meaning, if you're going to get yourself into trouble, I will steer you clear, and I'll be required to punish you if you get out of line."

Whoa. What the hell was I supposed to do at this point? Either spend two plus days with Lincoln or obey a gorgeous, rugged man? I'd opt for the latter.

Exhaling, I nodded. Then as he opened the door, I realized I'd just opened Pandora's Box. I had a terrible feeling my plan would blow up in my face.

* * *

Phoenix

What the hell are you doing?

Not thinking. That's what I was doing. Why the hell had I agreed to go to some damn wedding? I hated them almost as much as I did wearing a suit. That wasn't me. My father, on the other hand, flew to Italy to purchase hand-crafted Dolce & Gabbana attire to the tune of twelve thousand a pop.

She had to be at least twelve years younger than me, her perfect face and bright eyes an indication of just how young she was. Hell, it almost felt like robbing the cradle.

I couldn't seem to get my mind off her for longer than a few seconds during the drive. Her scent lingered on my skin even after taking another shower. She was a feisty little thing, but the fire burning inside of her was almost as bright as the flames I'd just finished fighting.

And spanking her had seemed natural. I wanted to laugh.

I needed to get my head out of the sand.

Women.

Now I knew why I wasn't good at the dating bullshit. They talked a lot. Too much. But hell, Wren was pretty to look at, and the way she'd felt underneath me, writhing as she moaned had awakened the beast inside. I wasn't entirely certain I could put him back in the cage at this point.

By the time I pulled into the driveway, I was already second guessing my decision to accept her offer. Hell, I didn't need the money, although she obviously thought I did. I was playing with the kind of fire that would burn me into ash and somewhere in the back of my mind, I knew better. However, her soliloquy had been endearing, like a deer caught in headlights. Did arranged marriages really exist nowadays?

Old. She'd made me feel old at thirty-five. Sighing, I rubbed my jaw, images of her voluptuous, young body shifting back and forth in my mind. I was a wicked man to be thinking of her with such… hunger.

At least my weekend should prove to be interesting. As long as Mother Nature and the pyrotechnics cooperated, that is. There'd been way too many fires as of late, although most of them were confined to a limited number of acres given the recent wet weather conditions. Still, my gut told me the smokejumping team was in for a doozy of a year, arson on the rise.

I grabbed my bag and jumped out, the front door opening almost immediately. As Justin rushed out without a coat as usual, I knelt down, hoping he'd come and give me a hug for a change. He stopped at the edge of the porch, glaring at me with such hatred in his eyes that it broke my heart every time. I had no business being a father, but neither the kid nor I had any other choice.

"Hiya. Can you give Daddy a hug?"

He never blinked as he stared at me, but finally he stomped down the stairs, which was a huge change from when I'd come home from fighting a fire. When he was within two feet, he wrinkled his brow. "You didn't come home last night."

Sometimes, he acted as if he was so grown up, but he had no method of coping after all he'd endured in his five short years on this earth. As Betty walked out on the porch, I glanced in her direction. She'd been a godsend, a woman with the patience of Job. Without her willingness to be flexible in her schedule, I'd never be able to continue being a Zullie.

"Justin. You forgot your coat," she told him as she held it out.

He didn't bother looking in her direction or acknowledging her. The poor kid was dealing with such vicious anger issues that his behavior precluded him from joining a kindergarten class. I blamed myself for not taking time off after he'd landed on my doorstep. I'd been in far too much shock over Dahlia appearing after five and a half years, dumping the kid and a single suitcase along with one toy in my lap.

My own fury hadn't gone away for a two solid weeks.

"You're right, little man. The snow kept me away." I balled some in my hand, holding it out, but he stood exactly the same, his stare piercing my soul. When I brushed the snow-ball against his cheek, he giggled. Only then did he allow himself to throw his arms around me. It was the first time he'd done so. I glanced up at Betty, noticing tears in her eyes. She'd been with me through every struggle, never saying a word when he smashed almost every plate in the house he could get his hands on, using his crayons to write all over the walls.

At least I'd gotten him into a damn good therapy program, but the psychiatrist had told me it would take time, a lot of time.

I picked him up, holding his small body tightly against me. "I drew you a picture," he whispered.

"You did?" I opened my eyes wide, pulling away so he could see the delight on my face.

He nodded several times as I walked up the stairs, Betty shaking her head. "Let's get you inside," I told him before hearing a vehicle pulling up the long gravel driveway. "Go get it for me. Then we'll have some hot chocolate. Okay?" He nodded, the anger leaving his eyes. After putting him down, I headed back down the stairs. It wasn't often I had company and I preferred it that way.

As the beat-up old Ford came into view, I took a deep breath. I never knew what to expect from the man. I'd been shocked like the rest of my buddies that he'd returned home alive, his rumored death haunting almost everyone. But he'd changed, just like everyone else who'd served in the military.

Myself included.

Sadly, he was a shell of a man, living in the past instead of forging his way into a new future. As he pulled up, stopping his vehicle, I walked closer as he climbed out. Then I threw out my hand, waiting as he debated whether he'd shake it.

Then he grinned, which was as rare for him to do as it was for me, accepting the gesture.

"Snake. It's good to see you."

"You too, buddy. I wish I was coming here for under more pleasant circumstances." He glanced at the house, having only accepting my invitation to come in once. Since his return from Afghanistan, he'd kept to himself, becoming more of a hermit than anything. While he'd purchased the ranch butting up to mine, he spent most of his time hiding out in a cabin in the mountains.

The day I'd heard he'd been killed in action, I'd envied him knowing the nightmares were over. What kind of asshole of a man thought that kind of thing? I couldn't imagine what he'd endured as a prisoner of war, scarred from a horrific fire that had stolen his identity for months and yet there'd been times I'd wanted to be him. Sighing, I rubbed my jaw, hating the awkward tension that had started on a dark day back when we had yet to turn eighteen.

"What do you mean?" I finally managed.

"I found some of your horses on my property this morning."

"Shit. Another fence needing repair."

Snake shook his head. "No, there are fresh cuts on the rails. Someone did so intentionally, but it gets worse."

"What?"

Exhaling, he shook his head. "Three of them were shot. There's nothing I could do for two of them. The one who's injured is safe in my barn. I didn't see your foreman so I did what I could on my own."

Shot? What the fuck? "Are you thinking poachers?"

"I honestly don't know what to think. They wandered onto my property before they were hit, though. Not sure if the asshole was going for you or me."

He eyed me carefully as he always did, hoping just like he'd done before that I had the answers. All I had was guilt and agonizing pain.

Great. First suspicious fires. Now this. "I appreciate you letting me know."

"I called the vet early this morning. Marshall came out right away. The other horse will be just fine."

Nodding, I scanned the property. I'd had issues with poachers the first day I moved onto the ranch, but nothing since then. "I'll come get her later today if that's okay with you."

"You should probably give her a couple days." He stood where he was, glancing toward the mountains. I knew instinctively what he was thinking about, the same thing that had kept me awake many times over the years.

"Yeah, you're right. How are you doing?" I asked after a few seconds.

"As well as to be expected. I need to figure out what the hell to do with the rest of my life."

"When the time is right, you'll know."

"Yeah, one day. When the shit in my head clears." He continued to stare in the same direction. "Do you ever wish you could go back in time?"

I'd asked myself that at least a dozen times, only I wasn't certain what we could have done differently. "Sometimes, but I got to a point I had to let the past stay buried."

I sucked at lying.

He turned his head, his eyes holding no emotion. It was as if his loss of memory and the time he'd spent recuperating had stripped him of everything he'd once been.

But not the ugly secret.

Karma was a fucking bitch in my mind.

Snake said nothing else before heading to his truck. While I'd been injured while serving in the Marines, it was nothing like what he and his team had suffered through. As he drove away, I glanced one last time toward the area where it had happened.

It.

I couldn't even put a real name to what had happened all those years ago. What I did know is that one day, the grim reaper would send his demons to collect my soul.

I deserved nothing less.

* * *

Wren

Snow.

I hated it, or at least I had until the night before. Shuddering, I bit my lip as I checked the godforsaken GPS application on my phone for the tenth time then glanced at the faded numbers on a small sign at the end of a gravel driveway. This had to be it. If not, I was going to call the company who'd rented me the cabin and tell them exactly what I thought about their shoddy directions and lack of detail.

As I made the turn, my stomach tightened. I'd never done anything so impetuous in my life. To ask a man I didn't know to pretend to be my boyfriend had to be on the top of my list of stupid things. And my list was getting long.

Kissing him.

Fucking him.

Those were right up there.

Good girls don't fuck men they don't know. They were words my mother had told me after drinking one too many martinis the day I'd turned eighteen. That had been her way of reminding me that I had a reputation to uphold. I was the daughter of a very important man.

Then she'd spent at least an hour berating me for everything I'd done wrong in my life. That's one reason I'd moved away as soon as possible.

Huffing, I allowed naughty visions of Phoenix to slide into my mind on purpose. He was certainly rough and rugged, which would likely force my father into drinking heavily. While I didn't want to ruin Cammie's wedding festivities, this had been her idea after all. And bringing a smoke-jumper as my date instead of a multimillionaire would give my father his just deserts.

And I didn't even know his last name.

I was crazy. Insane.

I couldn't help but grin. I needed to have a little fun after all. I was due. As I glanced into the rearview mirror, I noticed a spark in my eyes. That hadn't happened in years. I was able to make light of paying a man money for his company. Who knew?

I'd worked twelve hours days for as long as I could remember, building up an impressive client list. I'd endured nasty phone calls, demands, and pompous attitudes for as long as I could remember.

At least Phoenix had been a gentlemen, digging out my car with a shovel he'd had in the bed of his truck, sending me on my way with a heated gaze and a 'so long.' He'd been right that the GPS had sent me via bumfuck, and I would never have made it anywhere alive given the distance to the small town where we'd stayed. He'd been my hero, a rugged savior in the night, but I wasn't planning on telling him that. He was already arrogant enough as it was.

But the fact he still went by his code name told me a lot about his character and his love of his country. Another small shiver skated down my spine. This was just a date and nothing else. He was too grumpy to care about. However, I did love a challenge.

As I noticed a clearing just up ahead, I held my breath, praying I hadn't been lied to about the condition of the cabin. When the structure came into view, I was pleasantly surprised, relief settling into my system. The cabin appeared rustic, but much like so many others I'd seen in the area. While the ground was covered in a blanket of white, I could sense the grounds had been well maintained. The porch wrapped around on one side, the oversized windows inviting.

I noticed a huge stone fireplace on one side and near a large shed was a stack of wood just waiting for me to light for warmth. Exhaling, I cut the engine, cursing the fact I hadn't packed snow boots. The closest I had included heels, which wouldn't work in this weather. I'd been forced to realize how stupid I was not coming prepared. I'd need to go shopping sooner versus later.

While Phoenix had been right and the roads had been cleared by the time he'd driven back to my car, I'd remained terrified I'd get stuck again. My mother had already called twice asking why I hadn't been able to make the lunch reservations she'd made for just the three girls of the Tillman family.

Not that I minded missing it.

I'd remained on edge the rest of the trip and what should have taken a little more than four hours had taken six. It was already after three and I'd yet to eat anything. Why hadn't I stopped on the way? Stupid me also hadn't thought about purchasing food before getting here either. I'd just wanted to lock myself behind closed doors, pretending my heart wasn't aching.

I carefully made my way up the stairs, pressing in the code to the lockbox. At least the key was inside. When I unlocked and opened the door, I stood in awe for a few seconds. The interior was gorgeous, the high ceilings drawing my attention immediately to the wooden beams. There was an incredible view from the huge back windows, and I moved toward them instantly, peering out at a majestic sight. Mountains covered in snow. Wow. Things were looking up.

I meandered through the furnished space, finding everything exactly as had been described. And the kitchen was to die for, stainless steel and granite. As I ran my fingers over the surface, I had to wonder why anyone would allow this beautiful location to be rented. Everyone had an ugly story buried somewhere in their world.

I knew that far too well.

After dragging everything inside, I returned to the kitchen, opening the cabinets. Food. Wait a minute. The cabinets were stocked. I moved from one to the other, finding an array of pastas and spices, flour and soups. Then I dared look into the refrigerator. Oh, my God. It had been fully stocked, the freezer as well. I did a happy jig, especially when I noticed a wine rack off to the side.

I needed to take back all the ugly things I'd said about the rental company. When I heard my phone, I laughed. My sister was persistent.

As I yanked out my phone, I sighed, given she'd done a face-time call. I doubted I looked my best after the long, delicious, crazy, sinful night. My thoughts remained on the rugged man as I answered, trying to act cheerful when I remained exhausted, whether from the cold or the three rounds of intense, passionate sex.

"I'm here safe and sound," I said, suddenly craving a glass of wine.

"You didn't call me. I was worried sick, and my calls didn't go through," Cammie admonished. I was thrilled she was so happy after everything she'd endured in her life. Still, I wanted to beg her not to get married, but that would be the bitchiest thing I'd done my entire life.

And she didn't deserve it.

"Well, I stopped for the night."

"Why didn't you call me then?" She leaned forward toward the phone, narrowing her eyes.

"I might have been stranded. And busy."

"What do you mean stranded? I told you that you shouldn't have brought the car. Are you okay? Are you hurt?"

"No, I'm not hurt. Hold on." I propped the phone against the toaster, taking a few seconds to select a wine. While at this point I would have sucked it right out of the bottle, I was thankful there were some very pretty wineglasses, too pretty to be left in a rental house if you asked me.

"Is that why you look rode hard and put away wet?" she teased.

No, that's because I was rode hard, kept wet and hot for blissful hours. "Very funny." I found a wine opener and knew it was my lucky day. As I started to open the bottle, she remained quiet. I finally threw her a look and sighed. "I drove into a ditch, but a guy came along and saved me."

"A guy?"

I waited until I'd popped the cork, pouring a hefty amount in the glass and taking a sip before leaning over the counter, unable to keep a smile off my face. "Let's just say they grow their men in Montana big, strong, strappin' and packin'."

She narrowed her eyes then slapped her hand across her mouth, giggling like some schoolgirl. "You're kidding me?"

"Not even a tiny bit. Of course, that was after I threatened to cut his balls off with an ax I found."

"Whoa. Hold on. You had an ax?"

"No, he did. I found it in his bag inside the motel room where he took me when I was unconscious."

"Wait a damn minute. Repeat what you just said," Cammie said, her expression full of horror.

I laughed. "It was a misunderstanding. I thought he was an ax murderer. Turns out he uses the ax for smokejumping. We threatened each other then we had sex multiple times." I couldn't believe I'd blurted it out just like that.

Her look of revulsion turned into one of shock.

"Wow. You took a plunge alright. I know what I said to you, but oh, my God."

"It was crazy, just one of those things."

"Just one of those things. Girl, you are an entirely different person. So, was he really hot?" Cammie asked, waving her hand in front of her face as she formed a perfect O with her mouth.

"You have no idea."

As I shifted from foot to foot, I was reminded again that he'd spanked me. I didn't think I could admit to that humiliating part. She knew me as a tough woman, taking on both wealthy male clients and arrogant financial advisors with glee in my eyes.

"Wow. I wish I could take after you," Cammie admitted. Why did I have a feeling she was second guessing getting married? How many times had I wanted to convince her that she shouldn't be marrying a stuck-up, rich prude who couldn't stand me? I'd learned the art of biting my tongue.

However… an evil thought rushed into my mind.

"Why don't you come out and play tonight?" I asked, although my tone was more of a purr.

"With you? You'll lead me astray. At least according to Mom."

"Well, you deserve a bachelorette party."

Cammie huffed. "Are you kidding me? Marcus would have a cow. We're going to dinner at his parents' house."

Marcus. AKA stuck-up dude.

"Did you ask this hot man to come to the wedding with you?"

"You're changing the subject," I told her. "Maybe, but you're going to need to wait to find out."

"You're terrible."

I held up my glass of wine, giving her a saucy grin. And for some reason I had butterflies churning in my stomach.

"Well, this should get interesting. Are you going to tell Mom before you come?" Cammie shook her head.

"Why spoil the fun?"

"You're one bad girl. Be careful. Mom took the liberty of inviting Lincoln to the rehearsal dinner. Assigned seats. Guess who he's sitting next to?" Her grin was almost as devious as mine.

All I could do was laugh. "I guess Mom and Dad are in for a rude awakening."

Now I couldn't wait to have the sexy man on my arm. We'd make quite a couple.

* * *

Phoenix

. . .

I scanned the perimeter of Snake's ranch before giving my dead horses one last look. They hadn't deserved to die like this. The horses had been grazing in the back pasture, which meant the assholes had come up the back road, the one few people knew about. It serviced both ranches, but the area was overgrown, not visible from any other road. The cut through the fences had been crude, likely made from a chainsaw. What I couldn't understand was why break through the fence? What the hell was the point?

I wasn't the kind of man to think conspiracy theories, but I'd had a bad feeling since returning to town that I should have reconsidered my decision.

Exhaling, as I rose to my feet, Gage was just returning from looking for any evidence that might have been left.

"I'm sorry about the horses, Phoenix," he said as he peered down.

I gave the vet a nod before he pulled the sheets over them. "The asshole who did this is going to die."

"Don't do anything rash," he advised.

"I'm going to do what I need to do." I noticed the vet was shaking his head. "What's up?"

"Well, you're not going to like this," Marshall said as he rose to his feet, his expression pinched. "I don't think the person responsible was a poacher." Marshall Lockwood was one of the best vets in the state and someone I'd call a friend.

"A handgun was used," Gage suggested.

Marshall nodded. "Do you want me to dig out one of the bullets?"

I glanced at Gage. "Why not. That might tell us if the hit was personal."

"Like I said. Don't go off halfcocked," Gage advised again.

"It's not about doing anything rash. It's about hunting down a fucking lowlife and providing payback."

"That's my job."

I turned my head in his direction. I'd known Gage for even longer than I had Snake. We'd been buddies since the first grade, but he'd taken a much different route than I had, almost landing in prison. He'd gone way off the deep end after the incident in the mountains, enough so he was almost institutionalized. Instead, he'd been forced by his father to join the Army to clean up his act. In my opinion, he was lucky to be standing here wearing a badge after the crimes he'd committed as a kid. "You have more important things to handle."

"You know how I feel about animals. And you do too, buddy. Let me know what you find, Marshall."

"As soon as I get the ballistics report I'll give you a call." Marshall clapped me on the back. "We should catch up sometime."

"We'll do that." I'd been saying that for months. I worked. I cared for my kid, and I fought nightmares. That's all that I had the energy to do.

"How's Justin?" Gage asked after Marshall had headed for his truck.

"Still adjusting. I don't know what I'm doing, and he knows it too. The kid is smart but uncontrollable."

"Sounds like somebody else I know." While Gage laughed, I could tell by the concerned look in his eyes that he knew how much the blow of finding out I had a child had hurt and angered me.

"Very funny. I just don't think I'm the right person for him."

"You don't have a choice."

"Yeah, well, his grandparents have started hounded me, telling me I'm unfit to be a father."

"Fuck them. After the damn daughter they raised, what the hell are they talking about?" He sucked in his breath, realizing he'd crossed a line. "That was shitty of me."

"It's fine." He was right. Justin's mother was a mess. No, she *had* been a mess. I closed my eyes, a moment of rage shifting into my system.

He patted my shoulder. "Day at a time."

"Like you would know, Mr. Confirmed Bachelor."

He laughed. "Some of the guys are going to Raunchy Ride tonight. I might even be able to get Snake out. Think you can swing by?"

As soon as he mentioned the weekend, another image of the naughty vixen slipped into the back of my mind. "Maybe." Justin had made a single friend and was going over to the kid's house tonight. Either I could sit around and worry that he'd make a scene, or I could try to enjoy myself. Hell, why couldn't I get her off my mind? Wren. My little bird.

Shut the fuck up. She's not yours.

"Oh, and there's the rodeo starting tomorrow."

I had to laugh. My buddy still fashioned himself to be a bull rider at his age. "As much as I'd love to see you fall on your ass, believe it or not, I have plans for the entire weekend."

"Wow. Some new chick?" His grin told me he wouldn't let it go until I said something.

"Do you ever meet someone and half of you wishes it would never have occurred because you know it's going to be a nightmare and the other half wants to explore that person top to bottom?"

"I take it something happened last night."

"Not just something," I said as casually as possible. "Someone."

He lifted his eyebrows, his grin widening. It was still amazing we could tolerate each other. I was a rule breaker and proud of it. He'd spent his adult life doing nothing but following rules, trying to make sense of criminal activity, and the usual bullshit that came with it. "Are you going to explain or are we playing the guessing game? Are we talking about a woman?"

"Not just a woman, but one whose behavior required a trip over my knee. And I didn't stop there."

"How is it possible that you leave a fire likely grimy as shit and you meet a woman in the middle of a snowstorm and manage to have wild sex when I can't get a woman to look in my direction?"

"Because I'm damn good looking," I chortled.

"Thanks. I'll keep that in mind. So, are you two gettin' hitched or did you bother to get her number?"

"I agreed to be her date for her sister's wedding."

"Wow," he snickered. "You're turning into such a romantic man."

"She's paying me too."

He burst into laughter. "I take it she doesn't know who you are."

"That never came up. We were a little busy."

As he leaned in, he winked. "What's her name?"

"Wren Tillman."

"Tillman?" he asked, laughing as he shook his head. "You're certain that's her last name?"

"That's what she told me."

Gage sighed as he scratched his chin. "I know you don't follow politics, but you have to know who her father is."

I narrowed my eyes, trying to figure out what he was talking about. Then I sucked in my breath. "Not that pompous son of a bitch who thinks he's God."

"If I'm right, then you might just get your ass handed to you. He's one gruff, belligerent man."

"Yeah? Well, I'm one badass man. He's trying to set her up with some old guy, as in an arranged marriage. That's just shit if you ask me."

"Wow. You like this girl. I can tell when your possessive streak comes out."

"Very funny." I hadn't realized I'd bristled when talking about the plans her parents had for her. "She just doesn't deserve that shit."

"Uh-huh. You like her. Lie to yourself all you want. Oh, and by the way. You're an old guy."

He took a step away as if I'd punch out his lights. "Asshole. Don't remind me."

"No. I'm wrong. You're the bad boy of Missoula just like all those years ago. At least some things never change." His expression hardened. "Now, tell me about the fire in Billings."

"Not much to tell. It was man made. There's no doubt about that."

"You're still thinking arson?"

"It's not a popular opinion with the Billings boys, but that's what I think. I caught a whiff of gasoline, but not enough to confirm my suspicion. Still, with the bodies, I think they were dumped, the fire started to cover up the murders. Why?"

"Did you check if there were any reports of missing people or abductions?" he asked.

"What are you getting at, Gage? Did something happen while I was gone?"

"A ranch burned. Shadowland." He allowed the information to settle.

"Shit." They were some of the nicest people in town, still talking to the wayward kids who'd nearly torn Missoula apart.

"Yeah, I know. Fortunately, it was contained by the fire-fighters quickly, but there were four casualties. Only two people live there. Did you realize I knew the owners my entire life?"

"Yeah, I know."

"God-fearing people, the husband a friend of my father's from a long time before. Hell, they bought the house from Pops when we moved into the new place."

I could tell he was putting some pieces together. If my memory served me, his parents had moved after Gage had gone overseas in the Army. There was a hell of a lot I didn't like in the world, but coincidences were close to top of the list.

"I didn't hear anything from the captain about any missing persons reports, but I came in on the tail end when they thought the wind was going to shift. I can give the man a call and ask what he found out about their identities."

"Yeah, do it. I'd be curious," he said as he stared down at the horses again, his jaw clenched.

"So, the fire was suspicious."

"Second one this week."

"There's been a hell of lot of suspicious fires over the last few months. From what Captain Hansen mentioned a few days ago, the percentage is up by eighteen percent," I told him.

"Yeah. Then this."

I was sickened from the thought of losing the animals. My gut told me their deaths had been sent as a warning. But to whom?

I glanced toward Snake's barn then back to my sprawling land.

Why did I have a feeling this was just the beginning?

CHAPTER 5

 hoenix

Raunchy Ride.

I'd purposely stayed away from the honky-tonk bar since the last time I'd had too much tequila, roughing up one of the regular customers. Hell, they'd deserved it, but the incident had added to my less than stellar reputation.

As I strode inside, I noticed two other Zullies had sidled up to the long bar. I snickered as I repeated the nickname that had been bestowed to the group of smokejumpers a long time before I came to work with the team. As much as I hated to say it, they'd been more like a family than I'd experienced my entire life.

Life was good at this point, no need to allow my mind to shift to the past. Unfortunately, I couldn't get Wren out of my mind, still second guessing going to the damn wedding. I'd heard far too many ugly stories about how my Pops had been best friends with Gregory Tillman. They'd been partners in the early days, determined to buy up a good portion of Missoula.

Then there'd been some kind of betrayal, which had led to my Pops leaving Montana but not before trying to destroy his former friend. After I'd heard the story a few times, I'd tuned out. The question was would Gregory recognize me after all these years? Then again, did I give a shit?

The answer was a clear no.

I noticed Gage and Marshall on the other side of the room and headed in their direction. It had been a long time since the three of us had been able to grab a beer outside of the house, our work schedules clashing. I pushed my way through the crowd, giving high fives to a couple of the other people I knew, including Jake Travers, otherwise known as Hawk. He'd had been overseas in Afghanistan at the same time I'd been, our respective teams working in collaboration on a couple of missions. Also a helicopter pilot, the shit he'd gone through with another team had hit me hard, Snake a member. We all had stories from serving our time, but his entire team had come through, which is more than I could say for a lot of them.

"How's it going?" Hawk asked as he grinned.

"Pretty damn well. How's married life?"

He was the person who gave me hope that one day I might find the right girl. That sure wouldn't come from Gage, the divorce he'd gone through more like a damn firestorm.

"Bryce keeps me on my toes."

I had to laugh. "Then she's doing a good job. Hey, is she still a reporter?"

"On and off while being a mother. Why?"

"I wondered if she'd caught wind of a possible serial arsonist."

"Not that she's told me. I'll check with her. You know Bryce. If there's some insidious mystery to be solved, she'll dig until she finds out what it's all about."

"That's what I was hoping for."

He frowned. "Is it anything I should be worried about?"

He owned a huge ranch that had been in his family for years. "No. Gage was asking."

After rubbing his jaw, he nodded. "I'll ask her to give you a call."

"I'd appreciate it. Good running into you."

"Yeah, dude. Don't be a stranger."

I moved through the crowd, joining Gage and Marshall at a table near the stage. As I sat down, I sensed Marshall had already been told about my night of raw passion.

"I took the liberty of ordering you a beer," he told me, his hand firmly wrapped around the base, the grin on his face one I'd normally wipe off with my fist. "For a price."

"You told him," I snarled at Gage.

"Hey. You didn't tell me to keep it a secret." Gage grinned as he sat back in his chair.

"Fine. Yes, I rescued a damsel in distress, and we had hot sex. Okay?"

"I'm jealous," Marshall said.

"If you'd step away from the animals long enough, maybe you'd find a hot chick yourself." The man took being a veterinarian seriously, so much so he had no life.

"Very funny. I'm happy at this point in my life. Loneliness has its benefits. I don't spend much money. I get to leave my dirty laundry on the floor."

I gave him a stern look. "Snake didn't bite for tonight?"

Gage shook his head. "That man is really suffering. Have you talked to Hawk or any of his other team members about it?"

"Not my place," I said half under my breath. "Besides, he won't let anybody help him."

"Yeah, I know." Gage leaned farther back in his chair, more pensive than usual.

The tension between us was thick.

"So, I called in a favor with a buddy of mine," Marshall said in passing. "The bullets I pulled from the horses were unusual."

"Soldier grade?" I asked, just guessing at this point.

"Yeah. You knew." Marshall looked from one to the other. "A Ruger. An MK to be exact."

"That's not the usual cowboy weaponry," Gage said as he shook his head. "I don't like this shit."

"Have you talked to the fire investigator about the Shadowland fire?" I lifted my eyebrows as his expression darkened. Marshall was an implant, not party to the burden Gage and I carried.

"Results expected any time. I'm sure he'll ask me to come to the scene."

Which I knew would be rough on him.

"I'd like to come with you when you talk to him." I grinned after making the statement.

Gage lifted his eyebrows. "Against protocol."

"I'm in the business." I took a gulp of beer, wishing I'd invited Wren out for the evening. The girl had managed to crawl under my skin. How the hell had that happened?

Marshall laughed. "Mr. Rule Breaker, you are the town sheriff."

"Yeah, yeah. Did you talk with Stoker?"

"He doesn't know anything definitive. A couple of the fires were ruled accidental anyway."

"I'll let you know when the investigator calls," Gage said absently, obviously more worried than he wanted to let on.

"So, about this girl," Marshall said, quickly changing the subject.

"She's cool." I tried not to make a big deal of it.

"Cool. We're not in high school," Marshall teased.

"He's got another date with her." Gage grinned like a kid.

Marshall laughed. "The man I thought incapable of feeling anything but anger found a woman he likes. The world must be coming to an end."

"Very funny." The truth was that spending time with Wren had made me feel so damn alive. The moment I'd looked into her lavender eyes, I wanted nothing more than to taste every inch of her. A woman hadn't done that to me in... forever.

I sat back, sipping the beer, trying not to feel sorry for myself, which I did far too often. Hawk was married, almost every member of his last team hooked up with the perfect woman, some with families or with ones on the way. It was at night I felt the loneliest, which allowed the ugly nightmares to set in. Maybe a shot of tequila would make me feel better. Maybe it would take three.

"I'm going to grab a shot. Another round?"

"I'll come with you," Marshall said. "Maybe I'll check out the hotties hanging around the mechanical bull. There's a special contest going on tonight."

Both Gage and I laughed. There were always cowgirls who used the bull as a way of grabbing some cowboy's attention.

"I'm afraid to ask," I huffed as I stood.

"Let's just say the highest bidder takes all."

What in the hell?

He moved through the crowd first, heading toward the other side while I headed for the bar. Still, my eyes were drawn to the ridiculous ride given the volume of noise. The joint was rowdy as hell even after being cleaned up a couple of years before. After ordering another round, I turned toward the stage, studying the entertainment for the evening. What did it say about a place when you had to hide the band behind chicken wire? I had to laugh. If only I could relax and get into the music. The only thing that took away the edge was fighting fires. It had become my drug, a need that furrowed deep inside of me. I might have become the killer Wren had feared if it hadn't been for being selected.

After tossing back a shot, I shoved the glass onto an empty table, the roar of the crowd surrounding the bull drawing my attention again. I couldn't help walking closer as the electronic wood and leather creature bounced and gyrated, spinning back and forth in an effort to toss off the rider. No wonder Gage loved coming here. He could practice to his heart's desire. I couldn't help but grin as I walked closer.

What the hell were they bidding on? To see if the rider fell off? An ugly feeling pooled in my stomach.

Then I heard a lilting female voice yee-hawing over the country music blaring on the speakers.

When the rider was tossed a few seconds later, the crowd started to cheer.

"More. More. More."

"Woohoo. She's mine," some dude screeched. Good for him for winning.

As I started to turn away, unable to keep from laughing, I heard the rider's voice clear as day and a combination of anger and frustration rolled through me like a firestorm.

"Get your hands off me."

There wasn't a chance in hell that I was right. No way.

"Come on, sweetheart. You know you want it. In fact, you've been asking for it all night," a man snarled. "Besides, I bid on you and won fair and square."

She was playing the damn game? Instantly, rage tore at my system, and I pushed my way through the crowd, determined to knock the asshole's head off. No other man would ever dare touch my woman. "What the hell is this?' I snarled as I tried to figure out what was going on.

"They have it every Thursday. They pick the hottest girls to ride the bull then get the customers to bid on them. Highest bid gets a nice little date while the girl gets the money. Everybody wins."

Oh, Jesus fucking Christ. That wasn't going to happen. She was mine. All mine. Fuming, I shook my head, trying to figure out what to do. When I noticed both Marshall and Gage were standing off to the side, I motioned for them, my attention immediately drawn back to the mess in front of me. My little bird had gotten in over her head.

"I swear to God, if you don't take your hands off me, I'm going to find a way to cut them off," she bellowed.

My anger only increased. *What the hell are you doing?*

I found my way front and center, clenching my fist, no longer shocked by the bad choices she made.

"Hey, Bart. Get your fucking hands off the lady," I snapped.

"What's it to you?" Bart hissed. "She's coming with me. I bought her for the night and she's gonna do exactly what I say."

"Like hell she is," I hissed, narrowing my eyes. The damn crowd was still cheering, closing in on her. I doubted she had any clue I was the only man who could rescue her from bad-ass boys who frequented the joint far too often.

"You didn't buy me, you son of a bitch," she yelled, acting as if she was prepared to take them on one by one.

I had to shake my head. What in God's name had she gotten herself in the middle of? Whatever she'd done to gain Bart's attention had worked. The little lady obviously needed a lesson in choosing her friends wisely.

"Get away or you'll be sorry," Bart snarled in my direction as his two buddies gathered around him.

Exhaling, I pushed up my sleeves as I advanced. It was apparent the boys needed to learn a lesson that they couldn't touch my lady.

Mine. Uh-huh. I was one possessive, dominating man who protected his own. It didn't help a hint of jealousy had slithered into my system either. The crowd stepped in front of her, making it impossible for me to grab her attention. Not that the feisty woman would listen to me.

Just after I closed the distance, Bart threw a punch, catching me in the jaw. I punched him twice and the crowd went wild.

But he wasn't done yet, coming out swinging.

And what did the little woman do? Decided she was going to retaliate.

And she did it, her hard right hook catching Bart against the cheek.

Fuck.

As all hell started to break loose, both Gage and Marshall stepped in the middle.

"This is gonna stop right here, boys," Gage snapped, glaring at me as he shook his head.

"I'm going to kick his ass for touching mine," Wren snarled, trying to get to Bart a second time.

I snagged her long hair, yanking her backward just as she decided to throw yet another punch. When it hit me square in the eye, she opened her eyes wide, finally realized who'd come to her rescue.

A second time.

"Phoenix," Wren gasped.

I took several deep breaths, the same vile thought I'd had before with her dancing in my mind. The girl shouldn't have messed with a man like me.

"Now you did it, sweetheart. I told you to be careful what you ask for."

* * *

Wren

No. No. No!

What had I just done?

The carnal look on Phoenix's face stated it in bold red letters.

I'd fucked with the wrong man. It didn't matter that it was accidental.

Fate had to be playing games with me. There wasn't a chance that the rugged, dominating savior was standing right in front of me and I'd managed to drive my fist into his eye.

Oh, yes, it was. Now this wasn't a game. Karma hated me.

And what was he doing acting so authoritative?

"Phoenix," I repeated, trying to figure out why my life continued to spiral into the toilet. Although seeing him again had brought up another wave of heat, the embarrassment from the other night as well as from the fact I'd cold cocked him weighed on my mind.

And I had a date with him the next night. No, it wasn't a date exactly, but it was obvious he thought of me as his possession.

"Yeah, darlin. It's me. How many times have I told you not to tease other men?" Phoenix wrapped his arms around my waist, pulling me close.

The two men who'd broken up the fight were all grins.

Wait a minute. He was already assuming the role of my boyfriend. Oh, what the heck. Why not? I could tell the three ugly men were out for blood. If I'd known that the highest bidder would win a date with the bull rider, I wouldn't have been coerced into riding the damn mechanical thing in the first place. Okay, maybe I didn't need to have my arm twisted, but I hadn't been told the rules.

Phoenix nuzzled into my neck, half laughing. "You're one very bad girl," he whispered, which caused me to tingle all over.

"Get used to it," I whispered back.

"Not on my watch."

I pushed away from Phoenix, giving him a hard glare even if he was even more handsome than the night before.

"This not so nice man assaulted me," I said in a pouty voice, glaring at the guy. "I was just ridin' the bull like you told me I could do." I could tell Bart was obviously drunk, slightly slurring his words. Then he lifted his fists, shifting from foot to foot as if he would be stupid enough to throw another punch.

"Sweetie," Phoenix continued. "I didn't say tonight. There's a big contest going on tonight." Then he lowered his head, whispering in my ear, his tone more dominating than I'd heard, sending shivers down my spine. "It's obvious you need to be disciplined more often. You don't know these boys."

Disciplined. Oh, no. That wasn't going to happen again.

"Need some help, bro?" one of the men who'd stopped the fight asked as he swaggered closer.

I'd been stupid enough to think that going out on my own would clear my mind of all the naughty thoughts I'd continued to have about Phoenix. Like that was going to happen any time soon.

"The man was messing with my girl. Maybe we need to show our boy Bart here a lesson, Marshall. What do you say?" Phoenix asked, grinning.

Phoenix pushed me behind him then glanced at the burly asshole who'd slapped me on the ass and cupped both breasts when I'd left the restroom before I'd gotten on the bull. While the dude was large, Phoenix was several inches taller and outweighed him with a solid thirty plus pounds of muscle. "I wouldn't do that if I were you, Bart. You won't like what happens if you do," he told the guy.

"Who do you think you are?" Bart asked. Why did I have a feeling a huge fight was beginning to form? "She ain't your girl, Phoenix. I know better. You think every chick is your girl."

"Ouch," Marshall said, laughing.

I couldn't continue this charade. If I did, then he'd think he had control over me. That couldn't happen.

"I can fight my own battles," I told him, pushing my way back to the center. As the crowd started to shift into a wide circle, I heard the chanting begin and cringed.

"Fight. Fight. Fight."

What were we, back in high school?

"Bart. You're either going to leave of your own accord right now or I'll have no choice but to arrest you for disorderly conduct. Which would you prefer?" the other guy said, obviously another one of Phoenix's friends.

"Ooh la la, the sheriff," one of the other girls chimed in.

"Fuckin' bitch," Bart said as he glared at me.

My natural tendencies kicked in and I lunged for him, getting off a hard right hook before Phoenix pulled me back.

"That's it, Bart," the sheriff hissed. "Get out of this bar right now."

"Come on, sweetheart. The party's over," Phoenix said as he pulled me away. Then he whispered in my ear once again and the same electricity from two nights before skittered through me like wildfire. "You should know better than to pick a fight with someone bigger than you."

"I just said that I can take care of myself." That's the lie I'd told myself for years. I'd taken martial arts years before, knew how to shoot a weapon. And put a bow in my hands and I could shoot an apple off the tin can three hundred yards away, but I couldn't tell a man from a monster to save my life.

"Hmm… I don't think you can."

When he grabbed me around the waist, pulling me closer, I pressed both palms against him, but my body's reaction was the same as it had been the first time I'd laid eyes on him. I was wet and hot all over.

Treacherous bitch.

He fisted my hair, the look on his face primal. Then he captured my mouth, dragging me so tightly against him my breath was stolen. I wanted to push him away, but the taste of him was incredible, more so than it had been before. He slipped his tongue past my lips, taking his time to sweep it back and forth.

"Whew," one of his friends said from behind us.

I couldn't help but think Phoenix was showing off for his buddies and that pissed me off once again even as he ground his hips against me. When he broke the kiss, sliding his hand down to cup my buttocks as if he owned me, the natural fighter in me made another appearance. But this time he was too quick, grabbing my arm before I could slap him across the face for being so forward.

"Hmm… Tsk. Tsk," he growled.

There was a different gleam in Phoenix's eyes and when he threw me over his shoulder, I immediately pummeled my fists against his back. "What are you doing?"

"Teaching you some damn manners."

CHAPTER 6

 *ren*

This just couldn't be happening to me.

What were the odds I'd run into the gorgeous man in such a big town? Was fate trying to tell me something?

"Let go of me," I snapped, pounding him on the back.

"Not gonna do it," Phoenix snarled, taking long strides down the corridor then kicking in the door to the men's room. Then he growled at the only man inside.

"Get out," he snarled.

I jerked up my head, wiggling with everything I had to get out of his hold. "Are you crazy?"

"That's what I've been told on several occasions." He eased me onto my feet, shaking his head. "But it's a good thing I came along when I did. Bart is a hell of lot crazier than I am. He's also a brutal asshole, a dangerous criminal."

"I told you I could handle him." I tried to push my way out from around him, but he fisted my hair again, narrowing his hooded eyes. "Besides, you're a dangerous man too."

"Sugar, from what I've seen, you're not capable of making the best decisions. I'm going to help change that."

"Excuse me, Mr. Big Shot. You're not my keeper."

When he wagged his finger in front of my face, his eyes twinkling, I almost did something irrational like slap him across the face.

Good. Just do that and see what he does.

"That's where you're wrong. I am through the weekend. And that starts now." As he started to unfasten my jeans, I was immediately frozen for a few seconds.

"What the hell do you think you're doing?" I slapped at his hands, almost laughing at myself. As if that was going to do any good.

"Giving you a hard spanking." He managed to yank down my zipper and I slammed my fists against him.

"Oh, no, you don't. I'm not a little girl, and you certainly aren't going to humiliate me." I wiggled with everything I had, ready to scream bloody murder.

Only I knew it wouldn't matter. Between the drunken, rowdy assholes and the band playing at full volume, there was no way anyone would hear me or care.

Maybe they'd sell tickets to watch me being spanked like a bad little girl.

"You certainly act like one. What the hell were you thinking?" He grumbled under his breath, snapping his head toward the door when some drunken fool tried to come inside. "Get out and stay out."

"Sure thing, buddy," the dude said, smiling as if he knew what was going to happen.

"I wanted to have some fun. To live dangerously, just…" I started to say just like him, but that was insane.

He managed to finish unfastening my jeans and I pummeled my fists against his chest again. The man was built like a carved stone statue. There was no way I could budge him.

"This isn't the kind of place for you," Phoenix growled, the sound just as primal as it had been before.

"But it is for you?" I almost got away from him only to have the brutal man grab my arm, swinging me around and tossing me over the edge of the counter so I could stare myself in the eyes as I was being punished.

This was crazy.

"Touch me and I'll cut off your fingers. Okay?" I snarled.

"God, I love your fire."

I threw him a hateful look. "I'll show you fire." The lighting might be shit in the ugly space, but his eyes were luminescent, drawing me in. For a few seconds, I was strangled by the intense connection we seemed to have, as if I was being sucked into a black hole. I purposely blinked, fighting again but I could tell it was no use.

Then I watched in near awe as he ignored me, unfastening his buckle and for some crazy reason, tickling sensations shifted all the way down to my toes.

When he yanked the thick material over my hips, I elbowed him. Then he fisted my hair, yanking back my head. "How many times have I told you to be careful enticing the beast?"

"You're a beast alright."

With that, he jerked my jeans and my panties at the same time, dragging them all the way to my knees. I was mortified, much more so than before. How could I not be? Anyone could walk i ı at any time.

"If you touch me, I'll…" I couldn't even finish the sentence.

Phoenix brought his hand down three times in rapid succession as I sneered at him in the glass. "Then you'll what?" His grin was positively evil. He was enjoying my humiliation far too much.

"Never mind," I said through clenched teeth.

"Uh-huh. I know you."

"You know nothing about me."

He yanked the strap from his beltloops, cracking it against the floor on purpose, the sound making me jump.

"You're such an asshole."

As he lifted his eyebrow, he crushed his full weight against me. My God. He was enjoying the hell out of this. "You have a caustic mouth. Not very ladylike."

"Yeah? I'm not a lady."

"You will be when I'm finished with you." He brought the belt down, smacking my bottom several times.

The pain was blinding, stealing my breath and my mind. "Damn you. Damn you."

"Adding five because you continue to curse."

"What are you, the curse word police?" I hissed, gasping for air.

"You need to learn you can't go around purposely poking the bear. One day, you'll do that with the wrong guy."

"You're not my daddy."

He stopped short, lifting his head and glaring at me in the mirror.

Why did I have a feeling he'd not only undressed me with his eyes, but had already positioned me on a silver platter with fruit surrounding my naked body?

And why did I gather a whiff of my own desire? Oh, God. This was bad. If I was able to gather the fragrance, then he certainly could.

No. I couldn't go down that hole. Or maybe I should call it quicksand.

"No, but for this weekend I'm your protector and the man who will keep you in line, which is exactly what you need."

The arrogance of the man was incredibly… sexy.

Phoenix caressed my skin, taking far too much time in doing so. When he took a deep breath, I cringed inside, but I kept my eyes open, watching as he shifted into the same intense need I'd seen more than once.

Then he started the spanking in earnest, one strike coming right after another. Even the cracking sound his wrist made was enough to stoke a fire deep within. I couldn't be enjoying this. Not being spanked inside a nasty men's bathroom.

Why, oh, why had I talked myself into going out?

"Ouch. Ouch!" I finally snapped, becoming more and more exasperated.

"Here's the thing, sweetheart. Spankings are supposed to hurt for them to do any good." He lifted an eyebrow then brought the belt down. Six. I even counted them in my mind before my knees almost buckled. Thank God I was gripping onto the edge of the counter.

I tried to kick out again, hissing through clenched teeth.

"Are those jeans bothering you?" he asked. "If they are, we can take them off."

Before I had a chance to object, that's exactly what he did, wrapping his arm around me and lifting me off the floor so he could drag the pesky material away.

"You are an asshole," I repeated, although I was surprised there wasn't any emotion in my voice.

"You aren't the first woman to tell me that and I doubt you'll be the last," he said, his voice dripping with lust, and the mirror told no lies.

He was fully aroused, and I couldn't take my eyes off the thick bulge between his legs.

Chuckling, he shifted his hold around my waist, keeping me in position, forcing me to lean further over as he cracked the strap against my already aching bottom so many times I lost count. His rhythm was perfect, just like a metronome. By the time he was finished with the volley, I was dancing back and forth from boot to boot, the explosive heat jetting down both legs.

That wasn't the only fire burning within me, my pussy aching, clenching and releasing several times. I stared at the mirror, watching my flush of shame turning into one of raw, unbridled lust.

"You're wet, little bird," he murmured. "Your pussy is glistening."

I couldn't deny it. My nipples were hard as rocks, the ache extending all the way into my stomach. Breathless, I blinked several times, uncertain what he was going to do. When he did the unthinkable, sliding his hand between my legs, it was all I could take. A single moan dripped from my lips as if the man had been a longtime lover. I slouched against the counter, my breathing so ragged stars were floating in front of my eyes.

"Do you know what they say about women who become wet when being punished?" he asked in a gruff voice, the deep baritone only adding to the vibrations humming in my tummy.

I couldn't speak for fear of falling down the rabbit hole all over again. He was so handsome, every square inch of him what fantasies were made of.

All the chastising I'd done about fucking a stranger in the middle of a snowstorm was tossed out the window. Now I was dancing in flames, about ready to be doused with gasoline.

And a part of me couldn't care less.

"Mmmm…" he continued as he rolled a single finger around my clit. "That only experiencing pain can allow them to have any kind of pleasure. Do you think that's true?"

I narrowed my eyes, trying to regain my resolve and what was left of my mind. I was clearly out of control. Maybe I needed the harsh punishment to get my act together. "Never."

"Maybe I should test out the theory." He cracked the belt four times in rapid succession, the pain now exhilarating.

It was crazy, the sensations unlike anything I'd ever imagined.

Or wanted.

When he returned his hand between my legs, pushing his palm into my swollen folds, he almost brought me to an orgasm. How was that possible? He rubbed up and down and another fog developed in front of my eyes. I tried to concentrate on anything else, but as I shifted my gaze from left to right, I was forced to accept just how much I wanted the man's touch.

His kiss.

His cock.

His mouth.

I was in way over my head, but I loved every second of it.

As he continued rubbing, he never blinked as he watched me, pushing me to the point I was digging my nails into the ugly Formica.

When he placed the thick strap on the counter, shifting his arm around the front of my legs and yanking me backward off my feet, I was forced to throw back my hands. As I tried to wrap my fingers around his thick thighs, another wave of desire kicked in.

The look on his face was carnal.

As if I was his possession.

Phoenix knew exactly what he was doing to me and the second he rolled the thumb of his other hand around my clit, it was all I could take.

"Oh. Oh. Oh..." As a climax rushed into me, the only thought that slammed into my mind was one of utter filth.

I wanted to suck his cock, tasting his sweet cum. This was pure heaven, even if I would go straight to hell for my behavior.

He nuzzled into my neck, forcing me to experience additional pleasure. As one orgasm swept into a wave, I allowed myself to be pulled into a vacuum, barely aware that he'd put me down.

Dozens of wicked thoughts raced through my mind, embarrassment making my cheeks as hot as my aching bottom.

The thought brought another ache in my nipples. Perhaps he knew what I was thinking as he yanked up my shirt, shoving the lace bra out of the way. Then he cupped my breasts, twisting and pulling my nipples before lowering his head. The first swipe of his tongue forced a shiver, the second a moan. When he pulled the tender tissue between his lips, sucking and biting, my actions became rougher, creating friction. I moved my hand down, stroking his shaft through the dense material of his jeans.

Between the gruff sounds he was making and the scent of sex, I remained in a sweet haze. But it wouldn't last for long. He forced my legs around him, pushing me against the counter.

His cockhead was already pressed against my pussy lips, and he smirked as he lifted me by a few inches then brought me all the way down.

I threw my head back, doing everything I could to keep from screaming. That's when he captured my mouth, cupping both sides of my head as he swept his tongue inside. I was shocked at the way my body contorted to his whims while he used his powerful thigh muscles, pumping in and out. I wrapped my arm around him, tangling my fingers in his hair. This was so wrong, but I was more excited than I'd been fucking him in the motel.

As he pulled away, he laughed softly, his eyes just as mesmerizing as they'd been before. His cock stretched my muscles, the ache the most incredible feeling. I was aware of noise, the door opening and closing at least three times, but I didn't bother looking and I honestly didn't care who watched what we were doing.

"I love being inside of you," he whispered. There was such need in his voice that I was taken aback. He eased me onto the counter, spreading my legs wide. Then he yanked me all the way to the edge, planting his hands on either side of me, daring me with his eyes to slide his cock back inside.

"Oh, yeah?" I purred.

"Yyeess…"

There was such a gruff command with his voice that I found myself obeying him. The moment I pressed his cockhead inside, he yanked me off the counter, stretching me even wider. I grasped for his arms, clinging to his shoulders as I wrapped my legs around his massive thighs. He was so muscular, and I adored the way he was staring at me.

He thrust hard and fast, the force vibrating every part of me, sensations exploding deep inside. Within seconds, he brought me into the fiery heat of an orgasm, my muscles clenching and releasing.

"Oh. Oh… Yes." I lolled my head, closing my eyes as the beautiful moment of bliss tore through me, my core turning into molten lava. I couldn't seem to stop shaking and he refused to slow down, plunging like a crazed animal, a predator of the night. I clung to him, doing everything I could to control my breathing, aware at least two other people had walked in and left. What did I care? I was floating on a sea of bliss, confused why the electricity soared between us.

"My good girl," Phoenix muttered as he finally slowed down. Then he eased me into his arms, cupping my face and rubbing his thumb across my lips roughly. "But we're not finished yet."

"We're not?" I could barely talk, my mind still foggy from the raw slice of ecstasy.

"Nope. You see," he said then whipped me around to face the mirror once again, "bad girls get fucked in the ass."

Even the way he stated the words was as filthy as the act he was about to perform. I fell into the moment, never blinking as I watched his facial expressions. He was so serious about what he was doing as he slipped the tip of his cock against my dark hole. There was no doubt about his heightened level of hunger, but I also sensed his possessiveness had reached a different level.

He'd hated seeing me around other men. He would have taken on every man who'd dared lay their hands on me. I wasn't certain whether to be thrilled or worried. But he was such a powerful man I remained mesmerized.

"So tight," he muttered and slipped his cockhead inside, allowing me to get used to his thick girth.

I panted as the blast of pain sent a vibrant display of colors in front of my eyes. Nothing seemed real any longer, the pleasure already turning into sheer rapture.

"You're so beautiful," he whispered, his tone huskier than before.

As he pressed another two inches inside my ass, pushing past the tight muscle, I couldn't hold back a sharp cry. Then

I bit my lower lip as he finished thrusting all the way inside. I'd never felt so full in my life, my mind spinning with just how delicious the sensations really were. This was by far the most incredible experience I'd ever had.

He wrapped his hand around my throat, holding me in position as he rolled onto the balls of his feet, fucking me in slow and even motions. But as his fingers dug into my skin, his eyes seemed to change color, an iridescent shimmer forming.

Moaning, I pushed back against him, arching my back. Then he started fucking me harder. Every sound was predatory, every breath he took as ragged as mine. In those few filthy moments, I couldn't help but think I could do this over and over again, enjoying every minute of his attention.

It was crazy, unthinkable, yet for a few minutes I was allowed a real sense of peace.

When his body tensed, I did what I could to meet every hard thrust, squeezing my muscles. There was something so beautiful about the serene look on his face before he threw his head back with a primal roar.

And as he erupted deep inside, I knew I was in deep trouble. It would be far too easy to fall hard for the man. That cemented a decision I'd wrangled with all day.

As soon as the wedding was finished, I was leaving town.

Hopefully, I'd never see him again.

If I didn't, I stood a chance of falling headfirst, hopelessly in love with him.

* * *

Phoenix

"You got everything you want to take with you, buddy?" I asked Justin as he popped around the corner carrying his new suitcase. I'd tossed the one that he'd had in his hand the day his mother had dropped him off on my doorstep. I'd spent a fortune taking him to toy stores and purchasing clothes. I'd allowed him to pick out his 'grownup' bed and sheets, painting his room the exact color he'd wanted. Then I'd filled it with books and an iPad, games and everything else I could think of that he hadn't experienced.

None of it mattered. He was still clinging to the stuffed bear he'd brought with him, clutching it in his arm as he lumbered toward me.

I'd heard from the great experts he was behind in both mental and physical development. They'd acted as if there was no chance the poor kid would have a normal life. That had pissed me off, enough so I'd screamed at his developmental doctor, firing the son of a bitch on the spot.

It hadn't been my finest hour, but no one fucked with my kid.

Just like I'd refused to allow anyone to mess with Wren.

I raked my hand through my hair as I tried to shove thoughts of the night before out of my mind. Hell, when I'd noticed Bart still hanging around outside as I walked her to her car, it had been all I could do not to beat the man to a pulp. I'd even followed her home, making certain the fuckers hadn't followed her.

Then I'd realized she'd rented Gage's old place, the one he'd swore he'd never step foot in again. Karma was really kicking my ass.

"Do I have ta go?" he asked.

"Oh, my goodness. You're going to have so much fun. You're going to the zoo. Remember how you like the animals?" Finally, his little face brightened up.

"Yeah." He stopped a few feet away, staring up at me. "You look weird."

"Weird?" I grabbed his coat from the closet, taking his suitcase from his hand. "How so?"

"Dunno. Happy. You don't have a mean look."

I had to fight to keep from laughing. I'd been surly the entire time he'd been with me, barely laughing when we watched one of the dozens of movies I'd bought for him. As a matter of fact, I couldn't remember the last time I'd laughed or smiled for that matter.

But I had around Wren.

"Well, maybe Daddy is happy. Come on, bud. Let's get going. I think Betty is having pizza tonight."

"Yay!"

As we headed for my truck, I said a silent prayer he didn't go into one of his violent rages. Betty had been an angel handling him, but he'd gotten worse lately. I wasn't certain how to handle him any longer and that pained me more than anything.

After settling him into the passenger seat, I scanned the perimeter. If only the gut feeling I had would go away. Would somebody dare try to seek revenge after all these years? Or was I just feeling more guilty than usual?

I put on his favorite station, trying not to think about Wren. I still hadn't decided whether I'd let the cat out of the bag with regard to my real identity. The asshole inside of me wanted to, but that wouldn't be fair to Wren or her sister.

When my phone rang, I was surprised Gage was calling.

"What's up?"

"How was your night?" he jested.

"Don't you go there."

"Where is my good buddy, Phoenix?"

"Maybe's he's changing for the better. I know you didn't call me just to give me… garbage."

He laughed. "Oh, Justin's with you. I shouldn't be doing this, but Investigator Nelson asked me to come to Shadowland. He has the results."

"Yeah. When?"

"Twenty minutes. But you aren't going to fuck with anything. Right?"

"Of course not."

"Uh-huh. I'll believe it when I see it. I'll meet you there."

Betty's house was only a few miles away and when I pulled into her driveway, I sensed he was having second thoughts about agreeing to come. "Hey. What do you say when you come home, we plan your birthday party?"

He blinked several times, taking a full minute before turning his head. There was nothing more agonizing than seeing the confusion in his little eyes as he tried to process what I was saying.

Fuck the drugs. Fuck what Dahlia had done to him.

Anger swelled for the fiftieth time, almost pushing me over the edge. I'd had a meltdown of my own after I'd realized the full extent of what he'd endured.

"Okay." The light switch had flipped again, and I exhaled as he reached for the handle.

Betty was already waiting on the stairs and God love the woman. She had a jar of bubbles in her hand, one of his favorite things.

I climbed out, grabbing his suitcase. He'd forgotten about the bear. As I walked closer, he was already running through the yard, happy as could be. "Thank you so much, Betty."

"Well, it's rare that you want to do something for yourself. Don't worry. We'll be just fine. I have a few surprises in store for him."

"You're an angel." I waited to see if Justin would notice I was leaving. I'd found it was best to allow him to enjoy whatever he was doing.

Even if it ignited the ache inside.

As I headed for Shadowland, my thoughts returned to Wren. She was a spark of energy, but she was right. I knew almost nothing about her. Maybe it was best that way. I certainly couldn't entertain getting involved with anyone and definitely not long distance. That would kill Justin. I wasn't even sure whether I could bring her to the house. However, I had a gut feeling the rehearsal dinner might be explosive.

Laughing softly, as I made the final turn leading to the ranch, I forced my thoughts back to the recent arsons. Setting fires to cover up a murder certainly wasn't unheard of but starting a forest fire was something else entirely. There had to be a connection between the recent murders and why the horses were shot.

The fire investigator had been working with the various fire departments and smokejumpers for years. Frederick Nelson was tough but given his background in fighting fires, he could sniff out an arsonist from a hundred yards away. That knack had given him a solid reputation. He also had no love for people, which was understandable after what he'd been through in his life.

At least we'd always had a decent relationship, both of us playing it straight. As I stepped out of my truck, the stench of charred wood assaulted my senses. I was also able to detect a hint of gasoline, but I had a feeling it had only been used as an accelerant after the fact.

I noticed his truck, but he was nowhere to be seen. After grabbing my flashlight, I saw Gage heading in my direction.

"Devastating," I told him as I glanced at the horrific remains.

"Yeah. They were decent people."

"There's something brewing in town. I'm certain of it."

He nodded. "You might be right. The medical examiner called. The weapon used to commit the murders was the same as what Marshall found."

"A Ruger. Just like the horses."

"I know. Marshall called with the findings. And I'll bet an accelerant was used on the fire in an attempt to cover up the murders."

"You know, I wonder if that's what the assholes were planning on doing, torching my ranch. Maybe they had a change of heart and wanted to free the animals," I suggested. There was a connection between the incidents. I just had to find it.

Gage frowned. "Or maybe the horses got scared, forcing the perpetrators to shoot them. Interesting theory."

Theories meant shit in my mind.

"Anyway, let's see what Frederick has to say," he said as he started to walk away.

"Wait. I thought you should know that Wren is renting your old place."

He took a deep breath, holding it for a few seconds before letting it out. "Wow. I had no idea. I never pay attention. I have a real estate company handling the rentals."

"Why don't you just sell the damn place? It's gorgeous. You'll get a pretty penny for it."

"I just can't do that, Phoenix. At least not right now."

"You're not thinking about going back with your ex." I heard the chastising tone in my voice and sighed. The fact he'd found her in their bed with one of his deputies was close to one of the worst things that could happen.

"Fuck, no. Are you kidding me? I thought I could move back to the place, but it's just not going to happen. Still, I'd hate to see it go to just anyone."

"I just wanted you to know."

"You followed her back there last night."

Half laughing, I could tell he was amused. "It was the least I could do."

"You do know Bart is a slime bag. Right?"

"Bart Michaels is a bully with far too much money since Daddy left him everything in his will. He already had a grudge with me from a long time ago."

"Yeah, I remember. He's moved up to being a dangerous asshole, accused of several blackmailing schemes in his attempt to buy up half the town."

I could tell Gage had an opinion on whether Bart was capable of murder. "I hear you."

"Uh-huh. I'm serious. He made a very lucrative offer on your father's property before you came back to town." He lifted his eyebrow, curious as to whether I'd heard.

"Fuck. Son of a bitch. No, I didn't know that."

"You need to talk to your father more often."

"Sounds like you're putting two and two together."

"Maybe. And I'm probably an idiot for telling you." Gage lifted his eyebrows again. "Don't do anything stupid."

"I don't plan on it."

"Famous last words."

Gage led the way, the stench making my eyes water.

We found Frederick just inside the burned-out shell, shining his flashlight around the crumbled space. As I crunched through the ruins, I realized I was usually lucky in that I never had to see the aftermath of people's lives destroyed.

"Frederick," Gage said as I took shallow breaths. "I thought I'd find you here. You remember Phoenix from the Zullies."

"Oh, yeah. I heard about your reputation too," Frederick said as he studied me carefully. "You're damn good, but the hot dogging is going to get you killed."

"So I've been told many times," I managed.

Gage cleared his throat. "This was an unusually hot fire."

"Yup. It stinks. Doesn't it?" he asked. The man was one of few words.

"More than usual. Why?" I piped in.

"Gasoline was mixed with chlorine trifluoride then reacted with something else I haven't figured out yet. Colorless and highly flammable, but the stench is ungodly. That's why the concrete disintegrated." The investigator broke a chunk apart with his fingers, crushing it into dust.

"Let me guess. You can't purchase it over the counter," I suggested.

"Hell, no, son," he said, laughing. "Which might mean good news for us, especially you, Sheriff. You can only purchase it through specialized dealers. Burns like a son of a bitch."

"How did it start?"

"That's going to be real tough to figure out given the level of destruction. However, it was concentrated to one specific area of the house, which could mean the victims were killed beforehand, their bodies dumped, or maybe they were locked in."

"Great. This isn't just an arsonist."

"Nope," he said mechanically. "Just so you know, Zullie, if you or your crew come across a fire with a greenish yellow substance, get the fuck out of the way."

Exhaling, I shifted the flashlight against the charred remains. Something continued to nag at me that I couldn't shake. "I'll keep that in mind."

"You got yourself somebody who knows exactly how much to use," Frederick added.

"Meaning what?" Gage asked.

"Meaning they could have started a fire you'd never be able to put out, but they used just enough. And for someone to go to this trouble, they wanted to hide something big."

I glanced at Gage as he shook his head.

Whatever was going on was about to get worse.

CHAPTER 7

*ren*

Embarrassment.

That's all I could feel most of the day. I could never set foot inside Raunchy Ride again, not that I'd want to. It was a little rough around the edges.

Well, at least I wouldn't have to worry about seeing their faces in the grocery store or at another bar since I was leaving, never to return to Missoula again. I just couldn't do it.

The first shock was the car Phoenix had, a sleek black Maserati. The second had been the way he'd acted as his tall, rugged body climbed out of the driver's seat, taking long strides in my direction. He seemed like an entirely different man, including the expensive Rolex he wore on his wrist.

And the third had been how dominating he was, yanking my bags from the car and grabbing my hand.

There were no words said, but I'd seen the lust-filled sweep of his eyes, the look of hunger explosive. I'd felt the thunderous bolts of current enshrouding our bodies as soon as he'd gotten within a few feet.

The man was raw power and sex appeal.

And he was my date.

After he'd settled me into the car, he'd said nothing, merely peeling out of the parking lot at an excessive rate of speed. He was the epitome of the tall, dark, and silent type. As I'd leaned into the seat, all I could think about was how looks could be deceiving. Who was this man? The only internet search I'd done was on the smokejumpers, finding his name on the roster. That had given me all the comfort I'd needed.

We sat in silence for a few minutes. Then I couldn't take it any longer.

"Who are you?" The edge in my voice was unmistakable yet he seemed amused, the waning like of the late afternoon doing nothing to hide the amusement in his eyes.

"You know who I am. At least you should by now."

"No, I have no clue obviously since you are an entirely different person than two nights ago or even last night." I knew him sexually, the raw passion he exuded keeping me awake the entire night. As I squirmed in my seat, I was also given a stark reminder that he was more dominating than any man I'd ever met.

"How am I different?"

"Did you steal the car?"

"I've done a hell of a lot of bad things in my life, Wren, but I'm not a thief." He had a wry smile on his face. My God. He was enjoying the hell out of my discomfort.

"So this is yours or you borrowed it from a friend?"

I could feel his heated gaze and almost read his thoughts.

He chuckled and as he shifted in the seat, I couldn't help but notice his hands. They were strong, his fingers long and perfectly shaped. But the pads of all ten were rough, obviously from the hard work of being a smokejumper. And the way they'd felt brushing across my skin had been dangerously close to the most incredible sensations I'd had in my life.

Stop it. You can't think that way.

"I own a Harley too, but I didn't think you'd want to arrive to a fancy dinner on the back of a motorcycle."

"You're not just a smokejumper, are you?"

"I'm many things, but I love fighting fires."

"It's dangerous."

When he turned his head, I could swear he was undressing me with his eyes. "Anything worth having is worth risking the danger. There's nothing more exhilarating than facing the beast, flames eager to consume everything in its path. Once you've looked something like that in the eyes and beaten it, then you know you can do anything."

The guttural sound of his voice ignited my pulse and suddenly my mouth was dry. "You're a danger junkie."

His deep chuckle returned, the sound reverberating in my ears. "As I said, I'm many things, but it would seem we have something in common." Then his tone changed. "As far as fires, I do it because I need to stand in front of the beast."

"Why do you call it a beast?"

Phoenix thought about what I was asking, the lights from outside flashing through the windshield allowing me to see his expression was completely different.

Another wave of tension crackled the air, my mind trying to think of anything to talk about instead of gawking at him. He was infuriatingly handsome, his aftershave tickling all my senses.

"Because it's living and breathing and if you dare take your eye off it for even a split second, it'll eat you alive."

"I don't understand how you do it, Phoenix. That sounds terrifying."

"It is."

He said the two little words as if facing the beast was a penance of some kind. I had no idea what to say to him.

"Where's the rehearsal?"

Exhaling, I folded my arms, shivering for about a bazillion reasons. "There isn't one, just the sanctimonious dinner. Protocol, you understand."

"Then why no rehearsal?"

I was exasperated, with no desire to endure the long evening. "The wedding is being held in the backyard of my parents' house. My father doesn't feel it's warranted."

"And you and your sister always do what your father says?"

He had me there. "It's not my wedding and my sister is still living in my father's house."

"So you'll do it your way."

"Don't worry. I'm never getting married!" I made the statement with far too much emphasis.

"What a shame."

"Oh, really? You don't seem like the marriage type or having kids for that matter." Why did he suddenly look so uncomfortable with my accusations?

Phoenix shifted in his seat, rubbing his index finger back and forth across his sensuous lips. And I couldn't stop watching his every action.

Bad girl.

Bad... girl.

"I ain't into marriage," he admitted.

Well, at least that was off the table. Whoa. What was I thinking? We were only compatible in bed, nowhere else.

"What do you want me to call you?" I finally asked as I threw Phoenix another quick look.

136

He turned his head, allowing his gaze to fall from my face to my legs. Then he appeared uncomfortable as hell. "My name would be an excellent choice."

"But Phoenix isn't your real name."

After he took a deep breath, I sensed he was losing patience with me. "No, but it's the name I've used for years."

"Fine. Do we have any pet names?" I gave him the same onceover he'd given me, realizing I was holding my breath while doing so. While the dinner was slightly more casual, he'd opted for black jeans and cowboy boots, a crisp white shirt opened to the middle of his broad chest and a leather jacket. He exuded dominance, his stature impossible to miss. I'd tried to convince myself that I could easily act my part and be able to turn off my attraction, but the crackle of electricity drifting back and forth between us was a clear indication I could be very wrong.

Nope.

I wasn't going to do it.

So what if his exotic spice, cedarwood, and deep earth after-shave had already stained my skin? I could ignore it. Easily.

"Not for me, little bird." The way he called me his little bird had been annoying at first, but at least for right now, the term of endearment brought me a smile.

Nerves.

They were like icy claws digging into every vein, sucking the life out of me. The closer it had come to Phoenix picking me up, the more anxious I'd become. The reason wasn't because there was a chance I could screw up my sister's wedding or that my father would likely have a hissy fit. My anxiousness was all about spending additional time with Phoenix.

He remained his quiet grumpy self after picking me up from the shopping center I'd insisted he meet me at. I had no idea why I was being cautious other than the fact I knew almost nothing about him.

Yet you paid him money to spend time with you, almost every bit of it up close and personal.

That wasn't technically true. I'd given him half the thousand dollars plus another five hundred to purchase a suit, even telling him where I thought he could find the best deals. He'd given me the same stare I'd seen multiple times, the smug look on his face one I'd wanted to wipe off.

Maybe the reason he remained quiet was that I'd insisted on his phone number, calling him twice to remind him of the time.

"Did you pack everything?" I asked. "Granted, it's not like we're going to be far away from a store if you forgot anything, but Mom has back-to-back events after tonight." He gave me another hard look. "You can turn right there. I used to go to this restaurant when I was growing up. I'm sure it looks the same. Did you know it's been in operation for over two decades?"

As soon as he turned onto the street leading to the restaurant, he pulled over on the side of the road.

"What are you doing?" I demanded, immediately glancing at the digital clock on the dashboard of his truck. We were already going to be late.

He cupped my face, rubbing his thumb back and forth across my lips. "Stop talking. Everything will be fine. Breathe for me, little bird. Just breathe."

"I know you probably haven't been to a place like this before, although I'm just assuming. I know that's shitty of me. And my father is going to grill you about where you went to school, what you do for a living, and how much money you make. I know he is because that's what he does to me. He managed to run off two different boyfriends when I was in high school. I just—"

As he'd done inside the motel, he captured my mouth, holding our lips in place. I'd never felt so lightheaded in my life, my mind immediately shifting into a beautiful haze of various colors, every one of them iridescent.

I slipped my arm around his shoulder, tangling my fingers in his thick strands. As he opened and closed our lips together, I could feel my blood pressure stabilizing, the dull ache in my stomach disappearing. He pulled me closer as he swept his tongue inside, taking his time to dominate mine. Then he pulled away by a few inches, his breathing as ragged as mine.

"What was that for?" I asked breathlessly.

"To calm you down before you had a panic attack."

After exhaling, I nodded, terrified he'd notice how hard my nipples had become. *No sex. Remember the deal.*

139

"I'm fine."

"Good girl. Now, you're going to let me grab your hand and take you inside where you'll smile and greet your family as if you're thrilled to see them. Then you're going to introduce me as a man you've been seeing on and off for a few months. Given the distance, we can't see other all the time. And I assure you that I can handle anything your father tosses in my direction. Is that understood?"

I'd never enjoyed being around dominating men. That had started with how strict my father had been throughout my childhood, barking orders as if we were new recruits in the military. He'd wanted to have boys, even pissed at my mother that she hadn't produced them.

"Fine. Just don't do anything rash."

"That's the second time I've been told that in as many days."

"You should know my mother is a brash bitch who'll come across as uncaring. Then she'll sidle up to you." My mother had always been flirtatious. I had no doubt she'd had several lovers over the years. All my father cared about was that she continued to have enough plastic surgery to look enchanting on his arm. In her eyes, that made her an expert on the subject, which often led to her telling me all the things that were wrong with me. I'd endured her nastiness my entire life, Cammie as well. Only my sister seemed unaffected by our mother's caustic behavior. "And my father will try and pick a fight with you. Also, my father is one of the most important men in the entire state."

"I'm well aware of who your parents are, Wren. Your father is a very conservative senator who will be up for reelection soon."

"I guess I should have told you."

He shook his head. "You weren't required to tell me everything about your life. I don't care who they are. I won't be trying to impress them because they don't mean anything to me. Only you do."

"That's nice, but we're just friends."

"Friends. Of course. I'm going to park now. Take a deep breath," he instructed.

Maybe because he was older, I felt calmer with him taking the lead. It was just for a couple of days. Then I'd return to the sanctity of my boring life.

As soon as he cut the engine, he slipped me another heated look. "By the way. You look incredible tonight, a stunning vision of beauty."

I was surprised at his words. They were so unlike him, as if my taunting him had turned him into a different man. I suddenly had the urge to go somewhere else, ditch the sexy car, and just have a glass of wine and talk. I didn't need him to be anything he didn't want to be.

He pressed his hand against the small of my back as he guided me toward the entrance, swinging open the door with flair.

"Where are they?" he asked.

"The private room in the back."

"Remember, relax and breathe."

Why were his words comforting? As we made our way toward the room, I pulled on his arm, forcing him to stop. When he turned to face me, I noticed a gleam in his eyes. He was enjoying my discomfort. Damn him.

"What is it, little bird?"

"Is there anything I should know about you?"

He lowered his head so only I could hear his answer. "All you need to know is that I'm a very bad man."

With that, he took my hand, leading me into the room.

Into the lion's den. That's the way I'd always described entering the parties I'd been required to attend, always required to be at my best. Tonight was no exception. While this was an intimate affair in comparison to the actual reception, all eyes were on us as we walked in. Within seconds, I noticed my father's look of disdain, his expression cold as he studied Phoenix as if he was an intruder to the party.

Only when Cammie squealed, racing in my direction did the tension ease, but only by minimal degrees. She threw her arms around my neck, the only one delighted to see me.

"I was worried you'd changed your mind," she said as she pulled away.

"Your sister knows better than to dare go against family rules," Mother said absently, immediately finishing off what I knew was her second martini. I'd never considered my family dysfunctional until now, but the term fit our protected world perfectly.

My aunt and uncle stood on the outskirts, watching the real show of the evening, the rest of Cammie's friends standing off to the side, already whispering about Phoenix's arrival. As I turned my head toward Marcus, who was standing with his buddies, every one of them in expensive suits, I gathered a sense they were immediately snubbing my date.

Then I noticed Lincoln, who'd obviously been holding court with my father, his look just as smug. I immediately wanted to turn around and leave. He was an avid supporter of my father's campaign, which is where I'd met him. If I was married to the man, my father would still have control over me. I wasn't interested in the least.

Phoenix pushed me closer to my parents and I wished I could glance at his face. As soon as he removed my coat, I was oh so warmly welcomed by the look of disdain on my mother's face.

"I thought I told you to dress appropriately," she said before throwing Phoenix a look. She was already flirting with him.

"And I thought I told you that I'm perfectly capable of selecting my own clothes," I retorted, which brought a chuckle from at least two of Marcus' friends.

My mother took it in stride then turned her full attention to Phoenix. "And just who did you bring with you?"

"He's a good friend of mine. Don't worry, Mom. Dad. He's not here to challenge your wealth. He's a smokejumper, a regular guy who you would say makes no money." Why was

I exacerbating the situation? I was already lying to everyone, including myself. I might as well get my full money's worth. "And Phoenix and I have been dating for months." I leaned against him, taking a deep breath.

"Phoenix? What kind of name is that, boy?" my father asked.

I noticed Phoenix's eyes lit up with fire, but he resisted lashing out. "I was in the Marines, stationed in Afghanistan. I flew choppers."

My father had never thought about serving our country in his life. I wanted to wipe the smug look off his face. "He's a hero, Dad. Oh, you don't know what that means." I was shocked the nastiness had popped from my mouth. Maybe my date was good for me.

"Wren!" Mother snapped.

I noticed Cammie slapped a hand over her mouth, turning away slightly.

"Let it be, Pamela," my father said.

"You should have told me you were bringing a... friend," my mother snapped. "We invited someone for you to sit with tonight."

"So I understand. I'm not eighteen and living under your roof any longer, Mother. I will date whomever I want."

"Phoenix. A fascinating name," my father said as he approached, holding out his hand.

"Mr. Tillman. I've heard so much about you," Phoenix told him as he shook my father's hand, the grip firm, my 'date' towering over the man.

"That's interesting since I've never heard anything about you. I wonder why that is." My father turned his head in my direction, peering at me with a knowing glint in his eyes, as if he knew I was faking it.

"Well, we thought we'd keep our little love affair a secret. That makes the desire that much sweeter," Phoenix said as he slipped his hand around the back of my neck.

Phoenix was playing my father like a fiddle, enjoying every moment of doing so.

"I didn't catch your surname, son. Surely you have one of those."

"Oh, of course. I'm sorry. Where are my manners? My name is Emerson Riggs Wentworth. I believe you know my father, William."

As soon as he said the name, a cold shiver raced down my spine. I should have asked about his family.

His father and my father were bitter enemies and had been for two decades or more.

Dinner had certainly just become more interesting.

Phoenix

"Why didn't you tell me?" Wren demanded after dragging me out of the room.

"Would you have asked someone else to be your date?"

145

"I… I don't know."

Hmmm… That meant she knew all about the bad blood between our two families.

"What good would it have done?" I eyed her carefully, especially the nervous tic that had formed on the side of her mouth. It was obvious she was anxious, yet the fire in her eyes was exactly the same as I'd seen in the motel room. I had a sick desire to tame her, requiring her full submission twenty-four hours a day. The thought went beyond Neanderthal and was one that I hadn't indulged in my entire life. But with her, everything was different, as if my senses had been awakened for the first time.

"Well, for one it would have warned me about what I was getting in the middle of." She threw a look over her shoulder after Camille popped her head out of the room, her chest rising and falling from her ragged breathing. "And second, it was the right thing to do, although I'm not entirely certain you know what that means."

I hadn't intended on creating additional difficulties. Or… maybe that's exactly what I'd intended. After learning who Wren's father was, it had taken all I had not to make a phone call to my father, even though doing so would have started a vicious argument. I wasn't a man who had any level of patience, nor did I tolerate bullshit for long. It had taken me two minutes after meeting Wren's father until I'd had enough.

Besides, I'd wanted to see the man's surprised reaction given my hunch about the fires. He was genuinely shocked to see me. I wasn't certain what that said, but I doubted he was trying to torch my place in order to purchase it at a fire sale.

However, he was an arrogant, insufferable piece of shit, at least in my opinion. Granted, I'd grown up listening to my father lamenting how Gregory Tillman had betrayed him, severing their partnership after a violent incident. However, I'd never expected to meet the man or to find myself in the uncomfortable position of already having fucked his daughter.

And enjoyed the hell out of myself in doing so.

While the man's notorious, unscrupulous activities had been a bone of contention for my family, what pissed me off the most was his arrogance in the way he treated his two daughters.

Especially the woman who'd hired me as her escort for the evening.

I'd been amused when she'd offered me money, as if there wasn't a red-blooded male on the freaking planet who wouldn't have agreed to the date without being paid a dime. It had been obvious she hadn't recognized my name, putting two and two together. And in truth, I hadn't cared in the least about hers. My dick had done the thinking, the first taste of her sealing some kind of fate that I hadn't looked for.

Now here I was, pretending I was something I wasn't.

Including decent.

To Gregory's credit, the pompous man hadn't reacted other than his eyes opening wide. Yet I'd seen the look in his eyes, the need for retaliation when he had no clue what I was doing with his daughter in the first place.

And who was I to disclose her little secret?

I was reaching the limits of my control, my anger ready to let loose. Every insult he made about Wren was being stored in a location in my brain that boded ill for any man. I'd been told more than once I had no conscience, that the error of my violent ways would eventually land me in jail. But right now, I didn't give a shit.

"Who my father is should have no bearing on tonight," I told her.

"You obviously don't know my father very well, Phoenix or Riggs. What do you really want me to call you? I have no idea why they hate each other, but this has to be the worst possible thing that could have happened."

"As far as I'm concerned, Riggs is dead." I thought for certain she was going to challenge me but she didn't.

"I like Phoenix. There's such an incredible story behind the image."

There were several of them, but I wasn't going to tell her why I'd chosen the name for myself. "Here's what is going to happen, Wren, and you won't fight me on this. We will make polite conversation. Then we are leaving."

She eyed me warily but said nothing. Somehow, I could tell she was trying to figure out how she'd gotten herself hooked up with a very bad man.

I walked us both inside and soon realized that nothing about the night would go according to plans.

As her father approached, his glare was harsh. "I'm afraid I'm going to need to ask you to leave, Mr. Wentworth."

"That's not a choice for you to make," I told him.

"Yes, it is. Now, you can do this without causing a scene, son, or I'll have you thrown out. I'm friends with the owner."

The man was actually going to throw that at me? I laughed in his face. "You're doing no such thing."

"Stop. Just stop! This is Cammie's rehearsal dinner, for God's sake," Wren snapped. "You're not going to spoil it for her. Or for me. I'm finished with playing the good daughter. I have my own life, which includes seeing anyone I want to without reservation as to who they are or what family they're from. And you're not going to set me up with a buddy of yours to keep me under control, which is exactly what I expect you're doing with Cammie. You can't control the world, Dad. You can barely control your kinky proclivities." She sucked in her breath, and I had to say I was proud of her.

"Wren. You apologize to your father," her mother snapped.

Wren turned her head ever so slowly. "No, Mother, I won't. You might not care about Dad's indiscretions because you're fucking the pool boy or the lawn maintenance guy, but it's disgusting all the way around."

While everyone else in the room gasped, I was more amused than ever.

"Make him leave, Gregory," her mother insisted, glaring at me as if I was the hired help.

As Lincoln walked closer, I jerked my head up and snarled. "I suggest you back away."

"Come on. Let's just go," Wren said. "I'm suddenly no longer hungry."

"No, you're not going anywhere. This is my party," Cammie insisted. "And Phoenix stays or I go."

"He's right, honey. He's not welcome here," Marcus said, trying to pull Cammie away.

I couldn't help but smile as her sister's fiancé got in the middle.

The look Cammie gave him was priceless.

"Come over here with me," Lincoln dared to come closer, attempting to direct Wren as if he owned her.

That would have been fine except he yanked on her arm.

"Get your hand off me, you prick!" Wren snapped, jerking her arm away.

"I'm warning you, son!" Gregory pointed his index finger in my face.

The moment Lincoln tried to pull her away was the exact second I lost my shit, returning to the bad boy that had always gotten me into a hell of a lot of trouble.

That's also the moment I took a swing at Lincoln's pretty face, hitting him square in the nose. When I heard the crack, blood spurting from both his nostrils, I had a feeling all hell was going to break loose.

And it did.

* * *

"Do you mind telling me what the fuck you thought you were doing?" Gage asked after he headed outside.

I remained leaning on the hood of my car, nursing a bruised ego more than anything else. Sure, I'd allowed the situation to get out of hand, but the pissant Lincoln deserved the broken nose he'd gotten. As far as Wren's father, I wasn't even going to talk about the way I felt about him. I'd managed to get in two solid punches to his face, which had tickled me pink.

All I could do was grin, even though I was worried about what was happening with Wren inside the damn place. "I guess I wasn't thinking."

"No, I guess you weren't." He paced the pavement in front of me, cursing under his breath. "He's a goddamn congressman, for the love of God. Do you understand what would have happened to your career if the man had decided to press charges?"

"Well, I knew you'd talk him down. Besides, I thought it best to confront him." I'd managed to put in a call to my attorney to try to find out the details regarding my father's interference with the ranch. Maybe that would provide a few answers.

"Jesus Christ, dude. How many times have I gotten your ass out of hot water before?"

"About as many times as I did when you were a kid," I retorted.

He took a deep breath, his glare evil looking in the shrill light of the parking lot. "Yeah, I know you did, but we were stupid kids then. You're a goddamn grown man now. You finally returned home, and you pull this shit."

I shrugged and pressed my hand against my split lip. The reason I was so pissed was that Wren's mother had gotten in the middle of the melee, slapping me hard across the face. Hell, my ears were still ringing.

"Your daddy might own half of Texas, but in Montana, Gregory Tillman is now king. Do you hear what I'm saying?"

"I hear you loud and clear."

"But you don't give a shit," he chided me.

"Not in the least."

"Fuck." He grumbled some more then looked over his shoulder. "I have to admit, she might be worth the trouble you got yourself into."

I gave him a hard look and he threw up his hands. "I'm not poaching. I'm just saying she is one fine-looking woman."

"Yeah, she is."

"You really like her."

"I'm too old for her, but yeah, I like her."

"That's right. You're an old man just like I keep telling you," Gage laughed. "The owner is going to want you to pay for the damage."

"Fine. Just have him send me a bill." When the door opened and Wren walked outside, I immediately stood, wiping my hands on my jeans.

He patted my shoulder. "You're lucky this time I was able to keep Gregory from putting your ass in jail. Sometimes I think that's what you need."

"Very funny. I appreciate you taking the call."

Chuckling, he headed toward his truck, and I suddenly wasn't certain what to say to her. She'd let loose a second time, telling off both her parents. Now she appeared angry, frustrated, and uncertain what she'd done had been the right thing.

She stood where she was for another ten seconds before walking closer. "About in there."

"Look, I know you want me to tell you I'm sorry, but I don't like your father and it has nothing to do with whatever background he has with my dad. What bothers me is the way he treats you, like you're his possession, not his daughter. Then that jerk who really believed you were going to listen to him. I'd break his nose all over again."

I hadn't realized during my dissertation and the way I was frothing at the mouth she'd moved closer. When she put her finger across my lips, I took a deep breath. Then she did exactly the opposite of what I thought she'd do. She rose onto her tiptoes, capturing my mouth.

There was something cathartic about the electricity that soared through us. I wrapped my arm around her waist, dragging her against my chest. I couldn't seem to get enough of her, the taste as sweet as ripe cherries. When she pressed her hand against my chest, I pulled her all the way off the ground, sweeping my tongue inside.

Holding her in my arms was entirely different than it had felt on the night I'd carried her to safety. I was no longer surprised how my body reacted around her, my cock aching and my balls tight, but tonight I had a sense that I would protect her no matter the odds. It was the most unusual feeling I'd had in a long time.

When she pushed away, she took a deep breath.

Then she slapped me across the face, backing away instantly.

"What the hell was that for?"

"That," she huffed, "was for making a scene at my sister's rehearsal dinner. Do you know what that girl has suffered to get to this point? Cancer. She was on death's door for years. Now, she gets a chance to live her life."

"No, I didn't think, I—"

"That's what I mean. You didn't think. That's not you. You barge into a situation as if you own the place, pretending to be something you're not. Then you take control, the big he-man planning on conquering the world. "

"Well, tell me this," I challenged, my tone gruffer than I'd wanted it to be. "Why did you bother asking me to take you to this soiree in the first place? Because I'm nothing but a goddamn smokejumper? No couth. No money?" I could tell by the way she sucked in her breath I was right. Fuck. I'd worried about women liking me for my money. Now this.

"Okay, so I wanted a normal guy that my father couldn't challenge with politics or the latest stock prices."

"You could have told me. That wasn't cool, lady."

She took another deep breath, nodding several times. "No, you're right. That was cruel of me and what you did was the nicest thing anyone has ever done for me. Coming up against my father isn't easy. He lords his position over everyone, including his own family, but you almost brought my sister to tears. And I'm certain I did. What was wrong with me?"

"You did what you thought was right."

"I'm not in tears, sis." The other female voice came from directly behind. "In fact, I was trying to keep from laughing the entire time. That was the best present you could have ever given me."

Wren took a deep breath, still glaring as me as she turned around to face her sister. "You're really okay?"

"Oh, hell, yes," Cammie laughed. "You should feel glad you have a man in your life who has no fear about challenging Daddy."

I looked away, uncertain what the hell to say at this point.

"I guess I should say something conciliatory," Wren said a few seconds later.

"Don't do it," Cammie stated. "I came here to tell you that your presence is wanted, without your date of course, but I'm going to say right here, right now. Leave. Go enjoy your evening. I'm just fine. In fact, I'm going to call off the wedding."

"Wha—at?" Wren almost choked on her words.

"All that crap you saw with Marcus, you know, the lovey-dovey shit. I was faking it. I thought that's what I was supposed to do. I mean heck, I'm a girl with no one else who's interested in her. Right? Mother made certain to remind me of that dozens of times. I have a limp because of the cancer, my organs are more fragile than normal, and the possibility I'm going to be able to have children is about ten percent. So, I settled. Marcus doesn't love me. He loves the money and power our marriage will bring."

"Wow. Oh, Cammie. Why didn't you tell me?" Wren asked, anguish in her voice.

"Don't be sad for me. I'm elated. I finally broke free of my shell. I might not live to be fifty or have kids, but I am going to find a man who loves me for me."

I had to admit, even to the gruff side of the man I'd turned out to be, the moment was touching as hell. As Wren moved forward, wrapping her arms around her sister, I leaned back against the car.

"I'm so proud of you, baby sister. So very proud." Wren pulled away, brushing hair from her sister's face. "Do you need me to stand by your side?"

156

"Nope. I need to do this all by myself, just like you need to get out of here and go somewhere with that man standing right there waiting for you. I witnessed more chivalry in Phoenix in five minutes than I ever witnessed in our father. Go. Just go." Cammie squeezed Wren's arm then headed for the door. Then she stopped and turned toward me. "But I will say this, Mr. Smokejumper. If you ever hurt my sister, I will kill you myself. Is that clear?"

I had to chuckle. "As a bell."

"Good." Cammie threw back her head and walked inside.

It took Wren a full minute to turn in my direction. When she lifted her head, I could tell she was still debating what she needed or if she even wanted anything else from me.

"So what now?" I asked.

"I paid for you. An entire weekend and that's what I'm going get. Take me somewhere for a nice dinner."

I crossed my arms and grinned. "I think I have the perfect place. But Wren," I told her as I walked closer. "Just remember that for this weekend, you belong to me."

CHAPTER 8

ren

Phoenix's words resonated in my mind, filthy images continually sending electric signals all the way down to my toes.

Fate.

My mother had never believed in fate. She'd told me more than once that I had to claw my way into or out of a situation to get what I wanted. That's what she'd done with my father. She'd set her sights on marrying him and she wouldn't back away until he'd shoved a ring on her finger, one worth millions. She'd come from the wrong side of town, her family poor, but she was beautiful and had won several beauty contests when she was growing up. Her incredible good looks and blonde hair became a commodity for the highest bidder. Imagine how she'd felt when her two daughters weren't so picture perfect.

I'd hated how she'd treated Cammie when she was given the news about my sister's cancer. That had put the final wedge between me and my mother. Selfish bitch that she was.

I'd been guessing about their affairs, but it had been obvious I was right. I honestly wasn't certain whether it angered or saddened me. It was another reason I would never allow myself to fall in love. As soon as I thought the words, I glanced at Phoenix, still wondering why he considered Riggs dead. However, I knew there were dirty little secrets hiding in everyone's home.

As I studied the road, I noticed he wasn't driving toward the city.

"Where are we going?" I asked.

"A place I enjoy."

"And you're not going to tell me."

"Nope."

Sighing, I shifted in my seat. "I am sorry I treated your job as…" I couldn't find the right words.

"A lowly job on the totem pole of life?" Phoenix asked.

"You just don't know my father."

"And I have no intention of getting to know him."

"I don't blame you." I hated the awkward silence between us. Not that he was a big talker. "Where are you from?"

"Missoula."

"Your parents are still here?" I don't know why I was pushing him. Maybe I needed to know his family was as fucked up as mine.

He took a deep breath before answering. "They're in Texas."

"Oh. They're *that* Wentworth family, the one who owns half of the state."

Chuckling, Phoenix glanced into the rearview mirror before making a turn. "My father has made it a point to purchase as much real estate as possible in the state as well as a few others."

"Why are you a smokejumper?"

"Do you mean why do something so lowly?"

I felt heat rising on my face. "That's not what I meant, and I know what you said about needing to face the beast. You are rich, powerful. Why not follow in your father's footsteps? Land development. Right?"

As he slowed down, the darkness didn't prevent me from seeing an ornate sign on the side of the road. Raging Thunder Ranch.

"Because I'm not my father and have no intentions of following in his footsteps." As soon as he made the turn, I tensed.

"Where is this?"

"What's wrong, little bird? You don't like surprises?"

"No. I like black and white."

"Well, you ain't gonna get that with me." He remained quiet as he drove up a well-lit road, fences on both sides.

"You own this."

"Yup."

"A working ranch?" I asked and I wasn't certain why I was more nervous than before.

"Yup."

"Why is talking so difficult for you?"

He slowly turned his head. "Are we back to twenty questions again?"

"Is there anything wrong with getting to know you?"

Before he bothered to answer, he turned onto another driveway. "Because you won't like most of what you learn."

"That's not true. Why bring me to your house if you don't want me to discover anything about you?"

"This was my parents' house before they moved."

"So you're saying it's not yours."

"I'm saying it's just a damn house," he stated flatly.

As the headlights splashed across the front, I was shocked. I'd expected an entirely different style of house, more rustic and meant for a cowboy or even a log cabin meant for a mountain man. The beautiful farmhouse with a three-sided wraparound porch wasn't at all what I could ever imagine him living in.

"This is lovely."

"This is my mother," he told me. He pulled the car near a four-car garage, parking in front. "She hated moving away, but my father insisted. Sound familiar?"

"I guess we come from similar backgrounds. Do you ever wish you could run away from your past?"

His exhale was ragged. "Almost every day of my life. Come on."

"Let me guess. You have a staff that provides everything for you, a chef standing by."

While he opened the door, he didn't bother looking in my direction. However, the overhead light allowed me to see that he'd clenched his jaw. "You might be surprised, Wren. I'm not who you think I am." He allowed me to get out of the car and I watched as he grabbed bags from the trunk, noticing he hadn't put a single duffle or suit bag into the vehicle for other wedding events.

"You never intended on staying at my parents' house. Did you?"

He said nothing as he headed for the porch, yanking out his keys. "I'd already planned on bringing you here."

"That's not fair. I was very specific in the reason I hired you." Even as I made the statement, I felt stupid for doing so. He could only have accepted the deal for one reason.

"Yes, you were. Have I mentioned to you that I don't follow rules?" There was such intensity in the way he looked at me.

He said nothing else as he guided me inside, flipping on a series of light switches. Small LED lights shimmered across the entire room, and I was surprised all over again.

"This is beautiful," I half whispered as I walked through the entrance foyer into one of the most incredible family rooms I'd ever seen. Between the floor-to-ceiling stone fireplace and the open floor plan, every piece of furniture designed perfectly for the space, I was enthralled by how he acted as if this was just a landing spot for him.

"It works. For now." He stood off to the side, his eyes never leaving me.

"What would you prefer, cold steel and all white furniture? No, you're the aging cabin type of guy, right? Or maybe you prefer camping out under the stars."

"Likely a combination of all three. If you don't want to be here, I'll take you home. However, you'd miss out on an incredible dinner."

The slight husky sound of his voice drew my attention, the thought of whatever dinner he might provide piquing my interest. I shifted to face him, planting my hands on my hips. "Dinner, huh? What do you have in mind, cowboy?"

His laugh was genuine. "I'm no chef, but I make a mean rare steak. You game?"

My mouth watered at the thought. "There is nothing I would like more." When I felt the heat of his gaze sliding ever so slowly down to my heels, a warm blush crept across my cheeks. "Well, maybe one or two things."

Chuckling, he motioned toward the kitchen. "Let me drop your things in the bedroom. Then we can have a drink and you can ask all those questions you're dying to find out."

"What are my limitations?" I asked just as he was starting to walk down the hallway. There was something so seductive about the way he tipped his head, his strong jaw clenching, the two-day stubble that was hard to take my eyes off of more pronounced in the dim light.

"None."

The challenge was on, and I had to admit, I was eager to learn more about him.

Including all the dirty little secrets.

* * *

Phoenix

The woman might be able to drive me crazy by the end of the weekend, but it wasn't just because of her incessant questions. It was the need to pick me apart that made me bristle one minute and long to tackle her to the ground the next. It was the carefree way she avoided all sense of normal dating banter, refusing to accept any terms but those she set for herself.

It had become obvious she'd lived a sheltered life, forced to become the perfect doll. Then she'd branched out on her own, a little bird in a big, bad world. She had no idea the evils that awaited her.

Including from a wolf like me.

I threw on another shirt, rolling up my sleeves, not bothering to tuck the tail in. This was my home, one of the few places I could be myself. While the reminders of my parents and my father's bullshit as I was growing up remained throughout the house, I'd done what I could in a short period of time to make it my own.

I pulled out the steaks first, allowing them to warm on the counter. By then, she'd already made herself at home, finding a bottle of cabernet I didn't know I had, assuming I wanted whiskey instead. She'd even poured me a glass, two ice cubes only. It was as if the woman had been able to read me in our limited time spent together.

Now, Wren stood in her bare feet at the end of the island, studying me as if I was a specimen she was prepared to dissect.

I grabbed my glass, lifting a single eyebrow as I turned toward her. Damn, the woman was beautiful, her long hair spilling over her shoulders drawing my attention. I wanted to wrap my hand around the thick strands, forcing her to her knees to suck my cock.

Neanderthal, buddy.

So what?

She'd been the first woman who'd broken through the protective layers I'd built around myself. But I was no romantic and this wasn't about starting a relationship. I'd likely need to make that perfectly clear at some point.

"Go ahead, little bird. I know you're dying to ask questions."

"How many acres?" At least her first question was a simple one.

"Ten thousand, give or take."

She almost choked on her wine. "Wow." I watched her subtle move as she wiped two small beads of wine from her lips and it was all I could do not to grab her fingers, sucking them dry.

Sighing, I swallowed hard, my cock aching already.

"Okay. What do you do with all that acreage?"

I had to laugh. For a girl who'd been brought up in Montana, she sure didn't seem to have a handle on what happened on a ranch. "I have horses, cattle. It's a working ranch. Yes, I have dozens of employees, but no one for the house."

"You're taking away all the fun of me asking questions."

As she walked around the end of the island coming closer, I forced myself to take a gulp of whiskey to keep from growling. The thin material of the dress did little to hide the fact she was already aroused, her luscious nipples announcing themselves. Shit. I had to try to think of something else. Anything else.

A fire burning in the fireplace.

A fire outside in the firepit.

A fire burning down several trees, claiming lives.

Fuck. As another image from two decades ago popped into my mind, I could feel beads of sweat forming along my hairline.

"Earth to Mr. Hunky Cowboy. Are you okay?"

A slight shiver slammed down my spine and I was sick of it. "Hunky cowboy, huh?"

"Very much so," she purred then caught herself, but if she came any closer, all bets were off as to whether I could calm down my raging libido. She looked away, stopping before she got within yanking her closer distance. "Which do you prefer, smokejumping or tending to the ranch?"

"Good question. The truth is I love fighting fires. It's in my blood, but my horses soothe the man inside."

She nodded, looking away briefly. "I used to have a horse. My father sold it because I got a B in senior high."

"Fuck. What a prick."

"He gave me a solid work ethic at least."

"What do you do?"

"Financial advising. I have several very wealthy clients."

I don't know why I wanted to laugh. "That doesn't seem like you at all."

"Well, it was either that or marry a rich guy by the time I was nineteen. You know the type, a man who was destined to run for president. Not like Lincoln. I refused and was given a list with a couple choices of careers I could choose. See, my father thought I'd meet a rich guy by giving him advice. Little did he know it turned me off on anyone with money." Two seconds later, her eyes opened wide and she slapped her hand over her mouth, laughing so hard wine sloshed over the edge of the glass, trickling down her fingers.

There was no hesitation this time. The big he-man she'd accused me of being reared his ugly head. I took a single step closer and took the glass from her hand, immediately bringing her fingers to my mouth. As I dragged my tongue down her index finger, her breathing became ragged.

Several growls erupted from my throat as I moved from one finger to the other, but I couldn't seem to help myself around her. She brought out the beast in me. When she pursed her lips, my eyes were drawn to them and there was nothing I could do to stop what happened next.

I barely managed to put her glass down on the counter before wrapping my hand around the back of her neck, yanking her against me and onto her toes. I gave her no time to think or breathe, capturing her mouth and immediately slipping my tongue past her voluptuous lips. God, the woman tasted like peaches and cream. All I could think about was tasting her more.

Licking every inch of her body.

Fucking that sweet mouth first before driving my cock into her tight pussy.

I was lost in a haze of lust, dominating her tongue as her long fingers clasped around my shirt. The sensations of having her so close was about to do me in. I was ready to sweep my arm across the counter, taking her like a wild animal. Her perfume had already stained my skin. Now I wanted to stain hers with my cum.

Shit. What was I doing? This was supposed to be a nice dinner.

We broke the kiss mutually, but I couldn't seem to let go of her. Our breathing was the same, scattered, the sound full of desire.

Wren closed her eyes, backing away and licking her lips. Then she turned her head toward the refrigerator. "What are we having with the juicy, blood-rare steaks?"

Damn if the way she elongated the syllables didn't keep me turned on. "Whatever you want, darlin.'" I watched as she found items to make a salad, even checking the pantry and finding potatoes for baking. Seeing her so comfortable in my kitchen was as strange as the way we'd gotten together.

Hold on. We weren't together. I'd need to remind myself of that. I came with too much baggage. And I was too damn old for her, set in my ways. We were like oil and water. Maybe if I kept reminding myself of that I'd finally believe it.

"What would you do for a living if you had the chance?"

She seemed surprised I'd asked her that question. "I don't know. Write a book, which is something I've tried to do several times. But what I really want to do is build a shelter for homeless animals. You know the kind. A beautiful sanctuary in the wilderness where they'd have lots of room to roam and play. Mountains. Lakes. Streams. They'd have snow and flowers, grass and hay. And they'd have shelter complete with comfy beds and even television. I love dogs, but all animals really. But it would have to be at least five hundred acres and the cost of building the facility, which would also need to have a veterinary clinic of course and a main house for the caretaker, although I'd want to live there. And maybe it could also be a working ranch to make money, not just need donations for food. And toys. Oh, God. They'd be lot of toys for them to play with all the time, not just every once in a while. And a huge pool. Yes, there would need to be at least one pool. Come to think of it, maybe two."

She took a deep breath and I was completely mesmerized.

"And maybe... Oh, yeah. How about if there was a play area for kids and we could teach them about all kinds of animals. How to be kind to them and take care of them. Oh, that's perfect." She clapped her hands, dropping a tomato on the floor, laughing as she scampered to pick it up. "Oops. I think I bruised it."

Suddenly, she stopped talking and I realized I'd been holding my breath. I'd never seen anyone so enthusiastic about something that sounded so incredible in my life. Holy shit. I could see the location now. My mind went to some very different places as I thought about the ranch. Hell, I'd sold off most of the cattle, laid off twenty-two employees over the last few weeks because I didn't want a working ranch. At least I'd been able to give them a year's salary, but it had made me feel like shit.

I realized the dead air between us was awkward as hell.

"I know. That's stupid. Just stupid."

After clearing my throat, I grabbed my glass and gulped down the rest of my drink. "No, little bird. That's the most incredible thing I've ever heard."

"Really?" Her entire face lit up and it became painfully obvious to me that she'd never been given any encouragement to do whatever she wanted or needed to do in her life. Fuck her father. I should have beaten him to a pulp.

Calm down, big boy.

"Yeah, really."

"I have some money, but not enough. Maybe I could get a loan." She was still lost in the haze of being told she was a good girl.

I wanted to see that happen all the time.

Stop it. You can't make her happy. You'll just give her nightmares.

That was the sick truth, and I wouldn't put her through that. However, maybe there was something I could do in order to help her make her dream come true. "I thought your father was rich."

She burst into laughter, grabbing the bottle of wine and refilling her glass all the way to the rim. "I have a trust fund I can access either when I marry or turn twenty-eight. However, if I'm not married by then, the amount gets cut in half. Granted, even five hundred thousand dollars would be a wonderful amount to start in building my dream, but not nearly enough. Plus, Daddy knows every banker in the entire state. If I had to guess, I'd say he'd make certain I never got a damn loan."

Now I wanted to put a bullet in the man's head.

Before I had a chance to comment, she lifted her head, staring me in the eyes. "Thank you for indulging me in my crazy fantasy for a few minutes. That meant a lot. Let's just stick to simple questions. Okay?"

Hmm... "Agreed." If only I wasn't the bad man I'd turned out to be. Maybe I could provide her with something that made her happy. Nope. That would entail remaining close and that just couldn't happen.

"What's your favorite color?" she asked, laughing again although I could see a new wave of pain in her eyes.

"Blue."

"Figures. You're a boy."

When my cell phone rang, I growled. This damn well better not be a fire I needed to race off to. "I'll be right back. Okay?"

"I might be here, big boy."

Now my balls were tight as fucking drums. Shit, I'd need relief soon.

"Hello?"

"I'm sorry to bother you, Riggs, but Justin is demanding he talk to you," Betty said, exasperation in her voice.

"Don't worry, Betty. You can call me anytime. I don't know what I would do without you in our lives."

"You're so sweet. Let me get him." I remained in the hallway, keeping my voice low. I'd never had to face telling someone about Justin. I knew it would put a wedge between us. Maybe that made me a damn coward, but I was also protective of my son. If I ever brought anyone into my life, she'd need to be special and the one, because he couldn't take another loss.

"Sweetie. How are you?"

"Daddy. I want to come home." He was already in tears. I could tell he'd had a tantrum.

"Soon. This is just something I need to do."

"Important?" he asked in his little voice. The kid tried to be so grown up. Sometimes he was like a little adult, able to put full sentences together. Other times he was in complete meltdown mode.

"Not important. Just something I need to do."

I thought I heard a sound and glanced over my shoulder seeing nothing. I lowered my voice even more, heading down the hallway. "Can you be a good boy for Daddy?"

"Hmmm… Don't wanna."

"I need you to get some sleep and I heard you're going to the park tomorrow." To see the animals. The small zoo offered him some comfort. Shit. Animals. My mind was churning again.

"Really?" Now he was more excited.

"Yes, really, but only if you go to bed and get some sleep. Can you do that?"

"O-tay, Daddy. Miss you."

"I miss you too, buddy."

"Thank you," Betty said. "I tried everything."

"You did the right thing. I'll call in the morning." As I ended the call, I held the phone against my forehead.

"You son of a bitch!" Wren said. "Who is she and why in the hell am I here?"

As I turned around to face her, I could tell there was nothing I was going to be able to say that would matter. So I did the only thing I could do.

I grabbed her wrist and dragged her down the hallway.

CHAPTER 9

Oh, my God.

What the hell was wrong with me?

I'd never asked him if he was involved. What I'd overheard was a clear indication that he had a girlfriend or maybe worse. I was just an inconvenience for him, or maybe because he felt sorry for me he'd allowed himself to be bought for the weekend?

I was sick inside, doing my best to pull out of his strong hold.

"I'm not doing this. You will take me back to my car right now or so help me God!" My demand was met with silence as he dragged me down the hall. If he actually thought he was going to fuck me, I'd find a way to knock him on his ass.

He stopped in front of a closed door, his chest rising and falling. I didn't need to see his eyes to know he was exasperated with me. So the fuck what?

"You two-timing pig!" I snapped, surprising myself when my punch landed against his jaw. But it was like hitting a brick wall.

All he did was grunt like the pig he was.

Then he yanked me so hard I thought for certain he was going to hit me. I winced and he seemed shocked, his eyes opening wide.

Exhaling, Phoenix looked away briefly, muttering under his breath. "Things aren't always as they seem, Wren. You need to stop second guessing me. I would never two-time a lady. I've done a hell of a lot of things I'm not proud of in my life. There are people in this town who will tell you in gory detail about how horrible I am, but I would never do that. I would also never hurt you." He twisted his handle around the knob, pushing me inside and turning on the light.

Then he stepped away, breaking his hold and allowing me to gasp at what I saw.

The room was set up for a little boy, complete with a rocket ship for a bed. There were posters of Spiderman and the Avengers on the walls, books in a wooden bookcase, and toys everywhere. But almost instantly I felt sadness in the room. Why?

"I…" There were no words to describe the way I was feeling. None.

"The phone call you just had to listen in on was with the woman I hired to be my son's part-time nanny. Betty has been a godsend, although I know she's getting tired of what she constantly has to deal with. My son refused to go to bed without talking to me. He throws temper tantrums that no damn psychiatrist or therapist has been able to help with. I took a chance that he'd like being away from his room and everything he knows for this weekend. But he's struggling and I am a terrible father because I can't break through to him."

There was such anguish in his voice, the sadness I'd seen in his eyes making complete sense. I moved further in, daring to touch the lampshade on the nightstand, the characters of racecars almost breaking my heart. "What's his name?"

"Justin. He's the sweetest little boy when he's not raging at everything around him."

"Why does he rage?" I felt guilty for even asking a single question. This wasn't my place. I couldn't provide any help or advice. My God. I was nothing but a damn spoiled brat complaining that I'd only get five hundred thousand dollars, money I'd never wanted.

He sighed and walked further into the room. "His mother was a drug addict. She was hooked on heroin when he was born so from what little I was able to find out, he was born premature and forced to stay in NICU for five months. He's borderline autistic, although the great doctors are hopeful he'll grow out of it. I don't have the skills to help him do

177

that. Not with my schedule and the anger I have inside of me."

Everything Phoenix said broke my heart. I turned slowly, walking closer, fearful of touching him or being able to find the right words. "I'm so sorry. I overreacted, which is a terrible trait of mine."

"Yeah, you're right. But I wasn't honest with you." He moved toward the bed, easing down and I could feel the weight of the world crowding around him.

"You weren't required to tell me about your family."

"Maybe I was afraid you'd realize what a horrible man I was. I am." He exhaled slowly and glanced around the room. "At least I can provide a decent home and all the therapy he needs."

"He just needs his father."

"Like I know what I'm doing. My Pops certainly didn't set a good example."

I sat down beside him, shifting to the side and placing my hand on his heart. "It's what you have inside here that counts. Justin knows what's in your heart. He can see the love in your eyes."

"Yeah, you don't know me very well, little bird. I ain't got much in there."

Whatever happened to him in his past was eating him alive. And I was interfering with his life. "Does he talk to his mom? Is she in therapy?"

Inhaling, his mouth twisted, and I could tell it was a question I shouldn't have asked. "She dropped him on my doorstep a week after I got back to town. She had a single bag of dirty clothes for him, a damn stuffed animal and nothing more. She told me I could have him and walked away. She just walked away. Fuck. She was strung out as hell. I tried to get her to stop so I could figure out a way to finally help her, but she vanished just like I'd done to her a long time ago. She never told me she was pregnant, but I wasn't the kind of guy who would have wanted to know, and I think she realized that."

"You were young."

He laughed. "No, I wasn't. I was just a hothead. Dahlia did her best, but the demons took everything away from her including her life. She overdosed a couple months ago. Justin doesn't know. I just can't figure out how to tell him. He can't handle rejection or loss. That's why I didn't tell you about him."

The ache in my heart was tremendous, but I had to find a way to soothe him. "You'll know when the time is right for both of you to mention his mother. Don't let him forget about her. Try and paint her in a light where he can have good memories."

"You're pretty smart for a girl," he teased.

"Ha ha. Maybe you should think about another career?" I half expected him to snarl and toss me out of the house, but he nodded several times.

"I've thought of it often and I wish I could explain why I need to fight fires."

"The beast is the manifestation of your very personal need."

He rubbed his knuckles across my cheek, forcing a shudder down my spine. "True. It's easier to deal with if you have something tangible to fight instead of demons who surface when you least want them to. As I said, it's tough to try and explain."

"Why don't you try?"

His expression changed, his face becoming pensive. "A lot of shit has happened in my life, Wren. I ain't going to bore you with the tragic details, but the only thing that allows me to fight the demons so they don't win is fighting fires. I'm good at it. I've saved a few lives over the years, but it's still not enough. I tried being something else. Hell, I was an EMT for a couple of years after moving away but something kept drawing me back. When I was offered a position on the Zullies team, I jumped at it. It wasn't a month after I'd passed all the damn tests when Justin came into my life. I thought I could juggle but I'm not doing any good for anyone."

We sat quietly for a few minutes and my heart remained in my throat.

"Maybe I could meet him someday. I mean I know that's presumptuous and I'm not mother material, but I really would love to meet him. If you don't think that's wise, I'll understand completely, but I'd love to get to tell him how great his daddy is. Protective. Grumpy but kind. A great man and a hero."

"I ain't no hero, Wren. No one should ever call me that." He bristled then took another deep breath.

"You served this country. Right? A Marine?"

"Yeah. I fought like I do everything else. With a vengeance. But so did a lot of men and women. Anyway, I wanted you to know that I'm not a two-timing son of a bitch. You can call me anything you want, but never that. It's one woman or nothing and at this point in time, I'm not good for anyone."

"Neither am I. I'm selfish, bratty, opinionated, and worth nothing in the grand scheme of things. I guess we're just two broken souls that should be tossed out." I was trying to bring some levity to the conversation, but I could tell I'd misstepped again. What bothered me was how much I cared about the man. I didn't really know him, but he was the first person in my life who'd allowed me to feel like me and enjoy it. But maybe he was right in that this wasn't the best decision. "Why don't you take me back to my car? Then you can pick up Justin. He needs you and I understand."

I could tell he was thinking about it. Then he shook his head. "That's not going to happen. I'm also a man of honor and I gave you my word that I would be with you for the entire weekend."

"I revoke the deal. I'll give you your money still. Okay? I can't do this, Phoenix. I can't pretend when I really want to be here with you. I want to stay but it's not right and I won't be able to look myself in the mirror." I jerked to my feet, trying to keep from bolting to the door.

He grabbed my arm as he'd done before, yanking me back with enough force I was pitched onto his lap. "Hear me, little bird. I'm in charge and you're staying right here with me. Period. I won't let you go. If I need to handcuff you to my bed, I will."

"Why? Is it all about the deal? I know it's not about the damn money."

"Stop cursing. You're a lady," he growled.

"I'll curse if I want to. Fuck you." Even as I said the awful words, I rubbed my fingers across his lip where Lincoln had gotten in a single shot. I expected him to wince, but he was one strong guy, refusing to act as if anything hurt him.

God help me, I wanted him more than I could ever imagine craving anyone. I couldn't help but laugh, racing away from him and into the living room. I should have known he'd catch me within seconds, yanking me by the arm. While his eyes were laced with mischief, his grin was practically evil. "You are a very bad girl."

I struggled, giving him a defiant look. "Yes, I am."

"Then we're going to need to do something about it." He pushed me backward, walking me further into the room.

"What do you think you can do about it?" I challenged. "And you didn't answer my earlier question." Everything about him was powerful, my entire body shaking from his firm hold.

There was an entirely different look in his eyes, as if the beast had come out to play. Then a wry smile drifted across his face and butterflies erupted in my stomach. "To answer your question, I want you here because that's what I need. You're the only woman who's lit a fire in me in five years and if you think I'm going to let you go, you've got another think coming."

"Really?" His words thrilled me, my heart racing.

"Oh, yeah, baby. But I got news for you. You're going to learn to be more obedient." The evil glint in his eyes pierced mine seconds before he plopped down on the couch, yanking me over his knees. I immediately yelped, struggling to get out of his hold.

"What are you doing?"

"Giving you a much needed reminder that you're a lady." He wasted no time yanking my dress over my bottom to my waist, dragging down my thong with such ferocity I heard the material rip. "You are one mouthy, bad girl, and I'm going to help you stop that."

I was breathless, shocked that he would do such a thing, but I should have known better. He was far too dominant and rugged. I'd never felt like such a bad girl in my life. He brought his hand down hard and fast, moving from one side to the other in rapid succession.

The wind was knocked out of me, my mind a fuzzy mess of desire and uncertainty as the pain swiftly caught up to me. Every inch of my body tingled, but the shock of what he was doing kept me from fighting to get away.

Then the usual girl took over, trying to claw my way out of his clutches.

I managed to get a few inches, but he dragged me back. "None of that or I'll be forced to take other measures."

"Other measures? This hurts like a son of a bitch."

"What did I tell you about cursing? Do I need to wash your mouth out with soap?"

"You wouldn't dare."

He chuckled, the sound sending a firecracker of desire into every cell and muscle. "You really don't know me very well, do you?" He cracked his hand against my naked bottom several times, the rhythm exactly the same as the ragged beating of my heart. Nothing could have shocked me any more than what he was doing.

Panting, I continued to struggle, kicking out my legs, cursing under my breath as the pain turned into agony. How could a spanking hurt so badly?

"Stop. Stop!" My pleading fell onto deaf ears. There was no doubt about it. When I wiggled even more, he'd had enough of my misbehavior. He was so strong that he rose from the couch, his arm firmly planted around my waist, able to drag me with him as he walked to the small cabinet. I watched in horror as he opened the drawers one by one until he found what he was looking for.

A damn ping-pong paddle. Was he fucking with me?

"No. No!" I screeched, frustration bringing tears to my eyes.

"This is what happens when you fight me." He brought the paddle down so fast that I felt as if I'd gone into suspended animation. How could he do that to me? Oh, God. I couldn't seem to stop tears from slipping past my eyelashes. I wasn't certain if it was because of the intensity of the pain or the frustration of knowing somewhere deep inside I deserved this.

He cracked the thick piece of wood down six times then stormed back to the couch, tugging me across his lap and immediately swinging his leg over mine. "This is what you need on a regular basis."

The brutal man sounded happy in what he was doing. I flailed even more, twisting to the point I thought for certain I could slide off his lap.

Nope.

Panting, when he stopped for a few seconds, I was hopeful the horrible spanking was over. The feel of the rough pads of his fingers sliding back and forth across my heated skin increased my blood pressure. I could tell I was wet, the heat expanding to every inch of my body. And my nipples were hard points begging to be twisted and plucked.

I was aroused by this? No way. None. Zero.

But his heavy breathing told me otherwise.

"Yes, you thrive on having a man in charge of you. That's good to know and I'm happy to give you exactly what you need." He dared to dip his fingers between my legs, teasing my pussy until I bucked hard against him, moans slipping past my lips at an increased rate. This was crazy. This was horrible.

This was amazing.

I closed my eyes as he continued the spanking, the anguish quickly turning into something I couldn't describe. Tingles flowed through my body, goosebumps everywhere. I was no longer the same girl I'd been when he met me, and I found that profound for some crazy reason.

Maybe all I'd needed was a firm hand, a man who acted like he cared about me.

Could this be the start of something amazing? No, I couldn't think that way. This was nothing more than two people needing someone else in a short period of time.

He disciplined me long and hard and when he tossed the paddle, my pussy was clenching and releasing over and over again. I was almost at the point of orgasming. How could that happen?

"You're wet, my little bird. Does that mean you're hungry?" The dark husky tone was far too inviting.

"Uh-huh."

"Would a rare steak fulfill your desires?"

"Um… No." The admittance was easy, the need building to a precipice.

"Then what will? Tell me and I'll know if you're lying."

"You."

He laughed softly and thrust his fingers inside. "That's not good enough, little bird. I need you to be very specific."

The man was frustrating as hell. "I need your cock."

"Where?"

"Inside."

He smacked my bottom again as another reminder. "More."

Tension and need, hunger and anxiety came bursting out of me. "I need your cock in my mouth, my pussy, my asshole. I want you to fill me with your cum. Then I want you to start all over again. I don't care about food. I just need you."

The startling admittance left me breathless inside. As he plunged his fingers inside, flexing them open, I did what I could to ride them like a wild stallion. I needed relief. Stars floated in front of my eyes, my heart racing and I concentrated on the sound of his breathing. As I rode his hand, coming closer and closer to nirvana, my moans increased in intensity. The man was going to drive me crazy.

"Please fuck me. Please." I'd never begged a man for sex in my life, but when I was with him, everything was different. I couldn't seem to control myself, either my hunger or my bad girl behavior. Why this man?

"I will. Trust me, baby girl. I will, but not until you come for me. Be my good girl and come."

Maybe it was the sound of his deep voice or the fact he'd driven me crazy for hours, but almost as soon as he uttered the command, a powerful orgasm swept through me like a wildfire. I was pushed straight into a moment of raw ecstasy, no longer able to think about anything.

Phoenix refused to stop, pumping hard and fast, rocking my body from his brutal actions. As the beautiful moment of release started to calm down, I thought for certain he'd stop, but the man was insatiable, requiring me to come again.

"More. Go ahead, little bird. Get my fingers nice and soaked."

When he jammed his thumb into my asshole, I lost it all over again. This time the orgasm left me breathless. I opened my mouth to scream but nothing came out. I couldn't think or breathe, move or talk. Nothing. The orgasm was that powerful and dear God, I wanted more.

He laughed softly, caressing my bottom for a few seconds before easing me back onto his lap, brushing away remnants of my tears. He was such a powerful, rugged man and I'd never felt safer in any other place than in his arms.

As he rubbed hair from my face, lifting my chin with his index finger, I noticed his eyes were dilated. The smile remaining, he yanked my panties down my legs, pitching them aside. "Now, I'm going to fuck you just like you want. And I assure you that it will go on all. Night. Long."

He gathered me into his arms, holding me close as he took long strides out of the room. When he kicked open the partially closed door, I couldn't resist running my finger under his shirt. I wanted to explore every inch of him, licking his skin and tracing his tattoos. I longed to suck him dry, savoring the taste of his sweet cum and I wanted to tangle my fingers in his hair.

I wanted him. Just him.

He didn't dump me onto the bed as I'd anticipated. Instead, he eased me down with care and consideration, but there was no doubt about the hunger swelling deep within him. I'd heard dozens of times that a man's eyes were a direct path to his soul, allowing a woman the opportunity to run when they had a chance.

But Phoenix's eyes were different than most men's, bearing an unspeakable level of anger as well as sadness, the combination creating a deep, luminescent quality. I could sit and stare into them for hours, but that wouldn't be allowed on this night of reckoning.

He had other, more desperate needs to fulfill.

As he backed away, leaving me in a sitting position, I tugged the dress from around my body, slowly lifting it over my head and tossing it aside.

Just before I turned on the lamp on the nightstand, he flipped a switch, the room bathed in a soft, warm glow. That allowed me the opportunity of watching as he undressed, the fact he was taking his time heightening the yearning crawling through me.

After he'd folded his clothes, placing them on the dresser, he advanced like a predator, enjoying the moment of watching my anticipation grow. He had no way of knowing what he was doing to me, the rush of adrenaline flowing through my system or the longing keeping my pussy aching. I'd never wanted a man this much, which kept me floating in the clouds.

As he crawled onto the bed, I tugged on the sheet, giving him a heated look. With a single snap of his wrist, he yanked the comforter and sheet away, most of it sliding off the bed.

"Never cover yourself," he told me, the dark husk in his tone providing another series of shivers.

I moved onto all fours, challenging him with my eyes, clawing at the bed as a low-slung growl erupting from his chest permeated the room. Vibrations skittered all the way down to my toes, the excitement building. We'd had rough sex before, but this was something different, a moment in time I'd never forget. As the electricity crackled between us, I tossed my head, smiling when his guttural sounds increased in volume.

"My perfect little bird," he whispered then fisted my hair, yanking me against him. "And all mine." He lowered his head, our lips almost touching, his hot breath cascading across my skin until I was lightheaded.

"I'm far from perfect," I murmured then fingered his tattoo, allowing my eyes to roam down his muscular arm.

"In my eyes, you are." He nipped my lower lip, pulling the tender tissue between his teeth. When he bit down, the slight pain was nothing in comparison to the sensations in my aching pussy. His touch had left me wanting so much more.

Somehow, the gruff man knew exactly the right words to say. I closed my eyes, allowing the tips of my fingers to dance across his heated skin. When he finally kissed me, he took his time keeping his lips pressed against mine, finally sliding his tongue inside. Where he'd been desperate to drink in a part of me before, this time he enjoyed exploring the dark recesses, the tenderness only pushing me closer to the edge. I wanted this to last, but the near desperate need was increasing.

Phoenix wrapped his long fingers around my hair, pulling me back into a deep arc, whispering words I couldn't understand as he brushed his lips down the length of my neck. Then he swirled the tip of his tongue around my nipple, his growls intensifying. How could a single gruff sound turn me on so much?

I struggled to hold onto him as he flicked his tongue back and forth, rolling his lips to my other breast, sucking on my hardened bud. I was shocked at the number of sensations flowing through my veins, still unable to think clearly. But that didn't matter any longer. Just being together was all that mattered.

There was no sense of time, no indication of how long he'd tease me, but I realized I just didn't care.

The man was surprising in so many aspects, so when he yanked me down on top of him, flipping me around so we were in a sixty-nine position, all I could do was swoon.

"Suck me, baby girl. Take all you want. I plan on filling you with my seed over and over again."

Why did his words thrill me, as if I'd been given the key to spending hours in a candy store all by myself? I barely had time to lean over before he grabbed my hips, lifting and yanking my pussy directly over his mouth.

This was filthy and delicious, a kinky little sexual position that I'd never tried before. What was I saying? I'd barely had any experience, the two times I'd enjoyed being with a man quick and barely dirty. This was on another level entirely. He was taking what he wanted without hesitation, refusing to allow me even a few seconds of control.

I teased him like he'd done to me, sliding the tip of my pinky across his sensitive slit. He responded by dragging his tongue all the way down my pussy only once as well, ending with smacking my bottom. The hint of pain added to the discomfort I was already in, making the entire moment more desirable.

He allowed me to feel free, uninhibited, and I wasn't certain why. I blew across his cockhead, shifting my body forward by a few inches. But as before, he was having none of it, yanking me back and driving his tongue past my swollen folds.

"Oh, God." I threw my head back, panting several times. The sensations were far too delicious, making me lose my train of thought. After licking my lips, I wrapped my hand around the base of his cock, pumping several times gently then tightening my hold, twisting and turning as I pumped him. I could tell the friction was getting to him, his breathing sounds even more guttural than before.

When he spread me wide open, swirling his tongue around my clit, I fell into a sweet abyss, unable to move. Another sharp crack against my bottom jolted me into action. I continued stroking him, using my other hand to toy with his thick balls. The man's cock was a magnificent creation, so long and thick that just getting my mouth around the girth was a feat. I rolled his testicles between my fingers before squeezing, smiling from the sound of his scattered moans.

Maybe I could have a small bit of control after all.

As he started to lick me furiously, I did what I could to concentrate, sliding his cockhead into my mouth, using my strong jaw muscles to suck.

There was no chance of interrupting him, his tongue licking me feverishly, moving up and down. I was at a loss for words.

But not for what I wanted.

I pulled two inches of his shaft into my mouth, savoring the explosion of flavors. When I was almost instantly rewarded with drops of pre-cum, I shuddered and sucked vigorously.

He pulled my clit into his mouth, sucking to the point I had to pull back, fighting to catch my breath, another wave of stars floating in front of my eyes.

"Keep sucking," he commanded, his voice barely audible.

"Yes, sir." Why the words came so easily I wasn't certain, but I took more of his delicious cock into my mouth, my head bobbing up and down. All time seemed to stop, the only sound our intense sucking. I could only imagine what we looked like. It was very naughty and exactly what I'd craved.

As he drove his tongue and fingers inside, I fought to keep the rhythm I'd developed. As he pushed me forward slightly, the angle changing, another raging orgasm swept through me. I managed to keep his shaft inside my mouth, even swirling my tongue. The only other thing I could do was moan around the thick invasion.

The climax seemed to last forever, and tiny beads of perspiration trickled down my cheeks, slipping onto the bed. When I stopped shaking, I was determined to make him come, filling my throat with his cream.

"Fuck. Your mouth is so damn hot," he managed, gasping for air as he used all four fingers to fuck me, teasing my asshole with his thumb as he'd done before. I fell into a lost moment, incapable of concentrating any further. I wasn't even certain I could move let alone think straight again.

He tossed me aside on my back, straddling my waist and planting his hands on either side of me. "Is something wrong, baby girl?"

"Uh-huh. I need you." I rubbed my hands against his chest, kneading his muscles.

"You're one insatiable girl."

"The insatiable one is you."

Laughing, he remained unblinking as I traced his tattoo. "You are fascinated by them."

"I am. What do they mean?"

"Life."

The way he said the single word left another haunted feeling deep inside. He'd obviously lost someone special to him, and I doubted it was the woman who'd given him a child. I had a sense this wasn't fucking to him. This was something else entirely. While that should terrify me, as with everything else around the man, I was excited, enthralled to the point I never wanted the moment to end.

He used his knees to ease my legs apart, taking his time rubbing his cock back and forth. "Are you wet for me? Are you hot and ready?"

"Uh-huh." I slipped my hand around his shaft, guiding the tip just inside my pussy lips. Then I wrapped my legs around his thighs, darting my eyes back and forth.

There was a moment of connection that was so different than before, the crackle of electricity keeping us in suspended animation. As he lowered his head, his eyes never leaving mine, I arched my back, forcing the tip of his cock inside.

"Be careful what you ask for," he whispered a split second before driving his entire shaft inside, my muscles immediately stretching, clamping around the thick invasion.

"Oh. Oh…"

"Goddamn, you're so tight," he muttered, throwing back his head, his strangled gasps matching my own.

I entwined my feet together, digging my nails into his chest as he lifted his hips, holding his cockhead just inside before thrusting down again. When he repeated the move, all the air was sucked out, the sensations building every second.

A smile remained on his face as he continued toying with me, driving deep inside then remaining aloft for several seconds.

"You're so mean," I half whispered.

"You're right but since I own you, I can do what I want, when I want. And I plan on taking my sweet time."

Own.

The word was so possessive. Normally I would argue, but the little word boosted the excitement.

As he continued to tease me, I used the leverage in my legs, able to drag him down. He laughed softly and jerked one of my legs up from the comforter, bending it at the knee. As he started fucking me in earnest, I remained breathless, refusing to blink. I wanted to see every moment, to bask in the way he pierced me with his eyes. I'd never been around a man so naturally dominating, and there was no doubt he had plans on devouring me.

I had no idea how long he lasted, but his stamina was incredible, pushing my boundaries to the point I could no longer breathe. Just when I was certain I couldn't take it any longer, he rolled me over, forcing me on top.

"Ride me, baby. Ride me like the wild filly you are." He cupped my breasts, holding me in place, rubbing his thumbs back and forth. The twinkle in his eyes was dark, even more authoritative than before.

I swung my hair across his chest, squeezing my knees against him as I bucked hard. When he pinched my nipples, the pain only added to the extreme pleasure. I rocked back and forth, rubbing my hands up and down his chest. He twisted my hardened buds to the point I let out a sharp cry. Then I threw my head back, blinking several times as the sensations continued to multiply.

"That's it, baby. Fuck that cock."

Every dirty word he said only turned me on even more. I became wild, bucking so hard against him the headboard slammed against the wall. As a climax came unexpectedly, all I could do was gasp, dropping my head as I struggled to catch my breath.

Phoenix sat up quickly, wrapping his hand around the back of my neck, pulling me down into a deep arc. I should have known he wouldn't allow me to maintain control for long. The angle was almost all I could take, another orgasm rushing into my system.

"Oh. Oh. Oh. Oh." Every moan I issued was strangled, every breathless sound full of exhaustion. I had no idea how he could keep from erupting deep inside. The man was a beautiful machine, capable of keeping me on the rollercoaster of ecstasy. But as my climax began to subside, I squeezed my pussy muscles, refusing to allow him to hold out any longer.

As he erupted deep inside, filling me with his seed, he eased me back into a sitting position. For a few minutes we remained where we were, holding onto each other as if there was no other place we'd rather be.

Yet as much as I loved being with him, I knew that the tragedy from his past would do everything to try to keep us apart.

And that scared me to death.

CHAPTER 10

 hoenix

"What happened on the mountain?"

"Who started the fire?"

"Have they been arrested?"

The crushing swarm of reporters was suffocating. I wanted to lash out, but my father had a firm hold on one arm, the family's attorney flanking my other side. I did what I could to keep from saying a goddamn word like I'd been warned, but it was almost impossible given the hatred tossed out by several people. When one of the reporters threw a microphone in my face, I growled like some crazed wild animal about to pounce, trying to jerk out of my father's firm hold.

"They were not charged!" the attorney bellowed above the yells and accusations.

"They're guilty."

"String them up!"

The insults came fast and furious.

"Get us the fuck of here, Barrett, or so help me God you're fired," my father hissed as he jerked me toward the parking lot.

Out of the corner of my eye, I noticed Ricardo, another crowd surrounding him and his parents. He had a blank expression, but our eyes locked, the pain evident. He hadn't said a damn word since the tragic incident, unable to process what had happened.

Or how much we'd sacrificed.

As we neared the waiting SUV, I finally yanked my arm free, charging the crowd. "You bastards!"

"That's enough, son. Goddamn it. Get in the car. Now."

Gasping, I jerked awake, blinking several times, my mind foggy as the images started to fade. Fuck. I took several deep breaths, realizing I wasn't alone. I glanced to my left, finally able to make out what I was seeing.

Wren.

She'd stayed the night.

Jesus. Thankfully, I hadn't awakened her. I wiped away beads of sweat, turning my head toward the window. Dawn was peeking over the horizon. There was no way I'd be able to get any additional sleep. At least I could smile thinking about the night before. We'd finally eaten dinner around eleven, the conversation light. She'd made me laugh more than once, which was something I hadn't done in a long time.

I rolled over, a smile crossing my face as I listened to her light breathing. She was so peaceful. Then for some reason, the story she'd told me about running away slipped into my mind. How could two damaged people ever find happiness? Shit. Now I was thinking about this in long term. Nope. Not possible.

After throwing back the covers, I slipped out of bed and padded toward the bathroom, grabbing my clothes along the way. As I closed the bathroom door, turning on the light, another angry memory popped into my mind, only one more recent. I would never forget the first time I headed into town. Maybe I was crazy because I wasn't the delinquent angry kid from almost twenty years before, but I'd seen the expressions on some of the old timers' faces. Their memories were long.

Maybe that's why I'd turned myself into a hermit. I yanked out my phone, thankful there'd been no calls in the night. As I was throwing on last night's clothes, I gathered a good look at the man in the mirror. What an angry face. I had to get some air in order to think more clearly.

I remained as quiet as possible as I grabbed my boots, heading toward the front door, yanking my coat from the closet. When I walked outside, I took a few seconds to stare at the sky, even as an ominous feeling settled into the pit of my stomach. There were clouds on the horizon, and it had nothing to do with weather.

One of the Marines I'd served with had been particularly religious, insisting that God had a plan for everyone. I'd thrown barbs at him, challenging him every time he'd brought it up. The kid was never flustered, never lashed out at me even though I'd prodded him to the point I wanted a damn fight. The rage had only been tempered with structure and rules, but just like now, it remained furrowed in the deepest, darkest portions of my mind.

He'd finally managed to get through to me, but it had been too late.

"The real meaning of life is how you live every day, Phoenix. It's not about money or possessions, only the love of people and animals. Once you realize that, there's no reason to fear death because you know you've lived the greatest life of all."

I hadn't thought about what he'd told me for a hell of a long time. "Maybe you're right, Ronny. Only I don't deserve peace." I muttered the words as I walked down the stairs, heading toward one of the two dozen barns I owned, the long structure housing several prized horses that I'd refused to give up. Even though I'd sold off almost half the livestock. There were already ranch hands at work, tending to the cattle. There were fences to be repaired, barns that needed new roofs. I hadn't given a shit. At least I had a foreman I could count on, even though we didn't see eye to eye on anything. Still, Jorge was a good guy and I paid him well to tolerate my lack of ambition.

The horses had been let out of their stalls to roam and run free. The thought of losing two of the precious beasts to some asshole continued to weigh heavily on my mind. Why would someone kill innocent creatures? To make a point? It pissed me off that my asshole of a father had tried to hide the fact he'd considered two separate offers for the property I owned.

I'd contacted my attorney and within an hour Adam had found out what lengths my father had gone to in order to try to finagle a deal. At least I knew what it was worth.

And I'd taken strides to shut him out completely.

As I leaned over the fence watching the magnificent beasts, I heard the tires of a vehicle rumbling up the gravel driveway. I turned my head, curious as to who the hell was coming to the main house this early.

As Snake pulled up with a horse trailer, I grinned. At least the injured horse was coming home. Sophia had been my horse for longer than I could remember, a precious mare that attached herself to me on the first day we'd met.

After cutting the engine, he jumped out, swaggering toward me. "You're up early," he said.

"So are you."

"I was just going to bring Sophia back and slip her inside the barn." He studied my expression, then glanced toward the enclosure. "Marshall pulled out the bullets. Soldier or assassin grade."

"That's what I figured."

"I don't like it."

I took a deep breath. "There are plenty of soldiers who still have their weapons after returning home." Pushing him into a conspiracy theory would only lengthen his healing process. He'd yet to address the fact another Marine was lying in a grave with his tombstone.

He shook his head, his jaw clenching. "There's something going on, Phoenix. You and I both know it. You know the four people who died in that fire at Shadowland Ranch? I'm going to guess they were murdered."

"They were." There was no sense lying to him.

"I know I'm stretching the possibilities, but those people were good to us, never turning their backs after..."

He couldn't even finish the statement. Very few people in town had dared talk to us or our families after what had happened on Sapphire Ridge. The owners of Shadowland Ranch had remained good friends with Gage's parents, mine as well, refusing to turn their backs. "Don't jump to conclusions, my friend." I wasn't prepared to suggest any possibilities at this point, although I was eager to find out what my attorney had discovered. I was still seething from learning how low my father had fallen to try to force me into working for him. It would never be a team effort. Hell, the man had admonished me when I'd told him about Justin. I'd learned he had no compassion early in my life. My father had certain rules that I would follow, or he'd cut me out completely. At this point, I wasn't certain I cared.

"You know my instinct is never wrong." Snake shook his head. "Never wrong."

I could tell he had something else on his mind.

"You knew I would have come and gotten Sophia. Why are you really here?"

Laughing, he shifted his arms on the top of the fence. "You could always read right through me."

"Yup. Don't you forget it."

He took a few seconds before answering. "There are some people asking questions."

"Who?"

"I dunno. One of my workers mentioned there'd been someone sniffing around the ranch. He's just a kid and if I had to guess an illegal, not that I care, but he was scared the guy was here for him. My foreman, Sawyer, saw the guy talking to one of the ranch hands. Nothing earthshattering, but I don't like people asking questions about me or the past."

"Yeah, I get it. What were the questions?" The hairs on the back of my neck were already standing up.

"How long he'd worked for me. If he'd known me for a number of years. Just weird. The dude was dressed in a suit but didn't identify himself. When my ranch hand finally started grilling him, the dude left. I thought I'd let you know."

I took a deep breath, uncertain what to make of it. "Maybe it just about undocumented employees. I've heard they're doing a sweep." Sounded like FBI to me. The question was why?

"Yeah, maybe you're right, but the timing is strange."

The timing. That's the only thing we could call it. The anniversary of when all our lives changed dramatically was coming up, something none of us had ever talked about. I glanced toward the mountains, thinking about that day. "Do you ever go there?"

He snorted, tossing me a look. "Not on my bucket list. Besides, what good would it do? And don't say that shit my therapist keeps telling me to do. Confront my past to erase the demons. The asshole has no clue what he's talking about."

"Maybe so, but the guilt's gonna kill you."

"A bit like the pot calling the kettle black." He lifted his eyebrows then something caught his eye. "You have a guest. I'm interfering."

I shifted my gaze in his direction and smiled. "Yeah, an unexpected pleasure."

He clapped me on the back. "It's good to see. Maybe you can finally be happy."

"Happiness comes from within."

"Shit. You've got a better psychiatrist than I do."

I laughed as Wren approached. She'd thrown on a dress meant for the wedding but surprised me by wearing cowboy boots. In the shimmer of the early morning light, the way the light breeze was flowing through her long strands of hair, she was a picture of beauty and my desire roared to the surface.

"I better get out of here," Snake said.

"Why don't you meet her? She's got a mouth on her, but I've grown fond of it."

"Maybe that's the kind of woman you need," he said, grinning.

"To hell with you," I teased then walked toward her, taking a deep breath. "You're a ray of sunshine."

She laughed, brushing a strand of hair from her face then glancing at Snake. "Am I interrupting?"

"Nah. Snake brought back a horse that was injured in a shooting," I told her.

"A shooting?" She glanced toward the trailer, her face pensive.

"Some asshole decided he'd kill a couple of Phoenix's horses," Snake told her.

"Why would anyone do something so horrible?"

"There's a lot of assholes who don't like us very much," Snake admitted then threw me a look, immediately shifting his gaze toward the barn.

"This is a good friend of mine. We go way back. Snake, meet Wren Tillman," I said, half laughing.

"Not to be rude, but please tell me your parents really didn't name you Snake." She moved closer, holding out her hand.

He wasn't one for handshakes or any physical contact since returning from his nightmare, but as he rubbed his hand on his jeans, his face lit up for the first time in months. "No, ma'am. Ricardo Garcia. I got the moniker while serving in the Marines."

"I'm afraid to ask why." Her sparkling laugh continued as she shook his hand.

"We all have different skills. This dude's a fly boy." Snake was nervous, which shocked the hell out of me.

"What's a fly boy?" She glanced into my eyes, a wry smile crossing her face.

"I can fly anything. Helicopters. Planes. I love being in the air. That's what I do for the smokejumpers sometimes. I fly the choppers that use weapons to start another fire." I laughed when confusion rocked her face. "That's a tactic to try and steer the initial fire in another direction. It's perfectly safe."

She nodded several times. "Uh-huh. You're a real danger junkie."

"She knows you too well," Snake chortled. "Good to meet you, Wren. Watch this guy. He's all attitude and mouth. I'm going to get Sophia. Do you want me to take her to the barn?"

"You're a load of laughs this morning," I told him, chuckling at the way Wren was nodding in agreement. "And I'll do it. Correction. We'll do it. Won't we, my wayward bird?" I pulled her to the fence, tipping my head toward the sky. "Besides, I thought maybe you'd like to see the ranch."

"I'd love to, but not on horseback. It's been years," Wren admitted. "Although I miss being around horses." The look in her eyes gave me pause. She was so enamored that it made me realize how much I'd taken for granted over the years.

"It's like riding a bike. Horses know when their human is scared. They are highly intelligent."

"Not a chance, cowboy. But they are majestic animals. Do you have any idea why someone shot two of them?"

"Not a clue." I wasn't prepared to get into any conspiracy theories at the point. I just might scare her away.

"Why do I have a feeling you're not telling me something?"

As Snake led Sophia toward us, I took a deep breath. "I'll never lie to you. That's not the kind of man I am. There's just no indication of why or who at this point. Gage is working on it."

"You're close with the sheriff."

"We go back a lot of years." As Sophia whinnied, I studied the smile on Wren's face. She was a ray of sunshine in yet another dark period of my life. I could almost see having her around for a long time.

The thought was as terrifying as it was riveting. We weren't a good match. It wasn't just about our age difference either or our families. She had her whole life to live and I was just uncertain I cared about living mine. Still, the weekend was turning out to be something entirely different than I thought it would be.

"Seems everybody knows everybody in this town," she said in passing.

That was part of the problem in my opinion.

As she brushed her hand down Sophia's muzzle, she took a deep breath. "Yes, I would love to see the ranch. Maybe one day I'll get to ride you, sweet girl."

Sophia snorted in response.

"She likes you. She's very special, the kind of horse who comes along once in a lifetime."

"I agree with you but be careful keeping ugly secrets." While she laughed, I sensed she was searching for answers, just like she'd done the night before and would do again.

Secrets were the only option at this point, although they were dark and ugly, and I had no doubt that one day they'd come back to bite all six of us.

* * *

Wren

There was no adequate way to describe the feeling of freedom that flowed through me as he drove the miles of roads and paths showing me his ranch. I'd gathered a sense of pride as well as the same haunting sadness I'd seen in him so many times. He was at a crossroads in his life, which wasn't entirely different than what I was going through. I'd even envisioned myself living here, which was absolute madness. We weren't well suited for each other, not by a long shot.

But what if...

Stop it. You're leaving in a couple of days.

The ugly thought brought me back to reality.

"Your ranch is just incredible." As he returned to the house, I eased against the seat, still staring at the mountains. "I'd forgotten how beautiful Missoula really was. Trees. Mountains. Rivers. Lakes. I miss it. You have a river running through the center of your property with green all around it and that tree is huge. Just gorgeous. You could do anything you want with the land. I don't think you want to be a rancher, right? So make something with it. I'm not talking about a development, but maybe a vacation spot or something."

"A sanctuary?" Phoenix asked, his laugh sending a chill through me.

I threw him a look. "No. That's not what I meant, but it's a shame you don't enjoy what you have."

"Yeah, I never thought about it. I learned my dad had a couple offers on the place. I checked his files. He was seriously considering selling it."

"You're kidding me? That would be a real crime. How did you end up with it?"

He tapped his fingers on the steering wheel. "I just told him I was moving back. The truth is that my grandfather willed it to me when he died, his only living grandchild. However, the will was complicated so I'm certain my father had his high-priced attorney figure out a way to use the property against me."

"And your father was going to sell it from under you."

"Oh, my father is a ruthless man. He's also a greedy son of a bitch."

"To get you back here."

He nodded, half laughing after he did. "I guess it worked."

"How did we manage to grow up with such uncaring parents?"

He laughed. "Just lucky, I guess. If you love Missoula so much, then move back."

Was that an invitation? I studied his face, and it was impossible to tell what he was thinking. He wore a mask as tightly as I had the armor I'd placed around myself the day I left Missoula.

"You know why I can't. With Cammie refusing to marry Marcus, my dad will try and set me up for marriage constantly. I won't marry unless I'm in love with the man and I don't see that happening. Ever. He'd just make my life miserable here." I gathered what I'd just said didn't bother him in the least. Was I just testing him?

Ugh. When I'd seen him standing near the fence, my first instinct had been to run into his arms. Then I'd reminded myself I wasn't living out some crazy fantasy that would turn into real life. There were no princes ready to scoop me up.

"What I know is that it's time for you to spread your wings, Wren. You're a grown woman with a love of animals. Do something with it."

"You're right. I'll think about it." An awkward moment settled in, both of us lingering in the truck. There were so many things I wanted to say to him, but nothing seemed right. So I took the easy way out and it hurt, my heart aching. "I know you need to get Justin."

"Yes, but I had a thought." He turned his head, his intense eyes twinkling.

"Uh-oh."

"The weekend isn't over. As I said, you still belong to me for a full day. Are you up for an adventure?"

I turned to face him, surprised to see an actual genuine smile cross his face. "What did you have in mind, cowboy?"

"I'm going to take you back to your cabin to get a few different clothes."

"Jeans?"

"Yep."

"Then what?"

"We're going to pick up Justin." His eyes searched mine.

"O-kay. Then what?"

I knew how huge it was for him to want me to meet his son. I was shocked, my heart lurching in my chest. Did this mean he cared about me? At least it had to mean he trusted me. Right? Oh, God. What if I fucked something up? What if the kid hated me? What if… shit. When I hesitated, all the light in his gorgeous eyes faded to black.

"Don't worry about it." He immediately turned away.

"Don't do that, Phoenix. Don't shut down. You don't have any idea what I was going to say." When he still wouldn't look at me, I grabbed his arm. "Please look at me."

He slowly turned his head, anger replacing joy. "What?"

"I am honored you'd think highly enough of me to allow me to meet your incredible son. You don't know what it means to me."

"Don't worry, sweetheart. It don't mean shit."

"Damn you! Just fucking damn you. You never want to listen to anyone else. You're pigheaded and opinionated and you think you're all that and a goddamn bag of chips. Well, you're not. You're an arrogant asshole who… who I care about and I don't want to fuck it up. Okay? I don't want to hurt you. Like ever. I don't want your son thinking I'm someone special to you when I'm just a girl you rescued from the side of the road who propositioned you for a terrible event. I just…" Geez. I was rambling again. I looked away, horrified that I had tears in my eyes. What the hell was wrong with me?

You love him, you idiot.

Love. Love…

My little voice repeated it over and over again. There wasn't a chance in hell that I could fall in love with a brutal savage like him. Certainly not within days. That was impossible.

But as the ache in my heart ballooned into a full dead weight, I started to feel suffocated. I needed space. I needed to go somewhere and let off a primal scream. When I moved to get out of the truck, he yanked me back with

213

enough force the wind was knocked out of me. He shifted the truck into park. Then he gripped my chin, digging his fingers into my skin. "You're going nowhere, lady. You hear me? Nowhere."

"Why? Why does it matter?"

"Fuck, woman. You could drive a man insane," he growled, his jaw clenched. "You're right. I'm an arrogant prick. But you're not going to fuck it up, Wren. You're one of the most caring women I've ever met. Just be you. And as far as why. Can't you see it? Haven't you felt the way it's been between us, the electricity and connection so damn strong that we can barely breathe when we're together? Don't you have a fuckin' clue how I feel about you?"

"No. I don't." I knew I was pushing him but there were so many emotions racing through me that I had to hear it from his lips. It was crazy and maybe wrong what we were both feeling, far too rushed to make rational sense, but I'd never wanted to be with a man as much as I did this rugged cowboy smokejumper who had a knack of taming the wild child inside of me.

"Fuck. Fuck. I'm falling for you, Wren. Not just because you have one hot little body, but because you have a swagger about you that's intoxicating. You have a lust for life that I've never seen before and it's catching. I want to do things with you. I need to be with you. Taste you. Kiss you. Fuck you. And I've never wanted that before in my life, not like this. You're staying right here. If you try and leave, I will find you. There ain't nowhere in this goddamn world you can hide from me. You got it, lady?" He didn't give me time to answer, capturing my mouth and dragging me even closer.

His powerful hold left me breathless, unable to think clearly, the taste of him igniting my core. My panties were damp, my pulse racing and I could crawl into his lap and never leave. As he slipped his tongue inside, I melted into his arms, wishing the world would just go away and leave us alone. I cupped his face, my fingers tingling from the feel of the glorious stubble covering his jaw. He was everything I'd ever wanted in a man. Dominating. Powerful. Caring. And I couldn't imagine spending another day without him.

When he finally broke the kiss, his husky growl kept me adrift in a sea of pleasure for several seconds. Finally, I dragged my tongue across my lips, the taste of him lingering. Then I realized I'd been crying. Not from pain. Not from unhappiness. From pure joy.

I rubbed the tears from my eyes and slowly reached down, intertwining his fingers with mine. "I'm not going anywhere, cowboy."

He gazed down at our hands then into my eyes, his features softening. Saying nothing, he shifted the gear into drive, turning around quickly and heading for the exit. As he rubbed his thumb across my knuckles, the closeness we'd shared returned, although I sensed he was still on edge. What was the man hiding not only from me but himself?

Within minutes, I realized he knew the location of the cabin I'd rented. As he turned down the last road, I sucked in my breath for a few seconds. "Did you follow me last night?" I noticed out of the corner of my eye he'd started to tap his finger on the steering wheel. "You did."

"Yup."

"Why?"

"Because you fucked with the wrong men, and no one touches my woman. Ever."

His possessiveness kept me floating on air, but he wasn't going to give me any additional information. "You don't need to take care of me."

"Is that what I'm doing?"

"I'm pretty certain you are. But I think I like it." My answer was rewarded with another full grin. Maybe Mr. Grumpy had finally met his match.

 hoenix

Emotions.

Why the woman brought out such intense emotions was beyond me. And what I'd said to her continued to drag a fog around my brain. I'd known Wren for all of what... three days? In that time the feisty little bird had driven me crazy, turned my life upside down, forced me to question my sanity, and she'd shoved me into some of the most uncomfortable, albeit hysterical situations I'd been in for a long time.

I hadn't been able to get her off my mind for even two hours at a time. Fuck. I had it bad for the woman.

I chuckled as she pointed out the driveway to the cabin she'd rented even though she knew I'd followed her home.

As I glanced over, I was surprised by the serene look on her face. Was it insane of me to have her meet Justin? No doubt. But it felt right, as if she would be a grounding force that Justin and I had needed all along. Maybe I was fantasizing about a life that I had no business trying to obtain.

As the cabin came into view, I tried to figure out the last time I'd been to the place. Years and only once after Gage had gotten married. How time flew. It seemed the Missoula Bad Boys, as we'd been called as young men, hadn't been able to grasp onto a decent relationship. Not one of us.

"I won't take long. I'm certain you're eager to get Justin," Wren said, already opening the door.

"Take as long as you need."

She gave me a wistful look before climbing out, walking gingerly in the remaining snow. There was another storm on the horizon, the weather patterns shot to shit this year. Later I'd build a fire and we'd make dinner together.

I couldn't help but laugh as I cut the engine. Since when did I want to curl up by a damn fire? For a few seconds, I could swear I caught a whiff of something. Bristling, I almost went to investigate then chastised myself. Now I was dwelling on the conspiracy theory. Fuck that.

After standing on the front porch for a few minutes, scanning the area several times, I headed inside, amazed the place looked exactly the same as what I remembered. As I walked through, a few memories of the day I'd been there popped into my mind. Dahlia had even been with me in celebration of Gage's marriage to Kelly. The four of us had laughed for hours.

Then I'd found Dahlia shooting up in the bathroom.

"What do you think of the cabin?" she asked, dragging me away from the rough memories.

"I always loved this place. Gage spent a hell of a lot of sweat and money on renovating it."

"What happened? Do you mind me asking?"

I glanced in her direction. "No, but Gage might. It was the place he shared with his wife. Then she betrayed him with a buddy of his."

"That's terrible."

"That's life."

"No, it's not. When two people love each other totally and completely, they would never do something intentionally to tear their relationship apart."

"I never knew you to be a romantic, little bird."

She rolled her eyes. "Obviously, I'm not, but I do believe that with all my heart."

As soon as I started to walk closer, my desires soaring to the surface, my phone rang. My attorney. "I need to take this."

"No problem. I'll finish up."

I turned away, heading toward the banks of windows overlooking a forest of pine trees. "Adam," I answered. Adam Reynolds and I had gone to college together. He was a man I knew I could trust. He was also my sometimes attorney, although I'd had very little need to hire one on a permanent basis.

"Riggs. I studied the will you sent me. Whoever drew it up was creative in the use of terminology and codicils."

"Meaning what?" I stared out the window, the fury already building against my father. I'd picked up the phone to call him several times, knowing I'd only start an argument that would get me nowhere.

"Your father was about to gain full control of the ranch because of your absence. When you returned, taking control, that stopped the clock."

"So, he tried to sell it." I fisted my hand, taking several deep breaths. I'd been so damn dead set on leaving Montana that I hadn't paid any attention to the will. I'd tossed it into a box after glancing at the bottom line. What a damn fool I'd been.

"Yes. And he had a few offers."

"Fucking asshole."

"There's more and you're not going to like it," Adam added.

"What?" As I continued to stare at the crusty snow, I couldn't help but notice footprints.

"You must keep it as a working ranch for the next ten years at one hundred percent capacity or your father will gain control."

What the fuck?

"If what you've told me is accurate, then you're in breach of your grandfather's will already. I'm not entirely certain what I can do to help you regain control. I hate to say this to you, buddy, but you should have paid closer attention when you received the gift."

A gift. At the time, it had seemed like a noose around my neck, the ranch keeping me from finding a new life. "And I can't sell it?"

"You need to understand that it was your grandfather's intentions of keeping Raging Thunder in the family. While there is some mention of it, I'm only reading between the lines, but I gather he suspected your father would sell it if the ranch fell into his possession. The short answer is no. You can walk away from it, allowing your father to take control, or you bring it back to a full working ranch within thirty days. Unfortunately, if that doesn't happen, he is perfectly free to do with it whatever he wants."

"Thirty days?" I asked, taking a deep breath as I moved to the back door.

"Yeah. The clock is ticking. You're at what, eighty percent capacity?"

I snorted. "Less than that now."

"Then you have some serious decisions to make about what you want to do. I can stall things if your father tries to put a sale on the table, but ultimately, he'll be able to sell it from under you."

"Why put me in a bind? What the hell was he trying to do?"

"I've known you for a long time. I met your grandfather only twice, but it was obvious you meant the world to him. He wanted you more than anyone to take his place, but he was smart enough to know that if you ignored the tremendous gift he gave you, then he'd be forced to accept the fact there was no hope of keeping the ranch going. He wanted you to have a legacy. In my opinion, you need to get your head out of your ass. Raging Thunder is a special place."

"Who asked you?" I taunted him, although he was right.

"Well, you did as your attorney."

I thought about the last few conversations I'd had with my grandfather before he'd passed. One of them remained in my mind and had while I'd served my country. He'd told me I had the spirit of Raging Thunder in my heart and soul. I had loved it, but Missoula had no longer seemed like home. On the day I returned after being rescued, he'd changed his will, which had put a final wedge between him and my father. Two days later he'd lost his battle with cancer.

Fuck. Fuck. I raked my hand through my hair, still fuming. I walked onto the deck, trying to figure out what the hell to do. The footprints drew my attention again. They were fresh, the ice crystals forming on the surface. I headed down the few stairs in that direction. "There's nothing I can do?"

"You can buck it up and start hiring some people and buying some cattle. But other than that, not really, unless you're willing to give it to charity," Adam said as he laughed.

Fuck.

"I need you to find out who made an offer on the property before."

"That may take some time. What does it matter?"

"I just have a bad feeling someone is trying to convince me to sell or forfeit, and I don't give a shit how long it takes and what rock you need to dig under. Find out."

"Convince you to sell? Is something going on you're not telling me about?"

As I headed toward the bank of trees, a strange scent assaulted my senses. What the hell was it? "It's just a hunch." I scanned the area then glanced down at the footprints. There were at least two different sets of them. What the hell? I bent down, realizing they'd likely happened the day before, firming up over night. As I glanced back to the cottage, I thought about how isolated the cabin really was.

Then I heard a scream.

"Fuck. I'll call you back." I shoved the phone into my pocket, sprinting toward the sound. As I rounded the corner of the house, a cold shiver slammed down my spine. There was no doubt it was Wren. Unable to catch sight of her, I turned in a full circle, noticing she'd dropped a suitcase near the truck, her footprints heading toward the woods. "Wren!"

I took off running, following the indentations as I darted through the woods, fallen limbs crackling under my feet. Still, I couldn't see her. Jesus. How far had she gone?

"Wren!" I heard her wails first before catching sight of her, hunkered down on the snow. I lunged forward, holding my breath as the stench of blood wafted into my nostrils. Then I heard another cry.

As I peered down, the sight of blood covering her fingers almost sent me over the edge, yet in her hands was a small puppy that she cradled against her chest, the soft mews mixing with her racking sobs.

PIPER STONE

She looked up, her eyes filled with horror. "Who could do something like this?"

While the coppery odor was distinct, given the blood had coagulated, that wasn't what I'd smelled before. As wind whistled through the trees, I caught another whiff.

And I knew exactly what I was smelling.

Chlorine trifluoride.

Fuck. Fuck. Fuck.

I had to think about what to do.

While the puppy wiggled in her hold, the horror of what the little creature had endured was like a stake shoved into my heart. The pup's mother lay dead in a pool of blood. I knelt, pulling both Wren and the shaking puppy against my chest, shielding her view. "It's okay." I scanned the forest again, hissing since I hadn't thought to bring a goddamn weapon with me. The fuckers could be waiting, watching.

"No, it's not okay. I heard a cry, and the puppy was just lying there... by... his mother... and..." She was close to becoming hysterical. "She has a collar on. She was someone's dog. Why?"

"Listen to me, honey. Do me a favor and take the puppy back to the house. Okay?" The last thing I wanted to do was terrify her.

She shot her head up again, gasping for air. "What if there are more puppies lost in the forest? What if they're injured or... Monsters."

"I'm going to take a look. Just go inside. Do it, Wren. Okay? Will do you do that for me?" There was no doubt by just glancing at the dog that she'd been shot. Was this another warning? Or had someone planned on hurting Wren? The only way for anyone to know she was here was from the rehearsal dinner or from being at Raunchy Ride. And how would they know she'd rented the cabin? There were too many strange occurrences for any of this to make sense.

"What's going on?"

"I'm not certain, little bird. Just go inside where it's warm. We'll take care of the puppy."

The puppy wiggled, lifting his head. "I don't think he's hurt, just cold."

"Then get him inside. We'll talk later."

"This is horrible." She kissed the puppy's head, allowing me to help her to her feet. "I tried to revive the mother. I tried."

I cupped her face, trying to drag her attention away. "Baby bird. It's okay. You did your best. Just cuddle the puppy and go to the cabin." *Now. Run. Don't stop.* My tone was more imploring.

Wren swallowed hard. "Find the motherfucker who did this."

"I plan on it." I waited, watching her closely as she headed back to the cabin before yanking my phone into my hand, dialing Gage. As I waited, I checked the dog's collar for tags. "I'm so sorry, Sofie." While the dog's name was proudly displayed on a golden metal tag, there was no other identification.

Goddamn it. Voicemail. "Gage. You need to call me as soon as possible. I'm at your cabin. Not only was at least one dog shot but there were visitors during the last day or so." I left it at that, hunkering down once again to take another look at the fallen baby. I'd seen some shit in my day but to hunt and kill animals was at the tops of my list for the most heinous behavior.

It was beginning to feel more like a vendetta or act of revenge. Bart came to mind. He was twisted enough to do something like this. Since I'd thrown out that Wren was my girlfriend, had he purposely hunted her down? Maybe so, but why kill a dog? I glanced in proximity to where the front of the house was located, and it was entirely possible the dog had been used as a warning. It took a sick bastard to do something like killing an innocent animal.

The entire situation was beginning to smell.

I trudged through the woods, moving deeper into them, quickly comprehending that there was no trail of blood. That meant the dog had been strategically placed along with her puppy. Wait a minute. There were other cabins within a couple hundred yards, but the area was very remote. Bart would have no way of knowing she wasn't coming home last night. And there was no way it had been a random dumping, not with the house positioned so far off the road. I listened for any sounds, walking at least fifty yards in either direction.

Then Gage returned my call, the connection shitty.

"You found what?" he asked, his tone incredulous.

I repeated what I'd said. "The mother dog has a collar." I noticed something closer to the back of the cabin. "Plus, I smell chlorine trifluoride."

"Hold on. You're certain of it?"

"I'm pretty damn certain. Once you get that shit in your nostrils, you can't get it out."

"Goddamn it," Gage hissed. "I'm on my way. Don't touch anything."

"Yeah, well, the puppy needs some attention, and I won't be here. I'm taking Wren to stay with me until this shit blows over."

Gage sighed. "Under the circumstances, I think that's a good idea. I'll need to call in hazmat as well as the fire department. There's no telling how much of the compound there is."

I walked another fifty yards. Then I stopped short. "Shit."

"What is it?"

"A body. A man. He's been shot." I studied the area, noticing additional footprints. Now there were three sets of them and from the distance each footstep was apart, I'd say they'd been running.

"I'm repeating myself, Phoenix. Do not touch a damn thing."

"You need to find these bastards, Gage, because I'm at the point of hunting them down myself."

"I'm working on it, and I don't need to issue you another warning. For all we know, the dogs could have been caught in crossfire with hunters." I heard the glitch in Gage's voice. He didn't believe it any more than I did.

"That's bullshit and you know it. Someone is sending a message. Work harder, Gage. This shit is getting personal and I'm not letting anything happen to my family."

He exhaled. "I'll have my deputies scour the area and give you a call."

"You do that. Incidentally, the dog's name was Sofie. Said so on a tag. Ring a bell?"

When Gage's breathing became ragged, I bristled. "What do the dogs look like, Phoenix?"

"What the hell does that matter?"

"What the fuck do they look like?"

"The dead one looks like a collie, the puppy shorter hair with the same markings. Why?"

"Ah, crap. Sofie belonged to one of the owners of the real estate company I used. He often came out and did sweeps of the cabins the firm rented, which included several on that road."

"Then where the hell is his vehicle? And why bring the dogs?"

"There's a service road a few hundred yards east. He loves the outdoors and his dog went with him everywhere. He's a nice older gentleman with no family. Sofie was his life outside of the business."

"Fuck. There's a sign of a scuffle or maybe he was running away after having interrupted whatever they were going to do."

"I'll be there in less than fifteen minutes."

"Okay."

I shifted around the body and sighed. While I didn't recognize him, it was obvious the guy wasn't a hunter by the way he was dressed, but he had been prepared for the elements, his boots meant for hiking. He must have surprised the perpetrators. I wanted to continue following the trail since the scent was stronger, but I couldn't risk Wren being attacked.

Still, I took another short sweep before returning to the cabin. By the time I walked in, the puppy was nestled in blankets on the couch, Wren standing over him. She slowly turned her head as I walked inside, her entire face pinched.

"He's not injured, but he needs food. I washed off his blood in the sink. He kept crying for his mother. He can't be more than six weeks old." While her words were flat, tears remained in her eyes, several drops spilling past her eyelashes. As she started to run her hands down her dress, I took long strides toward her, pulling both into mine.

"The female dog wasn't his mother."

"How do you know that?" Wren's tone was demanding, full of anxiety.

"I just do. Okay?"

"Why won't you tell me anything? I'm not a little girl. I can handle it." She rubbed her hands more roughly, her chest rising and falling from exertion and fear.

"The blood is gone."

"No, it's stained my skin. I can't stop thinking about it. Why? What is going on, Phoenix? You need to trust me enough to talk to me."

I kissed the knuckles of one hand then the other, lowering my head. "I'll tell you in the truck. Go change and get everything you think you'll need for a few days."

"Why? Are you trying to tell me someone was coming after me?"

Exhaling, I glanced back at the puppy before answering, "It's possible. There have been several murders recently, fires used to cover them up."

"What does that have to do with me?"

"I think there's something more personal going on."

"You're scaring me."

"I'm not trying to, Wren, but this is a dangerous situation. Please get your things."

She backed away, nodding then pointing to the puppy. "Stay with him."

Sighing, I moved to the couch, looking down at the little guy. "Looks like you have a new family." The same ominous feeling remained.

* * *

Wren

Terror.

I'd been afraid several times in my life, but not like this. I couldn't get the images of the poor dog out of my mind. Cruel, heartless people. No, they couldn't even be qualified as humans. While we'd agreed not to talk further about it until Justin was settled back in the house, I could tell how worried and anxious Phoenix had become.

Every move he made was stilted and he'd glanced into the rearview mirror at least a dozen times since leaving the cabin. I'd grabbed everything I owned, tossing it all into my bags haphazardly, he'd terrified me so much. He'd returned to the protector mode, which scared me even more.

Now he was stoic as I'd been forced to experience far too often.

I nuzzled the puppy against my chest, grateful that at least he didn't seem any worse for wear. As I sensed Phoenix was looking at me, I closed my eyes. "We need to find his owner. He's not a stray. The other dog had a collar and he's well fed."

"I know who the owner was. Unfortunately, the puppy is an orphan now." There was almost no emotion in his voice.

"How do you know that?"

"I just do," he said.

"You're infuriating."

"And you don't need to worry about it."

"Damn it, Phoenix."

As he slowed down, he rubbed his hand across the puppy's head. "What are you going to name him?"

"You're avoiding the subject."

"Am I doing a good job?" His grin was only half what it had been before, his eyes still holding tremendous concern. "By the way. It's tough for Justin to meet new people. I think he feels like they're going to take him away. He spent some time in a foster home before his grandparents finally came to offer some help when Dahlia was in and out of rehab. I'm only telling you this because he'll probably reject you at first. He might even do something like hit you. I'm trying to teach him how to be a gentleman, but sometimes he doesn't listen. I don't think he'll hurt you, but I can't be certain."

I was surprised he was the one rambling. After unfastening the seatbelt, I scooted a little closer, the puppy whining as soon as I did. "Did anyone ever tell you that you talk too much?"

He burst into laughter. "I can't say I've had that one before."

"Don't worry. I won't be offended. Maybe the puppy will break the ice."

"He loves animals."

When he pulled up to a house, the door was thrown open immediately, a young boy racing outside.

"I'm not going to name him. Justin is because it's his puppy."

When Phoenix gave me a stern look, I winked then blew him a kiss.

"You're a damn handful, Ms. Tillman."

"Which is why we're made for each other."

I eased the puppy onto the seat, slipping out and tugging the coat tightly around me. The sun was warmer than the day before, additional snow already melting, but I wasn't certain I would ever feel warm again. How could I? A woman came onto the porch. She was older, reminding me of the perfect grandmotherly type. By the smile on her face, it was obvious she cared for Justin deeply. I felt terrible that I'd been jealous of her.

Jealous.

I hadn't realized that's the way I'd felt but it was true.

As the little boy raced toward his father, I sensed the moment he noticed me out of the corner of his eye. He stopped short, his face pinched. I had a bad feeling he was about to throw a tantrum or start crying. Instead, he walked over to me with purposeful steps.

"What are you doing, Justin?" Phoenix called.

I held out my hand, shaking my head at the same time. Then I hunkered down to be at Justin's level, allowing him to come to me.

He held out his little hand and I sensed Phoenix had slipped behind the truck. "Who are you?"

I took his hand into mine and the strangest feeling rushed through me, a warmth unlike anything I'd felt before. "I'm Wren Tillman. I'm a friend of your daddy's."

As he cocked his little head, he wrinkled his nose as if trying to figure out if it was okay I could be a friend. "You're pretty. I think I like you."

"I think you're handsome as well. And I have something for you."

"You do? For me?" He tugged his hand away, clapping both together as he giggled like only a kid could do.

I rose to my feet, giving Phoenix a sly smile. "Absolutely. Now, you have to promise me that you'll care for him with all your heart, never letting anything bad to happen to him. Do you think you can do that?"

Justin nodded several times, his grin exactly like his father's. Even his tousled hair was a reminder of the growly man, who'd I'd learned had a big heart.

Even if he didn't want to show it.

"O-kay." I opened the door, gathering the puppy into my arms. He immediately licked my face, obviously no worse for wear from the horrible experience he'd been through.

Justin's squeal could be heard from several hundred yards away. As he held out his arms, Phoenix walked closer, acting as if he needed to interfere to make certain Justin didn't hurt him. Somehow, I had a feeling the puppy was exactly what the little boy needed.

"Back off, Daddy," I said under my breath as I handed Justin the pup.

While Justin giggled and squeezed, maybe a little too hard, the puppy didn't seem to mind. His happy little yapping barks managed to take away some of the ugliness from before.

"Is he really mine?" Justin asked, laughing as the puppy licked and wiggled.

"Be careful with him, buddy," Phoenix said.

"Can I play with him?" There was nothing like seeing the delight in the kid's eyes.

"Just for a few minutes. We need to get a few things for the puppy before we go home." Phoenix turned his head, giving me another stern look, but his eyes were twinkling with crackling lust. The man was so dominating he took my breath away.

"O-tay! Come, puppy."

As they raced around the yard, Phoenix walked closer. "You're a brat. You know I can't keep the puppy."

"I guess you have no choice."

"Think of my work."

"Yeah. I am." I scooted out of his way before he could grab me. Then I headed toward Betty, holding out my hand. "I've heard a lot about you. I'm Wren Tillman, a friend of Phoenix."

She smiled and it was one of those smiles that had years of knowing behind them. As if she knew I was trying to be polite by telling a little white lie.

"Well, anyone who can make a hit with Justin is a pretty special person in my book," Betty said, laughing. "The puppy is an interesting idea."

Phoenix lumbered closer, the grin on his face highlighting a dimple on his chin I'd never seen before. Maybe it was because he rarely smiled. Or maybe the sunlight was hitting it just right. Or maybe the scruffy beard he was now sporting was to blame for my sudden awe.

Whatever the case, I couldn't seem to take my eyes off his face, even if I felt like a terrible person for all the filthy thoughts racing through my head. Especially with Justin nearby.

"I kinda didn't have a choice," Phoenix said.

"How's that?" Betty asked, still chuckling.

"We found him. He'd been abandoned," I quickly said.

She frowned. "That's terrible. That makes you very good people."

"How did the partial weekend go?" Phoenix asked.

"Can I speak to you alone for just a minute?" she asked.

"There's nothing you can't say in front of Wren."

His statement shocked the hell out of me.

"Very well," Betty said, her voice turning more serious. "I'm not going to lie to you, Riggs. His behavior is getting more difficult, enough so I'm not certain I'm going to be able to handle him on a fulltime basis."

Phoenix stiffened, his jaw clenching.

I pressed my hand against his arm. "Do you have any suggestions of anyone else?" I asked for him.

"I started putting together a list. Please don't get me wrong. I love that little boy, but one day he's going to do something that we'll both regret. My son is begging me to be careful."

I could tell just how much that bothered him. He looked away, his chest rising and falling. "Can I ramp it down? He can't handle losing anyone else. He just can't."

"I understand completely. I'm not telling you that I'm walking away. I wouldn't do that to you, but I wanted to let you know to start looking for other options." Betty folded her arms, her tension evident.

He nodded then grabbed Justin's suitcase. "I appreciate you giving me some time."

"Of course. Wren, it was lovely to meet you."

"You as well."

"Bye, Justin," Betty called but the little boy wasn't paying any attention. She backed away, giving me another nod then retreated behind her front door.

At least Phoenix waited until she'd closed to door to explode. "Goddamn it!"

"Lower your voice. Justin doesn't need to hear you."

He acted as if he was going to say something else then took a deep breath. "I don't have anyone else. No school will take him. I went through three different people until the therapist recommended Betty. She's had experience before, a full-time teacher of troubled kids before she retired from the school system. And he's too much for her. What the hell am I supposed to do?"

"You'll figure it out. My only advice is to remind you that he's the only family you have."

"Not true. I've been thinking about letting his grandparents raise him. They'd good people, a little religious for my tastes, but maybe that will help him." The anguished look on his face was heartbreaking.

"You're his father. You're who he needs, Phoenix. No one will be able to replace that. No one. I understand you're a busy man, but you need to ask yourself what's more important to you."

As he shook his head, I watched so many emotions cross his face that I wanted nothing more than to reach out to him. It saddened me that he wasn't that kind of man who would let me in. If only he would share with me what had happened in his life, the horrors he'd been through. I wasn't certain I could help, but he needed to talk to someone.

"I appreciate your advice, Wren. I really do, but you're in way over your head with this."

"Understood." As with everything else in his life, he was shutting me out. At least this time was for good reason. I had no business trying to offer advice of any kind. What did

I know about parenting? My role models belonged on *Millionaire Housewife* and the *Most Wanted Files*, respectively.

At least the thought of my father behind bars gave me a chuckle. How many people had he swindled in order to get where he had? *What a terrible thing to say about your father.*

I shushed my inner voice. It was all true, the old boys club I'd known existed protecting him. Sighing, I walked toward Justin, leaning against the truck.

Then I was shocked when Phoenix crushed me against the hard metal, planting his hands on either side of me.

"That was the arrogant prick talking," he said as he lowered his head, the look in his eyes carnal.

"Careful, big boy. You might just be getting close to an apology."

He took a deep breath and his scent wafted through me like a wildfire. I lifted my head until our lips were dangerously close, crumpling my hand around his shirt.

"I am sorry for being such a shit. I've never known anyone to take the time to care the way you do," he said softly.

"Be careful, cowboy. I might just fall in love with you."

I hadn't intended on saying the words. They slipped out of my mouth naturally, but when they did, an immediate awkwardness settled between us. The second he dropped his head by another two inches, I pushed his chest, skirting around him, more uncomfortable than I'd felt before.

He remained where he was for a few seconds then headed around the front of the truck. "We should get home. I need to make a few phone calls."

"Don't forget, new puppy owner. We need to make a pitstop for puppy food, bowls, a bed, and all kinds of toys."

When he tipped his head, lifting a single eyebrow, all I could do was laugh.

Home.

Why did I have to wish that it could be our home?

CHAPTER 12

 *ren*

"Peeese, Daddy. Just ten more minutes," Justin begged for the third time.

I'd almost forcefully taken over getting the plates and glasses in the dishwasher, which had allowed me to watch their interactions. The puppy had made Justin a happy kid, at least for now. I'd seen none of the behavior I'd heard about, although he'd been a bear to try to get to eat. At least Phoenix had made the best cheeseburgers I'd had in a long time.

That had allowed Justin to get ketchup everywhere, including on the puppy's face since the kid had insisted on feeding him French fries. I'd never seen Phoenix laugh so hard as trying to catch the puppy when he'd snagged the brawny man's phone.

And Justin had giggled for almost ten full minutes.

As I put away the last item into the refrigerator, I stood against the kitchen island, enjoying every minute of their interactions. They were ones I'd never experienced with my father. He'd acted as if he'd had no time to play with his two girls, although even as a child, I'd suspected that if we'd been boys, he'd have taught us how to ride and shoot, play pool and football. If I knew my father, he'd have taken us to a brothel to get laid the first time.

"Just ten more minutes and I'm serious this time," Phoenix told him.

Justin gave him the exact same kind of look Phoenix had given me several times. The kid was going to be just like his dad.

I couldn't help but laugh.

Which caused Phoenix to slowly turn his head in my direction, his eyes piercing mine. "You find something funny?" he asked, his tone far too husky for while his kid was still racing around the house with the puppy.

"Absolutely."

"Careful. Them's fighting words."

"I'd like to see you try it." When he took long strides, crowding my space, I tried to race around him and he grabbed me, yanking me against his chest, cupping my jaw as he took several deep breaths.

"I'm going to do really bad things to you," he growled lowly into my ear.

"I hope you will."

"Dad. Is Wrennie your girlfriend?"

The little voice came from only a few inches away and I immediately pressed my hand over my mouth to keep from making a single sound. When I looked down, he had such a serious look on his face I had to bite my tongue.

"Yes, she is," Phoenix said without missing a beat. "Does that bother you?"

I was shocked when Justin rolled his eyes. "Bout time."

Then he stomped off and I almost lost it, forced to cling to Phoenix's arms. "He's adorable and just like you."

"Uh-huh. What does that mean?"

"Stubborn. He says what's on his mind without thinking."

"Hmmm... Do I do that?"

"Constantly."

The sound of his phone put a pensive look on his face, and he immediately let me go, grabbing it before the second ring, immediately heading out of the room. It was the second call he'd received since we'd returned; one of them I'd learned had been from the sheriff about the dog we'd found. From what little I'd overheard, I suspected the dog's owner had been a victim as well.

While I didn't want to eavesdrop, since he hadn't told me anything about what was really going on, I was getting antsy. I grabbed my glass of wine, inching closer to the doorway when Justin started to sing at the top of his lungs. I quickly moved to the living room, making certain the little boy noticed I was standing close.

"Justin. Can I ask you a question?"

He kept singing, even louder this time.

"Justin," I said his name in a singsong voice.

He kept singing.

"Justin. What's your puppy's name?"

The sudden silence was jarring. Justin looked at me then down to the puppy, his nose wrinkling. "Chewy."

"That's a great name." I heard footsteps and turned slightly.

"Hey, buddy," Phoenix said to his son. "Do you mind if Miss Wren tucks you and the puppy in bed?"

"Chewy," both Justin and I said at the same time, which put Justin into another fit of giggles. Phoenix still had his phone in his hand, his expression one I couldn't read.

"I would love to," I said, sounding a little happier than the way I felt.

Justin finally cocked his head. "O-tay, Daddy. This one time."

"One time," Phoenix repeated then mouthed 'thank you' to me before heading back out of the room.

"Come on. Let's introduce Chewy to your room."

"Yay! Come on, puppy," Justin said as he skipped out of the room, the puppy trailing behind him.

I took a deep breath, lingering in the doorway for a few seconds to try to hear something. Anything. But Phoenix had moved onto the front porch, closing the door behind him. As I headed toward Justin's bedroom, I realized there wasn't a single picture of Justin or anyone else for that matter. He didn't have photos of his buddies or a football scholarship. I hadn't seen a single truly personal item. It was as if Phoenix didn't think he deserved to live.

Justin was already in his PJs, the little space crafts adorning them too adorable. The puppy had been walked, but I had a feeling it was going to be a long night. As the puppy struggled to get on the bed, Chewy's little barks almost as adorable as Justin's giggles, I let the little boy handle the situation, making the decision whether he wanted to have the puppy sleep with him or not. Which he did.

We'd gone a little crazy purchasing three dog's beds, at least twenty toys, and a fifty-pound bag of puppy food. Justin had enjoyed every second of it.

And I'd felt like Phoenix and I were a couple.

That wasn't fair of me, especially since he hadn't said a word about my exclamation from before. Now I was tucking his kid into bed when I had no clue what I should do. Read him a story? Leave a light on? Play music? What? The timeclock I'd heard most women talk about hadn't been installed in me. That was for certain.

At least he seemed to know what to do, pulling down his covers. The puppy was certain he was supposed to take the second pillow, moving in four circles before settling down. I finally moved closer, feeling like a fish out of water. "Do you leave a light on, Justin?"

"Uh-huh." He pointed to the one on his dresser.

"Ah." I turned it on, smiling at the transparent shade covered with various superheroes. I wondered if he knew just how much of a hero his daddy was. When I came back, he had an expectant look on his face. "What now?"

"You weed me a story."

"Well, how about if I tell you one I know by heart? Would that do?"

He thought about what I was asking then finally nodded enthusiastically.

As I sat down on the edge, he curled onto his side, the puppy crawling closer so he could put his little head on Justin's shoulder. For a few minutes, all was right with the world.

But what about tomorrow?

Why did I feel as if there was evil lurking in the darkness?

Phoenix

"I appreciate you calling me, Bryce. I really do." Hawk's wife had done some digging, her tenacious attitude coming across as vivacious on the phone. What she'd learned was disturbing as hell, although not a smoking gun.

"The one thing about these real estate developers," Bryce said. "They like to keep the big projects under wraps until everything is in place and it's not unheard of that they develop a second, third, or fourth dummy corporation in an attempt to keep the information private. At least I couldn't find anything on Blue Waters. It's like they don't exist."

"But you're certain about the victims in the Billings fire?" I asked, memorizing the corporation's name.

"I have a good friend in the sheriff's department here. The two victims had been very vocal with the county about not allowing them to approve the sister resort being considered. They got themselves on television more than once."

"They were killed on the land they were trying to protect."

"Which has led to accusations being thrown around that they started the fire to make the area undesirable. I know what you told me, but from what my buddy discovered, there are two distinct sites for the proposed resort. I wish I could tell you more, including identifying the owners," she said as she sighed. "I hate sharks."

"So I've heard, and you've really helped."

"Good. I'll let you know if I find anything else."

"Thanks again." As I ended the call, I stood staring out at the night sky for a few seconds. This was all about developing resorts? While greed played a significant role in big business all the time, there were too many oddities and red flags I didn't like. Well, it wasn't going to be solved tonight, but at least I could provide some meat for Adam to chew on.

Then I would call my father.

Exhaling, I walked back into the house, half expecting to hear Justin in an uproar. When I heard absolutely nothing, my curiosity got the better of me and I walked toward his room as quietly as possible.

Seeing him with the puppy had reminded me just how much he loved animals. As I neared, I heard Wren's voice. She was telling him a story.

"So he eased down the mountain carrying not one but two puppies in his arms," she said.

"He saved them from the fire?"

"Yes, he did. He risked his own life doing so. That makes him a hero."

I moved closer, trying to catch a glimpse of the two of them. What in the world was she reading to him?

"Hero," Justin repeated.

"So remember those nights when Daddy goes away, he's going to be a hero all over again." There was so much emotion in Wren's voice. She was talking about me.

I leaned against the wall, closing my eyes. I'd never told Justin what I did. I'd been too afraid he'd be terrified, but she'd made my job sound like I was some kind of superhero.

She had no idea just how wrong she was.

"And the puppies lived happily ever after in their new home," she whispered. "Good night, Justin. Good night, Chewy."

When Justin didn't say anything, I couldn't resist popping my head inside just as Wren was getting up. She turned to face me and realized she'd been caught. As she smiled, the way she looked at me shot straight to my heart.

Just like the words she'd said earlier, the ones I'd refused to acknowledge. God, I was a shit for a man.

As she walked closer, her eyes never left mine. She turned off the light and I pulled the door closed. We remained silent as we headed for the kitchen. She said nothing as she refilled her wine, not asking before pouring another whiskey and sliding the glass in my direction.

We stared at each other for a few seconds. When she walked out of the room, I followed behind her, smiling as she tossed her head over her shoulder before heading out the front door, but not before beckoning me with a single finger. Who was I to deny the lady?

I walked out, moving beside her as she stood leaning over the railing.

"You were telling a pretty powerful story there, little bird."

"Mmm... You listened in."

"Only the last part. What made you tell the story?"

"Because you are a hero," she said without looking in my direction. "You protect nature and animals, people and beautiful locations at the possible expense of your life. I think that qualifies you as a hero."

Sighing, I glanced up at the moon. "That just means I take my job seriously. If you hang around long enough, you're going to learn I'm not the person you think I am."

"Look, I don't know what happened overseas, but given other horror stories I've heard, I can't begin to imagine what you suffered. Were you a prisoner of war?"

"Yeah, I was. Held captive for a few months, but I considered myself luckier than others."

"How so?"

"The torture the insurgents performed wasn't as bad for one thing. They lost interest in me when they thought I was nuts, which I was effective at making them think that I was."

"Do you have nightmares?"

"Sometimes."

"But that's not what's haunting you completely. Is it?"

The woman was too damn smart for her own good. "You want answers, but there's only so many I'm prepared to give. What you do need to know is that there is a serial arsonist using a highly flammable accelerant. If too much of the chemical is used, the fire is virtually impossible to put out. Gage is coordinating trying to track down where it could have been purchased from. A cannister of the substance was found near the cabin you rented. There'd been several controlled burns started in the forest, which tells me whoever is behind the fires was testing the chemical in their attempt to keep it from getting away from him."

"That was the nasty stench," she said.

"Yes. And the owner of the dog you found was also murdered, just like several victims of recent fires, all with use of the same military-style handgun."

"Close range."

"Yes."

She exhaled, taking a few sips of her wine. "The horses? The same?"

"It looks like it."

"Why?"

"Well, for one thing, my land, Snake's as well. But I think the horses were used as a warning."

Wren huffed. "That doesn't make any sense. Why warn you?"

"The only reason I can think of is to get me to default on my grandfather's will."

"I don't understand."

As I explained what both Adam and Bryce had learned, I sensed she finally understood why I was so concerned about her safety, Justin's as well.

"Do you think your father is capable of doing this to you?" she asked after a few seconds had passed.

"I honestly have no idea, Wren. My father isn't the man I thought he was. That's for certain."

I could tell she was mulling over everything I'd told her.

"Then we're going to figure it out together," she said in her usual defiant tone.

"No, *we* are doing nothing. I'm going to do everything in my power to protect you whether you like it or not."

"I can take care of myself. I'm sure you have a gun or two lying around here. I told you I know how to shoot."

"And I'm not doubting you, but you're not doing a damn thing."

"Bet me."

I turned to face her. She wasn't going to pay a damn bit of attention to me. The last thing I needed her to do was go off halfcocked. She'd get herself killed. "Listen to me. Whatever is going on, I don't want you to get in the middle of it."

"I'm already in the middle of it. I know some people. I can help you."

"I told you. It's not going to happen, Wren." What in the hell could I say to her to stop this crazy crusade?

"I appreciate your concern, but I want to help. There's got to be something I can do."

"You're not understanding what I'm trying to tell you."

"Which is?" she demanded as only she could do. There was so much fire in her eyes that I swear they glowed in the dark.

What I'd heard her say to Justin had sent a sharp blade through me. She wouldn't stop digging until she peeled away every layer of protection, the thick armor that had allowed me to continue functioning. I couldn't do this to her for so many reasons that I could barely breathe just thinking about what needed to happen. She was a firefly, an incredible light that I refused to have snuffed out because of my past or the wretched actions of some crazed bastards.

"You're going back to Texas," I told her.

"I was but I'm going to stay right here. To hell with my father."

I fisted my hand, trying to find the courage to send her away.

"You don't understand, Wren. I've enjoyed the hell out of the time we've spent together. Don't get me wrong. You're a great girl, but I'm not the kind of guy who wants to be in a relationship. That's something I told you from the start."

"You're right. I don't understand. First you act like you want to cocoon me here to keep me safe. Now, you're telling me to go back to the cabin?"

This was the hardest thing I'd ever had to do, so much so my heart was thudding in my chest, the feeling suffocating, but if I didn't end this right now, there was a chance she'd lose her life. And it was something I refused to risk for the woman I'd fallen in love with.

"No, that's not what I'm saying. I'm telling you that I don't want you here. Period. You deserve to know the truth, just like you did about the fires and what happened at the cabin."

"Okay, so…"

Goddamn it. She was going to make me say it.

"It's over between us, Wren. I've made my decision and it's best for both of us. You were right. I can't have you getting close to Justin right now. It's not fair to him. I'm taking you back to your car in the morning and you are going back to Texas." As the words sank in, she didn't recoil or make a single sound.

And I'd never felt so much like an asshole in my entire life. Fuck. What had I done?

She backed away, tossing the remainder of her wine in my face. Then she walked to the door, remaining silent as she headed inside, closing it with a soft click.

As I stared at the stars, my chest heaving, I told myself that it was the right thing to do.

But I was lying.

Anger and heartache swelled from deep inside of me, swirling like a fire devil threatening to consume my very soul. I took several deep breaths, my entire body shaking. As soon as the glass cracked in my hand from the pressure, I threw it against the house.

I'd just lost the best thing that had ever happened to me.

 *ren*

An explosion of heartache.

I was stunned, so much so a fog had drifted around my eyes. I stumbled into the house, somehow making it into the kitchen where I struggled to place the empty glass on the counter. As my fingers gripped the edge, I took several deep breaths, trying to decipher why everything had changed in a few short minutes. Was this what Phoenix really wanted, or had I dropped into some kind of crazy dream?

More of a nightmare.

Spending time with both him and Justin had made me realize just how much I cared about the man. Somewhere in the back of my mind, I'd tossed aside all my fears and reservations, longing to spend the rest of my life with him. While a small, rational side of me still existed, the inner voice debating whether or not we could make a go of a relationship, I'd wanted to take the biggest risk of all.

With my heart.

Then he'd crushed it with a few ugly words, tossing me aside as if our passion had meant nothing to him. I could either fall apart or fight for what I thought we'd had, but what good would it do? I wasn't the kind of girl to beg for anything. Certainly not to force a man to care about me.

Nope.

I wasn't going to do it.

As I threw my head back, determined to maintain what was left of my resolve and sanity, tears trickled down my cheeks. I furiously wiped them away as I headed for the bedroom to grab my bags. By the time I reached the hallway, I raced the rest of the way before I broke out into sobs. Just closing the door was difficult, my entire body shaking. I was angry. I was frustrated.

I was stricken with grief for something that had barely begun.

Stop it. You're a big girl.

No, I was the fairy princess looking for her gorgeous prince to take her away to a special place, a creation of beauty and love.

And I was a fool.

As soon as I grabbed my bag, I felt stronger, certain I could walk out the door, demanding he take me back to my car now, not waiting for the morning. When I reached for the second one, I almost lost it again, choking back tears.

Then the door was kicked in, the bastard storming inside.

"Just leave me alone!" While I tried to keep my voice down, knowing Justin's room was just down the hall, my chest heaved from the ridiculous agony swirling like a rapidly growing hurricane.

"No," he snarled. "I'm never going to leave you alone." He slammed the door then rushed forward taking three long strides. As he grabbed my arms, digging his fingers into my skin, his eyes lit up with the kind of fire I'd never seen before. "I can't. I won't."

I pushed hard against his chest, doing everything I could to shove him away, but his hold was too strong. My tears became waterworks, blinding me as I tried to keep my eyes locked on his. "Why? What does it matter? You don't want me. This. Us."

"Wrong, little bird." His voice held an edge, his body shaking as much as mine. "I'm a fool. I was trying to protect you when all I did was drive a wedge between us."

"I get it. Just take me back to my car." What was he trying to say to me? I pushed him again, but the feel of his muscles through my fingers ignited the same fire that was obviously sweeping through him.

"No. I was wrong, so fucking wrong. I don't want you to go anywhere. Do you hear me? Not now. Not ever. You awakened something inside of me I thought was dead. You've brought me more joy than I knew was possible. I don't just want your body, little bird. I want everything, including your heart."

I clenched my fingers around his shirt, the sounds I emitted strangled and angry. "Why? Why? I'm not your toy or your little bird. I'm a woman who... who... who loves you." There. I'd said it, the words that could never be taken back. The ones that could change or destroy everything. I'd found the courage.

He fisted my hair, dragging me closer and onto my toes. "Goddamn it, Wren. I don't know why you dropped into my life, but I'm glad you did. I love you. I'm not a perfect man, but I love you." As he crushed his mouth over mine, the sense of despondency and desperate need rushed through both of us, sparkling like the electricity we'd felt every time we'd engaged in blissful passion. But this was entirely different, as if neither one of us would ever be able to breathe again without the other. As if our lives depended on being together, forming a bond that could never be broken, even in death.

I wrapped my arms around his neck, arching my back as he slipped his tongue inside. We were both so needy, our tongues slamming together. My heart raced, thudding to the point of echoes, desire raging to the surface, refusing to be denied.

He brushed his hand down my back, cupping my bottom, lifting me off the floor. Then he swung me around in a circle, growling into the kiss, every sound increasing the hunger. I'd never felt such extreme emotions, one colliding into the other, leaving my body a shivering mess. But he was here, my protector. So strong and so powerful, refusing to let anything happen to either one of us.

When he broke the kiss, yanking back my head, he raked his teeth from one side of my jaw to the other before nipping my lower lip. "I want you. I need you. You're mine. Mine."

His possessive words forced another round of live current into every cell and molecule. I was lightheaded, wrapping one leg around his muscular thigh. As he brushed his lips down my chin to my neck, my pulse increased. And when he bit down, the rush of pain brought another sense of freedom. This man allowed me to be free from all the chains I'd placed around myself, free from the tyranny of being a senator's daughter.

Free from all the fears that had kept me from enjoying life.

This man. This marvelous, sensual rogue had captured my heart.

He ripped at my shirt with his teeth, managing to drag it down, exposing the cleft between my breasts. Then he dragged his tongue down the center, every sound he made guttural, animalistic. He would devour every inch of me, claiming me once again, only this time it would be final. As if I would be his mate for life.

Filthy thoughts drifted through my mind as he ground his hips against me. I managed to slip my hand between us, sliding them under his shirt. My fingers were instantly seared from the touch of his skin, sizzling every one of my senses as only he could do.

Phoenix pulled away long enough to yank the shirt over my head, tossing it aside then engulfing my nipple through the lace. His mouth was so hot and wet, my nipple hard as a tiny pebble, and I could no longer catch a decent breath as excitement tore thought me. Gasping, I slid my hand to his back, allowing my fingers to dance across his scars, a moment of heartache almost taking over. But he'd endure the pain only to come out a stronger man, capable of fighting all the odds.

My beautiful, damaged hero.

As he sucked on my nipple, his tongue sweeping back and forth, I raked my nails down his back, shivering from the explosion of sensations. My pussy ached, my panties soaked from the raging desire. He slowly lifted his head, allowing me to look him in the eyes. His pupils were dilated, his irises shimmering in gold, and his look of lust was amplified by the warm glow in the room.

There were no words needed, no statement of what we wanted. We were primal, our needs the same. He cupped both sides of my face, a dangerously evil smile crossing his face. Then he ripped at my bra, snapping one of the straps in his effort to remove the unwanted lingerie. His husky laugh sent another wave of shivers down my spine.

I tore at his belt buckle, dancing my fingers along the leather before unfastening his button, tugging on his zipper.

"No," he growled. "You're not in charge."

My laugh was nervous, but I was fully entranced by his dominance. I wanted him to take control, to use me however he wanted. I needed to feel the crushing weight of his body over mine, driving his cock so deeply inside that I screamed out his name.

He took a step back, yanking his shirt over his head, his chest heaving as the desire continued to increase. He didn't need to say a word, only lower his gaze, instructing me to remove the rest of my clothes.

I backed away, tugging off my boots, my fingers fumbling to unfasten my jeans. I refused to take my eyes off him as I slowly lowered the dense material over my hips, wiggling back and forth just to tease him. Every sound he made was a clear indication he was running out of patience.

When he kicked his jeans aside, standing in all his delicious naked glory, I drank his gorgeous body in for a few seconds, mesmerized by just how handsome he was. Only then did I finish removing my jeans. As I rolled the tip of my finger around one nipple, I licked my lips and his nostrils flared. Then I rubbed the flat of my hand down my stomach, flexing my fingers open before sliding it between my legs.

I issued several moans as I gyrated my hips, digging my fingers in through the lace just to drive him wild.

He cocked his head, narrowing his hooded eyes. "Don't tease me."

"Mmm…" I rubbed up and down for a few seconds before easing my fingers under the thin elastic, finally rolling them down my hips to the floor. As soon as I was free of the tight confines, I dropped to my knees, staring up at him as I crawled a few inches closer. Then I tossed my head back and forth, stopping briefly to gauge his reaction.

The man had turned into a beast, incapable of controlling his actions. When he beckoned me with a single finger, I purred.

His laugh floated around me like a soft blanket, but I knew I would pay for my teasing sins. I continued crawling closer, taking my time even though my hunger was exploding. When I was within two feet, I stopped, offering a mischievous smile.

"Come here, little bird."

"No."

"Mmm… You tease your master?"

"Yes."

He laughed but with a single stride, he wrapped his hand around my throat, pulling me toward him. "Bad girl." He was so strong, his needs too great and as he eased his other hand down, cupping my bottom, I knew exactly what he was going to do.

As the tip of his cock slipped inside, I bit back a scream. Then he yanked me all the way down, my muscles screaming as they expanded. There was nothing like the feel of having him inside. His shaft throbbed, pulsing to the beat of my heart. I clung to his shoulders, taking shallow breaths as he held me in place. When he shifted his hips back and forth, driving his cock in even deeper, I couldn't stop from whimpering.

"You don't have a choice," he said, half laughing as he pulled out, driving into me again. And again. With every hard stroke, he seemed to go deeper, dragging me to the point of ecstasy. His lovemaking was so powerful, as if he knew exactly what my body needed.

I rolled my hands down his back, biting on his shoulder as the pleasure continued to expand. How could anything feel so incredible? He pumped deep inside for several seconds before suddenly dumping me onto the bed, dropping to the floor as he opened my legs wide, lifting and bending them at the knee, pushing them until I was wide open.

I clamped my fingers around the comforter as he blew across my aching pussy. The anticipation was incredible, pushing the sensations to an even higher level. When he peppered the inside of my thigh with kisses, my body quivered. I couldn't catch my breath. I couldn't think straight. But I allowed myself to fall into the moment of bliss.

Phoenix rolled his fingers along the insides of my thighs, tickling me as he continued to blow across my pussy. As I lifted my head, the sight of the carnal look in his eyes forced goosebumps across my skin. He knew exactly how to keep me excited, dipping his tongue into my wetness then rolling the tip around my clit.

"So bad," I muttered, biting my lower lip the second he pulled the tender tissue between his lips, sucking as he rolled a single finger up and down the length of my pussy.

"Mmm... so good." His retort made me laugh nervously, stars in vibrant colors dancing in front of my eyes.

He kept me wide open, allowing his fingers to touch my swollen lips, his actions driving me crazy. There was something about being so exposed that heightened the vibrations skimming through me. He knew he was driving me crazy, yanking on my desire as he built the anticipation.

My pussy clenched and released several times, almost to the point of having an orgasm. When he finally slipped his tongue inside, I jerked up, dragging the covers with me.

"Oh, God. Oh…" It was almost impossible to keep from moaning at the top of my lungs, but I did everything I could do to control my reaction, laughing softly when he finally buried his face into my wetness. No man had ever brought me this much pleasure, knowing exactly what I craved without me muttering a single word.

As he started to growl, the sound low and husky, I fell into the sweet lull of raw bliss, turning my head to the side. I struggled to keep my legs wide open as he feasted, trying to be a good girl, although the wicked part of me wanted nothing more than to try his patience. Maybe I craved his firm hand more than I could comprehend, hungering for the crack of his belt against my backside. That would never make any sense to me, but it didn't matter. I was his for the taking.

The tasting.

The fucking.

A soft laugh escaped my lips as he drove two fingers inside, thrusting in a slow and even rhythm. The combination was almost too much, my legs trembling as the pleasure intensified. He knew exactly what he was doing, guiding me close then yanking it away. There was no sense of time as he licked me, his actions becoming more aggressive, every sound he made barbaric.

When two fingers became three, I couldn't hold back any longer, a climax jetting into me, electrifying every muscle.

"Yes. Yes..." I ripped at the comforter, jerking up, gasping for air.

He pushed my legs up from the bed, dragging his tongue up and down aimlessly. Then he sucked on my clit again, which sent me into another mind-bending orgasm. There was something even more possessive about his hold, as if letting me go would break the magic we shared. Only when I stopped shaking did he ease back, kissing my thighs then rolling his lips up to my stomach.

Blinking, I adored the way he was looking at me, his eyes as magnetic as the man. As he crawled onto the bed, he yanked me up further, centering me perfectly. Then he took his time tasting my stomach, my chest, licking up one arm then down the other. When he drifted to my breasts, I bit my lower lip. As he'd done before, he teased me, swirling his tongue around one nipple then the other before biting down.

The pain was instant, pulling me into a moment of ecstasy. I envisioned having my nipples clamped, a thick metal chain between them so he could pull on it anytime. And as crazy as the thought was, I wanted to be branded with his name, so everyone knew I belonged to him. The thought was filthy and sinful, but I craved belonging to him in every way.

As he shifted between my legs, he hovered over me, twisting his head as he stared down, eyeing his possession as if determining what to do to me.

I had to touch him, to marvel in his perfect physique. He said nothing as I brushed my fingers down his neck, kneading his chest before lowering them ever so slowly to his beautiful cock. Laughing, I rolled the tip of my finger across his sensitive slit, rewarded with a few drops of pre-cum. I slipped my pinky through the glistening string, pulling it to my mouth.

The corner of his mouth turned upward as I sucked, every sound exaggerated.

"I could drown you in my cum, little bird."

Even the way his chest was rising and falling was sexy as hell, the taste of him sweet yet salty. When I finally wrapped my hand around his shaft, he let out a series of growls that penetrated the room. The sound turned me on, reminding me that he was all male. He pinched my nipple, twisting it as I stroked him, the wry smile remaining on his face. But I knew this wouldn't last for long, his hunger far too great.

"Put my cock inside of you, Wren. Now." His commanding words sent another shiver down my spine, and I did as he directed, but not without teasing him for a few additional seconds. I rolled the tip up and down my slickened pussy, savoring the way he was looking at me. But the second I finally slipped it inside, he thrust his hips upward, driving the length further.

I opened my mouth, but no sound came out, only my ragged breathing as another wave of pleasure tickled my senses.

He ground his hips until he was fully seated inside then wrapped first one of my legs around his hips then the other. When he grabbed my arms, I thought he'd pin them over my head. Instead, he intertwined our fingers together, clasping his tightly around mine. As he rolled his hips, pinning me under his full weight, I shuddered to my aching core.

Exhaling, he held me in place, squeezing my hands as he studied me, his eyes never blinking. This wasn't about fucking any longer. This was making love, increasing our connection, throwing away all the fears and concerns. This was about exploring each other, needing what only the other could provide. This was about... love.

An explosion of feelings mixed with the intense sensations, and I became emotional, tears slipping past my lashes, rolling down the sides of my face to the comforter. He looked concerned for a few seconds then smiled, as if understanding what I was going through. As he pulled out, lifting his hips, I dug my fingernails into his hands.

"Don't worry, little bird. I'm not going anywhere."

His soft words only allowed the tears to flow harder, spilling down my cheeks as he drove into me again. His cock continued to swell, filling me completely. Within seconds, I was close to another orgasm, but I wanted this to last all night long.

"You're so beautiful," he whispered, lowering his head until our foreheads were pressed together. For those blissful seconds, we were as one, our bodies joined in every way possible. When he lifted his head again, I could tell something had changed within him, a dam broken or his armor slipping away. He was with me, not lost in a haze of guilt or shame. If only he would tell me what was wrong, I would go to the ends of the earth to make it right.

"I love you." I don't know why I felt the need to tell him again, but his eyes sparkled with the same fire from before as soon as I did.

"I love you. My perfect, sexy little bird." As he plunged in and out, taking his time with every hard stroke, I fell more and more into the man.

Within seconds, I couldn't hold back any longer and as soon as the wonderful wave of ecstasy began to spill through me, he captured my mouth, holding our lips together. He was allowing me to scream in pleasure, which I did, my body trembling under his. He slowed the rhythm, shifting his hips again, the angle pushing me to another climax, this one so intense the stars returned, butterflies swarming my stomach.

I was alive and on fire, breathless in wonderment. And I knew this was the man I wanted to spend the rest of my life with.

As he pulled away, he never blinked as he thrust harder, his needs starting to build. I squeezed my legs, holding him in place, trying to meet every hard thrust. When his jaw clenched, his muscles tensing, I could tell he was close. And the second I squeezed my pussy muscles, he threw his head back, calling out my name.

"Wren…"

He erupted deep inside, filling me with his seed and I eased my head to the side, imagining all the wonderful things that could happen in the future.

Even though the sense of danger remained, crowding in on the happiness I felt. And for some reason I knew, he was the target.

Why would fate bring us together then threaten to tear us apart?

* * *

Phoenix

Love.

I'd never wanted to be in love. Hell, I was the guy who laughed when a couple of buddies in the war had fawned over pictures they'd received in the mail. I'd made fun of the guys as teenagers who'd fought over a girl in school, as if she would be with them for the rest of their lives. The high school sweethearts had made it less than a year, already in debt to their eyeballs, the divorces bitter and expensive.

And I'd professed more than once I'd never fall in love.

Then Dahlia had challenged my beliefs, swarming into my life like a little firecracker. It wasn't until now, this very moment of holding Wren in my arms, staring up at the ceiling that I realized what I'd thought was love before had only been lust and infatuation. Dahlia had never loved me, and I'd just wanted a conquest.

This was entirely different.

That's why it scared the hell out of me.

I'd acted like some fucking cowboy in my attempt to send her away, pretending it was all about her safety, the need to protect her. It was true, but only partially. I hadn't wanted to allow myself to feel the love I'd sensed after spending twenty minutes with her. Nope. It didn't make any sense, but I couldn't deny the way I felt.

Now I had to figure out what the hell to do with it.

Especially since the weight of my past continued to drag me down, more so after returning to Missoula.

When Wren made a slight sound, I pulled the sheet up to her shoulders, kissing the top of her head. She'd fallen asleep in my arms, which had been a first. But it felt natural, as if she was supposed to be here. With me. In this house. What the hell was I doing? I couldn't help but smile as I grabbed the glass of whiskey I'd brought to the room, stopping just inside the door when I'd returned with our drinks.

She'd been glowing, her skin shimmering. I'd been in awe for several seconds, confused as to what the hell was going on with me. Then she'd patted the bed and I'd become an animal all over again, ravaging her for another full hour.

As soon as I put down the glass, she shifted, lifting her head. She said nothing, but as she used a single finger, swirling it in a circle on my chest, I took a deep breath. Then something changed inside of me, a need to tell her the reason I was such a fucked-up asshole.

"There's a gorgeous mountain range not too far from here. It's called Sapphire Ridge."

"I know it," she whispered. "I hiked there a couple summers with some girlfriends. It's beautiful, but you can tell there was a massive fire there years ago."

I bristled and she lifted her head even more.

"What's wrong, Phoenix? Did something happen there?"

As I took a deep breath, I brushed my hand through her hair. "Yes."

"Do you want to talk about it?"

"No. But I need to."

Wren eased to a sitting position, reaching over and taking the glass from the nightstand into her hand. After taking a sip and returning it to the same position, she rose to her knees, pressing her lips against mine, kneading them until I opened my mouth. As the liquor flowed from hers to mine, I realized she was reminding me that she wasn't going anywhere.

She pulled away, tugging the sheets over her legs, taking my hand into hers. Then she looked away, also giving me space. For a girl so young, she understood me more than anyone else ever had.

I took a deep breath and found the courage to admit what would haunt me for the rest of my life. And for some crazy reason, I knew she wouldn't run away.

"I killed a woman."

CHAPTER 14

 *hoenix*

"I want those kids brought up on charges!"

The cry hadn't come from the girl's parents, her father in prison and her mother a drug addict. The demand for justice had come from her last foster parent, a home she'd run away from only two days before the tragedy. The woman had thought there'd be a civil suit and she'd get the money, the story fading into the dust when she didn't.

As I thought about the horrible time, I closed my eyes. With a nudge from my father, the cries that had embroiled the news for two days had ended. He'd managed to convince the powers that be that we'd been victims as well, lucky to be alive, the fire set by lightning.

But I'd always known better.

The great Missoula Bad Boys had ceased to exist after that day.

After taking a deep breath, I lowered my gaze toward Wren.

She lifted her head briefly and I stared into her eyes. There was no admonishment, no fear in them. Just love. I never knew that could be possible. I was a bad man. That's what I'd always believed. I didn't deserve happiness. I didn't deserve to live after what I'd done.

"She was a friend of mine. Well, she was a friend of a group of guys. We all ran together in school. We were the delinquent kids your parents told you to stay away from. We got into trouble, but in looking back, what we thought was badass shit was just kid's crap. Pranks and small thefts. We were bullies, which I'm not proud of, but this one girl refused to buy our bullshit. She insisted she be a part of our bad boy club."

"There was such a thing?"

The slightly accusatory tone in her voice made me chuckle, although the story had nothing in it to laugh about. "Yeah, or so the six delinquents thought of themselves as. We ruled the school. Hell, even the teachers were afraid of us, but Belle had nothing to lose. She'd been a loner, which was something all of us had been. Even though the rest of us had come from decent or prominent families, we were castaways for various reasons."

"What happened?" she asked so quietly I had to strain in order to hear the two words. I noticed she was continually rubbing her thumb back and forth across my knuckles, the gesture soothing.

But not enough to keep my heart from racing.

"Belle was a difficult person. She had a foster mother who couldn't care less about the girl, taking the money the state awarded her to party with her boyfriends. We accepted Belle into our motley group and within a couple months, she was as much a part of us as anyone could be. Somehow, we became her protectors, her champions. She was a tough girl, but inside her heart had been ripped apart more times than I could count. It was summer just after some of us graduated high school. Only a couple of us had any clue what we wanted to do with our life, but not Belle. She wanted to become a veterinarian. She loved animals."

"You were in love with her."

"I think we all were."

"I remind you of her."

Wren's statement wasn't accusatory. I dropped my gaze, allowing myself to touch the side of her face, even though I didn't deserve to feel such joy inside. "A little, yes. She could hold her own. She had a caustic mouth and she refused to follow authority." I laughed, rubbing my hand down my face. It almost felt good to talk about this.

"A rule breaker just like you."

"Yeah, she was. But she wanted to forge a life, to help inno-cent animals. Anyway, she'd already gotten a job and was enrolled in community college. We went on the mountain almost as a last hurrah. A couple of the guys had already enlisted in the military and would be leaving Missoula in a month or so. I was still floundering at that point. Gage had gotten himself arrested for stealing a damn car."

"The sheriff?" She half laughed.

"Gage is an entirely different man now. We all are." I looked out the window before continuing. "It had been a really dry year and it was still cold in the mountains in May. So I had the bright idea of starting a campfire, only I didn't know what the hell I was doing."

"Oh, shut up. I know what I'm doing," I snarled at Colt, fucking furious that he was questioning me.

"Come on, dude. You've never started a fire with two stones in your life," Maverick shot out, laughing at me as I tried for the fourth time to get the damn shit lit.

I glared at him, grumbling under my breath as I jerked to my feet, heading to get a few more dry twigs, moving deeper into the forest. Still cursing under my breath, I knocked a few loose, dropping to the ground and gathering them into my arms. Then I noticed Belle out of the corner of my eye, the look on her face one I'd never seen before.

She walked toward me, glancing toward the others. "Why don't you come swim with me?"

"Swim? It's dark out here."

"I ain't afraid of the dark. Are you?"

I swallowed hard as I gazed at her, the last remaining light of the afternoon creating shadows across her face. But as she pulled down one side of her sweatshirt, exposing her shoulder, I froze.

"Come on. Come play with me."

My cock twitched as if had done so many times when she was close by. But I knew better than to break the sacred pact we'd made with each other. "I can't do that, Belle."

"Why? Because of the others?"

"Because we're all friends. That's very special for all of us. Why don't you come back. I'm trying to build a fire."

A look of hurt crossed her face before she shut down all her emotions. "Suit yourself. I'm going for a swim."

The memory was too fresh, the jab of pain almost too much to bear. "Then she disappeared, and I didn't go after her."

"That doesn't mean you killed her."

I laughed, raking both hands through my hair. "Don't you get it? I did start the fire, but I was a fool because I had no freaking clue how to contain it. After drinking a couple beers, I fell asleep. When Gage woke me up, the trees were already on fire and Belle was nowhere to be seen. I killed her."

She scooted closer, taking my other hand into hers. "No, that doesn't mean you were responsible. Besides, if the campfire you started had anything to do with the forest fire, it was an accident."

"I don't buy that, Wren. You don't understand. She was an innocent girl."

"Who wandered into the woods at night. You've been on those mountains. You know there are wild animals."

"And you don't know Belle. She could take care of herself. I taught her how to shoot and tie a rope. And I helped her purchase a switchblade and..." What the hell was I doing?

"Hmmm... She sounds an awful lot like a girl who'd tried to convince you more than once that she could handle herself just fine. It's funny how you told that girl that she had no clue how to take care of herself just because she'd been taught how to shoot and had taken martial arts courses."

I tipped my head, allowing a smile. "I guess if I tell you that it's different you won't believe me."

"Not a chance, buster."

As I cupped her face, she leaned in. "Losing her nearly destroyed me."

"Did you ever find out for certain that she was killed by the fire and not something else?"

Sighing, a feeling of exhaustion made it difficult to think clearly. "No. The fire burned so hot that trying to dig through the rubble in order to find her remains wasn't possible."

"I'm certain you did everything in your power to save her."

"I guess I did. My buddies had to pull me out of the flames. We were cornered by the flames, a slim chance of getting down the mountain. Then we ran out of time."

"Have you been back on the mountain since then?"

Half laughing, I finally shook my head. "I don't think I can face getting anywhere near Sapphire Ridge."

"Until you do, you'll never be free of the noose you tied around your own neck. You need to forgive yourself, Phoenix."

"Easier said than done."

"I understand." She crowded next to me, resting her head on my chest. Having her close allowed me to take a deep breath. "That's why you don't use your given name any longer."

"That's one reason."

"The war the second."

"Go to sleep, little bird."

She playfully punched my side. "I had a teacher I admired and respected around the time I was fighting with my mother on a daily basis. That was right before I... well, it doesn't matter. Anyway, she told me that peace of mind can only come from within and only after you've let go of the anger, replacing it with doing good for someone else. I didn't really understand what she meant or maybe I didn't want to believe that I should stop being enraged with my mother, but I get it now. I can't change my parents or the past. All I can do is to try and give back to those who are really in need. I hope that makes sense."

"More than you know, my sweet girl. More than you know. I want you to understand something very clearly. The way I feel about you has nothing to do with Belle. Nothing. You are the light I've needed for a long time."

"Thank you for saying that."

As she snuggled close, I stared at toward the wall, shadows forming in the darkness. I'd been spending my entire life sulking, wallowing in self-pity, fighting against demons that I'd never beat. Maybe it was time to do something else."

I pulled the covers tightly around her then closed my eyes. For the first time in as long as I could remember, I had a feeling I'd get a good night's sleep.

* * *

"You can't save him," my buddy called. The buzzing sound of gunfire all around us was a clear indication we were in significant danger, the enemy closing in.

"We're not leaving him out here!" I yelled through gritted teeth, the pain from the bullet wound in my side agonizing, but I refused to leave my teammate out here to die.

The motherfuckers would torture him first.

"Come on, Ronny. We can do this together," I told him, trying to hold my shit together as blood spewed from his mouth.

"Leave... me, Phoenix," he managed, the gurgling sound a clear indication his insides had been ravaged.

"Not a fucking chance." I hoisted him over my shoulder, ignoring the blinding pain. The darkness was oppressive, the shouts coming from the insurgents getting closer.

"Go. Go. Go!" I heard the sergeant yell from behind us.

As I trudged through the mud so thick it made moving quickly impossible, I could sense my buddy's life was hanging on a razor-thin line, his breathing ragged. "Stay with me, Ronny. We're almost there."

Bullshit. I had a solid half mile before I'd find a defensible position. As the barrage of bullets continued, Ronny started wheezing, his body shaking. Jesus Christ. I refused to lose him. Not now.

Panting, I heard movement and threw out my arm, issuing rapid fire. Another asshole was right behind him, but my reflexes were quicker, dropping the son of a bitch before he had a chance to get off a single shot.

I heard more yelling and ducked behind a tree, taking several gasping breaths. Ronny was becoming dead weight. Fuck. As I took off again, a single crack in the forest drew my attention to another area.

Pop!

Pain exploded in my side, the force of the close-range shot pitching me forward. As I lost traction, tumbling to the ground, I could feel the earth vibrating under me just seconds before...

"Boom," I spat out, gasping for air, smoke strangling me. I jerked up, the sound too real, the stench overwhelming. Panting, I was immediately disoriented by the darkness.

But there was no fire.

No explosions.

Just darkness.

And it was almost as overwhelming as the visions.

When I heard a noise and I reacted, immediately jerking toward the sound, noticing a figure on the ground. As another series of visions rushed into me, I wrapped my hands around the insurgent's throat. We'd been ambushed. "Die, you fucker."

"Phoenix. Stop. It's me. Wren. Your little bird. Remember?"

Gasping, I immediately jerked my hands away, horrified at what I'd done even as the ugly visions continued to ravage me. "Oh, God. What have I done." I jerked away, stumbling off something. A bed. That's right. Wren. No. No. No.

"Hey. It's okay. I'm fine." Her voice was so soft, comforting.

"I hurt you."

"No, you didn't."

What the hell? Was it real? It had to be real.

Calm down. Breathe. Count to ten.

One. Two. Three…

I couldn't make it.

Fuck. The images were bloody, more detailed than they'd been for a long time. I backed against the window, trying to catch my breath. The ugly visions had started to pick up in intensity, now so often I was terrified of closing my eyes at night. As I blinked, beads of sweat trickled down my face. Goddamn it. There couldn't be anything worse than if this happened while I was out in the wilderness somewhere, my smokejumping team counting on me.

I counted to ten again, raking my hands through my hair, trying to concentrate on the sound of her voice as I blinked furiously. "I'm so sorry." I jerked away, tumbling toward the door.

"Don't go. Please. Stay with me, Phoenix. Phoenix. Listen. I'm not going anywhere. Come back," Wren said so quietly, I strained to understand her words.

"You don't want me here. I need to get away from you." Jesus. Why had the dream seemed so real, as if I was reliving it all over again? I'd managed to suppress the ugliness for years.

"It was a nightmare. That's all."

I stayed where I was, my fingers digging into the dresser. When I felt her fingers pressed against my back, I tensed, forced to remind myself that I was no longer in the damn trenches, fighting to stay alive long enough to be found.

"Listen to me, Phoenix. I'm not hurt or upset. You have a lot of anger inside of you, demons that manifest in these nightmares. I know you weren't trying to hurt me. You're lashing out at what you couldn't control. Come back to bed." Refusing to take no for an answer, she slipped her fingers in mine, tugging me gently back to bed. I watched as she pulled down the covers, easing me into a sitting position, even taking the time to slide my feet onto the sheets. Then without hesitation, she crawled over me, cuddling against my legs and chest, her arm tenderly placed around my waist.

How could this girl stand being in the same room with me? I'd almost choked her to death.

I grabbed the glass of whiskey I'd brought to bed after the second time we'd… fucked, gulping down the rest. The slight burn did nothing to make me feel any better.

Maybe she was giving me space or maybe she was as confused as I was, but she remained quiet, rubbing her thumb back and forth across my stomach.

Just like she'd done when I'd told her about Belle. Her sensitivity and understanding amazed me. How much baggage could this girl handle? Exhaling, the asshole inside of me wanted to pull away, retreating to the same shell I'd lived in for years. I'd been damn good at it too, ignoring the rest of the world.

"I'm sorry, Wren. I'll take you home in the morning. It's not because I don't want you here. It's because…" Hell. I needed another drink, although I knew an entire bottle wouldn't settle the rage that surfaced every time I was faced with any difficulty. What had I been thinking, telling her about what happened on the mountain?

"Only if that's what you need to do, not because of what happened. And that's only for space for a little while. You're not getting rid of me that easily."

I kissed the top of her head, more surprised than ever she was able to tolerate being this close. "I don't know what to say."

"I'm here if you want to talk about it, but I won't push you. Whatever you endured in the war lingers in your mind just like what happened with Belle. They're connected. Maybe not in reality but in your mind, you've made them one and the same. Like I said before, until you can find a way to free the demons, you'll never be at peace."

"How old are you, twenty-two?"

"What does that have to do with anything?" Her rebellious side was still intact, where I hoped it would always be.

"Cause you're not just too smart for your own good, you're the only person who's been able to pick me apart and I don't like that. I've had three professionals try and do so, none of them effective." I was too old for her. Hell, I was too a lot of things, including unstable. This was such a bad idea. I cared a lot about the woman, which meant I should make it a point of never seeing her again.

I just didn't think I could allow that to happen.

The darkness hadn't always been comforting, but lately it had helped enough I thought I'd gotten better. I'd thought the demons couldn't find me in the shadows of my mind or the stark contrasts of color in the early hours of morning.

But I was wrong, as I'd been about so many other things in my life.

"Age is all relative. It's all about the experiences in your life," she said with such confidence that my cock ached all over again.

I lifted my arm, instinctively wanting to stroke her soft skin and tell her that I wasn't crazy, but I fisted my hand instead. While I sensed she'd realized what I was afraid to do, she nuzzled closer, letting a sigh escape, her hot breath dancing across my skin. It had been a hell of a long time since I'd had a woman in my arms like this. This felt as natural as when she'd been in my kitchen.

God, why couldn't I be normal?

"Do you remember I told you about my horse?" she asked quietly.

"Yeah. Shitty thing to happen."

"What I didn't tell you before was that I ran away after I learned about what my father had done."

"You did what?"

She laughed softly. "Believe it or not, I thought I could survive on my own so that was it, my decision made. What pushed even more was that after my father got rid of my horse, my mother and I had a vicious argument. That's when she called me the worst thing that had ever happened in her life."

Jesus Christ. I should have beaten the crap out of her father. And her mother was a real tool.

"I packed a bag, grabbed the money I'd been saving for a new computer, and crawled out the window. Trust me that my parents never handed me anything."

Tensing, it was all I could do to remain quiet. "What happened?"

"Nothing for a few days. I stayed with a girlfriend until her parents got back into town. Then I was on my own, trying to use the money sparingly. I even attempted to get a job, but no one would hire me. I ended up hitching a ride halfway to Billings. Then I got picked up by a couple of boys. You know, kids partying. I was into bad boys at the time, rebellious as hell. Wearing black. I'd dyed my hair pink. They were as far removed from what I'd lived as I could get and for a little while, it was pretty good being with them, but one night they got drunk, high, and furious that I refused their advances, so one of them hit me."

I bristled, immediately pulling her tightly against me. "The motherfuckers."

"At that point, I knew it was time to get away, but they wouldn't let me go, calling me their little fuck treat."

"Please don't tell me they… violated you."

"Almost. I was screaming and fighting them, but one of them kept hitting me until I almost passed out. I guess somebody heard my screams and called the police. Then my parents were called. I'd been so scared, so angry with myself. And I couldn't wait to get back home."

Exhaling, my gut told me there was a lot more to the story. "What did your father do?"

"It wasn't just him. My parents had spent the days I was gone stripping my room of everything. Every single stuffed animal and poster on the wall, every CD I had, my iPad. It was all gone. I didn't even have my favorite pink blanket any longer. They'd tossed out everything."

"You've got to be kidding me." What the fuck was wrong with her parents?

"Nope. And I was angry. God, I was so mad I wanted to run so far away they'd never find me, but that wasn't the worst of the punishment I received because I…" Her voice started to trail off and I squeezed her even tighter, rubbing her soft cheek with my other hand.

"Fuck that man."

"No, the reason I was so angry, guilt eating me alive had nothing to do with my parents. The horrible sense of shame was because of what I'd done to my sister. She'd thought I'd abandoned her forever. I was her only real support system. I'll never forget seeing Cammie's face. She was crying and screaming, so hysterical that she had to go to the hospital the next day, suffering from a seizure. It was touch and go for almost two days. Because of what I did. I was a bad person and my sister almost died because of me. So, I never said anything about my things. I never asked for a single Christmas present or birthday gift after that. The punishment I'd received wasn't nearly enough for what I did to her."

No wonder the girl knew exactly what to say to me.

"You're being too hard on yourself," I told her.

She lifted her head, the slender moonlight streaming in through the blinds allowing me to see the concern in her eyes. "That's something you have a full understanding of. Isn't it?"

I shook my head, easing it back against the bed. "It's different, Wren."

"Is it really? Aren't you suffering because of blaming yourself wholly and completely for what happened to Belle when you were with a few other boys?"

When I shook my head again, she cupped my face with both hands, her eyes imploring.

"You're incorrigible," I managed.

"I'm right. I'm always right."

She could always make me laugh. I rolled her over onto the bed, my heart aching for so many different reasons. "You are so beautiful, my little bird."

"There's nothing you can do that will scare me."

"If only that was the truth." I hovered over her for a few seconds then climbed out of bed, opening the blinds all the way so I could see the moon.

I could tell she'd sat up but remained where she was. I'd told myself that I'd never trust anyone ever again, but it was easy with her. She was fractured, broken in a similar way, a part of her soul stripped away at a young age. Maybe that's what had attracted us to each other in the first place. All I knew is that my heart ached like it hadn't in one hell of a long time.

"I told you before. I'm not a good man."

"Why do you continue to want me to believe that?"

"Because it's the truth."

"I don't buy it for a second," she insisted.

"I also left a man to die. You've heard the old adage. History always repeats itself." She didn't make a sound or flinch at all. The woman was stronger than I'd originally thought.

"When you were overseas?"

I couldn't stand the thought of telling her everything. "Yes, and not something I'd wish on just anyone. Don't get me wrong, I loved serving my country. I felt great pride in doing so, but the choices we had to make, the horrors we faced almost every day sucked the life right out of you."

"I know it hurt you tremendously, but I won't try and tell you that I understand. What I do know is that you did everything in your power to do the right thing both times. I don't need to hear the story to know that much about you already. There's no way I can understand what you went through, but just like with Belle, you can't go back. You endured violence and loss more so than most people can comprehend. Stop beating yourself up, Phoenix. Live."

I heard every word she said. "Ronny was a good kid who shouldn't have been sent to the trenches. He wasn't ready. I did what I could to nurture him, but he wasn't like the rest of us. He didn't have a penchant for killing, the kind of anger burning inside that a Marine needs in order to easily take another life. I did what I could to protect him at the cost of a mission."

"What happened?"

"He was shot multiple times and even though I did what I could to get him to safety, the conditions were treacherous. I failed. Eventually, I was taken prisoner, the base nearly destroyed. And no, I wasn't blamed given circumstances, but losing Ronny was just another blow."

"I'm so very sorry," she whispered. "That's where you got the scars."

I laughed bitterly. "Not just during the war, Wren. In my delinquent youth, I also got into a lot of fights. The story you told me about what you went through could have been something my buddies and I did."

"Not a chance."

Laughing, I couldn't take my eyes off the moon. "Believe it."

"You might think I'm very young, but I was forced to grow up at an early age. I've learned how to spot integrity and you are one of the most honest men I've ever known."

There were so many other things I wanted to say to her. I needed to scream at her that she should run far away from me, but I didn't have the courage to watch her walk away.

The love was even more terrifying now that I'd exposed the ugliness.

She leaned against me, caressing my shoulders. "Thank you for trusting me."

"I do with my life." I took her into my arms, wishing that releasing the heavy burden had brought me any peace. Maybe she was right in that I would need to face the demons head on.

As I heard my phone ring, my instinct kicked in. "Shit." Easing away from her, I grabbed my jeans, yanking my phone from the pocket.

"What's wrong?" she asked.

"It's the station. Just hold on." As I answered, the bad feeling only intensified. "Wentworth."

"Phoenix. We have a situation. I need all hands on deck," Stoker said, distress in his voice.

"Where?"

"Base of the Sapphire Range. Gonna need you on the bird."

Jesus. Fucking. Christ.

Was karma trying to kick me in the balls?

"I'm on it, Cap'n." As I ended the call, Wren had already turned on the light.

"A fire?"

"On Sapphire Ridge."

She frowned. "You're thinking someone is seeking retaliation for what happened with Belle. Right?"

"I don't know, Wren, but the coincidences are starting to mount up. I don't like anything I can't control." I yanked the gear bag from my closet before grabbing a fresh tee shirt. "I need you to do something for me." I had no other choice at this point. My initial hesitation wasn't about trusting her. It was about the fact I was now positive that somehow, some way, the value of the land had put me square in the target mode. Maybe this had something to do with the events at Sapphire Ridge or maybe it was a ploy to fuck with my mind. Yeah, maybe they wanted to drive me away from Missoula. Whatever the case, the asshole or assholes would use anything against me possible.

Including the woman I loved.

"What do you need?"

I grabbed the bag where I stored my weapons behind the shoeboxes on the top shelf. I'd been conscious of Justin's curiosity, keeping the ammunition in a lockbox in another location. As soon as I wrapped my hand around one of the pistols, she sucked in her breath.

"What's that for?"

"Just in case, little bird." I forced it into her hand, placing my other one on top. "I need you stay here until I get back. I can't promise you when that will be. A day. Five days. There's enough food, but you can call Gage if you need anything. I'll also leave the keys for my car in case you have an emergency." I didn't wait for her to answer, grabbing a pen and a piece of paper from the drawer of my nightstand.

"Whoa. I don't know how to care for a child. And now we have a dog. I mean you have a dog. I mean…"

"Stop worrying. After what I saw with Justin earlier, you're going to do just fine. Listen to me. I'm going to give you two magazines of ammo, but you need to find a place to store them where Justin can't get to them and the kid searches everything when he gets in one of his moods. Okay?"

She said nothing as I unlocked the box, grabbing two magazines, loading one for her then returning the weapon.

"Phoenix. I'm afraid."

I grinned to try to calm her nerves. "You're going to be fine." I yanked on my fire-retardant jumpsuit before grabbing the paper, writing down both Gage's and Betty's numbers. "Here you go. I put Betty's phone number on there as well. I'm sure she'll come to your aid if you just can't handle

Justin, but I have faith in you." I patted my hand on the note I left on the dresser before double checking I had everything in my bag.

"No, I'm afraid for you."

When she remained quiet, I turned to face her. "There's no need to be. I love you, Wren Tillman."

"I love you, Riggs Wentworth." As she walked closer, a look of fear crossed her face. "Don't do anything risky."

"Risk is my middle name, little bird. Don't worry. I know what I'm doing."

"Just come back safe. Okay?"

I'd never thought I'd ever have to worry about doing that for a single human being, let alone two.

"You're going to be just fine, little bird. And I need to be able to rely on someone."

"I…" She wore a panicked expression but closed her hand. "Just don't die on me cause I'll be pissed. And I'll put a crazy hex on you, making you one of the undead."

"I don't plan on it, sweetheart, but I think it's the other way around. I'll haunt you, baby. No man will ever be able to touch you again." I pulled her close, hating the way she was trembling. As I rubbed her back, she clung to me and I doubted the ache I felt inside would ever go away. God, I loved this woman. "Just remember that Justin can get cranky. Try not to lose your patience. He loves music and movies and the sound of your voice." I tapped my finger on her nose, bile forming in my throat. The bad feeling just wouldn't leave. "Oh, and if you want to use my computer, my call sign is the password."

"A little too easy, fly boy. Don't take one of those helicopters to a tropical island."

"Not without my best girl."

"I better be your only girl, or the fire is the least of what you'll need to worry about."

At least she was trying to take it all in stride. "Take care of yourself, little bird."

She nodded, but there was no doubt by the look in her eyes that she had more questions than the answers I'd already given her.

And at this point, I had none to give. Being with her made me realize one thing for certain.

I was a shell of a man, not good for anyone, including my own son.

"Jesus Christ," the Zullie snarled. Riker Sheffield was a tough son of a bitch, barely tamed by the woman he'd fallen in love with a few years before. He was also one of the few men I highly respected. Most of the team had been together for years, which had made my addition more difficult. There was a hell of a lot of competition, including with the other local jumpers.

We weren't drinking buddies, but I could place my trust in the man and that's all that counted.

I glanced at him before lifting my head toward the magnificent range. I'd loved the area, going there as often as possible when I was younger. I'd introduced the Bad Boys to the trails. And Belle. Sighing, I tried to put what had happened out of my mind. Maybe this was fate trying to force me to handle the situation. Besides, I had a team that would be counting on me not to lose my shit.

The Sapphire Ridge had some of the prettiest scenery around. The thought of losing additional acreage was disgusting. While the valley had experienced more rain this year, the mountains were dry as a bone, far too much debris covering over a hundred miles. The first could get out of hand quickly.

Stoker jogged closer, ready to give directions. "You two need to coordinate your actions. You're going to use the helitorch to start backfires on either side of this bitch. We need to head it toward the river. That's the only chance we have of keeping the flames from eating up dozens of homes on the south ridge. Riker, take the east, Phoenix, the west. We need to get it under control as soon as possible."

Starting fires to alter the direction of an existing one confused the hell out of people, but I'd seen the technique in action enough to know when it worked, it did like a charm.

"I'll send in the jumpship after that," Stoker added. Maybe use of the plane would be able to douse a good portion of it.

"The wind is picking up," Riker snarled.

The mud dropped from the DC-3 was only effective if the wind stayed low. I was beginning to wonder about that myself.

"Yeah, I know. Which is why I need your birds in the air ASAP. Just be careful." Stoker had a strange look on his face.

"What?" I asked.

"There are reports of campers. And don't go off halfcocked, Phoenix. You have your job for the day."

I glanced at the captain, taking a deep breath. I'd been through enough of these to know what he was concerned about. A fire devil. The whirlwind of fire was like a tornado blast. That would drive every jumper out of the trees.

"Let's get going, partner," Riker said, jogging toward one of the helicopters as I headed for the other. It was risky business what we were attempting to do.

I jumped in, immediately starting the engine. As I checked the airspeed, I cringed. If the wind caught the flames, carrying them toward one of the birds, we could get sucked in. As the blades started to turn, I yanked on my headset, adjusting the station so I could hear both Stoker's communication device as well as Riker's.

Riker was off the ground first, immediately heading toward the mountain range. I checked the fuel, gave the 'ok' sign to Stoker and allowed the bird to lift. As I headed toward the designated ridge, a location I knew far too well, I was forced to take a deep breath.

I'd lived to fly in the Marines, loving every day of flying a chopper. I hadn't experienced a single flashback while serving.

It seemed like time stood still every time I flew. For the most part it was a peaceful feeling, but I hadn't lost the gnawing in my stomach since finding the two murdered victims. Over thirty minutes had passed, and I was getting antsy.

I adjusted the throttle, climbing as I studied the fire. It was burning hot, the crown fire already exploding. As soon as I reached the right altitude, I made a wide arc, trying to find the best spot. I peered down at the flames hopping from one tree to another. From where the helicopter was positioned, I could see the firebrands raining down on the thick canopy of threes, the large chunks of embers almost immediately starting another smaller fire.

"Phoenix. Is everything set?"

"Almost." I swung around to the other side, trying to get closer. When the warning light went off, Stoker immediately came on the line.

"Don't hot dog this, Phoenix. The guys are getting their asses handed to them." I could tell he was in a vehicle, likely heading in the direction of the fire. This one required all hands on deck.

"Don't worry. Just trying to make certain we can contain this mother." I positioned the controls, sensing the heat was building. I couldn't risk more than a few hundred additional yards. But my gut told me if I found the right shot, we could turn this baby.

"Come on, baby. You can do this for me." The bird was straining, embers flying, the stench of acrid smoke filling the small cabin. Damn if it didn't have the same stench I'd smelled on the last fire.

Concentrate. Just fucking concentrate.

"Take the shot, Phoenix!" Riker yelled.

"Almost. Almost."

The entire bird started to rattle, the engine coughing. Fuck. I'd gone too deep. As I wrapped my handle around the controller, I shook my head, the beast looking me directly in the eye.

"Now!"

Then I fired the shot, immediately trying to head into a deep arc to get the hell out of there. As the engine continued to chug, I glanced at the controls.

Fuck. Fuck.

As I swung around, I heard the sound no helicopter pilot wants to hear.

An engine had failed.

CHAPTER 15

 *ren*

Sunshine.

I hated it this morning more than usual. The why was easy. Anytime now Justin would wake up and I'd be forced to tell him that his daddy was working, and he was stuck with me. I felt sick inside, already worried that Phoenix wouldn't return. I wasn't certain how a military wife could do it. I wouldn't be able to handle the constraints or the constant anxiety.

On my third cup of coffee already, there'd been no additional sleep after he'd walked out the door. I'd stood there on the front porch, freezing to death until his headlights faded in the distance. While Phoenix had tried to be light about leaving, as if he was headed out to meet a client, hoping to sell him a fractional share of a condo in Hilton

Head instead of facing the 'beast' as he'd called it, I'd been numb.

Oh, sure, fighting a raging fire was a typical day at the office.

Suddenly, the cheap coffee he had in his house tasted nasty and I tossed it into the sink, almost dropping the cup after doing so. Why was I already so nervous when it had only been a couple of hours? There'd been nothing on the news, so I'd turned off the television. I certainly didn't want Justin to start thinking his daddy wouldn't be coming back.

When I heard scampering feet, I braced myself for an immediate backlash. The puppy rounded the corner first, Justin second, immediately heading for the coat closet. I followed him, curious as to what he was doing.

"Good morning, Justin. What's going on?"

He gave me a sideways glance. "Puppy gotta go out."

I was pleasantly surprised, laughing to myself as I headed toward the door, grabbing my jacket as well. "Then let's go together." As I stood on the front porch, my chest tightened just from glancing toward the mountains. Sapphire Ridge was two hours away by car. But it felt like he was a million miles away.

"Where's Daddy's truck?" Justin finally asked.

Here we go. I took a deep breath and walked down the stairs. "Daddy got called to a fire. He's going to put on his hero cape and save the world."

As Chewy scampered around his legs, he contemplated what I was saying. Then he nodded once before returning his attention to the puppy.

Meanwhile, never-to-be-mother-of-the-year was shaking in her boots. Maybe I could do this. How long could it take? Right?

As I allowed them to play for a little while, I thought about what I'd been able to discover regarding the information Phoenix told me about. I'd put a list together as I'd sat in front of the computer, including the name of the dummy corporation. From what I'd been able to find, Blue Waters had been formed several months before. While I'd yet to find the officers on the Montana Secretary of State's listings, there were other sources I could check later. Fortunately, I had managed to find their registered agent, a name I didn't recognize. After making Justin and the puppy breakfast, I planned on spending time digging deeper.

I'd learned in my days of being an advisor that people often hid their dirty laundry in plain sight. I'd made it my business to thoroughly check any potential new client against their claims of fortune. That had prevented me from wasting time and money several times.

What I had found was the report on the murder victims in Billings, the two men providing reports on what the resorts would do to the terrain, the forest and wildlife in their hopes of squelching the projects.

The reason they'd been in what had seemed like an unusual location was an easy answer to find. One of the men owned a significant piece of property with a log cabin on it nearby, the place registered as a corporate retreat.

Plus, the area had been outlined as a possible secondary location for one of the winter sports arenas almost proposed in the project. They had personal reasons to hate Blue Waters, which had gotten them killed.

"Come on. Let's get you guys inside. Time for breakfast." Thankfully, both came running without me being forced to drag them in. I closed the door, still caught in the thought that there was a missing piece that would thread everything together.

When I'd looked up the land Snake owned, I was confused at first. He only had two hundred acres, which was nothing in comparison to what Phoenix owned. However, it was the position of his property that mattered. It would be smack in the middle of where the developer would likely need to put the main road entering the property given the existing water and sewer lines.

If only I could get my hands on whatever the proposed resort was. Maybe that would provide me with some answers. As I thought about it, I realized that I was missing a golden opportunity. Cammie worked for a law firm who handled real estate transactions. While it was still the weekend, she might be able to find out something on Monday.

I made mental note to give Cammie a call after breakfast. For now, I had to try to learn how to be a mom.

If only for a little while.

* * *

Over five hours had passed. I'd never realized just how exhausting a puppy could be, let alone a kid who could race around me at five hundred miles an hour. So far, Justin had remained happy with the fact I was babysitting him. I'd come to realize the kid was smart, so much so I was surprised so many people had such concerns about him. Maybe I was missing something, but he'd set the table at breakfast, helped me feed Chewy, and even brought his milk glass to me.

Then the perfect little boy had turned into a hellion, but only like a typical kid would do. We'd played a board game. I'd let him play on his gameboard. Then he'd begged me to allow him to watch a movie while eating lunch. At least a peanut butter and jelly sandwich had made him giggle with delight. I wasn't the best cook and in truth, I had no idea what I should feed him.

Wasn't I the posterchild for being a babysitter?

Fortunately, I'd been able to make a few phone calls, albeit needing to leave messages given it was a Sunday. Maybe the assessor's office would have some information. I'd even called the county clerk's office, giving them details of what I was looking for. And I'd risked contacting the single phone number I'd found attached to Blue Waters, although the recording made it sound like an answering service was being used. At least I'd accomplished something that might be useful.

Or so I hoped.

Sighing, I glanced at the clock, wondering if five-year-olds took naps. I certainly wanted to. After putting the knife in the dishwasher and wiping the counter, I glanced at my phone, wishing it would ring. Another wave of anxiety was setting in, so much so that I started to pace the kitchen, which wasn't like me.

Something was off. I could feel it in my gut.

"Can I pway in my room, Wrennie?" He'd taken to calling me that, which I thought was cute.

"Sure, you can."

As soon as Chewy dutifully followed, I grabbed my phone, touching the screen and glaring at it, hoping he'd tried to call, and I hadn't heard it ring.

No such luck.

I debated dialing him, but my nerves couldn't take it any longer.

So I did.

When it went to voicemail immediately, I didn't panic, convincing myself that it was a requirement that all phones needed to be turned off or that he had a locker where he stored his personal items when working. It wasn't good to panic in this kind of situation, especially when I had my hands full.

Sighing, I put the phone on the counter, tapping the surface as I debated what I should do. Research. That would keep me busy. I grabbed the laptop, placing it on the kitchen table, preferring to be closer to Justin's room. On a whim, I googled Phoenix's father. I knew little about him or why there'd been such a big fight with my father. Not that I really cared.

Except for what Phoenix had told me, which remained stuck in the back of my mind. It was still unfathomable that his father would be so cold. Then again, it sounded like something my father would do.

What I found was all the glossy items that a man of Mr. Wentworth's influence would want seen. The charity events he'd gone to, the private functions with celebrities. Then there were ribbon-cutting ceremonies of the various developments he'd crafted, utilizing funding from what I had to guess were his close friends. He seemed to have a presence in several states, but Texas he'd spent the last few years carving a piece of it for himself. He was reported to be worth billions.

I wrote down several notes, including the names of some of his supporters, a few of which rang a bell. Then I sat back, uncertain where to go from there. On a whim, I typed in my father's name, scrolling through google until something interesting caught my eye.

Before I had a chance to explore it, I heard a knock on the door. Almost instantly, my heart fell into my stomach. My mind went to a dark place, as if there would be a police officer behind the door, prepared to tell me that Phoenix had died in a fiery crash. Swallowing, I rose to my feet, debating whether to answer it. What if he'd called Gage, asking him to check on me? That made more sense.

I took a deep breath, glancing down the hallway before heading to the door. When I opened it, I wasn't expecting to see a nice-looking older couple standing on the deck.

"Can I help you?" I asked, able to tell by the woman's eyes she hadn't been expecting me either.

"And you are?" the woman asked.

"A friend. Who are you exactly?" Why did I have a very bad feeling about this?

The woman glanced at the man, her expression smug. "You must be the new girlfriend."

"I'm sorry. I still didn't catch your names." My instinct told me to put my foot behind the partially open door.

"I'm Abigail Foster, my husband Roger, and we've come here to collect our grandson."

Oh, shit. This was Justin's grandparents. I fought several nasty urges inside of me in seeing the smirk on her face, as if I wasn't good enough for her grandson. That brought out the tigress in me.

"Oh, I'm sorry. Phoenix didn't mention you'd be stopping by. If what you mean is to see him, I'm sorry, he's taking a nap. And I do apologize but I don't know you from anyone else on the street."

"Is Riggs here?" the male asked, his tone just as harsh.

"Why, no, he's working, which is why I'm here, a good friend of his. Now, I'll be happy to mention to *Phoenix* that you stopped by, but I will need to ask you to leave as I have work to do."

"I don't think you understand, Miss…" Abigail threw at me.

"Tillman. As in Senator Tillman's daughter." I allowed the information to settle in, smiling as it did. I was quite happy with my response, although I could see Abigail wasn't going to be daunted by me throwing around my father's name.

"As I said, we've come here to collect our grandson. Please step aside." When she dared to try to come in, I bristled, enough so a strangled sound erupted from deep in my throat.

"And I think it's time for you to leave. No, I know it is." As I started to shut the door, I could swear I heard the pitter patter of little feet. There wouldn't be anything worse that could happen today than if Justin saw me arguing with his grandparents.

When the man stuck his foot in, I was floored in realizing their intentions. They'd come here to take him by force. Over my dead body.

"If you don't take your hands off the door, I'm going to contact the sheriff, who is a personal friend of Phoenix's."

I'll be damned, the man still tried to get in.

"Get out. Now!"

After I screamed, that's the moment I heard Justin's little voice. At least it startled the man enough, I was able to slam the door in their faces, immediately engaging the lock. Then I backed away, turning toward the little boy. His face was filled with horror and immediately tears welled in his eyes.

"We'll see you in court!" the man yelled.

My stomach flipped.

I raced toward Justin, scooping him into my arms as Chewy jumped all over us, barking incessantly. *Why aren't you here, Phoenix?*

When the assholes had the nerve to pound on the door, I was mortified, immediately heading to the backdoor, snapping the lock into place. Would they try to climb in through a window?

Now the kid was full-blown crying, the dog yelping and I was close to hysteria. What was I supposed to do?

"It's going to be just fine, Justin. Nothing is wrong. Just a disagreement." As he became more and more panicked, he started to flail. That's when I had to let him down for fear of dropping him.

He started to pound on my legs with his little fists and tears slipped past my lashes. Oh, God. Oh, God. What had I just done?

Don't break down. Don't do it. You need to be strong.

The little voice wasn't helping.

"Where's Daddy? I want my daddy!"

"Hey, Justin. Do you want to watch a movie?"

He continued to cry, wailing at the top of his lungs. I was certain the Fishers were recording his outburst, likely to use it in court. What had I just done to Phoenix? I rubbed the top of Justin's head then dropped down to eye level. If the kid wanted to give me a black eye, so be it.

"Justin. How about a soda?" Did Phoenix allow him to have one? Shit. I had no idea.

As the crying continued, I was starting to become far too emotional. "How about some ice cream?"

Oh, my God. That did the trick. He immediately stopped crying, although his little sobs remained. I wasn't cut out for this. I guided him to the kitchen, my hands shaking as I grabbed a bowl from the cabinet, dishing out a nice helping.

I hated to admit I needed to bribe him just for a little while. When he sat down without being asked, I tousled his hair, taking a deep breath. I watched him for a few seconds before heading toward the front window, daring to glance out. The Fishers were gone, but I had a feeling they'd be back soon, only this time with a court order. Why hadn't Phoenix stopped them before this?

Who was I to judge.

As I returned to the kitchen, I had to admit that I was exhausted. I slumped against the doorway, digging the piece of paper Phoenix had left me into my hand. "Justin. I'm going to make a quick phone call."

"O-tay."

I moved around the corner, dialing Gage's number. As I suspected, I was forced to leave a message.

"Hi, um, Gage. This is Wren Tillman. Phoenix is at a fire and asked me to stay with Justin. His grandparents just stopped by. They threatened me and tried to take Justin with them. I locked them out, but I didn't know what else to do. This is my number. When you get a chance, will you call me?"

After rattling off the number just in case, I took a deep breath, holding the phone to my head. Then I sucked up my tears and walked back into the kitchen.

Only to find his little head down on the table, his hand still wrapped around the spoon. Sighing, I walked toward him, shaking my head. Children could easily define what was important in life. I pushed the bowl away and gathered him into my arms, thankful he wasn't fighting me. Then I headed into his bedroom, easing back the covers. As Chewy scampered on top, I took a deep breath. The little boy was safe, and no one was going to get to him.

I only closed the door partially after checking the locks on his windows. Then I headed back into the kitchen, giving myself an okay to have a glass of wine. One wouldn't hurt me at this point, and I needed something to calm my nerves.

I'd wanted to wrap my hands around the woman's throat. With the wine poured, I dialed Cammie. I needed a friendly voice to talk to and I was determined to get answers before Phoenix returned.

"Cammie. How's non-married life?"

She laughed. "You should have been there for the fireworks. I had a blast. I know that sounds horrible, but I did. Guess what else I'm doing?"

"I'm afraid to ask."

"I'm moving out of the house. Anyway, I know you didn't call me to talk about my lack of love life. I'm really sorry what happened."

"I'm fine. We had a glorious time together after leaving your rehearsal dinner." After laughing, I heard silence on the other end. "What's wrong? Did something happen?"

"Oh, God. Where are you?"

"I'm at his house. He went to work a fire and he asked me to stay with his son. Justin is a cutie pie. Oh, and we now have a puppy. At least, I think. It's a long story and it's really not mine, but Justin's at this point. I know I'm rambling. And I do need to ask you a favor, a big one this time. I want you to check with your associates, that favorite attorney you've been crushing on, to see who is behind the recent push for building a couple of huge resorts in Montana. Specifically, check the Wentworth Corporation and I know you might not want to do this, but I want to find out what our father has been doing and investing in. Do you think you could do that for me? Pretty please?"

When she didn't say anything, I leaned against the counter. "What's wrong, Cammie? Tell me. If you don't want to do that, I'll understand but I have a hunch and it needs to be played out. Too many bad things are happening around Phoenix and his ranch."

She still remained silent. What the hell was going on?

"You haven't been listening to the news?" Cammie asked in a soft voice.

"Not recently. Why?" I was already moving to the living room, turning on the remote for the television, searching frantically for any news program.

"You said Phoenix went to a fire?"

"Yes, in the Sapphire mountain range. I think that's what he said. Why? Tell me why?"

"Honey, there was a huge fire up there and—"

"I know that!" I snapped, interrupting her. "I'm sorry. I've had a trying day. Please just tell me."

"There was an accident with one of the men. Now, they haven't said who it is so I'm certain he'll call you."

"What accident? How? Do you know how?" As I finally found a news program, I waited, my heart thumping out of my chest.

"Um, a helicopter. It crashed, but they haven't said if the person is injured."

"Crashed? A helicopter?" No. No. No! As the lead in the story switched, the scene on the ground near the mountains came into view. There were firetrucks and ambulances.

Shock and anguish tore through me, my mind whirring as thoughts drifted in and out.

"Wren. Are you there? Come on. Talk to me. Please."

"I need to call you back, Cammie. Okay? I promise I will." I ended the call, no longer able to recognize my voice. As I stared at the screen, I could no longer breathe. He had to be alive. He just had to be. This was all a horrible dream. I knew it.

I dropped the phone twice before I was able to dial his number. Then I stood shaking, swaying as the reporter droned on about how they didn't know the cause of the crash, but it was under investigation.

When it started ringing, I held my breath.

Then as it had done before, it went straight to voicemail.

"This is Phoenix. You know the damn drill so do it."

Beep…

I collapsed, the phone dropping before I hit the floor. I clasped my hands over my mouth to keep from screaming.

And I knew in my heart that he was gone.

Gone…

CHAPTER 16

"*S*ome things cannot be fixed; they can only be carried.
Grief like yours, love like yours can only be carried.*"
—Megan Devine

Wren

I'd heard somewhere that you knew when the life of
someone you cared about ended abruptly, almost as if you
yourself were stabbed with a sharp knife. I'd felt that and so
much more over the last few hours, afternoon turning into
night. I'd never expected to find love in my hometown, least
of all with a man I'd hired for a date.

It seemed surreal now, so much so that I was completely
numb inside. I'd managed to keep it together, even
pretending there was nothing wrong after Justin had awakened from his nap. He hadn't mentioned his grandparents

and I hadn't either, although that was the only other thing that weighed heavily on my mind. Now he'd be forced to live with them. I couldn't seem to convince myself that it would be better than foster care. Maybe Phoenix's parents would take the child.

Was that any better?

I wasn't thinking clearly, the fog settling in for the long haul. Although there was nothing definitive on the news, including whether anyone had died from the Zullies, I didn't need confirmation. Phoenix hadn't called and I couldn't feel him any longer. All I was able to feel was a frigid cold that had turned my blood to ice.

I'd given Justin a bath and now he was in his PJs. And I knew at any moment he'd ask about his daddy. What the hell was I supposed to tell him?

"Are you going to wead to me?" he asked in his little voice. "Or tell me another hero story? I liked that. Daddy a hero."

I almost lost it, thankful when there was a knock on the door. "Stay right here. Okay? I'll be back in a jiffy." I wanted to grab the weapon just in case, but with my shaking hands and the fact Justin would be curious, I couldn't risk it.

But fear churned deep inside.

"O-tay."

When the pup jumped off the bed, racing after me, I thought for certain Justin was going to fly off the handle. Instead, he laughed. The kid amazed me. I headed for the door, my stomach churning.

"Who the fuck is there?" I used the most growly voice I had.

"Wren?"

It was Gage. After taking a deep breath, I opened the door, immediately noticing several faces staring back at me, including Snake's.

"I got your voicemail and um… I'm certain you've heard the news?" Gage's eyes flicked back and forth across mine.

Chewy went nuts, barking at everyone, nipping at their shins.

"Chewy," I scolded before nodding. "I heard. Anything new?" My voice was barely audible.

He shook his head. "We thought we'd keep you company, if that's alright. What a cutie pie. How's the pup doing?"

"Company would be good right about now. I'm just…" I backed away from the door, allowing the group in. "Chewy is doing great. Any news on what happened to the agent?"

Gage glanced toward Hawk who exhaled.

"We'll talk later. Okay?"

"Yeah, I get it. It doesn't matter right now," I half whispered, closing the door behind them.

"Hi, I'm Bryce Travers," the woman said. When I held out my hand, she grabbed me for a hug instead. "We're all family here."

"I'm Hawk Travers. Phoenix and I have been friends for a while."

As Snake moved closer, I could tell he was almost as destroyed as I was. "I don't know what to say, Wren."

"It's okay. I'm glad you'll all here. Justin doesn't know and I…"

"Don't tell him," Gage suggested. "It's a wait and see. We'll get some information soon. I do know there were two choppers up on the mountain."

I allowed the information to sink in, the cold chill turning icy.

"Make yourself at home. I need to tuck Justin in," I half whispered, another round of tears forming. Maybe I wasn't strong enough for this.

"Of course."

I was still numb but at least I knew that Justin would safe. As the pup trailed behind me, I put on my game face, determined to try to tell him a story about his daddy.

Even if it broke my heart.

Time had no meaning any longer as the minutes and hours slipped by. There was no news. Not on the local television stations or with Gage contacting the folks he knew in the fire department and smokejumpers' facility. From what I could tell, it seemed no one wanted to do any talking.

So I paced.

And had wine.

And paced more.

And looked in on Justin, who thankfully was sleeping peacefully.

Meanwhile, I was a complete wreck, barely able to think straight let alone function. At least I wasn't alone. Bryce was a godsend, searching the computer in an attempt to find out information that I wouldn't begin to know where to look.

But I was exhausted, tears forming every few minutes. I knew they were pointless, but I'd never felt so alone or helpless in my life. What I did know without a shadow of a doubt was how much I loved the grouchy man with the arrogant attitude and the need to hunt for danger. He'd carved his way into my heart, and I doubted I would ever be the same.

Now I was standing at the front window, where I'd been several times in my hope of seeing headlights. When I felt a presence, I almost lost it all over again.

"Hey. Why don't you get some sleep," Gage suggested.

"I can't. I have Justin to worry about and the puppy might need to go out at any time and… And if I close my eyes, I'll see his face."

He touched my shoulder. "Wren, there's nothing else you can do, and you need your strength for that little boy in there, especially if…"

I knew why he wasn't finishing his sentence, but it didn't matter. The ache and reminder were the same.

Devastating.

"What happens to Justin if we find out that… you know."

"Do you really want to talk about this?"

I nodded. "I need to know what to do."

Sighing, he rubbed his jaw before answering. "If there's no will or papers defining his welfare, then Justin will go to the closest living relative, which could mean his grandparents. I don't know if Phoenix made any alternate choices if something should happen to him."

I turned slightly so I could look into his eyes. "Is there a chance an outsider could adopt him?"

His eyes opened wide, a slight smile crossing his face. "There's always a chance, but I can tell you that most court systems want a child to be with living relatives."

I nodded, realizing my question was not only out of the blue but also likely sounded ridiculous. "They aren't good people. I can tell."

"I've made some calls. They'll need a court order to come and get him and… I might have prevented that from happening immediately. I know a judge or two." His grin became wider.

My reaction was instant and unlike me. I threw my arms around him. "Thank you for everything."

"Hey, it's going to be alright. You might not know Phoenix that well, but he's tough and a fighter."

"You're a good friend," I said as I eased back, wiping my eyes for the tenth time.

"We've been through a lot."

"He told me, at least a little bit about Sapphire Ridge."

He was silent for a few seconds then looked away. "He really likes you. He's never talked with anyone outside of our group about what happened."

"He's hurting."

"We all are. Now, let us take care of Justin or the puppy if need be. Just try and get some rest. Okay?"

After thinking about it, I sighed. "Just for a little while. Call me if you hear anything. Please?"

"Of course I will."

I glanced at the others, who were busy talking, still so thankful they were here. As I walked toward the bedroom, I glanced into Justin's room one more time. Chewy lifted his head for a few seconds but was completely comfortable with his new best friend. As I closed the door, I said a silent prayer, which was something I hadn't done in a long time.

Just walking into the bedroom where we'd made love was another crushing blow. Being in his house was both comforting and just another way of destroying what was left of my heart. Without bothering to take off my clothes, I slipped under the covers, leaving the light on by the bed. Maybe I should put a candle in the window to guide his way back home.

As I closed my eyes, images of Phoenix popped into my mind, especially when I was barely conscious the night he'd found me in the snow. My hero. I nuzzled into the pillow, yanking the covers over my head, doubting there was any way to block out the anguish. At least I could try.

After taking a few deep breaths, I felt another tear trickle across my nose toward the pillow.

All I wanted to do was curl into a ball and sob.

"What do you think?" Phoenix asked after he removed the blindfold.

"Oh, my God. It's beautiful."

"I thought you'd like it. This is my favorite place on the ranch."

I turned in a full circle, amazed we were in the same location. Green pastures surrounded a trickling brook, the water tumbling over rocks creating a peaceful sound. A majestic oak tree prevailed over the beautiful location, the light breeze tickling the full branches. And there were wildflowers just off to the right in vibrant colors captured by the sun.

"So amazing."

"Yes, you are," he whispered as he gathered me into his arms. "This is where I'd like to get married."

A shiver trickled down my spine. "Married?" He turned me around to face him, wrapping his arms around my waist.

"That is if you'll have a broken-down cowboy as a husband."

I touched his check, his stubble tickling my fingertips. There was so much love in his eyes, and I was floored, my heart bursting with joy. "Are you asking me?"

"My silly little bird. Wren Tillman. Will you marry me?"

Mmm... I snuggled under the warmth as the vision started to fade, happiness swelling deep within. I was tingling all over, butterflies in my stomach. Marriage. I'd be married to the most wonderful man in the world. From somewhere I heard a voice, deep and husky. Where had he gone to?

"Wren."

"Where..." *Sleep. Dream.* I suddenly couldn't find him. "Phoenix."

"I'm right here. I'm right here, baby."

Slowly, I opened my eyes, the bright red LED lights of the clock staring back at me. I'd been dreaming. Just a damn dream. As a sob started to form, I sensed a presence.

"Wren. Are you awake?"

No, I was just hearing things, in a horrible fog. I felt a pull, then a touch so warm that I was instantly on fire. As I rolled over, I blinked several times. This couldn't be real. "Phoenix?"

"I'm right here, baby. I told you I'd be back."

As he peered down at me, I took several deep breaths as I touched his face. He was covered in soot, a gash on his forehead, but he was alive. I jerked up, throwing my arms around him, allowing the tears to fall.

"You're really alive? I thought something happened. I couldn't feel you any longer."

He pulled me onto his lap, squeezing me tightly against him. "I was always with you, just like I'll always be. You're the air I breathe, the electricity that fuels me. I love you, baby."

He pulled away, cupping my chin. Then he captured my mouth, holding our lips in place. There was nothing like the feel of being in his arms. As he slipped his tongue inside, I couldn't stop shaking, tears staining my cheeks. And I still prayed this wasn't just some horrible dream.

The kiss was passionate, yet more emotional than any we'd shared together. Together. The word held an entirely different meaning. Life was precious. Time couldn't be wasted on anger or hatred. The only things that were important were friends and family.

The way his dominated my tongue was comfortable, soothing the ache inside. I could do this for hours, needing nothing else but the strength of his arms holding me. When he finally broke the kiss, he pressed his forehead against mine.

"I'm so sorry, little bird. I didn't have my phone. Things were chaotic. I got back to you as soon as I could," he said with such sadness in his voice.

"What happened?" I clung to him, still shaking in disbelief.

"The engine of the other helicopter failed, his chopper going down. I wasn't going to let him die."

I pulled back, able to laugh. "You never will follow rules, will you?"

"Not a chance, little bird."

"Is he okay?"

"Riker has a broken leg and is cut up pretty badly, but he'll be fine. He's a tough guy."

"Just like you." My voice cracked.

He chuckled, but his eyes were filled with anguish as he rubbed his thumb through my tears. "Yeah, maybe a little bit like me."

"Why didn't they provide any updates? Nothing. They said nothing."

"I had a hard landing, which destroyed the communications system. I had a few seconds to get him out of the chopper before it exploded. We were in the middle of a damn firestorm, so no one knew anything. I got him out of there, but it took time."

"You're his hero."

He took my hand, kissing my fingers. "I'm no hero, just a man doing my job."

"You can keep telling yourself that, but we all know better. Your friends. Your family. They know the truth, even if some of them don't want to admit it."

"I need to say something, Wren, so please listen to me."

"O-kay." I was still in shock, unable to think clearly, my heart pounding. But fear remained, his eyes distant and haunted.

"I'm really not a good guy, no matter what you think. You need to know that. I'm too old for you. I'm pigheaded and set in my ways. I don't understand how to be romantic or even a good boyfriend, let alone a husband, but I can't see spending another day without you in my life permanently. I know it's too soon and we barely know each other. Hell, a lot of people will call us crazy, but I know what I feel. There was a moment I was almost sucked into the fire because I was taking a risk. I did so because I thought that's what I needed to do. That's all I was good for as a person because life meant nothing to me. Not really. Until you."

I pressed my fingers across his lips, stopping him from continuing. "Did anyone ever tell you that you talk too much?"

Laughing, he pulled my hand to his cheek, rubbing it back and forth. "You can tell me that anytime."

"What are you trying to say?"

He took a deep breath. "This ain't romantic and not the way you deserve, but will you consider becoming my wife? I don't have a ring, but we can get one, whatever you want. Money is not a problem and—"

This time, I crushed my mouth over his as I wrapped my fingers around the back of his neck. I'd never known such a rollercoaster of emotions. This man was everything to me. When I pulled away, I took shallow breaths. "Let me answer."

"Okay."

"Yes."

There were moments that would be forgotten because of time, but this wasn't one of them. This very moment I would remember for the rest of my life.

Shared with the man I loved.

And not even death could tear us apart.

* * *

Phoenix

"Hello, Father," I said, trying to keep my tone even.

"Riggs. My God, son. How are you? I heard about your little mishap all the way here in Texas." The fact my father laughed after faking concern answered a few of the questions I was seeking.

Including an admittance of his guilt.

"My name is Phoenix, Pops, something I've told you a dozen times. Let me get to the point of my call. I learned about your attempt to invoke the codicil of my grandfather's will while I was away. It's funny how you didn't have the nerve to tell me that once I returned."

He paused, half laughing. "I'll be damned. You can't trust anyone nowadays, can you?"

Adam.

I'd unearthed as many rocks as I'd been able to, including on my attorney, a man I'd thought I could trust. He'd been working with my father for years. I was surprised the son of a bitch was such a good actor, pretending he cared about my concerns. "You're a real piece of work. Did you think I wouldn't find out, or had you instructed Adam to wait as long as possible? Was it a game to see how long it took? Or were you hoping you'd drop by, announcing the ranch no longer belonged to me?"

My words were edgy, but I didn't care. I was finished with our relationship, what little there had been.

"It's not like that, son."

"Bullshit!"

"You didn't have any interest in following in your grandfather's legacy and I have no interest in hanging on to an albatross. I thought it would be a win-win for the both of us. I thought you'd thank me."

Oh, for the love of God. The man was delusional.

As the waning sun splashed across the sky in various colors, I was reminded how often I'd taken the ranch for granted. "And you didn't have the courtesy to tell me."

"You had your damn head in the clouds, son. You wouldn't accept your responsibility in coming to work for me, so I was forced to take matters into my own hands."

"By giving me no options? Is that what you were thinking? Do you honestly think I give a shit about the money or your company, Pops? Not in the least, but you refused to realize or accept that. Yeah, I admit I originally had no desire to return to Missoula and you know why."

"A bunch of hogwash if you ask me."

"A woman died on that mountain. I'm responsible. You shoved it under the rug to keep the Wentworth name out of the mud."

He seemed flabbergasted. "I didn't shove it under the rug, son. In case you need a lesson in the law, if the authorities would have pressed charges, all six of you would have likely spent time in prison. I had a lot of enemies back then, son. They were chomping at the bit to use the tragedy against both of us. I couldn't allow that to happen. So I called in a few favors. If I hadn't, your life and that of your friends would have been ruined."

"Nice performance, Pops. It almost sounds like you give a damn."

"Jesus Christ, Phoenix. I wanted the best for you."

"And you wanted the best for you!" I snapped, closing my eyes to try to calm down. "Was selling the ranch punishment for tarnishing your life or was there another reason?"

"As I said, you'd shown no interest. What was I supposed to do? You would have made a hefty profit, allowing you to jump out of planes or whatever it is you do. I knew at some point you would come to your senses."

Bristling, I wrapped my hand around the railing, trying to keep the rage from my voice. "My senses? I protect some of the most beautiful terrain on earth, Pops. Sometimes I save lives, which is what I did in serving our country. But you never gave a shit. You acted embarrassed by my choices."

"That's not true," he said after a few seconds had passed. "I'm very proud of you. I want you to be happy."

"Happy. You never ask about my personal life because you don't care. Did you know I met a wonderful woman I asked to marry me? Did you know I also almost died in that fire? And did you know that my son, who you've refused to meet and likely don't even remember his name, is a wonderful little boy who grieves for a mother who never loved him? Meanwhile, he has one set of grandparents who are trying to take him away from his own father and another who treats him as if he doesn't exist. That's my life, Pops. I own a ranch that I don't want because you're right, I'm not a goddamn rancher. That's not me, but you tried to make me into a carbon copy of you. I have news for you, Pops. I'm not going to be forced off this land. It's precious and beautiful. I'm going to turn it into something special."

I don't know why I bothered. He couldn't care less. Laughing softly, I was ready to end the call.

"I'd love to meet Justin."

The few little words shocked me. "I hope you will one day."

"I will, son, and I'm very happy for you."

"Then why, Pops? Why? Grandpops wanted me to have this place for a reason, one that I was never told. So now, I'm asking you for once in your life tell me the damn truth. Was this all about greed? Money? Or did you just want to spite your own father because he didn't leave you the goddamn ranch in the first place?"

My father never seemed at a loss for words. Twice in one evening meant he'd been lying to me for years.

"Talk!" I demanded.

"It's not what you think, son. Just hear me out. There are some things you need to know."

* * *

I'd heard him, some of what he'd told me I'd anticipated.

I wasn't certain whether to remain angry or be appreciative of what he'd done. What I knew is that if everything he told me was true, it could potentially destroy a good portion of my life.

My thoughts drifted to the recent fire. Fortunately, it had been contained quickly, only losing a thousand acres. Sadly, a portion of the forest that had burned had been the same area where Belle had lost her life. I'd seen pictures of how the area had recovered, in part thanks to Parks and Recreation volunteers who'd spent countless hours replanting trees. To have it wiped out again was devastating.

It was sacred to me in so many ways. I rubbed my eyes, trying to control my breathing, my thoughts all over the place.

The thought of death had never bothered me.

Until now.

I'd almost allowed the need to find salvation to drag me straight into the depths of hell. Perhaps the only thing that had saved me from losing my battle with the beast had been the realization Riker's engine had failed and that he was going down. I'd reacted instantly, the shot from the helitorch fired only seconds before I'd made a change in course, heading for the crash site.

He'd managed to maneuver the helicopter, descending at a controlled speed, still crash-landing against the side of the mountain. Thank God it had been at the base, which had allowed me to climb the craggy rocks, dragging him from the twisted metal seconds before the chopper had burst into flames. I remembered little about what had happened next, both my training as a Marine as well as the grueling eight-week instruction course once I'd joined the Zullies taking over.

The task of bringing him to safety had been dangerous, but I hadn't given a second thought about what I was doing.

At least until we were safely away from the fire.

Then my mind and body had collapsed, all thoughts shifting to my son and the beautiful woman I'd left behind. The moment had been cathartic. Life altering. And I'd made certain we remained alive.

Just standing on the front porch of the house I'd barely given two shits about seemed entirely different. Maybe some psychiatric asshole would say I'd seen the light, choosing life over the possibility of death. Whatever the case, I'd made the decision to change, refusing to allow the woman I adored out of my life.

The thought of not being with her, of never being able to brush my fingers across her skin or kiss her soft lips had nearly broken me. For the few women I'd been with inti-mately, none had left me craving a lingering touch, a longing look like Wren had. She'd awakened the man inside, forcing him from his dark crypt. Then she'd refused to allow him to fall into the suffocating abyss of rage and self-hatred.

All in a few days.

I'd made a few phone calls, ensuring that the future would be entirely different than what I'd once wanted or believed was the only thing I deserved.

In doing so, I'd learned a few things that had provided a clearer picture of what was going on. What I had trouble dealing with was just how far certain people had gone in order to obtain my ranch and the reasons why.

However, I remained uneasy, angry that the sections of the puzzle hadn't been pieced together. For all the efforts Wren had put in making calls, in the single day that had passed, there was nothing concrete that would lead either the fire investigator or Gage to any conclusions about who was responsible for the recent murders and that pissed me off. At least they'd discovered where the chlorine trifluoride had been purchased, able to trace the cannister left outside Gage's cabin to a processing plant in Idaho. While Gage had informed me of the news, he refused to tell me any other details.

"What's up, cowboy? Just watching the setting sun?"

The sound of Wren's voice took the frown off my face. "Yup. Just admiring the view," I told her as I turned around.

"Um. So am I." Her smile could light up the darkest night. As she stood in the doorway, allowing her heated gaze to fall to my boots, she took a deep breath. "I love it here."

"Good. Cause you're staying."

"I have a job. Well, I guess I had a job. Maybe someone will hire a broken-down financial advisor."

"Nope. You're forbidden to work for stodgy old guys with money."

"You think you own me now, huh?" She moved closer, giving me one of her rebellious looks.

"Oh, I owned you the moment I dragged you out of the snow." I couldn't help but grin. She had the face of an angel, the body of a goddess, and the mischievousness of a vixen. The combination was explosive. As I walked closer, my desire roared to the surface.

"You just think you do. Never underestimate me."

"I won't, but you need to quit your job."

Wren narrowed her eyes. "You're serious. I was thinking about getting references from my boss."

"As a freaking heart attack. You're my woman now."

"That doesn't mean I'm going to lounge around the house waiting for you to arrive. Although…" She slipped her arm around my neck, laughing before her expression turning serious. "I can't stop working forever, Phoenix. That's not me."

"I get that."

"Then let me do it at my speed." She glanced toward the barn. "How's Sophia?"

"She's doing just fine. Marshall was out late yesterday and gave her a clean bill of health."

"She's lucky."

"I know. What do you say we take Justin to the zoo tomorrow?"

Her face remained pensive for a few seconds. Then she smiled all over again, which pushed my cock against my jeans. The woman had the ability to erase the shitstorm we were embroiled in. "I'd like that." She glanced away from me, so many emotions in her eyes.

A shadow fell across her face. "What's wrong?"

"What if the asshole keeps coming?"

"He won't."

"How can you be so certain?" she asked.

"Because I won't let him."

She tilted her head. "You've already my hero. Don't be a martyr. Let Gage do his job."

"He's not doing it fast enough."

"The people responsible took great strides in hiding their activities. If they resorted to illegal methods of obtaining your land, Gage will find that out."

Both she and Bryce had filled in details about what they'd found, including confirming Wren's thoughts regarding Snake's property. There were detailed plans for a road extension that had yet to be approved by the county. Bryce had been able to locate the plans, although from what she'd told me, she'd had to call in a few favors. The only name attached to the proposed project? Blue Waters. Who the fuck were these assholes? More important, how had they managed to stay so far below the radar that I'd received zero notification of what was supposed to be presented to the county for their vote at the end of the month?

Only my attorney might be able to provide the answer. I'd called Adam three times since early morning, only to have his secretary provide one excuse after the other. I was getting angrier by the minute.

"You're right, Wren. One way or the other, the truth will be found."

"And you're not going to do anything stupid. Remember?"

Laughing, I slid my index finger down the side of her face. "I don't plan on it."

"Good. Cause hell hath no fury like a pissed-off woman." She smiled, rising onto her tiptoes to kiss my lips.

"I need to make one last phone call. I also have a work thing I need to take care of. I won't be gone for long. I've called my ranch foreman. He's going to hang around until I get back."

"You're worried."

Exhaling, I brushed my knuckles down her arm, enjoying the way she was trembling from my touch. "I'm just being cautious. Keep the doors locked. I'll have my phone with me."

"Are you certain you need to? Justin's asking for you."

"He had a huge couple of days. I'll put him to bed early so you don't need to worry about it."

"I don't mind actually." When she smiled again, there was nothing I wanted more than to curl up with her in my arms by the fire. We'd be able to do that soon enough.

"How about we both do it?"

"Deal. I'll get him ready for bed," she said, immediately retreating. "Oh, and don't be gone too long. I need you."

Issuing a slight growl, I waited until the door closed before making the call.

Adam answered on the third ring.

"Adam Reynolds."

"I find it infuriating that I need to track you down on your personal cell phone."

He paused. "I was just about to call you."

"Right. I'd forgotten what good friends your father was with mine. Let's see. Were you strong-armed into working for William Wentworth or did you do it willingly?" I allowed the words to sink in. "I was scratching my head trying to figure out why you hadn't gotten back to me when my fiancée and a reporter were able to find certain aspects of what I hired you to do without breaking a sweat."

"Look, I can explain, Riggs. Your father wanted to make certain your interests were kept intact. And I was pushed into doing so."

"That a crock of shit, buddy, and you know it. My interests? What would those be? In this ranch? What was your cut if it sold?"

"That would be unprofessional of me," Adam insisted. "I could get disbarred."

"I'll keep that in mind. Are you working with Blue Waters?"

"Hell, no. From what I found out, the two men who were killed in Billings were about to go public with accusations regarding them and their business activities."

"For what reason?" I'd heard all about what Bryce had discovered.

"Attempted extortion. They owned several large pieces of property Blue Waters was interested in. They made several offers that weren't accepted. So they began a crusade that ultimately ended in their murders. This is all hearsay at this point. However, there's no doubt they became a sharp thorn in the developer's side. Sadly, there's not enough evidence to prove the men were murdered, but that's the working theory. There won't be unless someone can identify the corporate members and a smoking gun. I do know the Feds have become involved."

"Because of the chemical used to start the fires?"

"Well, that's one reason."

"What aren't you telling me?" I growled.

"If I provide you with that information and I'm wrong, I won't be allowed to practice law getting people out of parking tickets."

Snorting, I lowered my voice to make certain Wren didn't hear me. "And if you don't, you won't have an opportunity to practice law at all. I'll make a few phone calls and let the attorney general know you're on the take. And trust me, he's a damn good friend of mine."

"You wouldn't dare."

"Watch me."

"Does the name Bart Michaels mean anything to you?"

Stiffening, I fisted my hand, taking several deep breaths. "Go on."

He hesitated, his ragged breathing an indication he knew I was serious. "Fine, but there's something else you need to know first."

"What's that?"

"As your attorney of record and your registered agent, I was served with a subpoena today."

"From whom?"

"Abigail and Roger Foster. You have a court date in one month. They're seeking full custody of Justin."

 *ren*

A cold chill remained in every muscle. I hadn't been able to get rid of it since Phoenix had left. He'd been entirely different than he had been on the porch just minutes before. Whatever had transpired in those phone calls had altered his mood. Now I was worried to death about what he was doing. He'd been gone only thirty minutes and already I was antsy.

Sighing, I finally walked away from the fire, grabbing my glass of wine and easing down on the couch. I couldn't relax enough to sit back. There was no reason for it. The foreman had dropped by not ten minutes after Phoenix had left, introducing himself, telling me he was going to take a ride around the entire ranch just to make certain everything was in order. He'd also given me his phone number.

The doors were locked, the weapon Phoenix had given me earlier tucked away where Justin couldn't get ahold of it. That wasn't why I was nervous. I had no problem defending this family, but the nagging had more to do with the suspicions that seemed to be spiraling out of control.

I'd made Bryce promise that she wouldn't repeat what she'd found to anyone until I'd had a chance to talk with Phoenix. I'd planned on doing so tonight, even if I felt sick inside, worried what it would do.

I placed the wine on the table, holding my head in my hands. When my phone rang, my stomach immediately lurched, fearful something else had happened to Phoenix. Seeing Cammie's number, I cringed.

"Hiya, girl," I said, zero enthusiasm in my voice.

"For a woman who's getting married to a hunky man," she said, laughing, "you sound terrible."

"I'm happy. I'm just worried."

"I know." The silence was awkward as if she had something on her mind.

"What's wrong? Did something happen? Don't tell me Marcus is trying to get you back."

Cammie snorted. "Actually he is, but that's not what I called."

"Then why did you call?"

"Do you remember asking me to talk to one of the attorneys in the office?"

I thought about it and had completely forgotten. "That was right before…"

"I didn't think you remembered, or you would have been grilling me this morning. Anyway, I made the call then met him for lunch to see what he found. He wanted to make certain our conversation was private."

"Why?"

"Because of what he discovered."

"That sounds ominous." It would seem we were both full of bad news.

"Are you sitting down?"

I stood as soon as she said that, grabbing my wine. "Yes. Talk to me."

As she started to relay the information, a strange vibration occurred under my feet. What in the hell was that? An earthquake? I rushed to the front window, scanning the perimeter. When I caught a glimpse of orange, I froze for a few seconds.

"Wren. Are you there?"

"Hold on. I need to go outside." I threw open the front door, racing onto the porch.

Oh, God, no. The barn was on fire. I could already hear the horses whinnying. "Cammie. Call the fire department. Get them to the ranch."

"What's going on?"

"Just do it. I need to go." I ended the call, my hands shaking as I tried to dial Jorge's phone number.

"Ms. Tillman. Is something wrong?"

"The barn's on fire."

"Shit. I'll be right there. Stay put. I'm ten minutes away," Jorge said.

"I can't wait that long. The horses," I told him as I bolted off the porch, running toward the fence.

"Just hold on. Hold—"

I cut him off, ending the call, fighting to shove it into my back pocket. The fire was already raging over the roofline. And the stench was ungodly.

The accelerant.

There was no time to waste or to contact Phoenix. I had to get the horses out of the barn. I jerked open the door, hissing as a blast of hot air hit me like a ton of bricks. Thank God the electricity was still working. As I raced to one of the gates, I struggled with getting the latch open. "Please, God. Let me do this." I finally got it open, jerking on the rail. But the horse was too terrified to move.

"Go, boy. You have to get out of here."

Other horses were kicking on the stall doors, rearing up as the flames started to crawl across the wall. I'd never seen a fire burn so quickly or so hot. God. There were so many of them. How could I release them all?

You can do it. You can do it.

I finally lunged into the stall, smacking the horse on the ass. "Go, boy. Go. Go!" When he finally bolted, I breathed a sigh of relief, heading to the next one, easily able to throw it open, the mare needing help in getting the hell out.

By the time I opened almost every stall door, the entire roof was engulfed in flames. The only horse left was Sophia. I'd seen Jorge with her. She was still skittish, terrified of any loud noises. Now she stood as if paralyzed in the back of the stall, her nostrils flared, snorting every few seconds.

"Come on, baby girl. You need to come with me." As soon as I placed my hand on the stall door, a loud cracking sound drew my attention, a thick beam heading straight for me.

Jumping aside, I barely avoided being crushed, the engulfed piece of wood setting the hay bales on fire. The rush of fire was tremendous, the stench so overpowering I couldn't breathe, the acrid odor burning my eyes. As I scrambled to my feet, I started to cough. "You have to... get... out." Now the roar was so loud it was like a freight train speeding down the tracks.

I fought my way through the smoke, doing everything I could to guide her out of the stall. When I managed, another beam came crashing down. This time I screamed. Then I realized both entrances were blocked off.

Sophia reared up on her back legs, whinnying as loudly as my scream.

Then she came crashing down and I...

Phoenix

Fifteen minutes earlier

Bart.

I should have beaten the asshole to death when I'd had the chance. Now, I would. I didn't give a shit who his father had been or who he was best friends with. He'd made the first offer on the ranch, but it had all been a ploy. Then he'd been paid to try to force me out, likely responsible for the murders of several innocent people in doing so.

While all the pieces had yet to be put into place, what I did know is that Bart had the key to the remaining answers. If what Adam told me was true, the son of a bitch could provide the names of the people who'd hired him, and I'd get it even if I had to beat the information out of him.

I floored the engine, twisting around curves at well over the speed limit. I wasn't in the mood to waste any time. At minimum, the son of a bitch would know I was onto him. Then he'd lead me straight to the remaining members of Blue Waters.

The man in charge of the corporation had already been identified. The fucker was going down one way or the other.

When my phone rang, I grabbed it within a split second. "Gage. Good. I'm going to confess right now that I will beat the shit out of Bart. You'll need to clean up the mess."

"Where the hell are you?"

"On my way to hunt down the pig."

"Turn the fuck around," Gage snapped.

"You can't talk me out of it."

"Stop fucking talking. Your goddamn barn is on fire. I caught the call. The fire department is on the way."

I slammed on the brakes. "What did you say?"

"You heard me."

"Shit. I'm headed there now." A fog developed around my head as I tried to dial Wren. As it rang and rang, rage bloomed inside of me. "Come on. Pick up the phone, honey. Pick it up."

When it finally went to voicemail, I tossed my phone, gripping the steering wheel with both hands, swerving around curve after curve, passing every car that got in my way. By the time I skidded onto the road leading to the ranch, I could see the flames licking into the air.

As I swung into the driveway, I slammed on the accelerator, pushing the car to the maximum speed. Then I noticed Jorge's truck and skidded to a stop. The barn was completely engulfed.

I raced out as he started running in my direction. Horses were everywhere, Jorge trying to get them further away from the barn. "What the hell is going on?"

"Ms. Tillman called. She mentioned the fire. I came as fast as I could."

I heard the fire engines in the distance and took a deep breath. "Is it contained?"

"As far as I can tell."

"Thank you for getting the horses."

Jorge shook his head, handing me the phone. "I didn't, Riggs. Ms. Tillman did. I think she's still in there. I'm so sorry. I tried to get through, but it's just too hot."

Everything faded into ominous shadows as I peered down at the phone in his hand. Time seemed to freeze as a dull ache built in my ears and even in the dim lighting, I would recognize the bright pink phone case anywhere.

As I lifted my head, I could tell he was still talking, but every sound became muffled, including the hard beating of my heart just before I took off running toward the flames.

"Wait! It's too hot!" Jorge yelled.

But I wasn't listening. She wouldn't die, not because of me.

As soon as I lunged over the flames, I dropped and rolled, the smoke so thick I couldn't see anything in front of me.

"Wren," I managed, coughing. The darkness was oppressive, the odds of finding her in time slim. Then I heard a slight whinnying sound and snapped my head in that direction.

From behind me I some light popped through the haze. Jorge must have turned on headlights. That allowed me to see shadows. I scrambled forward, sweeping the area. When I was able to make out the horse, I realized it was Sophia. I could tell the muted look of her hide marks.

And she was standing over Wren.

"Wren. Baby." I crouched down and as soon as I rolled her over, my hand was slickened with blood. Fuck. "Come on, baby." I gathered her into my arms, narrowly avoiding a falling beam. The entire building was crashing down and from the creaking sound, I could tell the entire roofline was about to go.

I had few choices, the flames too high and took thick to run through, not without risking her life. With zero options, I did the only thing I could think of. I tossed her over Sophia's back, forced to grab her muzzle. As I leaned in, I tried to keep my voice even. "I need you, girl. Only you can save us. Can you do that for me?" Sophia was still injured, limping from being shot.

But I'd known the mare for years and knew her strengths. While she was shaking, terrified of the elements, I had faith in her. When she snorted, I patted her flank and carefully swung over her back, leaning over to capture Wren under my body weight and tangling my fingers in Sophia's mane.

Sirens sounded off from everywhere, but they wouldn't be able to help. "This is it, Sophia. We can do this." I eased her back, turning and guiding her to as far back in the barn as safely possible. Then I said a silent prayer before pressing my knees into Sophia's sides. "Go, girl. Go!"

Horses were magnificent, intelligent creatures. They felt every emotion humans did, but their natural instincts to stay alive often won over whatever their rider told them to do, unless there was complete trust.

I had it in her. Would she have enough for the three of us?

As she took off galloping, there was nothing else I could do but continue to pray. If she stopped short, she'd toss us both into the flames. If not…

In those few seconds that seemed like hours, a few memories of my life flashed in front of my eyes, every image spiraling, moving faster and faster as if God wanted me to remember every aspect of my life. The good, the bad, and the tragic. And in those precious seconds, the last frame was of Wren and the first time I saw her beautiful face.

Fly, little bird. Fly…

As Sophia sailed over the flames, I could swear I witnessed a shooting star high on the mountains. And in the last few seconds as she landed, I could feel the noose that had been wrapped around my neck so tightly I hadn't been able to breathe slip away.

Several pairs of hands grabbed us off the horse, pulling us to the ground, blankets tossed over our bodies. I pulled Wren against my chest.

"Jesus Christ," Gage said from a distance. "Did you fucking see that?"

"You don't see that every day," Snake said from somewhere in the darkness.

I pushed away, taking several gasping breaths. Then I felt for her pulse. She was alive, but her breathing was so shallow. "Come on, baby. Wake up for me." When she didn't stir, I bellowed over the fire. "She needs help!"

Then I felt her small hand pressing against my chest. Then… her voice.

"Phoenix."

As I peered down into her eyes, I made my peace with God for saving the woman who'd brought me back to life.

The true definition of a phoenix rising meant to emerge from a catastrophe stronger and more powerful. But to me it meant rising from the dead where I'd been for half my life.

All because of a woman who refused to believe that I was anything but a hero.

* * *

One week later

"Are you certain you want to do this?" I asked Wren before climbing from the truck.

"I'm positive. Stop worrying about me." She gave me a sideways glance, the smile on her face one she'd had for days, although I wasn't certain how she'd managed after the ugliness of what we'd faced, unannounced visits from the FBI and the press camping outside our door. She'd handled it with grace and intelligence, never losing her cool.

I, on the other hand, had been a grumpy fool who'd wanted to protect her from the evils of the world. I'd confronted Bart before he and his buddies had been arrested, but they'd been smalltime players, replaced by professionals.

Now, I sat on the charred-out road leading to Sapphire Ridge, a location I'd avoided since the incident all those years ago. However, this was the right thing to do, letting go of the past in order to make way for the future.

She opened the door first, stepping out into the sunshine. While the fire had been considered contained for days, the area had remained blocked off to tourists and hikers for fear of unearthed dangers. We had the area to ourselves. In her arms was a bouquet of flowers at her insistence. I wasn't certain what she had planned on doing with them, but I didn't object. How could I?

As I replayed the last few days, everything still seemed like a whirlwind of information. Secrets. Lies. Greed. Power. At least the resorts were no longer on the city council's agenda.

And the ranch was all mine.

Still, none of that was as important as the woman standing next to me.

Sophia had trampled her in fear, leaving Wren with a mild concussion. But she'd been lucky, no bones broken or internal injuries. And Sophia had saved our lives, the horse receiving only minor burns.

The fire had been contained to the barn, another warning sent by the two people hired to try to force several individuals to sell.

From what Gage had told me, the owners of Shadowland had called the FBI, but someone from Blue Waters had learned they were being investigated, sending the assassins they'd hired to the ranch, trapping all four inside. Their planned visit had been documented, but as an ongoing investigation, the FBI wasn't obligated and had no plans of supplying any additional information at this point.

There were rumors all over town, speculation there were other members of the elite group of men who'd formed Blue Waters. There were even reports other resorts had been planned. Then I'd heard the resorts were merely legitimate businesses as fronts of the mafia. Nothing was concrete.

What Gage had been able to learn as factual was that the people involved had used blackmail and extortion in an attempt to get what they wanted. That had included two prominent members of the city council, who'd always voted in approval of the resort projects, even though it would mean destroying several historical pieces of property on top of the group of ranches that had been targeted.

At least the two assassins hired, both ex-military with one serving time for arson, had been arrested and were facing long prison terms.

As far as the other men who'd been arrested, Missoula would be embroiled in a circus for a long time to come.

"Are we close?" Wren asked.

She'd waited until I'd flanked her side, looking up at me then taking my hand. While I had a general comprehension of the location where Belle had been lost, the terrain was too scarred, and my memory too fucked up to know for certain. But Wren had reminded me that Belle's spirit wasn't in one location.

"Close enough."

We remained silent as I guided her through the fallen debris, watching carefully to make certain there weren't any remaining hotspots or other dangers.

"Why was the agent killed outside the cabin?" she asked out of the blue.

"From what Gage mentioned, the assassins hired were staying in another cabin not too far away. He and his deputies found an area where it appears they were burning various substances to try and get the formula right."

"Because it could get out of control."

"Exactly. I think he just was in the wrong place at the wrong time. I'll venture a guess he smelled the chemical and went to find out what it was."

While she nodded, I could tell she wasn't entirely convinced. Then again, neither was I. There were questions that wouldn't be answered within the next weeks or months, at least not until the information came out in trial. Or so we hoped.

She threw her hand in front of me, forcing us both to stop. "Do you hear that?"

"What are you talking about?" Forests were always eerily quiet after a horrific fire.

"Do you trust me?"

I laughed as she gave me her mischievous look. "With all my heart and soul. However, you need to tell me what you're doing."

"Nope. Follow me." She slipped her hand from mine, taking long strides over the fallen limbs. The woman had no fear, which could be a problem.

"You're a danger junkie," I told her as I followed.

"Ha! Come, little boy. You'll see."

Then I knew what she was talking about.

She'd found an active brook, water trickling over rocks. After giving me an I-told-you-so look, she moved to the side, crouching down. I advanced slowly, the ache in my heart entirely different than it had been all those years go. While still painful, it was slowly fading, replaced with more moments of happiness than nightmares.

I noticed she was picking at the rocks.

"What are you doing, looking for gold?"

She laughed, the sound floating toward the bright sky. "Hardly. Something much better. Come here."

How could I not smile around her? She had so much life. I moved to her side, hunkering down. When she pointed toward the water, a strange tingling sensation shifted through me.

"Life," she whispered, pointing to two perfect purple flowers that had been protected from the fire by mud and water. "This is the spot."

"For what?"

She rose to her feet, peeling away the tissue paper surrounding the flowers. As she started to pick the petals off one at a time, I watched in fascination. Then she held out her arm, allowing them to float in the light breeze toward the water.

"Where there is death, there is life. Where there is hate, there is love. And where there is despair, there is happiness. They can coexist, but only one can flourish. I choose life, love, and happiness." She tilted her head and a stream of sunlight shifted down from the sticklike trees, showering her skin with a luminescent glow. And for a few minutes, I knew I'd been right that she was an angel.

No, she was my angel.

Together we pulled the petals, allowing the light breeze to cover the brook with vibrant colors of the rainbow. She'd brought me back to my life. Now she was bringing it to the barren forest.

Six young men had ventured into a forest, underestimating the power of nature.

Six broken boys had left, angry at the world around them.

Anger.

Guilt.

Sadness.

Denial.

There was no way to change the past, but there was a chance at altering the future.

For me, the time of healing had begun.

* * *

Wren

Three weeks later

Life had a funny way of keeping you on your toes. Just when you think you know what's going to happen, everything changes. Often, the changes are painful or unwanted. In my mind I was celebrating the possibility of a wonderful future while mourning a past that had never been kind to me. The two were colliding, but I was determined not to dwell on things I couldn't change.

Besides, on this day Riggs Phoenix Wentworth needed me. I knew Gage and Hawk, Bryce and Snake were already here, promising to give testimony regarding his character since the Fishers had challenged him on his reckless and dangerous behavior, using that against him as well as his long hours in their affidavit. Their kindness and friendship gave me a needed sense of comfort since we'd learned the Fishers had pulled out all the stops, hiring a top-level attorney. Still, I felt confident we would be successful.

"Are you ready?" Phoenix asked as he parked the car. Both of us were glancing around us at the huge crowd.

I almost felt as if hands were wrapped around my throat, digging into my windpipe, but I would never let him know how anxious I was. He hadn't slept in three days, other than when I'd found him curled up in Justin's room.

"We are going to be just fine, Mr. Wentworth. Right, Justin?" I asked.

"Yay!" Justin clapped his hands. Even though Phoenix had tried to prepare him for what was going to happen, how can you explain to a five-year-old that his whole life might be turned upside down all over again? I was angry and bitter, doing everything I could to keep it together.

We'd done everything we could to avoid the reporters asking questions about my family. His family. They'd talked about his service record and shoved what had happened on Sapphire Ridge into his face. It had been a free for all for almost two weeks. Now this.

Sadly, as we stepped out of the car, I knew that the past wasn't ready to let me go just yet.

And certainly not without a fight.

"Ms. Tillman. What's it like to have your father, the senator behind bars?"

"Ms. Tillman. Did you know that your father was involved with Blue Waters?"

"Ms. Tillman. Did your father mention that he had several people murdered?"

The questions came fast and furious but at the most inappropriate time. I grabbed Justin, bringing him against me and when his little hand slipped into mine, I almost broke out into tears. It would be the first time since learning my father had been one of the men involved in trying to destroy Phoenix and his grandfather's legacy. While part of the reason had been because of the stupid vendetta he had against William Wentworth dating back almost fifteen years, the other part had been all about greed.

William had won a bid for land that he'd never wanted in the first place, something my father had had his eye on for two years. The betrayal of their friendship had left both men bitter, but to go to the lengths of attempting to get the ranch in retaliation disgusted me. Phoenix wrapped his arm around me, guiding me toward the courthouse.

"Mr. Wentworth, what does it feel like to be engaged to the daughter of a murderer?"

"Don't," I whispered, trying to keep Phoenix from reacting. I noticed Gage was heading in our direction, several of his deputies trying to disperse the crowd.

"I'm going to kill him," he hissed.

"Think of Justin." I tried to steer us away, but the same jerk jumped in front of us again.

"Ms. Tillman. Are you considered a beneficiary of your father's estate?" the reporter asked, jamming a microphone in my face.

"That's it," Phoenix growled, all my rugged man could take. As he issued a hard punch, the cracking sound as the reporter's nose was broken was caught on camera. In the next few minutes, all hell broke loose.

"Get her out of here," Phoenix barked to Gage.

"I'm getting you both out of here. Do not throw another punch," Gage snarled, doing everything he could to block the crowd as the asshole reporter who'd been hit was screaming that he was going to sue.

"Wrennie. Wrennie!" Justin squealed.

"It's alright, honey. Just hold my hand." Why had this happened? Why?

Justin clung to me, and I tried to push my way through the crowd. This was the last thing the little boy needed to see. Goddamn the judge for forcing him to be here. I was angry, finally at the end of my patience.

"Just stop. All of you. Now!" Somehow, my voice cut through the din. "This isn't the time or place. Don't you see there's a child here?" I pulled Justin into my arms just as he started to cry. Then I handed him off to Phoenix so that the fucking reporters could get a good shot of how much the two of them loved each other.

As Justin put his little arms around his father's neck, the cameras were rolling.

Gage guided us up the stairs, additional deputies already waiting side by side to help.

"It seemed you called out the cavalry," Phoenix managed.

"Anything for my best friend," Gage said, nodding as he opened the door. "Just, for the love of God, stay calm."

A feeling of dread rolled into my system as we headed for the assigned courtroom. Phoenix pulled me to him, still holding Justin as he cupped my face.

"We're a family. Whatever happens. Right?" He looked from Justin to me, and I couldn't stop a tear from rolling past my lashes.

As Justin clung to him and I held Phoenix's arm, we walked inside the courtroom together.

When Phoenix stopped short, I followed his gaze. "Who is it?" I asked.

"My parents." The glitch in his voice made me smile. I'd called his father, encouraging them to show up. At least the man had the decency to listen to me. "That's Stoker, my captain and Riker, the guy I saved from the helicopter. That's Colt and Maverick," he continued, the tone of his voice as if he was surprised just how many friends he had.

"See. You have a huge family that you didn't know about," I whispered.

He shook his head. "I love you."

"I love you."

Then I noticed Cammie and almost lost it. She nodded, her smile huge. The attorney she had started seeing had suggested a very good family attorney to help with the hearing.

We were led to our seats, and I glanced at the Fishers. They had the same looks on their faces as they did the night they almost took Justin away.

"All rise."

I felt sick inside, keeping one hand on Justin and the other on Phoenix.

As the proceedings began, there were far too many people that painted Phoenix as a dangerous man capable of doing anything. Reckless. Prone to violence. And when the fact he'd beaten up a reporter outside came up, it was all I could do not to lunge over the railing.

Then one by one, his friends and colleagues told a different side. One of courage and dedication, one of respect and admiration. But I could tell the judge wasn't swayed. He kept looking at Phoenix as if he was a bad man.

And I was angry.

Livid.

So when it was my turn, I wasn't the nice girl who always followed the rules.

I came out fighting.

And once I was given the chance, no one was going to shut me up.

"Ms. Tillman. Please state your full name and relationship to Mr. Wentworth."

"My name is Wren Carmella Tillman and I am his fiancée."

The basic questions were asked, the Fosters' attorney trying to sway the conversation. I did what I could to keep my patience, my eyes never leaving Phoenix.

"Ms. Tillman. Have you had the opportunity to see interactions with Mr. Wentworth and his son?" the judge interrupted.

"Yes, Your Honor, and I'm going to tell you the real story behind Riggs Phoenix Wentworth, a man with more integrity and honesty than I have met in my entire life. This is the kind of man who would give you the shirt off his back, never expecting it back. He's kind and giving, enough so he made certain on a cold, snowy night that a woman he didn't know was protected from the elements, brought to safety, at the risk of his own life. A man who thought nothing of racing through a burning wall of fire in order to save my life. And a man who made certain every night that he tucked his son into bed, reading him a story. A man who enjoyed taking his son to the park and the zoo, making certain he had a beautiful puppy to love and cherish and who hired the best nanny in the world to care for little Justin when he worked those long hours that the Fishers' attorney called proof of being an irresponsible father."

I took a pause, expecting to be challenged. When I wasn't, I turned my head, staring into Phoenix's eyes.

"Phoenix is the kind of father that every child should be lucky enough to have. And if you take him away from his beautiful baby boy, you will break him because he loves that child more than any possession, any person, or any job. And I couldn't be prouder to stand by his side as Justin becomes an amazing young man. Do not take them away from each other. That perfect, sweet little boy needs his father in his life every day."

There were murmurs in the courtroom then one of the smokejumpers shouted the Marine battle cry.

"Oorah!"

Several others did the same and I couldn't stop the tears from falling.

"Quiet. Quiet in this courtroom!" the judge bellowed, smashing his gavel down.

Finally, everyone settled down. Then the strangest, most beautiful thing happened.

Justin broke away from Phoenix, heading toward the judge, his eyes never leaving the man. I held my breath, uncertain what I should do. When the bailiff started to come forward, the judge threw out his hand.

"What do you have to say, young man?" the judge asked, leaning over his bench.

Justin's face wrinkled as I'd seen so many times before and he said clearly and without reservation, "Can I please go home with Daddy and Mommy so I can see my puppy?"

I pressed my hand over my mouth, unable to stop crying.

"We're going to see what we can do to make that happen, Justin," the judge said.

When I looked over at Phoenix, I witnessed something I never thought I'd see.

Tears were running down his face.

EPILOGUE

W ren

One month later

A beautiful spring day followed a night of rain.

My wedding day.

The windows were open in the room, the light breeze bringing in the scent of flowers. I'd never felt happier.

"You look beautiful," Cammie said breathlessly. "Perfect."

"I'm so glad you're here."

"Where do you think I'd be?" She laughed. I knew it been hard for her the last few weeks, but I'd also seen her flourish, getting a house of her own, lovingly decorating every room.

"How's that new hot man of yours?"

"Dreamy, but we're not here to talk about me." She giggled, her eyes lighting up. "I'm glad you'll finally get to meet him today."

"I'm glad you brought him."

We both heard a knock on the door and she winked. "I'll get it."

When Phoenix tried to walk in, she did her best to block him.

"You can't see her before the wedding!" Cammie hissed.

"Rules were meant to be broken," I told her. "Can I have a few minutes, dear sister of mine?" In his hand was a huge envelope. I felt like bad news was going to crash the wedding.

"Okay. Five minutes. Not a minute more," she told him as she walked out the door.

I couldn't help but laugh. "She's tough."

"Just like her sister." He walked closer, shaking his head. "You are gorgeous. Let's skip the wedding and go straight to the honeymoon part."

"Not a chance, buster. So, what do you have there?"

"Hmm... This? Oh, it just might be your wedding present. Do you want to see?" He held it over my head, his eyes twinkling.

"Of course I do, although it doesn't look like gold."

"It's much better." He grinned as he handed it to me.

I took a deep breath, easing open the flap then pulling out what looked like concept photographs. As I flipped from one to the other, I realized that I was looking at detailed computer-generated pictures of the sanctuary I'd described months before. "What is this?"

"Well, in truth it's only in the beginning stages but it's yours."

"I don't understand."

He lifted his eyebrows. "For the highly intelligent woman, you are…"

"Don't say it!" I laughed. "Seriously. What are you talking about?" I remained unblinking as he took a deep breath.

"The ranch is going to become an animal sanctuary. A lot of work needs to go into building the various facilities and I will need you full time working with the designers and architects since it's your vision, but I think you can handle it." His grin widened.

What? What did he just say?

"The ranch? But the animals? The staff?"

He shook his head. "The animals aren't going anywhere and I'm keeping all the employees and hiring other professionals. We'll have a full-time veterinarian on staff, several vet technicians. We have an advisor who'd planned a few of these across the country."

I remained in shock.

"I… I don't know what to say."

"Well, say something."

"You're serious," I whispered, my hand shaking as I glanced at the pictures again.

"Absolutely."

I flipped to a couple of other pages then flew toward him, wrapping my arms around his neck, unable to stop the tears. "I love you."

"You better cause I'm going to be around a lot."

"Meaning…" I pulled away, narrowing my eyes.

"Well, I took a leave of absence from the Zullies."

"Oh, Phoenix. You didn't need to do that."

"Yes, I did. I need to get to know my wife and my son. I learned the hard way what's most important in my life and I'm not going to fuck it up again."

"Did I tell you how fabulous you are?"

He cupped my chin, his eyes darting back and forth across mine. "My little bird. Thank you for coming into my life. Without you, none of this would matter nearly as much. You are in every breath I take, every scent and every taste."

"That's almost… romantic." I teased, unable to stop crying, my heart ready to explode.

"But," he said as he whipped me around, smacking me several times on the bottom. "You will learn to follow my rules. You break them all the time. Not that I'll mind keeping you in line. You thrive on discipline."

"Not a chance." I pulled away, whipping around to face him. When he beckoned with a single finger, a series of shivers coursed down my spine.

I had a feeling he was going to ravage me later.

"Come on, my little bird. Sophia is waiting to take us to our wedding."

So, on a cloudless day in May on the grassy knoll near a beautiful stream, we were married under a magnificent oak tree, our friends and family in celebration, Justin our ring-bearer. And just after we said our vows, a rainbow appeared somewhere over Sapphire Ridge.

And in my mind, it was Belle's gift...

The End

AFTERWORD

backside, then she'll scream my name as she takes every single inch of me.

This naughty girl needs to be put in her place, and I'm going to enjoy every moment of it.

Mustang

I tried to tell him how to run his ranch. Then he took off his belt.

When I heard a rumor about his ranch, I confronted Mustang about it. I thought I could go toe to toe with the big, tough former Marine, but I ended up blushing, sore, and very thoroughly used.

I told her it was going to hurt. I meant it.

Danni Brexton is a hot little number with a sharp tongue and a chip on her shoulder. She's the kind of trouble that needs to be ridden hard and put away wet, but only after a taste of my belt.

It will take more than just a firm hand and a burning bottom to tame this sassy spitfire, but I plan to keep her safe, sound, and screaming my name in bed whether she likes it or not. By the time I'm through with her, there won't be a shadow of a doubt in her mind that she belongs to me.

Nash

When he caught me on his property, he didn't call the police. He just took off his belt.

Nash caught me breaking into his shed while on the run from the mob, and when he demanded answers and obedience I gave him neither. Then he took off his belt and taught me in the most shameful way possible what happens to naughty girls who play games with a big, rough Marine.

She's mine to protect. That doesn't mean I'm going to be gentle with her.

Michelle doesn't just need a place to hide out. She needs a man who will bare her bottom and spank her until she is sore and sobbing whenever she puts herself at risk with reckless defiance, then shove her face into the sheets and make her scream his name with every savage climax.

She'll get all of that from me, and much, much more.

Austin

I offered this brute a ride. I ended up the one being ridden.

The first time I saw Austin, he was hitchhiking. I stopped to give him a lift, but I didn't end up taking this big, rough former Marine wherever he was heading. He was far too busy taking me.

She thought she was in charge. Then I took off my belt.

When Francesca Montgomery pulled up beside me, I didn't know who she was, but I knew what she needed and I gave it to her. Long, hard, and thoroughly, until she was screaming my name as she climaxed over and over with her quivering bare bottom still sporting the marks from my belt.

But someone wants to hurt her, and when someone tries to hurt what's mine, I take it personally.

BOOKS OF THE EAGLE FORCE SERIES

Debt of Honor

Isabella Adams is a brilliant scientist, but her latest discovery has made her a target of Russian assassins. I've been assigned to protect her, and when her reckless behavior puts her in danger she'll learn in the most shameful of ways what it means to be under the command of a Marine.

She can beg and plead as my belt lashes her bare backside, but the only mercy she'll receive is the chance to scream as she climaxes over and over with her well-spanked bottom still burning.

As my past returns to haunt me, it'll take every skill I've mastered to keep her alive.

She may be a national treasure, but she belongs to me now.

Debt of Loyalty

After she was kidnapped in broad daylight, I was hired to bring Willow Cavanaugh home, but as the daughter of a wealthy family she's used to getting what she wants rather than taking orders.

Too bad.

She'll do as she's told or she'll earn herself a stern, shameful reminder of who is in charge, but it will take more than just a well-spanked bare bottom to truly tame this feisty little rich girl.

She'll learn her place over my knee, but it's in my bed that I'll make her mine.

Debt of Sacrifice

When she witnessed a murder, it put Greer McDuff on a brutal cartel's radar… and on mine.

As a former Navy SEAL now serving with the elite Eagle Force, my assignment is to protect her by any means necessary. If that requires a stern reminder of who is in charge with her bottom bare over my knee and then an even more shameful lesson in my bed, then that's what she'll get.

There's just one problem.

The only place I know I can keep her safe is the ranch I left behind and vowed never to return.

BOOKS OF THE KINGS OF CORRUPTION SERIES

King of Wrath

After a car wreck on an icy winter morning, I had no idea the man who saved my life would turn out to be the heir to a powerful mafia family… let alone that I'd be forced into marrying him.

When this mysterious stranger sought to seduce me, I should have ignored the dark passion he ignited. Instead, I begged him to claim me as he stripped me bare and whipped me with his belt.

He was as savage as I was innocent, but it was only after he made me his that I learned the truth.

He's the head of the New York Cosa Nostra, and I belong to him now…

King of Cruelty

Constantine Thorn has been after me since I saw him kill a man nine years ago, and when he finally caught me he made me an offer I couldn't refuse. Marry him and he will protect me.

Only then did I learn that the man who made me his bride was the same monster I'd feared.

He's a brutal, heartless mafia boss and I wanted to hate the bastard, but with every stinging lash of his belt and every moment of helplessly intense passion, I fell deeper into the dark abyss.

He's the king of cruelty, and now I'm his queen.

BOOKS OF THE SINNERS AND SAINTS SERIES

Beautiful Villain

When I knocked on Kirill Sabatin's door, I didn't know he was the Kozlov Bratva's most feared enforcer. I didn't expect him to be the most terrifyingly sexy man I've ever laid eyes on either...

I told him off for making so much noise in the middle of the night, but if the crack of his palm against my bare bottom didn't wake everyone in the building my screams of climax certainly did.

I shouldn't have let him spank me, let alone seduce me. He's a dangerous man and I could easily end up in way over my head. But the moment I set eyes on those rippling, sweat-slicked muscles I knew I needed that beautiful villain to take me long and hard and savagely right then and there.

And he did.

Now I just have to hope him claiming me doesn't start a mob war...

Beautiful Sinner

When I first screamed his name in shameful surrender, Sevastian Kozlov was the enemy, the heir of a rival family who had just finished spanking me into submission after I dared to defy him.

Though he'd already claimed my body by the time he claimed me as his bride, no matter how desperately I long for his touch I vowed this beautiful sinner would never conquer my heart.

But it wasn't up to me...

Beautiful Seduction

In my late-night hunt for the perfect pastry, I never expected to be the victim of a brutal attack… or for a brooding, blue-eyed stranger to become my savior, tending to my wounds while easing my fears. The electricity exploded between us, turning into a night of incredible passion.

Only later did I learn that Valentin Vincheti is the heir to the New York Italian mafia empire.

Then he came to take me, and this time he wasn't gentle. I shouldn't have surrendered, but with each savage kiss and stinging stroke of his belt his beautiful seduction became more difficult to resist. But when one of his enemies sets his sights on me, will my secrets put our lives at risk?

Beautiful Obsession

After I was left at the altar, I turned what was meant to be the reception into an epic party. But when a handsome stranger asked me to dance, I wasn't prepared for the passion he ignited.

He told me he was a very bad man, but that only made my heart race faster as I lay bare and bound, my dress discarded and my bottom sore from a spanking, waiting for him to ravage me.

It was supposed to be just one night. No strings. Nothing to entangle me in his dangerous world.

But that was before I became his beautiful obsession…

Beautiful Devil

Kostya Baranov is an infamous assassin, a man capable of incredible savagery, but when I witnessed a mafia hit he didn't silence me with a bullet. He decided to make me his instead.

Taken prisoner and forced to obey or feel the sting of his belt, shameful lust for my captor soon wars with fury at what he has done to me… and what he keeps doing to me with every touch.

But though he may be a beautiful devil, it is my own family's secret which may damn us both.

BOOKS OF THE BENEDETTI EMPIRE SERIES

Cruel Prince

Catherine's father conspired to have my father killed, and that debt to the Benedetti family must be settled. Just as he took something from me, I will take something from him.

His daughter.

She will be mine to punish and ravage, but when she suffers it will not be for his sins.

It will be for my pleasure.

She will beg, but it will be for me to claim her in the most shameful ways imaginable.

She will scream, but it will be because she doesn't think she can bear another climax.

But when she surrenders at last, it will not be to her captor.

It will be to her husband.

Ruthless Prince

Alexandra is a senator's daughter, used to mingling in the company of the rich and powerful, but tonight she will learn that there are men who play by different rules.

Men like me.

I could romance her. I could seduce her and then carry her gently to my bed.

But that can wait. Tonight I'm going to wring one ruthless climax after another from her quivering body with her bottom burning from my belt and her throat sore from screaming.

She will know she is mine before she even knows she is my bride.

Savage Prince

Gillian's father may be a powerful Irish mob boss, but he owes a blood debt to my family, and when I came to collect I didn't ask permission before taking his daughter as payment.

It was not up to him… or to her.

I will make her my bride, but I am not the kind of man who will wait until our wedding night to bare her and claim what belongs to me. She will walk down the aisle wet, well-used, and sore.

Her dress will hide the marks from my belt that taught her the consequences of disobeying her husband, but nothing will hide her blushes as her arousal drips down her thighs with each step.

By the time she says her vows she will already be mine.

I belong to him now, and he plans to keep me.

King's Possession

Her father had to be taught what happens when you cross a King, but that isn't why Genevieve Rossi is sore, well-used, and waiting for me to claim her in the only way I haven't already.

She's sore because she thought she could embarrass me in public without being punished.

She's well-used because after I spanked her I wanted more, and I take what I want.

She's waiting for me in my bed because she's my bride, and tonight is our wedding night.

I'm not going to be gentle with her, but when she wakes up tomorrow morning wet and blushing her cheeks won't be crimson because of the shameful things I did to her naked, quivering body.

It will be because she begged for all of them.

King's Toy

Vincenzo King thought I knew something about a man who betrayed him, but that isn't why I'm on my way to New Orleans well-used and sore with my backside still burning from his belt.

When he bared and punished me maybe it was just business, but what came after was not.

It was savage, it was shameful, and it was very, very personal.

I'm his toy now, and not the kind you keep in its box on the shelf.

He's going to play rough with me.

He's going to get me all wet and dirty.

Then he's going to do it all again tomorrow.

King's Demands

Julieta Morales hoped to escape an unwanted marriage, but the moment she got into my car her fate was sealed. She will have a husband, but it won't be the cartel boss her father chose for her.

It will be me.

But I'm not the kind of man who takes his bride gently amid rose petals on her wedding night. She'll learn to satisfy her King's demands with her bottom burning and her hair held in my fist.

She'll promise obedience when she speaks her vows, but she'll be mastered long before then.

King's Temptation

I didn't think I needed Dimitri Kristoff's protection, but it wasn't up to me. With a kingpin from a rival family coming after me, he took charge, took off his belt, and then took what he wanted.

He knows I'm not used to doing as I'm told. He just doesn't care.

The stripes seared across my bare bottom left me sore and sorry, but it was what came after that truly left me shaken. The princess of the King family shouldn't be on her knees for anyone, let alone this Bratva brute who has decided to claim for himself what he was meant to safeguard.

Nobody gave me to him, but I'm his anyway.

Now he's going to make sure I know it.

She will be used mercilessly, over and over, and every brutal climax will remind her of the humiliating truth: she never even had a chance against me. Her body always knew its master.

Claimed as Revenge

Valencia Rivera became mine the moment her father broke the agreement he made with me. She thought she had a say in the matter, but my belt across her beautiful bottom taught her otherwise and a night spent screaming her surrender into the sheets left her in no doubt she belongs to me.

Using her hard and often will not be all it takes to tame her properly, but it will be a good start…

Made to Beg

Sierra Fox showed up at my door to ask for my protection, and I gave it to her… for a price. She belongs to me now, and I'm going to use her beautiful body as thoroughly as I please. The only thing for her to decide is how sore her cute little bottom will be when I'm through claiming her.

She came to me begging for help, but as her moans and screams grow louder with every brutal climax, we both know it won't be long before she begs me for something far more shameful.

BOOKS OF THE EDGE OF DARKNESS SERIES

Dark Stranger

On a dark, rainy night, I received a phone call. I shouldn't have answered it... but I did.

The things he says he'll do to me are far from sweet, this man I know only by his voice.

They're so filthy I blush crimson just hearing them... and yet still I answer, my panties always soaked the moment the phone rings. But this isn't going to end when I decide it's gone too far...

I can tell him to leave me alone, but I know it won't keep him away. He's coming for me, and when he does he's going to make me his in all the rough, shameful ways he promised he would.

And I'll be wet and ready for him... whether I want to be or not.

Dark Predator

She thinks I'm seducing her, but this isn't romance. It's something much more shameful.

Eden tried to leave the mafia behind, but someone far more dangerous has set his sights on her.

Me.

She was meant to be my revenge against an old enemy, but I decided to make her mine instead.

She'll moan as my belt lashes her quivering bottom and writhe as I claim her in the filthiest of ways, but that's just the beginning. When I'm done, it won't be just her body that belongs to me.

I'll own her heart and soul too.

BOOKS OF THE DARK OVERTURE SERIES

Indecent Invitation

I shouldn't be here.

My clothes shouldn't be scattered around the room, my bottom shouldn't be sore, and I certainly shouldn't be screaming into the sheets as a ruthless tycoon takes everything he wants from me.

I shouldn't even know Houston Powers at all, but I was in a bad spot and I was made an offer.

A shameful, indecent offer I couldn't refuse.

I was desperate, I needed the money, and I didn't have a choice. Not a real one, anyway.

I'm here because I signed a contract, but I'm his because he made me his.

Illicit Proposition

I should have known better.

His proposition was shameful. So shameful I threw my drink in his face when I heard it.

Then I saw the look in his eyes, and I knew I'd made a mistake.

I fought as he bared me and begged as he spanked me, but it didn't matter. All I could do was moan, scream, and climax helplessly for him as he took everything he wanted from me.

By the time I signed the contract, I was already his.

Unseemly Entanglement

I was warned about Frederick Duvall. I was told he was dangerous. But I never suspected that meeting the billionaire advertising mogul to discuss a business proposition would end with me bent over a table with my dress up and my panties down for a shameful lesson in obedience.

That should have been it. I should have told him what he could do with his offer and his money.

But I didn't.

I could say it was because two million dollars is a lot of cash, but as I stand before him naked, bound, and awaiting the sting of his cane for daring to displease him, I know that's not the truth.

I'm not here because he pays me. I'm here because he owns me.

BOOKS OF THE CLUB DARKNESS SERIES

Bent to His Will

Even the most powerful men in the world know better than to cross me, but Autumn Sutherland thought she could spy on me in my own club and get away with it. Now she must be punished.

She tried to expose me, so she will be exposed. Bare, bound, and helplessly on display, she'll beg for mercy as my strap lashes her quivering bottom and my crop leaves its burning welts on her most intimate spots. Then she'll scream my name as she takes every inch of me, long and hard.

When I am done with her, she won't just be sore and shamefully broken. She will be mine.

Broken by His Hand

Sophia Russo tried to keep away from me, but just thinking about what I would do to her left her panties drenched. She tried to hide it, but I didn't let her. I tore those soaked panties off, spanked her bare little bottom until she had no doubt who owns her, and then took her long and hard.

She begged and screamed as she came for me over and over, but she didn't learn her lesson…

She didn't just come back for more. She thought she could disobey me and get away with it.

This time I'm not just going to punish her. I'm going to break her.

Bound by His Command

Willow danced for the rich and powerful at the world's most exclusive club… until tonight.

Tonight I told her she belongs to me now, and no other man will touch her again.

Tonight I ripped her soaked panties from her beautiful body and taught her to obey with my belt.

Tonight I took her as mine, and I won't be giving her up.

on his face to the fact that mobsters call him Blade. But I was drawn like a moth to a flame, and I ended up burnt... and blushing, sore, and thoroughly used.

Now he's taken it upon himself to protect me from men like the ones we both tried to leave in our past. He's going to make me his whether I like it or not... but I think I'm going to like it.

Prey

Within moments of setting eyes on Sophia Waters, I was certain of two things. She was going to learn what happens to bad girls who cheat at cards, and I was going to be the one to teach her.

But there was one thing I didn't know as I reddened that cute little bottom and then took her long and hard and oh so shamefully: I wasn't the only one who didn't come here for a game of cards.

I came to kill a man. It turns out she came to protect him.

Nobody keeps me from my target, but I'm in no rush. Not when I'm enjoying this game of cat and mouse so much. I'll even let her catch me one day, and as she screams my name with each brutal climax she'll finally realize the truth. She was never the hunter. She was always the prey.

Given

Stephanie Michaelson was given to me, and she is mine. The sooner she learns that, the less often her cute little bottom will end up well-punished and sore as she is reminded of her place.

But even as she promises obedience with tears running down her cheeks, I know it isn't the sting of my belt that will truly tame her. It is what comes next that will leave her in no doubt she belongs to me. That part will be long, hard, and shameful... and I will make her beg for all of it.

Dangerous Stranger

I came to Spain hoping to start a new life away from dangerous men, but then I met Rafael Santiago. Now I'm not just caught up in the affairs of a mafia boss, I'm being forced into his car.

When I saw something I shouldn't have, Rafael took me captive, stripped me bare, and punished me until he felt certain I'd told him everything I knew about his organization… which was nothing at all. Then he offered me his protection in return for the right to use me as he pleases.

Now that I belong to him, his plans for me are more shameful than I could have ever imagined.

Indebted

After her father stole from me, I could have left Alessandra Toro in jail for a crime she didn't commit. But I have plans for her. A deal with the judge—the kind only a man like me can arrange—made her my captive, and she will pay her father's debt with her beautiful body.

She will try to run, of course, but it won't be the law that comes after her. It will be me.

The sting of my belt across her quivering bare bottom will teach Alessandra the price of defiance, but it is the far more shameful penance that follows which will truly tame her.

Taken

When Winter O'Brien was given to me, she thought she had a say in the matter. She was wrong.

She is my bride. Mine to claim, mine to punish, and mine to use as shamefully as I please. The sting of my belt on her bare bottom will teach her to obey, but obedience is just the beginning.

I will demand so much more.

Bratva's Captive

I told Chloe Kingstrom that getting close to me would be dangerous, and she should keep her distance. The moment she disobeyed and followed me into that bar, she became mine.

Now my enemies are after her, but it's not what they would do to her she should worry about.

It's what I'm going to do to her.

My belt across her bare backside will teach her obedience, but what comes after will be different.

She's going to blush, beg, and scream with every climax as she's ravaged more thoroughly than she can imagine. Then I'm going to flip her over and claim her in an even more shameful way.

If she's a good girl, I might even let her enjoy it.

Hunted

Hope Gracen was just another target to be tracked down... until I caught her.

When I discovered I'd been lied to, I carried her off.

She'll tell me the truth with her bottom still burning from my belt, but that isn't why she's here.

I took her to protect her. I'm keeping her because she's mine.

Theirs as Payment

Until mere moments ago, I was a doctor heading home after my shift at the hospital. But that was before I was forced into the back seat of an SUV, then bared and spanked for trying to escape.

Now I'm just leverage for the Cabello brothers to use against my father, but it isn't the thought of being held hostage by these brutes that has my heart racing and my whole body quivering.

It is the way they're looking at me...

Like they're about to tear my clothes off and take turns mounting me like wild beasts.

Like they're going to share me, using me in ways more shameful than I can even imagine.

Like they own me.

Ruthless Acquisition

I knew the shameful stakes when I bet against these bastards. I just didn't expect to lose.

Now they've come to collect their winnings.

But they aren't just planning to take a belt to my bare bottom for trying to run and then claim everything they're owed from my naked, helpless body as I blush, beg, and scream for them.

They've acquired me, and they plan to keep me.

Bound by Contract

I knew I was in trouble the moment Gregory Steele called me into his office, but I wasn't expecting to end up stripped bare and bent over his desk for a painful lesson from his belt.

Taking a little bit of money here and there might have gone unnoticed in another organization, but stealing from one of the most powerful mafia bosses on the West Coast has consequences.

It doesn't matter why I did it. The only thing that matters now is what he's going to do to me.

I have no doubt he will use me shamefully, but he didn't make me sign that contract just to show me off with my cheeks blushing and my bottom sore under the scandalous outfit he chose for me.

Now that I'm his, he plans to keep me.

Dangerous Addiction

I went looking for a man working with my enemies. When I found only her instead, I should have just left her alone... or maybe taken what I wanted from her and then left... but I didn't.

I couldn't.

So I carried her off to keep for myself.

She didn't make it easy for me, and that earned her a lesson in obedience. A shameful one.

But as her bare bottom reddens under my punishing hand I can see her arousal dripping down her quivering thighs, and no matter how much she squirms and sobs and begs we both know exactly what she needs, and we both know as soon as this spanking is over I'm going to give it to her.

Hard.

Auction House

When I went undercover to investigate a series of murders with links to Steele Franklin's auction house operation, I expected to be sold for the humiliating use of one of his fellow billionaires.

But he wanted me for himself.

No contract. No agreed upon terms. No say in the matter at all except whether to surrender to his shameful demands without a fight or make him strip me bare and spank me into submission first.

I chose the second option, but as one devastating climax after another is forced from my naked, quivering body, what scares me isn't the thought of him keeping me locked up in a cage forever.

It's knowing he won't need to.

Interrogated

As Liam McGinty's belt lashes my bare backside, it isn't the burning sting or the humiliating awareness that my body's surrender is on full display for this ruthless mobster that shocks me.

It's the fact that this isn't a scene from one of my books.

I almost can't process the fact that I'm really riding in the back of a luxury SUV belonging to the most powerful Irish mafia boss in New York—the man I've written so much about—with my cheeks blushing, my bottom sore inside and out, and my arousal soaking the seat beneath me.

But whether I can process it or not, I'm his captive now.

Maybe he'll let me go when he's gotten the answers he needs and he's used me as he pleases.

Or maybe he'll keep me...

Vow of Seduction

Alexander Durante, Brogan Lancaster, and Daniel Norwood are powerful, dangerous men, but that won't keep them safe from me. Not after they let my brother take the fall for their crimes.

I spent years preparing for my chance at revenge. But things didn't go as planned...

Now I'm naked, bound, and helpless, waiting to be used and punished as these brutes see fit, and yet what's on my mind isn't how to escape all of the shameful things they're going to do to me.

It's whether I even want to...

Brutal Heir

When I went to an author convention, I didn't expect to find myself enjoying a rooftop meal with the sexiest cover model in the business, let alone screaming his name in bed later that night.

I didn't plan to be targeted by assassins, rushed to a helicopter under cover of armed men, and then spirited away to his home country with my bottom still burning from a spanking either, but it turns out there are some really important things I didn't know about Diavolo Montoya...

Like the fact that he's the heir to a notorious crime syndicate.

I should hate him, but even as his prisoner our connection is too intense to ignore, and I'm beginning to realize that what began as a moment of passion is going to end with me as his.

Forever.

Bed of Thorns

Hardened by years spent in prison for a crime he didn't commit, Edmond Montego is no longer the gentle man I remember. When he came for me, he didn't just take me for the very first time.

He claimed my virgin body with a savagery that left me screaming… and he made me beg for it.

I should have run when I had the chance, but with every lash of his belt, every passionate kiss, and every brutal climax, I fell more and more under his spell.

But he has a dark secret, and if we're not careful, we'll lose everything… including our lives.

BOOKS OF THE DANGEROUS BUSINESS SERIES

Persuasion

Her father stole something from the mob and they hired me to get it back, but that's not the real reason Giliana Worthington is locked naked in a cage with her bottom well-used and sore.

I brought her here so I could take my time punishing her, mastering her, and ravaging her helpless, quivering body over and over again as she screams and moans and begs for more.

I didn't take her as a hostage. I took her because she is mine.

Bad Men

I thought I could run away from the marriage the mafia arranged for me, but I ended up held prisoner in a foreign country by someone far more dangerous than the man I tried to escape.

Then Jack and Diego came for me.

They didn't ask if I wanted to be theirs. They just took me.

I ran, but they caught me, stripped me bare, and punished me in the most shameful way possible.

Now they're going to share me, and they're not going to be gentle about it.

BOOKS OF THE ALPHA DYNASTY SERIES

Unchained Beast

As the firstborn of the Dupree family, I have spent my life building the wealth and power of our mafia empire while keeping our dark secret hidden and my savage hunger at bay. But the beast within me cannot be chained forever, and I must claim a mate before I lose control completely…

That is why Coraline LeBlanc is mine.

When I mount and ravage her, it won't be because I want her. It will be because I need her.

But that doesn't mean I won't enjoy stripping her bare and spanking her until she surrenders, then making her beg and scream with every desperate climax as I take what belongs to me.

The beast will claim her, but I will keep her.

Savage Brute

It wasn't his mafia birthright that made Dax Dupree a monster. Years behind bars and a brutal war with a rival organization made him hard as steel, but the beast he can barely control was always there, and without a mate to mark and claim it would soon take hold of him completely.

I didn't know that when he showed up at my bar after closing and spanked me until I was wet and shamefully ready for him to mount and ravage me, or even when I woke the next morning with my throat sore from screaming and his seed still drying on my thighs. But I know it now.

Because I'm his mate.

Ruthless Monster

When Esme Rawlings looks at me, she sees many things. A ruthless mob boss. A key witness to the latest murder in an ongoing turf war. A guardian angel who saved her from a hitman's bullet.

But when I look at her, I see just one thing.

My mate.

She can investigate me as thoroughly as she feels necessary, prying into every aspect of my family's vast mafia empire, but the only truth she really needs to know about me she will learn tonight with her bare bottom burning and her protests drowned out by her screams of climax.

I take what belongs to me.

Ravenous Predator

Suzette Barker thought she could steal from the most powerful mafia boss in Philadelphia. My belt across her naked backside taught her otherwise, but as tears run down her cheeks and her arousal glistens on her bare thighs, there is something more important she will understand soon.

Kneeling at my feet and demonstrating her remorseful surrender in the most shameful way possible won't bring an end to this, nor will her screams of climax as I take her long and hard. She'll be coming with me and I'll be mounting and savagely rutting her as often as I please.

Not just because she owes me.

Because she's my mate.

Merciless Savage

Christoff Dupree doesn't strike me as the kind of man who woos a woman gently, so when I saw the flowers on my kitchen table I knew it wasn't just a gesture of appreciation for saving his life.

This ruthless mafia boss wasn't seducing me. Those roses mean that I belong to him now.

That I'm his to spank into shameful submission before he mounts me and claims me savagely.

That I'm his mate.

BOOKS OF THE ALPHA BEASTS SERIES

King's Mate

Her scent drew me to her, but something deeper and more powerful told me she was mine. Something that would not be denied. Something that demanded I claim her then and there.

I took her the way a beast takes his mate. Roughly. Savagely. Without mercy or remorse.

She will run, and when she does she will be punished, but it is not me that she fears. Every quivering, desperate climax reminds her that her body knows its master, and that terrifies her.

She knows I am not a gentle king, and she will scream for me as she learns her place.

Beast's Claim

Raven is not one of my kind, but the moment I caught her scent I knew she belonged to me.

She is my mate, and when I claim her it will not be gentle. She can fight me, but her pleas for mercy as she is punished will soon give way to screams of climax as she is mounted and rutted.

By the time I am finished with her, the evidence of her body's surrender will be mingled with my seed as it drips down her bare thighs. But she will be more than just sore and utterly spent.

She will be mine.

Alpha's Mate

I didn't ask Nicolina to be my mate. It was not up to her. An alpha takes what belongs to him.

She will plead for mercy as she is bared and punished for daring to run from me, but her screams as she is claimed and rutted will be those of helpless climax as her body surrenders to its master.

She is mine, and I'm going to make sure she knows it.

one climax after another until she is utterly spent and satisfied.

But something shady is going on behind the scenes at Dominick's company, and when Jenna draws the wrong conclusion from a poorly written article about him and creates an embarrassing public scene, will she end up not only costing them both their jobs but losing her daddy as well?

Conquering Their Mate

For years the Cenzans have cast a menacing eye on Earth, but it still came as a shock to be captured, stripped bare, and claimed as a mate by their leader and his most trusted warriors.

It infuriates me to be punished for the slightest defiance and forced to submit to these alien brutes, but as I'm led naked through the corridors of their ship, my well-punished bare bottom and my helpless arousal both fully on display, I cannot help wondering how long it will be until I'm kneeling at the feet of my mates and begging them take me as shamefully as they please.

Captured and Kept

Since her career was knocked off track in retaliation for her efforts to expose a sinister plot by high-ranking government officials, reporter Danielle Carver has been stuck writing puff pieces in a small town in Oregon. Desperate for a serious story, she sets out to investigate the rumors she's been hearing about mysterious men living in the mountains nearby. But when she secretly follows them back to their remote cabin, the ruggedly handsome beasts don't take kindly to her snooping around, and Dani soon finds herself stripped bare for a painful, humiliating spanking.

Their rough dominance arouses her deeply, and before long she is blushing crimson as they take turns using her beautiful body as thoroughly and shamefully as they please. But when Dani uncovers the true reason for their presence in the area, will more than just her career be at risk?

Taming His Brat

It's been years since Cooper Dawson left her small Texas hometown, but after her stubborn defiance gets her fired from two jobs in a row, she knows something definitely needs to change. What she doesn't expect, however, is for her sharp tongue and arrogant attitude to land her over the knee of a stern, ruggedly sexy cowboy for a painful, embarrassing, and very public spanking.

Rex Sullivan cannot deny being smitten by Cooper, and the fact that she is in desperate need of his belt across her bare backside only makes the war-hardened ex-Marine more determined to tame the beautiful, fiery redhead. It isn't long before she's screaming his name as he shows her just how hard and roughly a cowboy can ride a headstrong filly. But Rex and Cooper both have secrets, and when the demons of their past rear their ugly heads, will their romance be torn apart?

Capturing Their Mate

I thought the Cenzan invaders could never find me here, but I was wrong. Three of the alien brutes came to take me, and before I ever set foot aboard their ship I had already been stripped bare, spanked thoroughly, and claimed more shamefully then I would have ever thought possible.

They have decided that a public example must be made of me, and I will be punished and used in the most humiliating ways imaginable as a warning to anyone who might dare to defy them. But I am no ordinary breeder, and the secrets hidden in my past could change their world… or end it.

Rogue

Tracking down cyborgs is my job, but this time I'm the one being hunted. This rogue machine has spent most of his life locked up, and now that he's on the loose he has plans for me...

He isn't just going to strip me, punish me, and use me. He will take me longer and harder than any human ever could, claiming me so thoroughly that I will be left in no doubt who owns me.

No matter how shamefully I beg and plead, my body will be ravaged again and again with pleasure so intense it terrifies me to even imagine, because that is what he was built to do.

Roughneck

When I took a job on an oil rig to escape my scheming stepfather's efforts to set me up with one of his business cronies, I knew I'd be working with rugged men. What I didn't expect is to find myself bent over a desk, my cheeks soaked with tears and my bare thighs wet for a very different reason, as my well-punished bottom is thoroughly used by a stern, infuriatingly sexy roughneck.

Even though I should have known better than to get sassy with a firm-handed cowboy, let alone a tough-as-nails former Marine, there's no denying that learning the hard way was every bit as hot as it was shameful. But a sore, welted backside is just the start of his plans for me, and no matter how much I blush to admit it, I know I'm going to take everything he gives me and beg for more.

Hunting Their Mate

As far as I'm concerned, the Cenzans will always be the enemy, and there can be no peace while they remain on our planet. I planned to make them pay for invading our world, but I was hunted down and captured by two of their warriors with the help of a battle-hardened former Marine. Now I'm the one who is going to pay, as the three of them punish me, shame me, and share me.

Though the thought of a fellow human taking the side of these alien brutes enrages me, that is far from the worst of it. With every searing stroke of the strap that lands across my bare bottom, with every savage thrust as I am claimed over and over, and with every screaming climax, it is made more clear that it is my own quivering, thoroughly used body which has truly betrayed me.

Primitive

I was sent to this world to help build a new Earth, but I was shocked by what I found here. The men of this planet are not just primitive savages. They are predators, and I am now their prey…

The government lied to all of us. Not all of the creatures who hunted and captured me are aliens. Some of them were human once, specimens transformed in labs into little more than feral beasts.

I fought, but I was thrown over a shoulder and carried off. I ran, but I was caught and punished. Now they are going to claim me, share me, and use me so roughly that when the last screaming climax has been wrung from my naked, helpless body, I wonder if I'll still know my own name.

Harvest

The Centurions conquered Earth long before I was born, but they did not come for our land or our resources. They came for mates, women deemed suitable for breeding. Women like me.

Three of the alien brutes decided to claim me, and when I defied them, they made a public example of me, punishing me so thoroughly and shamefully I might never stop blushing.

But now, as my virgin body is used in every way possible, I'm not sure I want them to stop…

Torched

I work alongside firefighters, so I know how to handle musclebound roughnecks, but Blaise Tompkins is in a league of his own. The night we met, I threw a glass of wine in his face, then ended up shoved against the wall with my panties on the floor and my arousal dripping down my thighs, screaming out climax after shameful climax with my well-punished bottom still burning.

I've got a series of arsons to get to the bottom of, and finding out that the infuriatingly sexy brute who spanked me like a naughty little girl will be helping me with the investigation seemed like the last thing I needed, until somebody hurled a rock through my window in an effort to scare me away from the case. Now having a big, strong man around doesn't seem like such a bad idea...

Fertile

The men who hunt me were always brutes, but now lust makes them barely more than beasts.

When they catch me, I know what comes next.

I will fight, but my need to be bred is just as strong as theirs is to breed. When they strip me, punish me, and use me the way I'm meant to be used, my screams will be the screams of climax.

Hostage

I knew going after one of the most powerful mafia bosses in the world would be dangerous, but I didn't anticipate being dragged from my apartment already sore, sorry, and shamefully used.

My captors don't just plan to teach me a lesson and then let me go. They plan to share me, punish me, and claim me so ruthlessly I'll be screaming my submission into the sheets long before they're through with me. They took me as a hostage, but they'll keep me as theirs.

Defiled

I was born to rule, but for her sake I am banished, forced to wander the Earth among mortals. Her virgin body will pay the price for my protection, and it will be a shameful price indeed.

Stripped, punished, and ravaged over and over, she will scream with every savage climax.

She will be defiled, but before I am done with her she will beg to be mine.

Kept

On the run from corrupt men determined to silence me, I sought refuge in his cabin. I ate his food, drank his whiskey, and slept in his bed. But then the big bad bear came home and I learned the hard way that sometimes Goldilocks ends up with her cute little bottom well-used and sore.

He stripped me, spanked me, and ravaged me in the most shameful way possible, but then this rugged brute did something no one else ever has before. He made it clear he plans to keep me…

Auctioned

Twenty years ago the Malzeons saved us when we were at the brink of self-annihilation, but there was a price for their intervention. They demanded humans as servants… and as pets.

Only criminals were supposed to be offered to the aliens for their use, but when I defied Earth's government, asking questions that no one else would dare to ask, I was sold to them at auction.

I was bought by two of their most powerful commanders, rivals who nonetheless plan to share me. I am their property now, and they intend to tame me, train me, and enjoy me thoroughly.

But I have information they need, a secret guarded so zealously that discovering it cost me my freedom, and if they do not act quickly enough both of our worlds will soon be in grave danger.

Hard Ride

When I snuck into Montana Cobalt's house, I was looking for help learning to ride like him, but what I got was his belt across my bare backside. Then with tears still running down my cheeks and arousal dripping onto my thighs, the big brute taught me a much more shameful lesson.

Montana has agreed to train me, but not just for the rodeo. He's going to break me in and put me through my paces, and then he's going to show me what it means to be ridden rough and dirty.

Carnal

For centuries my kind have hidden our feral nature, our brute strength, and our carnal instincts. But this human female is my mate, and nothing will keep me from claiming and ravaging her.

She is mine to tame and protect, and if my belt doesn't teach her to obey then she'll learn in a much more shameful fashion. Either way, her surrender will be as complete as it is inevitable.

Bounty

After I went undercover to take down a mob boss and ended up betrayed, framed, and on the run, Harper Rollins tried to bring me in. But instead of collecting a bounty, she earned herself a hard spanking and then an even rougher lesson that left her cute bottom sore in a very different way.

She's not one to give up without a fight, but that's fine by me. It just means I'll have plenty more chances to welt her beautiful backside and then make her scream her surrender into the sheets.

Beast

Primitive, irresistible need compelled him to claim me, but it was more than mere instinct that drove this alien beast to punish me for my defiance and then ravage me thoroughly and savagely. Every screaming climax was a brand marking me as his, ensuring I never forget who I belong to.

He's strong enough to take what he wants from me, but that's not why I surrendered so easily as he stripped me bare, pushed me up against the wall, and made me his so roughly and shamefully.

It wasn't fear that forced me to submit. It was need.

Gladiator

Xander didn't just win me in the arena. The alien brute claimed me there too, with my punished bottom still burning and my screams of climax almost drowned out by the roar of the crowd.

Almost…

Victory earned him freedom and the right to take me as his mate, but making me truly his will mean more than just spanking me into shameful surrender and then rutting me like a wild beast. Before he carries me off as his prize, the dark truth that brought me here must be exposed at last.

Big Rig

Alexis Harding is used to telling men exactly what she thinks, but she's never had a roughneck like me as a boss before. On my rig, I make the rules and sassy little girls get stripped bare, bent over my desk, and taught their place, first with my belt and then in a much more shameful way.

She'll be sore and sorry long before I'm done with her, but the arousal glistening on her thighs reveals the truth she would rather keep hidden. She needs it rough, and that's how she'll get it.

Warriors

I knew this was a primitive planet when I landed, but nothing could have prepared me for the rough beasts who inhabit it. The sting of their prince's firm hand on my bare bottom taught me my place in his world, but it was what came after that truly demonstrated his mastery over me.

This alien brute has granted me his protection and his help with my mission, but the price was my total submission to both his shameful demands and those of his second in command as well.

But it isn't the savage way they make use of my quivering body that terrifies me the most. What leaves me trembling is the thought that I may never leave this place... because I won't want to.

Owned

With a ruthless, corrupt billionaire after me, Crockett, Dylan, and Wade are just the men I need. Rough men who know how to keep a woman safe... and how to make her scream their names.

But the Hell's Fury MC doesn't do charity work, and their help will come at a price.

A shameful price...

They aren't just going to bare me, punish me, and then do whatever they want with me.

They're going to make me beg for it.

Seized

Delaney Archer got herself mixed up with someone who crossed us, and now she's going to find out just how roughly and shamefully three bad men like us can make use of her beautiful body.

She can plead for mercy, but it won't stop us from stripping her bare and spanking her until she's sore, sobbing, and soaking wet. Our feisty little captive is going to take everything we give her, and she'll be screaming our names with every savage climax long before we're done with her.

Cruel Masters

I thought I understood the risks of going undercover to report on billionaires flaunting their power, but these men didn't send lawyers after me. They're going to deal with me themselves.

Now I'm naked aboard their private plane, my backside already burning from one of their belts, and these three infuriatingly sexy bastards have only just gotten started teaching me my place.

I'm not just going to be punished, shamed, and shared. I'm going to be mastered.

Hard Men

My father's will left his company to me, but the three roughnecks who ran it for him have other ideas. They're owed a debt and they mean to collect on it, but it's not money these brutes want.

It's me.

In return for protection from my father's enemies, I will be theirs to share. But these are hard men, and they don't just intend to punish my defiance and use me as shamefully as they please.

They plan to master me completely.

Rough Ride

As I hear the leather slide through the loops of his pants, I know what comes next. Jake Travers is going to blister my backside. Then he's going to ride me the way only a rodeo champion can.

Plenty of men who thought they could put me in my place have learned the hard way that I was more than they could handle, and when Jake showed up I was sure he would be no different.

I was wrong.

When I pushed him, he bared and spanked me in front of a bar full of people.

I should have let it go at that, but I couldn't.

That's why he's taking off his belt…

Primal Instinct

Ruger Jameson can buy anything he wants, but that's not the reason I'm his to use as he pleases.

He's a former Army Ranger accustomed to having his orders followed, but that's not why I obey him.

He saved my life after our plane crashed, but I'm not on my knees just to thank him properly.

I'm his because my body knows its master.

I do as I'm told because he blisters my bare backside every time I dare to do otherwise.

I'm at his feet because I belong to him and I plan to show it in the most shameful way possible.

Captor

I was supposed to be safe from the lottery. Set apart for a man who would treat me with dignity.

But as I'm probed and examined in the most intimate, shameful ways imaginable while the hulking alien king who just spanked me looks on approvingly, I know one thing for certain.

This brute didn't end up with me by chance. He wanted me, so he found a way to take me.

He'll savor every blush as I stand bare and on display for him, every plea for mercy as he punishes my defiance, and every quivering climax as he slowly masters my virgin body.

I'll be his before he even claims me.

Rough and Dirty

Wrecking my cheating ex's truck with a bat might have made me feel better… if the one I went after had actually belonged to him, instead of to the burly roughneck currently taking off his belt.

Now I'm bent over in a parking lot with my bottom burning as this ruggedly sexy bastard and his two equally brutish friends take turns reddening my ass, and I can tell they're just getting started.

That thought shouldn't excite me, and I certainly shouldn't be imagining all the shameful things these men might do to me. But what I should or shouldn't be thinking doesn't matter anyway.

They can see the arousal glistening on my thighs, and they know I need it rough and dirty…

His to Take

When Zadok Vakan caught me trying to escape his planet with priceless stolen technology, he didn't have me sent to the mines. He made sure I was stripped bare and sold at auction instead.

Then he bought me for himself.

Even as he punishes me for the slightest hint of defiance and then claims me like a beast, indulging every filthy desire his savage nature can conceive, I swear I'll never surrender.

But it doesn't matter.

I'm already his, and we both know it.

Tyrant

When I accepted a lucrative marketing position at his vineyard, Montgomery Wolfe made the terms of my employment clear right from the start. Follow his rules or face the consequences.

That's why I'm bent over his desk, doing my best to hate him as his belt lashes my bare bottom.

I shouldn't give in to this tyrant. I shouldn't yield to his shameful demands.

Yet I can't resist the passion he sets ablaze with every word, every touch, and every brutally possessive kiss, and I know before long my body will surrender to even his darkest needs…

Filthy Rogue

Losing my job to a woman who slept her way to the top was bad enough, and that was before my car broke down as I drove cross country to start over. Having to be rescued by an infuriatingly sexy biker who promptly bared and spanked me for sassing him was just icing on the cake.

After sharing a passionate night, I might have made a teensy mistake in taking cash from his wallet in order to pay the auto mechanic, but I hadn't thought I'd ever see him again...

Then on the first day at my new job, guess who swaggered in with payback on his mind?

He's living proof that the universe really is out to get me... and he's my new boss.

ABOUT PIPER STONE

Amazon Top 150 Internationally Best-Selling Author, Kindle Unlimited All Star Piper Stone writes in several genres. From her worlds of dark mafia, cowboys, and marines to contemporary reverse harem, shifter romance, and science fiction, she attempts to delight readers with a foray into darkness, sensuality, suspense, and always a romantic HEA. When she's not writing, you can find her sipping merlot while she enjoys spending time with her three Golden Retrievers (Indiana Jones, Magnum PI, and Remington Steele) and a husband who relishes creating fabulous food.

Dangerous is Delicious.

* * *

You can find her at:

Website: https://piperstonebooks.com/

Newsletter: https://piperstonebooks.com/newsletter/

Facebook: https://www.facebook.com/authorpiperstone/

Twitter: http://twitter.com/piperstone01

Instagram: http://www.instagram.com/authorpiperstone/

Amazon: http://amazon.com/author/piperstone

BookBub: http://bookbub.com/authors/piper-stone

TikTok: https://www.tiktok.com/@piperstoneauthor

Email: piperstonecreations@gmail.com